WRECK'S WAKE

WRECK'S WAKE

JOF CROXFORD

First published by Jof Croxford in 2023

ISBN 978-0-6456534-0-3
ISBN 978-0-6456534-1-0 (ebook)

All design & typesetting by Jof Croxford

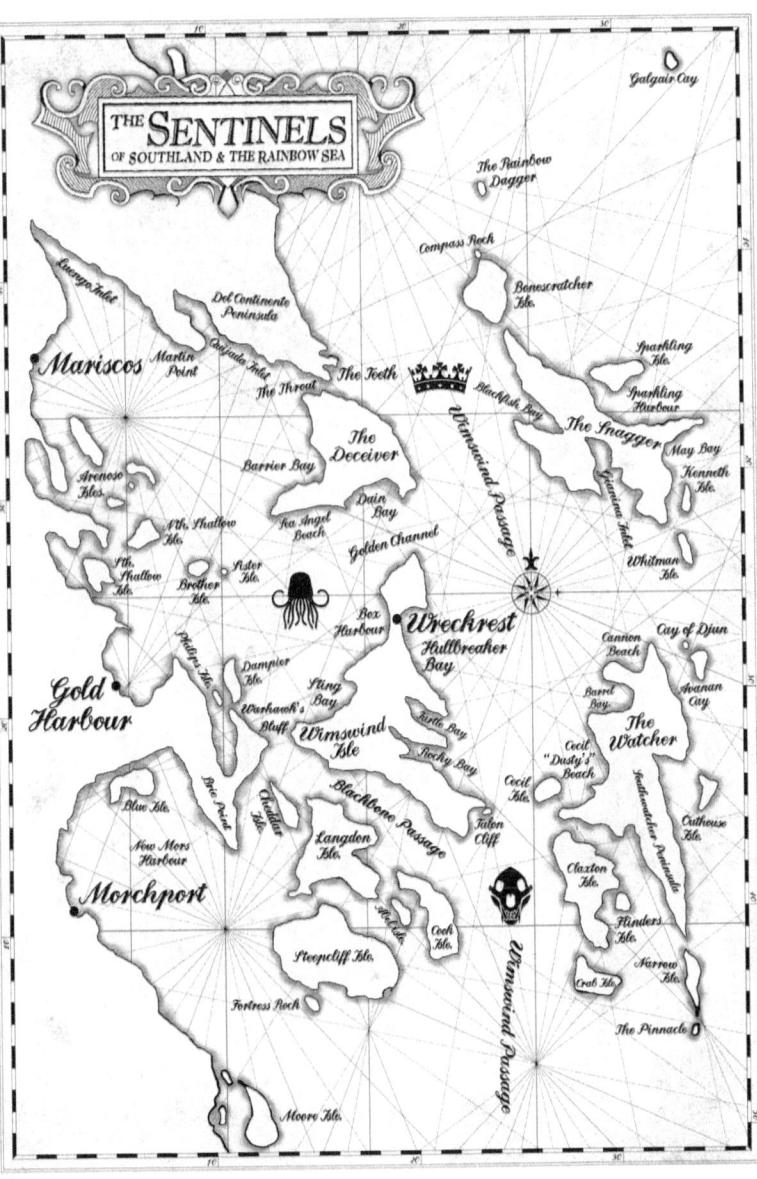

1

Dusty black sails vanished over his head. Slowly, the Blood Hammer eased to a halt amongst the turbulent waters of the Rainbow Sea. Its polished oak deck creaked in strain as the heavy sun fell unfiltered onto its dry surface. They were a long way out from the Sentinels here, the islands that stood guard about the Golden Coast of Southland. Even as they left their post, some brave little vessels would be slipping into the Wimswind passage, hoping to make unadulterated trade with Mariscos or Gold Harbour. But it did not matter. Not today. The dead needed to be treated with the proper respect.

Sebastian peered through squinting eyelids at his dear brother. The crew hoisted him out onto the Blood Hammer's gangplank so that his bulky arms flopped down over the waves. He looked even more dead than he had earlier. The cut that spilt his life was still visible, and repulsive. No longer was it flowing with red, or dribbling with death; now it had taken on a rubbery, dry quality, making poor Bartram seem no more than a tanned hide stuffed full of marrow and salted pork. His cutlass was placed beside him, for all the good it had done. The curved sword was chipped from use, and still red.

This was the way the Seabloods always sent off their regarded dead. Bring them out into the middle of the ocean and dump their carcass into the depths, to be forgotten forever. The reason they did so was lost, but Sebastian knew it was somehow important, a ritual maintained so that some half-rotted fish might come along and nibble at his brother's cock, hence adopting the robust and headstrong immaturity Bart was so exceptional at demonstrating. When Sebastian was to die, he wanted none of this rubbish. He had told Liz to make sure his lifeless body was carved up and roasted, so the crew had something somewhat hearty to chew on for a change instead of the usual vegetables. Liz had only shrugged it off, saying 'don't worry my love, when you die you'll be given as much respect as Bart will.'

Seb chuckled lightly to himself, making sure no other sailor heard. In the end it was Bart who had died first. The fact was unable to surprise him, but it had made a hefty impact on the remainder of the vessel's residents. In a way, this was what the young man had always dreamed of, though now that he was faced with its reality, he was not so sure he had struck gold.

Sebastian leant his elbows against the railing, his gaze darting from the blue sea to the hunk of hot meat that once was his brother, not sure where to linger. A few of the more prominent crewmembers were pronouncing their undying love for Bart while the rest listened in silence. Though Seb stood at a distance he pretended he was one of them, while in truth he did not care for a single word any of those foul-smelling men could speak. His own goodbyes were rustling through his head, but even there he could not form full sentences.

He had loved his brother, and he had hated his brother. Perhaps he only hated him so much because he loved him so much. Or maybe Bart was just an utter idiot on whom proper love could never rest. Seb knew nothing of which was true, only that when he stood back-to-back with his older sibling, surrounded by a hoard of surprisingly well-equipped merchant pests, he had been quick enough to cut his way free, and Bart had not.

All that bravado, Bart! And for what? It seems you listened to our father more than you listened to reason. Now look at you. Though I suppose I can't decide who got the better deal, you terrible excuse for a brother! Sebastian wiped some of the sweat from his brow. *Let me know—when you're down on the sea floor—if it's quite so hot there as it is up here. If not, I might come to join you a few decades sooner than father should like.*

Seb chuckled again. A funeral was no time to laugh, but he could not help himself. Somewhere above the masts and the rigging of the great wooden Blood Hammer, way up in the thick hot Southland sky, the god of justice was laughing too. *See what an intricate web I am weaving for you?* the god chortled. *Now go and make the most of it. Don't waste this rare gift!* The thought troubled Seb to the core. Troubled him with every pumping of his salty blood.

The captain was speaking now. His righteous voice thundered over the deck and sprayed into the surrounding ocean. Seb was not close enough to see whether there were any tears in his eyes. He hoped there were. He would feel too horrid if there were none.

The speech finished quickly enough, if nothing else could be said for it. Then the men holding the gangplank gave it a turn and Bart's limp body fell straight to the waves and disappeared with a plop.

And there goes my brother, Seb sighed. It felt as though a weight had been lifted from one shoulder, and an even heavier weight had been dropped onto the other.

When it was over, the gathered crewmen began to disperse, returning to their posts or their beds were they scheduled off duty. Fortunately for the Blood Hammer, Bart had filled no particular role aboard its hardy deck, meaning life could continue as if nothing had ever happened. The same could be said for Seb himself, making the waves below appear terrifyingly hungry.

Sudden shade fell over his sunburnt cheek, bringing with it a nasty chill. Seb straightened from his slouch to tower over the captain, who stood now well below his chin.

Though the man was short and plump, the captain's reputation made his shadow larger and darker than any other sailor's. His unreasonably huge wide-brimmed hat helped too.

Seb shuffled backward so as to spy his company's glaring pupils. With the sails furled, the sun glistened unfiltered from the man's golden ornaments, causing his appearance to match his name in grandeur. Captain Theodore Seablood he was called, or Ted, commander of the Blood Hammer and the Seablood fleet. He dressed himself up like a proper Sirlish lord—stockings and all—and wore an illustrious white wig with curls that hung well below his saggy, naked jowls. Nobody knew exactly why he wore that wig; there had been theories tabled before, though no sailor had ever thought to ask him in person. Not even Seb.

Ted's thin lips barely opened when he spoke, but his kingly voice found a way out nonetheless. 'Well boy. You're my eldest now. That was your plan all along, wasn't it?'

A lump found its way into Seb's throat. 'Father, if you think I wanted Bart to die, then—'

'Aaah, shush. You always take it the wrong way. But what I said's still the truth, isn't it? You're my eldest, and you'll have to carry on the Seablood name when I die.' He said the words like it was his duty.

'Yes, father,' said Seb.

Ted groaned. 'I thought he was better than you. More of my blood… Or… Something. Perhaps I was wrong. He was stronger, at least. And bigger.'

'But not as slippery,' Seb added. Salvino betrayed a snicker. That man was standing nearby, eavesdropping. If Theodore Seablood was said to cast the biggest shadow of them all, Salvino was said to posses the curious ability to hide in the smallest of them all. The black-haired Dorian quartermaster was thin and cooked bronze by the Southland sun. He wore a simple black cloak and kept his face as freshly shaven as his captain. If one ever held Captain Seablood in their sights, they could usually expect to see Salvino as well. He was a bit of a lurker.

Ted ignored him and pressed on. 'Nevertheless, you'll need to be trained for command, else I'll have to try squirting a boy into Agatha's dried up belly, God help me. You'll take the reigns of first mate, and I'll have a swabbie shoulder your old duties. Remind me boy, what were they?'

'Little and less, father.'

Salvino snickered again.

Captain Seablood shuffled forward, pushed his chest into Seb's stomach and raised a stern face, pointing a fat finger at the younger man's nose. 'I'll have no more of your funny, funny wits,' he growled. 'Today I sank my favourite son. You will respect my mourning and you will respect me. That's the end of it. Salvino, find Rob and have him sail us back to the Wimswind Passage. I'm bloody sick of this business today.'

Rob was there before even Salvino could summon him. 'Ah, Rob,' Ted grumbled. 'You heard what I said didn't you? Now get to it. Drop the sails.'

'Drop the sails!' Rob shouted. The Blood Hammer came swiftly back to life with the sound of 'aye aye's and the heaving of thick ropes. Ted subsequently waddled off towards the sterncastle.

Salvino passed Seb a brief look, raising his eyebrows in amusement. Seb disregarded the man and strode off in Ted's wake.

Sebastian's private chamber was cramped and dank by any land dweller's standards, but when compared with the hammocks afforded other crewmen, he lived like royalty. The room was compacted into a narrow slice of the sterncastle between the gun deck below and the luxurious captain's cabin above. He used the same entrance as his father did, but where the elder went up, the younger went down.

To make matters somewhat less comfortable, Liz could be found in Seb's bed more often than not, given her distaste for sleeping amongst the Blood Hammer's lustful crew. She rathered allow the desires of only one man disturb her sleep: Sebastian. It was a nice sentiment, though it came at the cost of a space—any space—where Seb could go to be truly alone. This very day, such a place was exactly what he sought for retreat. For this reason, when he swung open the creaky wooden door, his gut twisted in frustration at the sight of his lover lying naked on the bed. Her pale body filled the tiny room with the reflected light of a single lantern, and left space for little else.

Her pose was unashamedly suggestive, and she held her shoulders back the way that he liked. It did not take long for Seb to feel the front of his breeches tighten, regardless of how disinterested the remainder of his body felt.

'I thought you'd need something sweet... After all that,' Liz said, squirming slightly so that her womanly figure was especially noticeable.

Seb chose not to react right away. He closed the door behind himself and hung his coat over the dresser by the bed before looking wearily into the woman's eyes.

'You don't want it?' Liz asked, annoyed. 'Maybe I'll go and offer it to the other boys then. They'll be happy to have it, at least.'

'Liz,' Seb groaned. 'That was my brother out there. You know that, don't you?'

'Yes, my love, that's why I—'

'You didn't think I might not be in the mood?'

Liz scrunched her knees up against her breasts and shuffled into the corner of the lumpy mattress. Her bare shoulders pressed harshly into the splintering wooden planks that separated Seb's own chamber from that of his dead brother Bart. Her face betrayed her frustration. 'For shit's sake, Seb,' she snarled. 'Crewmen die all the time.'

Seb fell onto the bed. 'He was my *brother.*'

Soft hands crept forward, slithering into Seb's clothes as Liz leant towards him and kissed his neck. She shifted the tone of her voice as if it were carried by the wind. 'I *know* he was your brother. Of course I do. You've always wanted this day to arrive, and here it is. Your Teddy's only son now, and the ship will one day be yours... my captain.' She stretched her fingers through Seb's belt. He paid them no mind.

'It just doesn't feel like I thought it would,' Seb commented.

'Forget how it feels,' said Liz. 'Feelings are for poets and sulky peasants. You're neither, my prince.'

Seb shrugged his lover aside. She recoiled promptly, fearful he might strike out at her. The wooden planks thumped as naked shoulders pounded against them, irritation palpable in Liz's jagged movements. 'You should knock down this wall,' she continued. 'Bart has no more use for his chamber, and you deserve something bigger than... *this!*'

'Aye,' Seb agreed, peering aimlessly into the flickering lantern. 'I should. But father would never allow it. He'd sooner cut a hole in me than cut one in his precious brig.'

'You've never waited for your father's permission before.'

'You're right... Too right. I'm the best bloody crewman he has. Not to mention the best boarder. I've never let a man get away! Not ever!' Seb turned to slide his palm up the woman's curved waist. 'He better start seeing it. For once. I'll make him!'

'Yes,' Liz assented. 'Yes, yes.'

Seb grew harder still, and a warmth began to run through his skin. He leant over the naked woman and kissed her cheek, then her ear. Liz began to fumble with Seb's breeches. 'I knew it was what you wanted,' she giggled. 'I knew it was what you *needed*.'

A shout burst in from somewhere atop the main deck, calling for Seb's attention. The sound of incredulity flavoured its hurried tone.

'What in bloody Southland is it now?' Seb huffed, peeling himself from his lover.

'It's nothing,' hushed Liz. 'Stay here, with me.'

'It's not nothing,' said Seb. 'It's never nothing.'

The floor creaked as Seb bounced onto it, hastily tying up his clothes and shouldering through his doorway. He moved quickly to the main deck, worried that something awful had happened to Bart's body. Perhaps it had come back to life. Such would have been in the bastard's nature. *If your corpse won't sink Bart, I'll push you down myself!*

When he stepped out beneath the open black sails, he saw that the marshalled crew was glued to the starboard bulwark, ogling at something over the sea near the distant Deceiver.

Swiftly, Seb whirled and clambered up the stairs to the helm, where he found his feet beside Rob, who was using one hand to shield his eyes from the sun as he too peered westward.

'What is it?' Seb asked, unable to locate the cause of the sudden commotion. Rob silently pointed his index finger towards the Southland coast on the horizon. There was a ship sailing humbly beneath it, Seb could see. It was a marked distance away, so it appeared little more than a silhouette, though its size and magnificence were obvious nonetheless.

The ship was no doubt larger than the Blood Hammer, a fully rigged vessel of near one hundred and fifty feet. It boasted an elaborate forecastle at its bow, three thick masts decorated with brilliantly bulging black sails, and two fanned wings resting beside the raised stern, carved delicately from Sirlish Oak like the rest of it. The vessel was beautiful, a shining testament to the age's finest craftsmanship.

There was no need for a scope; Sebastian knew this ship, and knew it well. 'It can't be!'

'Yet there it is!' Rob exclaimed.

Seb found himself truly and deeply breathless. 'But I watched… As that ship sank to the bottom of the ocean.'

Rob's one-handed grip on the helm held strong, along with his stare. 'We all did,' he said.

2

The governor lowered his paper with meagre effort. He peered at them over the top of it, his eyes narrow with scepticism. 'And you said your names were?'

'Wesley,' replied Wesley. 'King. And this is my wife, Rosa— Rose King. And my sister, Alice—'

'King?'

'Yes… sir.'

Beneath his fading wig, the governor's forehead scrunched up as if to match the wrinkles covering the rest of his face. He scanned the paper again, grumbling to himself.

Rose's hand twisted into Wesley's. It was lathered in warm sweat. She squeezed. Wesley thought he might look back at her, though he knew already the look she would return, and he had well and truly had enough of that look.

The governor's forehead straightened again. 'Well, it does seem as though…' he announced '… everything is in order.' A heavy hand thumped the paper down onto the desk. The tension in his rigid posture visibly eased, and he folded his fingers together, passing a cursory smile to his three guests. His moustache curved upwards with the corners of his dutiful smile.

'They're only rags, but these should do better than what you've got on. The property itself is on the west side of the Waterman road. The fifth along. Shame we don't have any horses spare to cart you up there. It's a good spot though. The dirt is fertile as dog shit, and if you're lucky you might even turn up a piece of gold while you're sowing whatever the hell it is you decide to plant there. But for God's sake, keep in mind we could all use something other than turnips and potatoes, if you've got the backbone. Something that suits this wretched climate... bananas, I'm thinking. What, what's wrong?'

Rose was sprouting tears from everywhere on her face whilst attempting to plug her gaping mouth with her free hand.

'Nothing, sir,' Wesley explained. 'If anything, I suppose, it's just... well... we *built* the houses up on Waterman Road. Sir.'

'Well that's nothing to cry about, by Wimswind! All the better, I say! You'll be aptly rewarded for your service to Gold Harbour, or appropriately punished depending on the manner of your handiwork. By the look of your papers here, the three of you were as good and straight a bunch of convicts as they come. Nothing like those drunk fools I've got knocking on my door night after night. But don't let me call you that name anymore; convicts, that is. You're free men now. And women, begging your pardon.'

Rose swallowed her sobs just in time for Wesley to notice Alice's audible sigh of relief.

'Now listen. If you turn enough profit from your property there,' the governor continued, 'I'll see to it that you have your own cons to work under you. Wouldn't that be swell?'

A shiver ran from the crest of Wesley's spine down to his

knees. He had made it! After three long years, he had come out the other end. Alive. 'We're just happy to be pardoned, sir. I cannot tell you how thankful—'

'Oh shut it. I couldn't care less about you. That's the truth of it. It just so happens the harbour needs more good Sirlishmen to drive it, and you fit the bill. It's not like the homeland is sending down any good stock to fill our here port. And I've got cons spilling from my ears! I gotta do what I gotta do, you know? Ah, and we're short of unmarried women too, so your sister there's going to be in high demand. Just keep her away from my sons, you hear? I won't have them lusting over someone so scrawny.'

The governor pushed the pile of sodden apparel towards the edge of the desk and slapped it twice with his fat palm. 'Here. Take your rags and get the bloody hell out of here. Get yourself washed up too; you carry that special stink God reserves for slaves and wet hounds.'

Wesley jolted into motion, throwing out another 'thank you, sir' before shepherding his two women through the cabin's doors with the clothes pinned between his elbow and ribs.

This time, when the three Kings stepped out into the thunderous sun of Southland's coast, it greeted them as its own. No longer were they prisoners of Gold Harbour; they were its kin.

Rose's arms crashed around Wesley's shoulders, knocking the wind from his chest. Her shoulder-length blonde hair stuck to the filth on his cheeks as she pressed her lips against his. 'It's over,' she said between kisses. 'We're free! We're—'

'One thing I can say for sure,' Wesley interrupted, gently

pushing his wife from his chest. 'Is that I never want to hear that word again. That thing that they called us. *Convicts*. We didn't deserve the name in the first place, and we don't deserve to be remembered by it.'

'Yes. I agree.' Rose nodded, her expression flickering alternately between squealing joy and uncontrollable sobbing.

Alice shielded her eyes from the morning light. 'Are we going to our new house now? It's on the Waterman road! I can't believe it!'

Wesley stopped short, staring at his sister. She was no longer a child, but a grown woman, a free woman. Her face was hard edged and life worn, with a spattering of freckles curtained by long sheets of dead-straight hair. She was not as voluptuous as his wife, nor did she sport her sister-in-law's unmistakably feminine features, but she was taller, and carried her slender frame with the true confidence of a fully grown Southland settler. Three years convicted had robbed her of immaturity.

'Didn't you hear what the governor said?' replied Wesley. 'We're filthy. We'll go down to the beach first and wash ourselves. We're settlers now. Proper citizens of Southland. We can throw these uniforms into the ocean while we're there.'

Alice smiled with pride, nodding as Rose slipped her arm around Wesley's waist to walk him down to the water.

They made their way from the Governor's quaint work cabin to the soft curve of the harbour where the Golden River met the Rainbow Sea. There the water was fresh, and the chances of being snatched up by a Southland croc were significantly lower than further upriver.

The women started undressing almost as soon as their feet pressed into the white sand by the bank. Before Wesley could even get his old uniform past his hips, the others had plunged headfirst into the warm water as it lightly slapped against the rocky ledges that stretched into the water all around the river's gaping mouth. Alice was bare chested, her small breasts as smothered in grime as the rest of her pale figure. Rose remained in her underwear however, as she rightly should have.

Soon enough, Wesley joined them. Being under the water had never pleased him so much as being over it, so he scrubbed away at his layers of dirt with bare hands until the pale bumps on his bony limbs were pink, then got back out onto the shore. Before the heat had a chance to suck the moisture from his skin, he eagerly ruffled through the governor's pile of cloth to find a pair of tan breeches to pull over his legs. Drops of salty water soaked into the fabric as he yanked them on, though it did not bother him in the slightest. The young man had perhaps never felt so wealthy in his life.

Once he had finished off his outfit with knee-high stockings, worn leather shoes and a dusty linen shirt, Wesley propped his moist hands against his hips and looked back down at the others. The morning sun was still hovering above the horizon. It glittered off the ripples as Rose and Alice teased each other, splashing about joyfully.

The beach was empty besides the three of them, of course. By this time, the cons of Gold Harbour would be hard at work further inland, and the settlers would only be watching distantly from the shade of their verandas, if not yet at work themselves. Southland was home to little recreation, and even less swimming. All over the hills and mountains that overlooked the harbour, men and women alike would be planting seeds, hammering nails or wading through streams with rusty pans, sifting for gold. Sometimes they would be digging for the stuff too, mining for it, or simply wandering the landscape with a long stick while watching for it. For all the hell that was the newly discovered continent of Southland, it was certainly full of gold. Especially in Gold Harbour, Sirland's prized settlement on the continent's eastern shore. Though it was difficult to reach by sea, and a world away from the homeland, Gold Harbour had become a hive of activity. Every Western Nation wanted a piece of it too, though there was not nearly enough room in the cramped bay to accommodate their needs, so they had each set up their own settlements along the nearby coast, hoping to build, trade and perchance discover some gold of their own. Along with the settlers, the land was one plagued by a terribly unstable tropical climate. When the rain chose not to belt down over the rugged terrain, the sun took its place. And when it did it hammered the soil with a heat so thick one could smell it.

The Harbour's proud trade centre stood, creaking, to Wesley's left. The port. It was the only part of the harbour he had not yet visited, though it had been ever in the corner of his gaze for the full length of the year he had served as a slave to Southland.

Not surprisingly, Wesley soon found himself wandering towards it, egged forward by his newfound liberty. The place was a metropolis of wooden docks and half-sunken wayfinding markers, populated by an impressive collection of grand sailing vessels amongst some smaller rowboats. Men scrambled all over it, wrapping shiplines hastily around cleats and hauling crates of goods up and down the numerous piers.

Wesley gave a start when the sole of his shoe tapped against the wooden planks of the nearest pier. For years, that sound had been reserved for the feet of free men. Men who were afforded both hard shoes and hard floors to stomp them on. He paused only for a moment before pressing on, too eager to gaze upon the wooden beauties that so effortlessly brought back memories of his former life. The rapping of his footsteps filled him with satisfaction, and he puffed his chest out like the proper Sirlishman he had always been at heart.

The first decent vessel he came across was small and trim, with a single mast and a single sail, fore and aft gaff rigged. Not much unlike the one he had sailed back in Sirland, his beloved country of origin.

The free man halted to admire the vessel. Its hull was polished smooth, and it sprouted a single cabin just aft of the bow. The perfect boat to be manned by a small crew. Wesley stepped toward the edge of the pier, wondering whether he had yet acquired the right to touch the beauty.

'Don' you get any ideas there, son.' A voice growled from somewhere behind him. A hardy sailor came after it to stand beside Wesley, a three-pointed hat atop his head that covered his face in a rigid darkness. 'It'll take more'n one man to sail this girl.'

'Oh, I wasn't…'

'I'm just kiddin' with ya!' the sailor chuckled.

Wesley produced a nervous laugh. 'What do you call her?'

'A yacht, son.'

'Sorry, I meant... Does she have a name?'

'Aye,' the sailor turned to face the boat. 'Second Chance, it be. Aye.'

'Really?' Wesley smiled, and for all he could tell Second Chance smiled back.

'I lost me fam'ly in Sirland,' explained the sailor, 'when the pox hit Barrowt'n. I figured I'd move to Southland and start over in a new world. A second chance at life, if ya get me meanin'.'

Wesley squinted through the rising sun's rays at the sailor. He was short and stumpy and gruff, and the scars on his stubbly chin seemed to open and close with his mouth. 'You're a fisherman then, from Sirland? That makes two of us,' Wesley remarked.

'Aye son, I was, but I haven' felt the waves 'neath me boots in half a century, to be honest. I manage these here docks now, and I barely ever leave 'em these days. Not that I don' want to. Second Chance here was built for pleasure cruising, you see. Of all things! I wanted to sail around the Sentinels, stoppin' by every island I could 'till I found ol' Halfeye's Hoard, or somethin' like that.'

Wesley sniggered. He had heard of Halfeye's Hoard, but almost every story mentioned how damn impossibly well it had been hidden. The chances of a lowly sailor like this one stumbling across it were laughable. Wesley raised his eyebrows at the stranger, as if to suggest something.

'Don't be a lunatic,' the man replied. 'God you're a bold one! Or stupid, I'll say! There be pirates out there, son. Haven't ya heard? And not just the savage kind; God knows those ones're easy to put in their place if you know how to handle a pistol. And know where to point it, of course. Nay, out there be lords of the sea, kings in their own right, sailing the straits with an eye on every piece o' land. Once you step off the dock, you're in their territory, and you better hope you've paid the right one of 'em your weight in gold, or they'll suck you up and spit you out all bloody like the cork of a Morch red. Aye, I thought it'd all ended when ol' Halfeye's ship sunk to the sea floor, but it went on, son. God, how it goes on. Halfeye's Hoard be tempting, aye it be, but a fantasy all the same. The danger's not worth the risk. Nay, not by a long shot. Only heaven'll give me me third chance now. Aye, and I'll expect it sooner than any man would hope for.'

Wesley sighed dismissively. He had not expected the man to get so worked up. 'Well it's not like you'd have found it anyway,' he said.

The sailor leant towards Wesley and swung a bulky hand up to the corner of his lips, as if to shield his speech from some invisible eavesdropper. 'I met a man said he'd seen it,' he whispered. 'Near enough to mad, but not so near ya couldn' hear him out, see. Said it was all packed up in chests in some rocky cave, on a small island just north of the mainland. He asked me person'ly to take him back ou' there, pile it onto one of me ships. Only thing is, I never saw him again. Gone, as if some ghost!'

'Sounds suspicious.' Wesley blinked, weighing the story for its worth.

'Ah, just a bloody story, see! It gets my blood pumping if ya get me meanin'.' The sailor laughed it off. 'Aye, I've gone on. What brings you to me docks, then? Apologies I didn't ask ya sooner!'

Wesley moved to speak but was cut short.

'I'm Val.'

Wesley moved to speak again. 'I'm just wandering,' he managed. 'My wife and sister are in the water over there. I thought I'd give them some time.'

Val swung around instantly to search for the half-naked girls in the distance. His eyes caught them lustily. From within the port, they appeared as no more than pale smudges in the shimmering water. 'Swimming! By Wimsworth, haven't ya got work to do? Who are ya anyhow, goin' wandering around like this? Ya drift up from Morchport or somethin'?'

'We were prisoners in Sirland,' said Wesley. 'Before we were shipped here for lack of space back home. We've been doing the governor's dirty work now for a year or so. Building, mostly. That's what I've done, anyway. But since there's more convicts here now than free settlers...'

'Ah, one o' *those* crew. Can't say I envy ya then. Ya must'a been real well behaved to get let off though, aye?' Val stroked his face with dusty fingers. 'What'd ya do back west, huh? To get ya fam'ly in chains?'

'I looked after them,' Wesley stated bluntly, ending the conversation with his tone. 'Just as I've looked after them here. And just as I'm going to look after them now, as a free man.'

'Alright, alright, didn't mean to get ya feathers all rustled up.' Val straightened, the shadow from his hat still shrouding his face in obscurity. 'Ya have to get off me docks though, if ya got no real business 'ere, aye? Can't have no stranger snoopin' 'round all the boats, see.'

'As you say. Although maybe—if the seas ever settle—I'll come back down and we can sail Second Chance after that treasure.'

Val smiled a warm smile, bending those scars in all sorts of uncomfortable directions. 'Aye, sounds like a real plan, son. I'll come find ya when the stories stop flowin', huh?'

Wesley's shoes tapped importantly along the wooden planks as he retraced his steps down the pier. *Maybe I'll come and find you sooner,* he thought, *when growing bananas has devoured the last remnants of my soul.*

3

It was the smoke that woke him, not the fire. At first it seeped into his dreams. A smell he could not escape. Tearing. Clawing. Suffocating. He was underwater, the smoky blue clogging his throat as he desperately gasped for air. Rose was nearby, shuddering in the blurry depths. Her eyes screamed for help. Wesley tried to swim to her, but his arms would not move. She thrashed alone in the water, drowning, drowning. Alice was there too, and their mother. The older woman was closer, but still Wesley could not touch her. They were above him now, reaching down. Wesley was drowning, not the others! They were safe. He was not. The sea was going to swallow him. Alone. The realisation hit so hard it thrust him upward from his sleep into the smoke-filled bedroom.

His eyes filled with water the moment they opened, his fists came flying at his face to rub out the sting. He let loose the cough that had been welling up inside his chest. His fingers reached out for Rose. He felt her asleep beside him, her skin hot and dry. He gave her a violent shake. 'Rose! Rose!' Another cough.

A deep crackle ascended through the air, and a muffled

crash sounded from somewhere down the corridor. All Wesley could see before him was the faint outline of the open doorway amid the grey mist and the black night. Shapes bubbled from the opening. Billows of dusty breath puffing vigorously into the room.

Rose rolled over and opened her heavy eyelids, scrunching them together again in discomfort as the smoke soaked in. 'Wesley, what's going on?!' Confusion coursed through her voice. And fear.

'Fire!' Wesley exclaimed. 'In the house!'

Rose stumbled to her feet beside the bed, only to crash into a wall and fall to her knees.

'Rose! Are you alright?'

'No!' screamed Wesley's wife. 'Get us out! Where's the fire? Where is it?! Oh, get us *out* Wes!'

Wesley's breath quickened. Adrenaline pulsed through his bones. He knew that even if he could pry open his aching eyes for long enough, there would be nothing to see. The smoke was pouring in now. He could feel it through the clothes he had worn to bed. The heat of it thrust against his skin over and over, growing, growing.

He fumbled his way down to the floorboards by Rose, collecting a few splinters as he collapsed onto the wood. Her soft body found its way into his palms. He ran his fingers along her arm until he had her wrist locked tightly within them. Then he pulled.

'Come on, let's go!'

'I can't see! I can't see!'

'It doesn't matter. Just come this way! We've got to get out.

Feel your way! Follow me!'

Rose's mouth started to form bubbles with all the juices it had accumulated. A whimpering sound dripped out with them before she finally yielded to Wesley's pull, scrambling along the floor behind him. Together they dashed out into the corridor like blind rats, bouncing from wall to wall. His feet kicked her in the chin more than once, but his hand never let go. The front door soon beckoned them with the cool breeze it generated as it sucked smoke through the gap beneath its solid mass. They raced along the boards towards it.

When Wesley reached for the handle he gave a shout, the metal in his palm so hot it almost burned him. His hand instinctively snapped free, though he grabbed at the lever again anyway, forcing the door open and kicking it away with his bare feet. Smoke rushed swiftly out from the new opening, as did the frightened pair. Rose immediately collapsed into the dirt before the house, then rolled onto her back and shuffled away hysterically.

An orange glow snagged the corner of Wesley's vision, yanking his head around. The building loomed over him, creaking in grief beneath the dark blue of the star-speckled sky and the rough black of the mountains. Its north wall brandished yellow flames almost twice the height of the roof. They seemed to pull on the frame of the house, as if attempting to lift away the only thing Wesley had to show for his lifetime of hardship.

Heat flushed over his features as he glimpsed the burning scene between rubbing his eyes and shielding his face. Somewhere off in the surounding foliage he managed to distinguish the excited crunch of feet from the whispering roar of the fire, accompanied by an unmistakeable hooting and howling. Wesley had no need to investigate; he knew too well who was out there, and what they had done.

Ijians! he silently cursed, but he certainly did not have time to linger on hatred. After all, the north side of his house—the flaming side—contained Alice's room.

Wesley spun to check that Rose had distanced herself from the fire, then turned swiftly back towards the front door.

'Wes!' Rose screamed, fully aware that she could not stop him now. She was right.

Bursting back into the house, Wesley could instantly feel how much the heat had grown. It bit into his skin so hard it almost knocked him back out the door. Nevertheless, he pushed forward through the searing pain toward Alice's wing.

The smoke was now black and utterly opaque, rendering Wesley's vision almost completely useless. He hence dropped again to his knees and scuttled along the corridor floor. Within moments he could see the hellish flames through his closed eyelids. The stink of burning wood became pungent as he neared Alice's bed. He coughed it out stubbornly and held his breath, lifting his hand through torturous heat to flick through Alice's flaming sheets.

She was not there.

'Wesley!' It was his sister's voice, distraught. 'Are you in there?! I was looking for you!' She was behind him. Closer to the door. A brief glimpse revealed she was clutching her arm, clearly hurt.

'Get out!' Wesley screeched. 'I'm fine! Get out!'

'Rose—'

'She's outside! Get out there! I'm coming!'

A pop sounded from somewhere above Wesley's head, shortly followed by a blunt and numbing thud in his thigh. 'Argh!' he cried. Something had fallen on him, probably afire. Wesley's body crashed against the smoking floorboards. The taste of blood filled his mouth. A cold knife of pain drove deep into his back just below the ribs, paralysing him momentarily.

The knife twisted, sparking a river of heat that surged through his body as if his very blood was boiling. He jolted, then struggled frantically, screaming, hauling the wooden beam from his leg. It crumbled as it came free.

The fire was right on top of him now, its temperature pushing its way fully through his flesh, cooking him alive. The knife in his back began to tear this way and that, arching his back.

A hot hand grabbed his shoulder. 'Alice! I told you to get out!' The words were little more than a string of coughs and spits. 'Get out!'

She would not. She refused to escape. 'Shit!' Wesley hissed. He leapt energetically from the floor and tackled his sister clean around the waist, hurtling her back into the corridor. The two of them clapped against the doorframe as their bodies flew from the burning house into the thick, woody air without.

'Wes! You're *alive!*' Rose's voice cut through the pounding beat of Wesley's own heart in his ears. He could still feel the knife in him. He looked down. A patch of fire was ripping away at the side of his shirt where the blade ought have been.

Wesley dropped immediately and rolled onto his back,

forcefully scrubbing the fire against the cold dust. The burn did not cease though the stabbing of the flame eventually cut out. Wesley ceased squirming. His body shivered on the ground while Alice toppled into Rose's embrace, heaving.

Half of their house had now almost fully collapsed, and the flames were sprouting from its every corner. It shone like a beacon upon the slope of Gold Harbour, illuminating the Waterman road with its orange light. Though none of the victims could see it—or cared to—their neighbours had begun to poke free of their own homes, wandering out into the night to view the spectacle. One of them eventually knelt by Wesley's shoulder and touched him tenderly. 'Are you alright?' The man's voice was soft against the sharp backdrop of crackling fire.

Wesley's eyes opened despite the bitter sting. 'I'm fine,' he spat, sitting up hurriedly. He shuffled over to his family in an awkward half-crawl, half-walk. The pain in his lower back pulsed horribly.

'What were you thinking?! You could've died!'

Alice looked out from Rose's ample bosom. 'So could you!' she snapped back.

'I was fine,' grumbled Wesley.

Rose wiped a hot trickle from her nose with her forearm. 'Oh, stop it! We're all okay. We're all okay.' The thump of a heavy wooden beam crashing through the kitchen drew their attention away from each other. They each looked over to the ruin of their home and watched helplessly as the fire consumed it. Dotted now around the building's stumps, a handful of Southlanders were shovelling dirt onto the flames. Preventing the madness from spreading was the only hope that remained; the river was too far away for quick water, let alone the fact that no settler yet had fought Ijian fire and won.

Wesley may have only been a true citizen of Southland for a few fleeting days, but he had lived and breathed its air for over a year, and had therefore seen his fair share of Ijian attacks. To him, the hostile native folk of Gold Harbour were little more than disobedient savages. The dark-skinned people lived in the mountains amongst the trees—mostly naked—catching their food with spears. From the day the people of Sirland had first landed in Gold Harbour, the Ijians had consistently proven themselves antagonistic towards them, popping out for destructive sorties whenever they could manage it. They would attack seemingly innocent settlers and convicts alike, most often without warning. Whether it was their plan to scare away the Sirlish newcomers or to eliminate them entirely did not matter, because it always ended up failing. Though they never gave up. As if it were some God-given mission, the native population continued to resist the colonisation of Southland with inconvenient aggression. And fire. It was always fire that they used. Their favourite weapon. The weapon they had used on Wesley's house. The thought of how unfair and untargeted their ruthless efforts had been tonight filled Wesley with a deep and scorching anger.

The now distant war cries betraying the attackers' identities faded into the shadows as the bustle of the curious contracted around Welsey and his little family. He fended them away despite their best efforts to offer assistance or comfort, choosing instead to let his anger fester unhindered. Rose was crying amongst it all, her sobs growing louder every time another piece of their house fell to the ashes. Alice, in contrast, was silent, stunned, her pupils watching carefully as the thick breeze fanned the flames high into the night sky, carrying little pieces of their new life off into oblivion.

'It isn't fair,' Wesley finally spoke, restraining his voice so that none of the onlookers could hear. He swallowed the lump in his throat and pressed his teeth tightly together to hold back the wailing he felt within. He touched the burn at his side, and then quickly pulled his fingers away from it. A terrible pain soaked into his flesh where the blaze had kissed him. He felt as though his skin was dissolving right off his body, allowing the radiant heat to claw directly into his veins. He clenched his teeth tighter. 'I'm burnt,' he said without moving his jaw. Rose let Alice go and leant over to Wesley. 'I need to get away from here,' he continued. 'This heat… Let's get down to the water.'

'What about our house?' Rose asked, her expression utterly flustered.

'What about it?' Wesley rebuked, somewhat breathless. The chaotic swirl of fire raged behind them, unceasing. 'Can't you see it? It's gone! Come on, let's get down to the beach… I need to soak in some water. This burn. It's… Bad.'

The girls did not argue further. They got painfully to their feet and followed Wesley as he paced swiftly and unsteadily down the Waterman road towards the mouth of the Gold River. There were a few comments to be heard from those standing around, though Wesley was not of a mind to pay them any attention. Only a week prior, he had walked the very same path, striding toward his pardon with his head held high. Now his bare feet dragged along the stony trail with tense dejection.

The three Kings completed the journey in silence. Every step of it drew them closer to the attractive chill of the ocean—and further from the furnace—which was enough for the moment. None of them looked back except to check that nobody was following them. And nobody was. Nothing followed them but the dark night and its suffocating warmth.

After the rocks between their toes had finally moved aside for grass and sand, the two women collided suddenly with Wesley's frame, which almost brought the whole group back down to the ground. The man had stopped moving right in front of the governor's mansion, and appeared to be stuck in thought. The elaborate house was the largest in the harbour, and looked out with pride over the docks and the waves below it. Somewhere inside, the governor was blissfully asleep, frustratingly ignorant of the trauma that had just razed the newly freed family's hopes of a happy, wealthy life.

'What are you doing?' Rose asked, concerned. She grappled Wesley's shoulders to regain her balance.

'It's not fair,' Wesley whispered to himself, swiping her away. 'It's just not fair. So impossibly unfair.'

Alice stepped ahead of the others. 'Wesley, come on. We're almost there.'

The sorrow in Wesley's chest twisted with the pain of his burn, blending with it to form in its place a fiery fury and a resounding desire for justice. And if the governor could not deliver them the justice they deserved, nobody could.

'It's not our fault. We didn't burn down the house. The governor will understand.'

'You're not going up there!' exclaimed Rose. 'It's the middle of the night! The governor will be asleep! Please Wes, we can find him in the morning! That's what we'll do.'

'And where will we sleep tonight?'

'She's right, Wesley,' Alice added. 'Let's keep going!'

It was too late. Wesley had already ascended the steps of the governor's porch and was rapping on the door, clutching his burn with his free hand. Too frightened and shocked to be left alone in the dark, Alice and Rose hustled up behind their limping leader and held their breaths.

Despite the hour, the door was swiftly attended by a long-faced man with a tiny moustache, dressed in a set of sodden clothes that may have once been black. He held a lamp stiffly by his chest that threw light right up his nose and over his shoulders. Behind him, Wesley could only just make out the shape of the governor's extravagant entrance hall. A curved staircase wrapped around the rear of the tall room, and varnished furniture crowded the floor. The mansion reminded him of his old master's back in Sirland, though out from this one spilt a foul waft of wet timber and mould.

'Have you any idea what time it is?' the butler complained, his posture unmoving. 'What business could you possibly have at this hour? I told Walt the hounds would be no more trouble.'

'We wish to see the governor,' Wesley blurted out.

'Keep your voice down!' the butler shushed. 'Edward is asleep, as he ought to be, and I expect he should not desire to be disturbed by the likes of *you*.' The stiff man peered sourly over Wesley at the two anxious women. If he was not so properly mannered, he might have spat at their feet.

'The likes of *us*?' Wesley questioned, completely ignoring the butler's request for quiet. 'We are free citizens; the governor gave us each our pardons just this week. We deserve to have his attention!'

The butler rolled his eyes. 'So you're convicts, then?'

'Not anymore!' Alice piped up from deep within her brother's shadow. 'And not ever again!'

Wesley nudged her backward subtly, letting her know he had the situation under control, even if he did not. 'Listen,' he said, 'we have been attacked by Ijians. They've burned down our new home with their fire. Just now! That's the same home that was given to us by the governor. Tell him that we need a new one.'

'Do you realise how ridiculous you sound?' the butler yawned into his free hand, his shoulders still and stiff as cast iron. 'Ijians attack us as often as the sun rises. Perhaps you should have sat outside your house with a blunderbuss. That would have scared them off. You shouldn't have even needed waste a shot on them.'

Wesley's features tightened. 'I don't have a gun. And even if I did, I can't stay up all night, every night. It's not our fault this happened... So... I'm demanding the governor come out and hear us!'

'Demanding?' The butler pursed his lips sarcastically. 'My, you have been set afire! Might I remind you that this house has not, and that there is evidently no suitable reason for this servant to be standing in this doorway with you? Sleep comes rarely to me, as it does to Edward, and lo, here you are, making it rarer.'

'What is all this blasted commotion?!' a third voice joined the argument, deep and irritated. It rattled down from the balcony atop the staircase. At its sounding, the butler finally broke his solid stance in the doorway to spin around and face the faint shadow cast by the governor of Gold Harbour, who leant now over the balcony railing in striped pyjamas. His presence and authority did little to ease the dank hopelessness of the expansive hall.

Wesley spoke up before the butler could mitigate the scene. 'Governor, sir, our house was burned down by Ijians!' He tried to ignore the pain of his injury as he addressed the town's most powerful figure.

The governor decided not to descend the stairs, but to remain in the distant murk at the furthest end of the hall where he could lord over the unwanted intruders. 'Who's that? William! Step aside so I can see them!'

The butler stiffly shuffled away from the door, allowing Wesley to see straight through to where the governor was hunched.

'Who are you and what do you want in the Goddamn middle of the night?! It better be bloody important!'

Welsey cleared his throat and repeated himself clearly. 'I am Wesley King. We met a few days ago when you accepted our pardon. The house you gave us. It's been burned down by Ijians. Just now!'

'Bloody Ijians!' the governor cursed. 'Can't they give me one peaceful night?! Just *one*?!'

'We were wondering if you could—'

'I get it, Winfred, or whatever your name is. You want some

sort of compensation. Compensation! Ha! Like it's ever *my* fault the Ijians do the shit they do! Maybe you should sit outside your front door with bloody blunderbuss next time! That'll scare them off good and right!'

'I don't have a gun and even if I—'

'Understand this,' the governor interrupted, his loud voice filling the overstated room. 'I care not for you or your stupid family or their stupid problems. Get me some trade or dig up some gold and I'll send a pack of cons to build you a new shack. Truth be told, it's Gold Harbour I care for, not its people! Now get off my porch and let me shut my eyes for long enough to imagine that my wife's not as ugly as she is!'

Wesley believed—for the brief moment before the door slammed in his face—that he saw a smile on the butler's rigid features. Whether or not he was right, what he spied next was nothing other than the wood grain of the governor's front door, illuminated by the soft silver glow of the night sky. The bite of his own protesting voice bounced straight back at him and echoed off the nearby water.

You bastard! Wesley thought. *You're meant to look after this place! You're meant to look after its people! That's what you're here for! You're nothing more than a greedy idiot who's never had anything taken from him in his life! Well I'll take something of yours then! I'll take it! I'll take it! I Will!*

Rose started to cry again, even as the three descended the front steps of the governor's mansion. It only served to make Wesley more frustrated.

'Our house, Wes!' Rose wailed. 'We didn't even get a chance to live in it! What are we going to do? Where are we going to sleep? Oh, Wes, what are we going to do?!'

Wesley pushed her clawing hands away from his chest. He did not want anybody to touch him. Not now. Not ever again. He had served his time for a crime he had no choice but to commit. He had served it with his head down and mouth closed. He had served for his family, the family he had forced into chains. He had served for his second chance. A second chance at life. A second chance at wealth.

'The land is still ours,' Alice consoled, 'we can still live on it. We can… Wesley, do you need to get to the water?'

The burn reignited itself quickly when Wesley paid it attention once more. A burn he did not deserve. It cut through his core, setting fire to his heart, his soul, his desires. His second chance had come and gone, and was now no more than a plot of rubble by the Waterman road. He needed a third chance. A real chance. Or a second second chance. One he deserved. One his family deserved.

'Wes… Do you?' Rose sniffled.

He had been good his whole life. Listened to his mother, took a wife while he was young, looked after his sister. He had spent twenty-five years trying to fit into the world around him. But where had it taken him? The homeless sands of Southland? He could not accept it.

'Let's go to the docks,' said Wesley.

'The docks?' Alice questioned.

'They've taken everything from us. It's time we took something back.' Wesley's tone had adopted a cruel, menacing timbre.

'What do you mean, Wes?' Rose sobbed, her fear obvious.

'I mean that we've come too far to be left with nothing. I know a way we can get the second chance we deserve. I have a hunch on where Halfeye's Hoard is, and I know a way to get there.'

'Wesley, is this the right thing to do?' asked Alice, but it was too late again. Wesley had made up his mind and was not turning back. The women had only the ultimatum he had handed them: to follow or be left behind.

They chose to follow.

The docks were guarded day and night, though under the cover of darkness only the harbour's most prized vessels were afforded the proper surveillance, and none of those were tied up on the southernmost pier. It was to that very pier Wesley led them.

As the family neared the ocean, a breeze lifted up from the water and licked the scorched clothes around Wesley's burn. The cool allure of a quick dip drove deep into him, but Wesley's drive had become so strong, so focused, that the water's call could not break him.

Face forward and accomplices behind, the freed man walked straight onto the pier. He figured that the sooner it was over with, the less time the port watchmen had to react, and the less time he had to change his mind. The quickened thuds of his bare feet against the pier's worn planks were not nearly as glamorous as the sound of his shoes days earlier. Wesley pushed the thought from his mind. Pushed all thoughts from his mind.

'Wesley, what are we doing?' Alice whispered, clutching her brother's arm. 'We shouldn't be here!'

Wesley whirled in her grip. 'We *should*, Alice,' he replied, his voice equally muffled though thick with adrenaline. He gestured towards the boat that was tied up beside them. A small, wooden yacht with a single mast and *Second Chance* painted on its hull in discreet lettering. The moonlight draped over it gently, and beamed off its furled sail. '*This* is the second chance we deserve. A chance to sail again, and to lay our hands on Halfeye's Hoard!'

'You want to steal it?' Alice gasped.

'I don't want to. I have to! Now get on and untie the lines. Before someone stops us.'

Alice swallowed hard, then leapt aboard. Her soles landed firmly on the yacht's deck, the sound not so loud as it could have been were she properly dressed.

Wesley was quick to follow. He scurried across the width of the small vessel to where the halyard was tied to a pin in the wooden railing. He unwound it as quickly as he could. His fingers were a little slow at first, but once they were moving they remembered only too well how to manoeuvre their way through rope, even after so many years.

A sob upon the pier distracted him. Wesley looked up to see Rose standing there, looking down through teary eyes.

Wesley growled. 'Come on, Rose. Get aboard! Quick!'

'This isn't you, Wes! What are you doing?!' Rose bothered not to restrain her voice.

'I'm taking my life into my own hands!' Wesley snapped back. 'Only this time, I won't get caught. So get aboard, Rose. I'm taking this boat!'

She broke out into tears again. 'I won't let you, Wes! You're just upset! This isn't right. This isn't *you!*'

Alice had already untied the lines that held Second Chance against the pier. Wesley held the thickly wound rope of the halyard now in his palms, ready to hoist. 'It is now,' he said, and bounded over to the yacht's port side where he lifted a leg to prop against the pier's edge. He glared at Alice and she soon did the same, spurred on by perplexed obedience.

'Wes, no!' Rose cried. Wesley pushed heavily against the wooden beam and the stern of the yacht began to swing out. He pulled his weight against the halyard. It creaked as it pulled the sail upward.

Then—just as Wesley had anticipated—Rose jumped from the pier to the yacht, crashing onto its deck. She rolled up to her feet and braced silently, sucking in her tears while Alice pushed the bow away. Second Chance drifted calmly towards the dark beach while Wesley eagerly eased the sail up the mast. At first it caught more moonlight than it did wind, though soon enough the magnificent white triangle was bulging comfortably, and the yacht, ever so slowly, set itself into motion.

None of them spoke. What they had just done was far worse than anything they'd done before. And more exciting.

Wesley peered back towards the southern pier as it grew steadily more distant. A pair of confused sailors appeared atop it, running about like headless chooks. It would not be long before they sent out a vessel to catch them. Wesley only hoped the wind would be kind enough to give him a solid head start.

He turned to his sister. 'Alice, let out the sheet, we need to pick up some speed.' Alice nodded and wordlessly swept across to where the line was tied.

And so the three Kings left Gold Harbour, free and sailing with the breeze. *Never again*, Wesley promised himself, *will we be locked in chains. We have our second chance, and I will see that it catches the wind!*

4

The sun was merely peering over the crooked tops of the distant Sentinels, the islands that stood watch over Gold Harbour and the eastern coast of Southland, itself a continent so massive it was a wonder so many years had passed before the Sirlish were to discover it. The islands may not have been very good at watching, as such, but they did a fine job of protecting the mineral-rich mountains of the mainland from ill-prepared adventurers. They were named the Sentinels after Sirlish voyager Winston Wimsworth wrecked his ship, the Wimswind, on one of their coral reefs, only to discover the golden bounty they were defending. Afterwards, his crew managed to repair the Wimswind well enough to sail it north to Brindia, where he used the gold he had found to barter passage back to his homeland.

The region was a rich archipelago of sharp, rocky and overgrown tropical islands, all broken and weathered like the skeleton of a great monster that dwelt in an age long forgotten. Its largest bones were tall and terrible. The Deceiver, the Snagger, the Watcher and Wimswind Island, the largest of them all.

Beneath the pulsing sail of Second Chance, the faint outline of these beckoning islands grew ever the less faint, and the bright sun rose ever higher into a sky thick with cloud, heralding a new day and a new life. Wesley had to shield his eyes to protect them from the glare that skimmed the surface of the calm waters ahead.

'They're getting closer!' Rose whimpered. Wesley spun around to see, keeping a firm grip on the yacht's wheel. His wife was right; the vessel that the harbour had sent after them was catching up. It was still too distant to see how many sailors were aboard, but near enough to make out its bulky shape. 'Don't worry,' he replied. 'Once we can see around that bushy point there, we'll take a sharp turn to port and ride the wind north, close to the shore. This boat is half their size, so we'll be able to cut the corner much closer than they can.'

'But what about after that? Are they going to stop chasing us? We stole a *boat*, Wes! Oh, what are we going to do?'

'Rose! Calm down!' Wesley barked. 'There's a bunch of small islands just up from here, north of this point.' He pointed. 'We can lose them in there. All we have to do is reach those islands before they catch us.' He grinned. 'And then we'll find Halfeye's Hoard. Treasure beyond measure!' *A small island north of the mainland,* Wesley remembered. *That's where the treasure is. God let that man Val be right, or we may be sailing the Rainbow Sea for the rest of our lives. Although I guess that would be better than waiting it out on a charred heap up Gold Harbour's sickening slopes!*

Rose noticed the strange and possessed look that had overcome her husband and eased away from it. 'Wes, I'm scared.'

'That's reasonable,' Wesley replied. 'But it's too late now. We've done what we've done. Right? Just help me sail this yacht as fast as I can and put that fear all the way behind you. There's no room for it on board this Second Chance.'

'I love you, Wes.' Rose added, insistently.

'Yes. I love you too. But it won't matter much longer if you don't help Alice with the ropes. I need you ready at the reef when we go around this corner. Can you do that?'

Rose nodded and slipped sheepishly away from the yacht's helm. Wesley's gaze then drifted to Alice, who was sitting by the end of the sheet where she could silently eavesdrop. She was just as scared as Rose, though she did a better job of hiding it. Wesley was scared most of all, he was sure, but he was not going to let his women see it. Not for one second.

He swallowed and cranked his nose back toward their heading. Despite the hungry vessel streaming after them, Second Chance sailed peacefully through the water as the sun slowly settled into the sky. The Rainbow Sea was shielded here by the Sentinels and their coral reefs, so the waves never grew too high. They lapped soothingly against the small hull of the yacht, each in perfect time, before whisking off in its wake.

It was only very early in the morning, but the atmosphere was already thick with warmth and humidity. In the sticky air, Wesley felt as groggy as he ever had, having not slept since he was rudely awakened by the Ijian fire. His eyelids kept trying to droop. He convinced himself it was because the sun was shooting through the gap beneath the yacht's sail and its deck to hit him square in the face. *Once the sun is higher in the sky, I will feel better,* he promised himself.

Wesley released a hand from the wheel to rub his aching burn. The wind was almost directly behind them, so there was no great breeze to cool his skin while the Second Chance sailed on its current course. Instead, the unimpeded temperature made the burnt patch of skin grow increasingly less comfortable. Wesley shuffled his bare feet against the deck. Light droplets of lukewarm ocean mist touched his flesh where his clothes were ripped and grey. *I'm a mess,* he thought. *It was almost better serving as a convict.* Welsey swallowed again. *...Almost.*

Just ahead, the dense green of the nearby peninsula had shifted aside to reveal a steep cliff, which glowed white in the shallow rays of the morning light. Wesley could see clearly around the point now, into the vast waters of the north. It was time to make the turn.

Steadily, Wesley coerced the yacht's wheel around. Since he was turning with the wind, the wheel was eager to align itself more abruptly than Wesley wanted. 'Alice, ease the sheet,' he called out. Alice responded swiftly by letting a few loops of rope off the belaying pin. The great white sail filled lustily with air. Wesley could feel the wood beneath his feet creak with joy as the yacht realised its full pace.

In a mater of seconds, Second Chance had turned near ninety degrees northbound, and was cutting through the waves like a knife through butter. The wheel loosened in Wesley's palms, easing the pain his palms still harboured from the fire.

To his left, the cliffs of the peninsula floated past at a comfortable distance, slowly but surely cropping their pursuers from sight and mind. The ocean opened up before them, wide, glittering and flat like a shaggy carpet laid over solid timber.

Rose looked over to her husband, concern on her face. 'When do I pull the reef, Wes?'

'It's ok,' Wesley replied, 'I don't need it now. You can relax.' He felt his own body ease, too. 'Here, look… Rose, come here.'

Rose wobbled across the yacht's cramped surface to the helm again, where Welsey took her gently in his arms, wrapping them warmly around the dirt-smeared rags that had been her night gown. 'Rose,' he said, 'we'll be fine, you know. Here, take the wheel for a bit, I want to see if I can finally get some water on this burn.'

Rose released a brief squeak of uncertainty.

'It's fine, Rose. You're fine. Just hold the wheel still, like this.' Wesley guided his wife's hands to the rounded handles of the yacht's wheel. 'See right over there, in the distance.' Wesley extended his finger. 'It's a bit hard to make out through the mist, but that island there. Just keep the bow pointed at that and you'll be fine.'

'What if something goes wrong?' Rose questioned.

'Come now, Rose.' Welsey chuckled. 'The yacht's not *that* big; I can hardly go far. But on a boat like this, it shouldn't matter anyway. See that line that Alice just released? That's the sheet. It controls how wide the sail turns. And the reef, that just pulls the sail in, if we need to lose some speed. The halyard, over there, that pulls the sail up and down.'

'I know what the ropes do, Wes. You've told me a million times.' Despite her assurance, Rose's eyes were swimming in anxiety.

'Listen, Rose, you can do this. It's good for you. You've got to be stronger, you know. Take charge, don't be so scared. I know you can do that, Rose. You've just got to *try*.'

'I can't *choose* the way I feel, Wes. If I'm scared, I'm scared.'

Wesley grumbled. 'Yes, but you can choose how you go about it, can't you? I know you can be stronger. I know you. You've just got to work out a way to admit it to yourself. If we're going to do this thing—which we *are*—then you're going to have to learn. And quickly.'

'I didn't want to do this, Wes! I was happy to live in our little house. Simple.'

'Our house was burned down… Or did you forget already?'

'We didn't have to steal a boat because of it!'

Wesley grunted. He felt the sting of his burn swell up and left Rose at the wheel alone. Surprisingly, she allowed him to walk away without spitting forth any further protests, her mouth instead zipped tightly shut in frustration. For the moment, her fears were suppressed.

On the yacht's current heading there was hardly any tilt to the thing, so Wesley had to hang low over the starboard railing just to get some decent water droplets onto his torso. From the moment he leant overboard, he could feel the heat squeezing out of his red back. The water here was not anywhere near as cold as it was in Sirland, but with every speck of it, a touch of imagined frost eased into his flesh. He had to adjust his contorted position several times, each arrangement anything but comfortable, but he found his mood clearing nevertheless, and his senses opening to the world once more.

As he hung there, Wesley's troubled mind was surprisingly

empty. The horrid decisions he had been forced to make that led him to this moment seemed suddenly trivial. All that mattered now was that their yacht reached those islands before the righteous of Gold Harbour caught up to them. It was a dangerous state of affairs, but a simple one. Wesley had always thought too long and hard about his actions, his self and everything in between. Now it seemed as though he could not be bothered thinking at all.

He lowered one of his arms to the water and let his fingers skim the white wash as it whipped by. *Is this what it feels like to be truly free?* He asked himself. *What a feeling! Perhaps I should have committed to life as a criminal long before now! I could've been here a year ago. Or sooner!* He pulled his arm back up to clutch the railing. *Although maybe I'm too tired to be thinking properly. Maybe that's it.*

Alice's face appeared over the side of the yacht, looking down at Wesley with a half-puzzled expression. 'Are you alright?' she asked.

'Yes,' said Welsey, yanking his torso up to the railing so his back was still exposed to the choppy water below.

'Good.' Alice brushed some of her long hair from her face. 'You don't seem to be very… worried… Or not as worried as you should be. You know this sea is full of pirates… Don't you?'

Wesley sighed. 'Yes, Alice. But where isn't these days? Back in Sirland, I watched plenty of greedy thieves shrink in my ship's wake. Why should here be any different? Really? This yacht's as fast as any.'

'But Wesley—'

'Alice, don't fret! It's not like we're heading out into the

Sentinels anyway, where they're more likely to grab us. We're hugging the coast, keeping clear of those dangerous places. The only vessel we've got to worry about is the one on our tail, and I promise you we'll outrun it.'

Alice drew back, unconvinced.

'Enjoy the breeze, Alice,' said Wesley. 'Doesn't it feel good to be free? *Really* free?'

Alice raised an arm to feel the air that glided by. Her muscles relaxed a little as cool, wet gusts coerced goose bumps from her skin. There was a strange sort of magic about. The chill she felt reminded her of Sirland, of her real home, before she was shipped away to Southland.

The breeze pushed lightly against her face, then puffed a little harder and ruffled her hair. The clouds grumbled loudly, their voice deep and wordless. She squinted her eyes in curiosity, whirling. Above her, the sail complained with a few uncomfortable flaps.

'Wesley, is the wind... blowing the right way?'

Her brother flopped over the railing like a wet fish and thumped onto the deck before raising his eyes. 'Alice! Duck!'

She dived to the ground just in time. The boom swung sharply overhead, pulling the sail to the other side of the yacht with a crash. The deck shook as the sheet caught the great white triangle, thrusting the vessel into a steep portside lean. Rose's grip on the wheel became vice tight. She pressed her heels into the yacht's planks to keep her feet and yelled after her husband for help. 'What happened, Wes?!'

Wesley bounded up to the helm, took the wheel from his wife. 'Just a gust.' His tone carried an unstable hint of exasperation. 'I can get it back' he declared, though he struggled to hold the wheel in place. The yacht wanted to turn in a new direction. Wesley would not let it.

The rising sun still glared at them from the east, though the accelerating winds blew across a fresh curtain of rain like only Southland knew. Within moments, sheets of water were flowing over the angled deck's surface, bubbling under the heavy assault of the tropical downpour. The sky transitioned into a murky white-grey with surprising speed, and jagged waves emerged from the Rainbow Sea like retractable spines.

'Damn this Southland weather!' Welsey shouted, shielding his face from the suddenly insistent rain. Rose clutched his arm with the characteristic vice grip she often relied upon in such frightful situations. Wesley let her hold him. Something about the sudden weather shift had shaken his resolve. It would have never happened in Sirland. That he knew.

'Alice, pull the sheet in!' Wesley shouted over the furious fluttering of the sail, his voice all wet and choked.

Alice slid across the deck into view, her long dark hair even longer and darker whilst soaked. 'We should take the sail down! The wind's too strong!'

'We're being chased!' rebuked Wesley as warm and sticky water splashed off his face. 'We cannot lose any speed! Bring the sheet in, we keep going.'

'But Wesley!'

'Bring the sheet in! Tighten it up! Now!'

Alice darted to her station. Rose's grip on Welsey's arm tightened even more. The boat began to rock harshly. She let out a gasp.

'Rose, we're fine!' said Wesley. 'This storm is perfect! We'll be able to lose the boat behind us if we play this right!'

Alice was yanking the sheet into a pulley so she could reel it in despite the violent weather, when the whole line snapped free of her grip and flung like a whip into the falling skies. Welsey cursed. 'Rose, keep the boat straight!' He released the wheel and leapt down after Alice and the runaway rope.

The sail flew free from its bounds and flapped vigorously in the ever-growing gale. Its pull on the mast halted immediately and the hull ceased its lean to wobble unsteadily in the turbulent sea. Rose watched helplessly as the wheel spun and the boat twisted. She fell to the deck and grasped the stern railing, squashing it between her wet breasts.

Wesley sprang from the deck to grapple the loose sheet, his feet flailing out over the waves as his fingers dug into rough rope. Alice screamed as he jumped, grabbed his ankles to pull him back into the boat. The sail was desperately jerking at the sheet in Wesley's hands, but the two siblings managed to pull it amidships.

Then it happened.

The sound and the light and the wallop came all at once. Like a hundred cannons firing in unison with an explosion of white flame. There was no time to react, or even to decipher what was happening. Not until after the lighting had struck, and its reverberating crash had boomed away from them in all directions.

The three Kings were flat against the deck of their Second Chance. Pieces of broken mast rained down with the water. The world shifted and shook. Loose lines slapped into the sea and the sail flopped over the cabin's roof.

Wesley glanced up to see fire for the second time in too short a while. Only now the rain was bound to put it out. The mast, however, was beyond repair.

Steadily the grey sky filled with despair and death. Wesley's ears were ringing, pulsing pain through his skull. *Of course!* he laughed. *How could anything go my way? There never was any chance! Never! Why did I have hope? It was impossible! Impossible!*

A flickering shadow scraped the corner of the sky. Wesley shot up. *Was that a ship?* He scanned around through the misty rain. Everything was rocking one way or the other. Half the mast was now leaning sideways over the sizzling deck. He felt sick.

'Rose! Rose, are you there?! We were hit by lightning!'

Alice was near the cabin. 'Did you see it?' she shouted, seeming to ignore the damage to the yacht. She got up suddenly and collided with the starboard railing, shivering as the storm swirled around her. Forgetting himself, Wesley stumbled up to her side, shaking his head. He could have sworn he had seen another vessel too—a huge one—lining up its broadside with their measly yacht. Now all he could see was the diagonal smudge of rain and smoke.

Were we hit by lightning or cannon fire? He rubbed his eyes with soaked, salty knuckles. *That's ridiculous! There's no ship there! The storm is giving me hallucinations!*

Rose screamed from behind them. 'Wes, the ship! It's caught up!' She wobbled to her feet, stepping frantically over the ruined deck towards the others while jabbing her finger at the dreary horizon to their left. Wesley spun to match her line of sight.

'Yes, there it is,' Alice yelled. 'The ship. But it's not the one from Gold Harbour. It's… bigger!'

'Oh Wes!' Rose replied. 'Our boat! They're going to get us, or we're going to drown! What are we going to do now?!'

Wesley shrieked in frustration. 'I can't see it! The storm must be playing tricks on us!' The burnt man had to reach for one of the loose mast stays to keep his feet while Second Chance swayed violently beneath them. Seawater sprayed up into his eyes, and Southland's heavens continued to spill down on him from somewhere high above. He cleared his throat. 'Gather up the loose lines and tie down the mast. Bring over what's left of the sail. Let's get this boat stable again. I'll get us through this, if— oh… Shit. There it is.'

Wesley's mouth ceased making noise as he made out what the others had already seen. His bottom lip hung open, stunned. Right before him, emerging from the menacing grey, was the pale silhouette of a fantastically regal, fully rigged ship, gliding effortlessly through the downpour. The giant beast shimmered in the storm, but sailed slowly past them with a solid and possessed pace as if it were flying. Columns of cannons blinked at him beside what appeared to be the outline of giant wings.

Wesley glimpsed through the rain to position life aboard the vessel. It was too hard to see. 'What is it?' Alice asked in a stunned whisper as her brother drew nearer. 'A ghost ship or something?'

There's no such thing, Wesley thought. Usually, he would have shared the thought aloud, though right now he did not feel the need.

5

He was at the main deck's bulwark again, hands stretched over the smooth and weatherworn wood. Privacy was denied him once more, even where a moment alone to gather his senses would be all he needed.

He shouldered the boarders beside him. They shoved back to give him some room. Every one of them was frothing from the mouth, salivating at the sight of their prey, yet they knew even now not to step on Sebastian Seablood's toes. He was their leader, and was not one to anger.

Seb tried to relax, so much as it was possible. With the black sails over his head full of Southland wind, the Blood Hammer was carving through the water at full speed. The deck rumbled beneath him, shaking his nervous knees. It was impossible not to feel nervous before a boarding. Seb knew at least one man would die. Last time it was Bart, Seb's brother. This time it could be any of the men crowding around him. Seb was not fearful for his own life, though. He neither held it in such high esteem nor doubted his own abilities so much that the danger troubled him. The simple adrenaline, however, rattled his bones.

Beyond the port flank of the Blood Hammer—where Seb and his crew stood waiting—a sizeable schooner was drawing nearer and nearer. The sleek boat looked young, flaunting a polished hull and unstained, snowy sails. It looked to be made in Danidor, though the visible crew were largely from Brindia in the far north or somewhere near there, based on the especially deep hue of their skin and hair. The schooner chopped desperately through the water while the Blood Hammer, a brig of far larger size, closed in on its starboard side to cast darkness over the former amid the afternoon light.

As the two vessels neared, Seb could see the terror of their prey's crew, as plain as an open sea. They scrambled about the deck of their schooner like ants whose hole had been plugged up, pulling at sails for more speed or hurriedly stuffing powder down the shafts of their pistols. It was hard to feel sorry for them, Seb reflected; they had brought this attack upon themselves.

Amongst the Sentinels of Southland, trade was abundant and fiercely profitable. But it was also dangerous, supposing any merchant neglected to keep the sealord families involved in their dealings. Usually, a ship heading through the Sentinels' northern waters would be protected by a trade agreement made with the Seablood fleet, or by a considerable Western naval force. Sometimes, if a vessel were small enough—and fast enough—it would attempt the passage unaided. For these intruders, the Seablood fleet had a fistful of smaller allies, though even then there was certainly no way of stopping every trader who sought free business with the relatively newly settled Golden Coast of Southland.

Consequently, word would sometimes get back to trade hubs in other parts of the world such as Brindia, or even Sirland, that a well-navigated voyage could see any fool get through the Sentinels and back out again without a run-in with pirates. When this happened, schooners such as the present one would leave port in all manner of confidence, dreaming that the Rainbow Sea had cleared up despite overwhelming evidence to the contrary.

As far as Seb could see it, the wisest course of action was simple: pay the Seabloods some of your profits and secure safe passage through to Mariscos. No one need then worry about the other two families, or even worry about the small-time pirate scum that would jump out from rocky harbours to sink any boat they saw once they were done raping it.

Seb slid his fingers down his side, checking for the flintlock pistol wedged in his leather belt. It held its position well, though the spray from the waves dampened it a little. On his other side, a sharpened cutlass dangled loosely, Seb's weapon of choice. By the end of the hour, its blade would surely need to be cleaned and resharpened.

Shouts echoed across the water from the victim vessel. They were close. Seb's grip closed around the guarded handle of his sword.

The schooner's crew were now loosing some of their sails, attempting to drop behind and let the Blood Hammer sail on ahead. *They really don't know what they're doing,* Seb thought, sadly. The poor merchants had fallen for the same trap that snared almost every boat that decided to sail through Seablood waters in a hurry. The schooner was obviously headed for the

Dorian town of Mariscos, one of the three major settlements along the Golden Coast. They had therefore wanted to cut as close to the outcropping Del Continente Peninsula as they could, since they had arrived from the north, and squeeze through the gap between the mainland and the Deceiver, the most northwest of the four major Sentinel islands. To the settlers, this gap was called the Throat, and it led straight in to the sheltered harbour beyond. But what these traders did not know was that with every throat comes a set of teeth.

The Teeth was a vast triangle of partially submerged rocks that stretched out from the tip of the peninsula. They were clearly visible once nearby and rarely wrecked any hulls, but they would force an unsuspecting vessel to rush into a sloppy course recalibration that would see them detour sluggishly through dangerous waters for about an hour. Such was more than enough time for the Blood Hammer to notice their presence and set up an ocean-borne intercept.

If the schooner had been more cunning, it would have tried its luck navigating *through* the Teeth, though intelligence was clearly lacking aboard the freshly built deck.

Seb braced as the target vessel finally pulled up to the Blood Hammer's side. The merchant rabble began to loose some of their pistols' shots. The Seablood crew ducked at the sound, rising shortly after. There would not be enough time for reloading.

'Grapples!' Seb shouted, drawing his cutlass from his belt and raising it ferociously. The men at the bulwark swung their grappling hooks onto the passing schooner's deck and into its rigging, drawing them back as quickly as they could so the hooks caught fast. They heaved lengths of rope back onto the Blood Hammer, forcing the schooner closer. Once the tension caught between the two vessels, the deck jolted. The seasoned crew held their feet with ease.

'Keep pulling!' Seb shouted, watching hungrily as the victim's ship splashed closer and closer. Almost close enough to touch.

'Guns!'

The pop of blunderbuss rifles filled the air, and smoke drifted into the eager wind. Several members of the merchant crew fell backward, either injured or dead. The others were quickly distracted by those that had been shot. Too distracted.

A woody thunder strike sounded as the schooner's gunwale thudded into the Blood Hammer's flank. Seb was now close enough to see the fear in the prey's very eyes, even as he stood above them, stepping up onto the railing.

'Board!' The final command was answered with a roar of enthusiasm from the rest of Seb's boarding crew. Pistols drawn and swords flailing, the Seablood men leapt aboard the schooner like a wave of blades crashing over sand.

Seb's feet landed softly on the merchant deck. Screams of pain and fright swept through his hair, cooling his sweaty forehead. He glanced from side to side, watching for any danger, or stray Seablood blade. It was soon apparent there was no real threat; the merchants were attempting self-defence at best, with some even opting to jump overboard. Relief coursed through Seb's veins, filling his heart with fire and violence. He lunged forward into the heart of the action, sought out a stray merchant and swept his blade through the man's dark-skinned face.

The corpse rolled onto the deck. A dagger fell from the sky and landed immediately in its chest. Seb looked up, surprised. A Brindian sailor had apparently tried to kill him by dropping the small weapon from the crow's nest, nestled high up on the main mast. Snickering, Seb sucked in a mouthful of moist, bloody air and skidded over to the ratlines on the schooner's port side. He joined half a dozen of his men in scaling the rigging while those below began to flood into the vessel's lower deck. Seb had always been quicker than the others, especially on the ratlines, so he found himself rising up into the thrashing sails far sooner than his comrades could.

Usually, Seb would not have put himself at the frontline of battle, but the fever had caught him and his steel was hungry for blood. He was at the crow's nest before he had time to reconsider, and found himself hanging below a trio of cornered Brindians wielding swords of their own. They poked them down at their attacker from over the edge of the oversized basket they were stuffed in, with as little reach as children. Seb moved about amongst the wobbling rigging as the mast jolted vigorously, throwing everybody up in the sails from side to side. He faked left and right, trying to find an opening to lunge up and disembowel his foes. Unfortunately, the sailors were not in such a hurry to die.

Way above the schooner's guts, the wind was exceptionally strong. The enormous sway of the mast was throwing off Seb's coordination. White sails and blue sky swirled around him. He wedged his boots between some of the ropes to gain some stability.

One of Seb's boarders pushed a blunderbuss up through the ratlines and blasted a hole in the base of the crow's nest. Splinters shot into Seb's arm. He braced first, then shoved his cutlass through the hole, unsure whether he had made any contact with flesh at all. A couple of other Seabloods had now made it to the wooden cage atop the vessel too, and were harassing its inhabitants with vicious, aimless stabbing.

Just as the Brindians became distracted with the other assailants, Seb swung his weight up to the side of the crow's nest and shoved his cutlass into the shoulders of one of them. Another turned to him. He ducked swiftly, avoiding an enthusiastic slash. He then stretched an arm through the side of the cage and yanked at an ankle. A Brindian toppled harshly into a companion. The effect allowed the other Seablood crewmen to pounce into the nest.

One of the Brindians managed to slip free unscathed, and dropped from his lookout into the rigging below with surprising agility. He flicked a dagger from his belt and whacked it into the arm of a nearby boarder who was still clambering up. The Seablood man grunted as his arm shook in pain and his grip on the ratlines came loose. He fell backwards from the ropes, scrambling, and bounced off the mainsail before crashing into the deck below.

Bill! Seb clenched his jaw. *It was you that had to die today.* He sprang from his perch and hurtled down after the offending Brindian. *I'll see that you were the only one!*

The merchant sailor noticed Seb's approach and readied his dagger, but Sebastian Seablood was not fool enough to openly meet an adversary in a glorious mid-rigging duel. When it came to fighting, there were no such requirements, Seb knew all too well. There was only death and life, killing and being killed. So Seb took his cutlass to the shrouds supporting the ratlines and hacked away at the rope. The Brindian cursed and scurried upwards to stop him, at which point Seb wrapped his sword arm around the rigging and used his now free hand to yank a boot from his foot. He threw it at the approaching man's face.

The Brindian was momentarily startled. Seb slid down the lines into his foe, then swung his cutlass into that foe's wrist so hard it almost completely severed the Brindian's hand along with the blade it held. Seb released his cutlass from his own fist and pushed his thumb into the other man's eye socket, grasping the brown face tightly in his palm. He kicked the man's legs free and thrust the limp head aside so that the Brindian flew from the rigging to land fatally beside dead Bill. After the thump, both bodies lay still beside each other in a growing pool of blood.

Seb let the air from his lungs. He felt his muscles ease. Below, the shouts and screams had all but ceased, and the boarders were assembling amidships, ready for the next act. The fight was over, the vessel was won. All Seb had to do was descend the ratlines and claim it.

He climbed down steadily, the whole while hoping it was only Bill that he would have to farewell this day. By the look of the blood-splattered deck beneath him, he decided it was most likely the case. The cut-down bodies of the Brindian crew were sprawled out all over the schooner's surface, and their ranks appeared to exclude any of the comparably pale-faced

Seablood boarders.

Seb's feet came solidly back down to the security of the main deck. The salty atmosphere mingled with the sweat in his eyes so that he had to rub them before he could see his crew properly. To his right side, the clattering of the two vessels filled the air as they rubbed up against each other. To his left, the excited waters of the Throat kissed at the schooner's hull. Before him—after he forced open his eyes—he saw that the Seabloods stood in a semi-circle around a single pleading merchant.

A few extra sailors were already spilling over from the Blood Hammer, reefing some of the schooner's sails to slow it down. It would not be long before Captain Seablood himself hopped aboard to properly claim his barely earned prize, so Seb had but a small window of opportunity to exert his dominance over the vessel. The Seablood heir intended to wring as much important information from the squirming Brindian as he could. His father would only get carried away with the trivial.

The lone merchant was still begging. As Seb stepped forward, the man grovelled at his feet, clawing at former's boots as a kitten would. 'Please, sir. Please, sir. Don't kill me, sir.'

The Bridian was supposedly the schooner's navigator. He would have hoped to be, at least. Seb had given strict orders to his boarding crew—as he always did—to keep the navigator alive. A ship's master could be killed without a second thought, or its captain, or its mates, but a ship's navigator was to be preserved as if they were part of said ship's cargo. That is, unless the ship was to be sunk.

'What's your name?' Seb asked, giving the Brindian a little kick. The navigator cowered back from Seb's feet, hyperventilating with his face down. The surrounding crew chuckled at the pathetic lack of backbone. Their menacing laugh was a terrifying sound to behold, and it appeared as though it caused the man to soil himself. It certainly smelt like it had, though there were a number of oozing dead bodies strewn about that could also have been to blame.

'Answer me! What is your name?'

'Pran... Sir. Please, sir. Please don't kill me. Please, sir.'

The Brindian's accent was thick, but it seemed his comprehension of Sirlish was adequate. That very fact alone possibly saved the man's life.

'Answer me properly, Pran, and you may live a little longer,' instructed Seb. 'What is your vessel carrying, and where to?'

The little Pran tilted his head up at Seb and spoke with his lip quivering. 'We going to Mariscos. But I don't know what we carrying. Food and... ah, I don't know! I just... I just... directions. They hire me, in Brindia. For directions.'

'Yes, yes. You just directions,' Seb mocked. 'Why were you headed to Mariscos, through Seablood waters, without our consent?'

Pran swallowed, offering brief respite from his frantic panting. 'I... I don't understand, sir, please.'

'Why were you sailing to Southland,' Seb clarified, 'from Brindia. Without making a deal with us?' A hint of irritation flavoured Seb's slow tone.

'Oh, ah. Please, sir, how we make a deal? We just come from home, and come here. We want trade with Mariscos. Please sir, I don't know.'

Seb grumbled. Perhaps this navigator was going to be less

useful than he had hoped. 'Who sent you with these supplies?' he interrogated further. Pran answered the question with watery, pleading eyes.

The probing was cut short by the sound of Captain Theodore Seablood's well nourished body slumping from the Blood Hammer to the schooner's trim deck. A number of mates assisted him and a number of others accompanied his heavy sides too. Salvino, the Blood Hammer's quartermaster, was right by his shoulder as usual, following his captain as a shadow would. The Dorian man wore the smug expression that was ever found upon his face.

Seb turned to Pran. 'Straighten up and stop shaking,' he ordered. 'This is Captain Seablood, commander of the Seablood fleet and Sealord of the Northern Sentinels.'

Captain Ted had dressed himself in his finest, sporting his characteristic curled wig beneath his wide-brimmed hat. He wore a clean ruffled shirt and an ornately decorated coat atop gold stockings and polished shoes. The man looked more readied for a fancy dinner party than for sailing the Rainbow Sea, though he commanded the respect he sought, regardless.

'Step aside, boy,' Ted snorted, shuffling past Seb with his entourage at his back. Pran had raised himself onto his knees, and was trying his hardest not to tremble.

The captain sniffed around obnoxiously. 'This filth is the sailing master, I assume?' The question was aimed at nobody in particular.

'It is,' Seb confirmed. 'He doesn't seem to—'

'You there, sailing master, there have been sightings of a vessel that ought not be striding above the waves. A full rigged ship with wings on its stern and a bird painted on its course sails. Have you seen it?'

Pran could not help but tremble. 'Please, sir. I don't think I see a ship with wings. Many ships, no wings. Please, sir.'

Ted cursed. 'Argh! That bloody ghost ship can't evade us forever.'

Seb cleared his throat. 'You don't think we should—'

'Good piece of wood, this!' Ted interrupted. 'New, big, and sturdy, by the feel of it. Pretty, too, once we clean away all this Brindian muck. It'll sell for a good price in Mariscos, or make for a good addition to our family.' He scratched his flabby chin. 'I'm of a mind to keep it. Sebastian, boy, what do you say? Want to captain this schooner?'

Seb puffed out his chest. He had never been offered a vessel before. Even Bart had been held too close to Ted's bosom for the honour, while he lived. *Perhaps things are different, now that father has only one son,* Seb wondered. Though there was little purpose in dwelling on it, Seb's answer was always going to be the same. 'If I were to leave the Blood Hammer,' he said, almost robotically, 'who then would continue leadership of the family once you are too old? Bartram is… no longer above the waves. My place is with my blood and kin, father: with you.'

'Your blood…yes. Of course.' Ted grumbled. 'I might dare call you ungrateful, boy. This is a fine boat.' The captain gave a nervous glance to his right and left. What Seb had said could not be faulted fairly. Ted had to be careful not to say anything that might help his crew decide that his son might be ready to take the reigns. The predicament showed clearly in the way his lips crumpled up. 'But I have others who will serve it well.

Salvino, you would make a good captain, I'm sure. The schooner is yours.'

'If I might,' Salvino interjected, his sweet styling both amused and overconfident. The plainly dressed man stepped out from Ted's shadow into the attention of all those gathered. His slender and dark-featured shape blocked Seb's view of his father's face. 'I have served you for six years, captain. I fear my place stands alongside that of your son. I would sooner call myself a true Seablood, if only I could, than a captain under your name.'

Ted cursed. 'Tell me, when did the fools about my waist become such honour-bound mongrels, scarcely short of Greyhide and his pack of wolves? Rob, are you about?'

A holler came up all muffled from behind the captain's entourage, and Rob began shoving his way through his fellow sailors towards the small clearing, where Pran still trembled on the deck. Soon enough, the rough-looking man slid in beside Seb, silently awaiting Ted's command. His hands were clasped together in front of him.

'Rob,' growled Ted, 'if you don't want the bloody thing, you can sail her in to Mariscos and bring me back her weight in gold.'

'Aye, aye.' Rob nodded, his cheeks red. 'I'll captain her under your name, Ted. All I need is an order, and it'll be done.'

'It better be,' said Ted. 'You can have twenty men from the Blood Hammer. That ought to be enough to get you by. Salvino, you can sort that out, yes? Keep the Brindian on as your sailing master too, but throw him overboard if he keeps whimpering like that. As for your order... You can head up the east coast of the Del Continente and reave those new settlements we spotted 'till I send any further word. Stay clear of the Teeth, and keep an eye out for our ghost ship. I don't care what bitch you've got your cock stuck in, if you so much as smell the thing, I want you sailing back to me before you soften up.'

'Aye aye,' Rob confirmed. Salvino twirled to rest a delicate hand on Rob's shoulder, and pressed him off towards the schooner's stern. With what little understanding he could muster, Pran hobbled after them.

Captain Seablood raised his voice, its deep authority cutting the thick air like a blunt knife. 'As for the rest of you, I want every piece o' loot back on the Hammer. No sense in giving Captain Robert a head start now, is there?'

The crew burst into action, quickly sinking into the schooner's lower hold, feet casually trampling the Brindian dead as they moved about. Seb looked down at one of the mangled corpses before him with a frown, then skipped over it after Ted. 'Father, don't you think you're getting carried away with the Frontiere? It could very well have been an illusion, no more.'

Ted Seablood snapped upright, turning his short façade sharply toward Seb. 'There have been other sightings, boy. The Frontiere has risen from the sea floor, and I plan to put it back there, before...' Ted shut his mouth and tenderly held his naked throat.

'I just mean to say, father... Ghosts are not—'

'Perhaps I should send your girl off with Rob,' Ted barked, changing the subject without even a blink. 'Maybe then you'll grow up, and stop clinging to me like you did your mother's breast. You know you near screamed me to deafness after I ripped you from her. Worse than she did when I poked her with my own little girl here.' Ted tapped his hip, where his prized dirk sat, strapped so tightly to his flesh that it almost sunk out of existence. 'There were times I thought of using it to cut my ears off, you know.' He glared at Seb, his lordly eyes betraying a mean sort of glee.

'Never mind,' Seb sighed, shuffling past his father to climb back aboard the Blood Hammer. *Search all you want, old man,* Seb thought. *Maybe you'll die sooner for it.*

6

It was morning. That abominable Southland sun was once again rising over the Sentinels, parading about amongst a chaotic swirl of clouds as it so often liked to do. Its position in the sky was now the only thing giving Wesley any sense of direction. No longer could he distinguish what was an island and what was mainland. No longer could he locate himself upon the simplistic map of the Sentinels he had pinned down in his mind's eye. And even worse than all that, Wesley could no longer control the movement of Second Chance, the ruined yacht.

A full night had come and gone since the storm that broke their yacht's mast. The three Kings had each taken turns attempting sleep throughout it, even as their wooden bed rocked unsteadily on the sea's currents. When it had been Wesley's shift, he could barely close his eyes. His burnt back radiated inexorable pain through his torso every minute he neglected to splash waves against it. Eventually, he found a rag aboard the yacht that he soaked in water and wrapped around his trunk. It was hardly a cure, but it felt better than the plain air did.

The moon had filled the long night with light enough for the small family to spy sparkling ripples in the sea that surrounded them, and little else. Wesley had kept watch for land, informing his wife and his sister that if they did not eventually wash into a beach, the broken pile of wood and rope on which they floated would eventually be carried out into the deep ocean, where full-sized swells would surely topple them. As a result, both Rose and Alice kept their gaze firmly upon the dark distance, though it did not stop them from chatting whenever they were both awake.

The two women maintained that they had seen a giant ship in the middle of the storm, sailing right by them in the thunderous rain, and they managed to keep discovering new ways to bring it up. It became Wesley's task to continually shepherd them back to reality, reminding them of their predicament's harsh truth, and how their ghost ship hallucination was no more than a false vision conjured by a mutual and desperate desire for hope, or something of the sort.

Despite his best efforts, Wesley spied no land that night, nor did he quench the others' wonder at what they thought they had seen. Instead, Second Chance had drifted aimlessly over the surface of the Rainbow Sea, peacefully undisturbed by anything but the constant slap of low waves against her hull.

Now that the morning had sprung, it was finally clear which direction they were floating. South. Ever since the first light of the day, Wesley had watched a few distant lumps of land edge slowly northward. To make matters even more frustrating, those lumps had crawled nearer and nearer until Second Chance floated right between them, never quite reaching land.

At the family's either side, those two enormous outcroppings of green rose high, allowing only a small channel of water to pass between them. It was almost impossible to judge the distance from one side of the gap to the other, though Wesley thought he could have perhaps swum to the shore had he needed to. He almost suggested that the three of them abandon the yacht to attempt the challenge, but by then the current had picked up in the channel and would almost certainly have taken them far away from anything they tried to swim toward.

Wesley turned from the glaring sun to gaze at the piece of earth that sat so temptingly close on the west side of the gap. There, the thick forest of the Sentinels was pushed up into the sky by a grey-brown cliff that leant over them like a dark tower. It contrasted with the relatively shallow slope of the jungle on the east bank, making this one seem especially tall.

The rock shone magnificently in the morning light, steaming as the moisture from the night before dried up. An eagle circled over its peak, huge wings stretched regally in front of its fanned tail. Wesley had seen an eagle like that before. A Warhawk, it was called, at least by the settlers of Southland. The regal birds were so named due to their propensity for engaging in fierce airborne combat any time one found itself in another's territory. The name was also shared by the region's fabled pirate legend, Halfeye Warhawk. The old convict was said to have commandeered the Frontiere, one of the very first Sirlish ships to land at Gold Harbour over a decade ago, shortly after the Sirlish settlement was founded. As far as the story went, Halfeye proceeded afterwards to plunder the Rainbow

Sea through its early years of trade with the Western Nations, at a time when the gold was flowing particularly freely. He was further rumoured to have stashed all of his accumulated reserves in a secret location within the maze of the Sentinels. Halfeye's Hoard, that treasure was called.

Usually, Wesley did not believe such stories, but when certain officers he had spoken to—and even other convicts—had witnessed the theft of the Frontiere first hand, it was near foolishness to deny the truth of it.

Alice came up beside her brother. 'It's pretty amazing, isn't it?' she said, tilting her chin toward the cliff.

'Sure.' Wesley brushed away the comment and turned his head, peering through the great gap to the distant islands ahead. 'I'm more interested in those. I think we might be able to run aground on that one.' He pointed at a medium-sized land mass on the horizon, directly to their south. It was a bulky shard of rock and jungle, like most of the Sentinels, steep, rocky and overgrown, though it had a ring of white beach circling its feet. There was a wide channel to either side of it, from what Wesley could make out, but with the help of the rudder it would be possible to steer the yacht's movements just enough to drive it right into the pale sand, he supposed.

'And what will we do there?' asked Alice. She was not trying to be condescending, or even rude. She was just asking. Nobody had yet dared speak a word of the horrible mistake Wesley had driven them into by stealing the Second Chance. Rose might have said 'I told you so', or something of that order, but it seemed the mood among the three Kings had become too resigned and melancholy for it. There were only so many times hope could be broken before that hope was replaced by sickening numbness. In a way, Wesley was glad for it; he had had enough trouble dealing with his emotions, let alone Rose's. He only hoped now that he could somehow transfer his numbness to the burnt patch on his back.

'It depends how far south we've drifted,' Wesley answered his sister, rubbing his hand slowly back and forth over the bandage around his waist. He accessed the map in his mind, but found no help in it. 'We might be able to wait for a trade ship headed into Morchport.' He smirked shrewdly. 'Or we could just live in the trees for the rest of our lives, like the Ijians do. What's it matter? Without a functioning boat we'll never be able to find Halfeye's Hoard. And if we're found by anyone from Gold Harbour... we're as good as dead.' He half-expected Rose to burst into another teary fit after hearing him, though it appeared she had finally composed herself. She was sitting at the bow of the yacht, watching the water churn through golden blades of uncombed hair. Her soft, pale feet were curled up beneath her sun-dried sleeping gown, accentuating her alluring figure.

Alice sighed. In distinct contrast, Wesley's sister stood by his side with her skinny limbs poised for action. Wesley yearned for a task he could put her to. Unfortunately, the only task any of them could busy themselves with was to take the helm and steer the rudder towards the island to their south, and Wesley was not about to give that responsibility away. He stepped across the deck to the wheel and took its handles in his palms.

Alice followed him to the centre of the vessel and stood

again by his side. 'Can't we steer towards that island there?' She pointed at the larger distant land mass just to the left of their heading. The second green lump could very well have been connected to the first, although from their current vantage point a narrow channel less than a mile in width certainly appeared to separate them into two islands, even if the other end of the channel was not yet visible.

'Why?' Wesley questioned. 'Because it's bigger?' He shook his head. 'We could steer there, maybe, but this one is closer to the mainland, I think. We should have a higher chance of reaching Morchport if we crash here.' He complimented his explanation with inexact hand gestures.

The Second Chance had cleared the great gap now, and was en route for an eventual beaching. From its solitary location in the middle of a vast cerulean seascape, islands could be spotted in almost every direction, rising out of the flat water like the tips of a jagged, sunken mountain range. The Sentinels were as a labyrinth to a sailor, complicated and dense; a collection of islands so twisted it was a wonder Captain Winston Wimsworth ever found the rich soil that they guarded.

Wesley guessed it would be short of an hour before the current drew them onto the target island's beach. The yacht was still closer to the cliff than their destination, but with every passing second it seemed less the case. Through the fresh morning air, their goal grew clearer and clearer, standing proud against the pale shadows of the islands behind and beside it. Soon enough, Wesley was sure that the boat would land ashore whether he continued to steer or not. He held the wheel tightly anyway, to be certain.

What are *we going to do once we land?* Wesley began thinking to himself. *We could hike straight to the island's south end and try to hail a Morch ship from there.* A rumble interrupted his thoughts, bubbling up from his stomach. The feeling was a welcome distraction from the stinging pain of his burn. *Maybe this island has some sort of food on it. Maybe coconuts.*

'Wes! Wes! A ship!' Rose's yelp tore through the wind as she got up from her slouch with a surprised jolt. 'Look!'

Wesley peered over the helm towards the gap between the smaller and larger islands ahead. Alice leapt to the front of the yacht, her own sleeping gown matching Rose's. 'Can we get their attention?' She was more excited than she ought to have been.

Wesley released the wheel involuntarily, his heart rate accelerating. This was no ghost ship. Rounding the corner into view between the two green lumps was a large sailing vessel, so clearly visible he could almost pick out the numerous sailors atop its main deck. The derelict monstrosity was a dark umber in hue, with a damaged upper deck and a boxy sterncastle. Flying smoothly over its jagged body were full sails, each bulging boldly. Even at a distance of near a full sea mile, a strange figure could be seen painted on each of the lower course sails and on the foretopsail. It resembled a squid, and it shimmered in white against the deep black of the sailcloth.

Black sails! Wesley had never seen a ship with black sails before, but he immediately guessed they could be nothing but a bad omen. He grappled the wheel again, suddenly unsure of what to do with it. 'Rose, Alice, get back here.'

The girls gave him a wary look, and moved across the yacht

towards him, hesitating only slightly.

'It's a pirate ship,' Wesley said, as soon as they were close enough to hear him say it quietly. Once again, Rose surprisingly refrained from erupting into a flood of sobs, though the fear hit her face like a heavy sack of potatoes nevertheless. She froze on the spot. Alice produced an odd noise at the suggestion, one laced with uncontrollable panic. She quickly whipped around to peek again at the oncoming vessel. 'Pirates?! Are you sure? Are they coming for us? Or will they just go by?' Her mouth trembled as she spoke.

Wesley grumbled, the numbness of his emotions starting to waver. 'It looks like pirates to me, I think. What trade ship would sneak between two islands like that? But... It's too big, maybe. And they may go past us still. I damn hope they do.'

Alice began to move about uncomfortably, her eyes fixed on the ship. It was already gaining on their position, veering so that its bow pointed right at them. The squids on its front sails glared back over the water.

'Just... keep calm,' Wesley said, as if he had the situation under control. 'They're still a ways away. If we can get to the island before they near us, we can run into the jungle... Just in case.' The words did nothing to comfort Alice, and they did even less for Rose, though there was no choice but to believe them. All three fell into deathly silence, listening timidly to the slop of the Rainbow Sea while their yacht floated serenely towards the island shore.

Time raced by as the Kings watched the pirate vessel draw nearer. Wesley stayed at the helm, pulling the yacht as far starboard as he could without turning it against the current.

Rose huddled up beside him, clutching his shoulders. Moisture seeped from her hands, adding to Wesley's discomfort, but he did not push her away. Alice was holding her breath, trying not to look at the ship lest its crew sees her doing so.

Minute after minute did little but bring the pirate ship even closer. The island, on the other hand, did not seem to get closer at all. By the time the vessel was a quarter-mile away, it made a slight turn eastward so that its course would take the thing past the Second Chance instead of over it. Despite the new heading, the presence and proximity of the strangers sent chills up and down Wesley's spine, yanking his body into involuntary shivers as he pushed emotion deeper and deeper into his gut.

At the great beast's approach, Wesley was able to make out much more of its detail. A row of open gunports stretched out below the main deck, though its cannons were withdrawn. Several ugly holes had been patched along its flank, while several others had been left untouched so the darkness of the gun deck seeped out. The squids on the sails became clearer too. They looked more like jellyfish.

Wesley swallowed hard, his mouth dry. The vessel now loomed over them with a dark and menacing authority, the top of its mainmast pricking the bowel of the sun. It was packed with ragged sailors, either standing at the ready or fussing about with their sheets. Some of them were running up and down between the waist and the quarterdeck. Some were resting their elbows on the railing, plainly ogling the three Kings and their battered yacht. Some others, near the stern, were...

Wesley's heart felt as if it missed a beat. His throat tried to turn upside down in his neck as a sudden flush of hot blood rushed through to his skull, chilling every hair that protruded from it. Those sailors near the stern were jumping aboard a sleek longboat that was supended over the edge of the vessel's gunwale. A handful of their fellow crewmen were lowering it into the choppy water.

The ship showed no sign of slowing, but the pirates continued to drop the ship's boat anyway. On the route the larger vessel was taking, it was as near Second Chance as it was going to get, a fact that only made the pirates work faster. They untied a couple of knots at either end of the longboat and let the lines slip through their pulleys, allowing the boat to fall down beside its parent and slam into the sea. The eight pirates aboard sustained the impact without fuss and each took up an oar. They began rowing… right in Wesley's direction.

'Shit shit shit, they're coming for us! They're coming for us!' Wesley's composure finally broke. He released his shaking arms from the wheel, shoved Rose aside and started hobbling around in circles. Rose was crying. She fell into a ball and rolled herself backward until she was pressed firmly against the wooden planks of the cabin wall.

Wesley leapt abruptly past the helm to lean over the yacht's bow. The island was still half a mile away. He could swim that distance, he knew, but could Rose? Could Alice? His sister was trailing behind him, bewildered but not incapacitated. 'What if they're not pirates?' she said. 'Wesley? What if they're not pirates? They could be traders! They could be trying to save us!'

Wesley turned towards her, dark shadows cast over his eyes. 'Unlikely.' He grimaced. It was still a possibility, but the odds were not strong enough to take the chance. *Black sails, battered ship, and they took the narrow channel. If they're merchants, I'm Captain Wimsworth!*

Wesley spun back towards the longboat. It was skidding over the waves at an even greater speed than he had anticipated, the bearded faces of its crew hungry and smiling. Their sharp teeth came horribly into view. They were yellow and sparse, and getting closer. And closer.

'Can you swim to the island?' Wesley forced the words out as quickly as he could.

Alice drew a sharp breath. 'I can swim it, I think. But they'll still get us! We can't get away, Wes!'

'We have to do it. They'll take the yacht, and leave us to drown.'

Alice darted across the deck and snatched up a piece of the shattered mast. It was a heavy chunk of wood with a splintered point on one end. She waved it about, her sleeping gown whirling up around her thighs as she twisted. 'We can fight them off. It's our only option.'

'It's not an option! Rose, get up, we have to swim to shore. Quick, they're almost on us!'

The longboat was near enough to smell. The two closest pirates pulled their oars into the wooden hull and stretched out their fingers, ready to grapple the yacht as soon it came within reach.

Rose shook herself and stood up, hurriedly snatching a smaller piece of broken mast to jab out in front of her chest like a dagger.

'No Rose, we have to swim! Come on!' Wesley grabbed at

his wife's wrist. She screamed and tried to break free. 'We can't get away, Wes! We can't get away!'

Wood slammed against wood, and the pirates scurried onto Second Chance like rats, slipping curved swords from their belts. Wesley jerked Rose towards the bow, where Alice was crouched behind her stick. He faced his sister and caught her eye, just for a moment. A painful moment. A moment where his true terror was revealed. The woman nodded, knowing at last the truth of their danger. 'Jump, Alice! Swim!'

There was a light splash. Wesley focussed back on his wife. 'Come on Rose, we have to jump! Three, two—'

'I'm not swimming Wes! I'm not! I won't make it! We'll surrender. We surrender! Please don't hurt us!' She threw her hands up, losing her grip on the makeshift dagger as the pirates circled them, swords raised.

Wesley made a move to abandon the yacht, but Rose's fingers clenched around his wrist and he faltered.

'Are you'se Blackbones?' One of the pirates growled. He tipped his half-bald head forward in nod, exposing the grime that had taken up residence there.

'Black bones?' Wesley whimpered. 'No. No! I don't know what black bones are. We've got nothing to do with them! Nothing!'

The pirate froze, puzzled. He held his blade out beside him to halt his companions. 'You say yer not,' he continued, leering at Wesley through lifeless eyes. 'But how'm I s'post t' know?'

'I've never *heard* of black bones before!' Wesley begged. He held his back to the bow, as did Rose.

'Ah, I see. Yer a liar, is it? Well we can argue 'bout it back on deck, then. Come on boys, grab 'em.'

Eight pirates lashed out, seizing the two Kings, forcing their submission. A couple of fists made sure Wesley was well and weak, but he welcomed their bluntness amongst so many swords.

Like spiders hauling prey into their nests, the pirates whipped Wesley and Rose into the longboat with absolute—and painful—efficiency. *They're leaving the yacht!* Wesley realised. *They didn't want it. They wanted us!*

Four of the eight took up oars while the others held their captives rigidly against the boat's wooden stools and bound their hands behind their backs. Rose had swallowed her sobs, choosing only to emit a yelp as the ropes were pulled tighter. Wesley refused to look at her, afraid beyond anything he had ever felt before. Afraid for his life, and for Rose's. He instead watched the remains of Second Chance as it floated away upon the Rainbow Sea, towards the island, towards freedom. He soon realised he could not spot Alice, so he shut his eyes tight in denial. *Let her get away! And let me live! God, let me live!*

The longboat chopped through the water, chasing the larger vessel it had come from. Once Wesley's hands were fully tied, a pirate grasped his hair and shoved his chin onto the boat's floor, holding it there with his boot. Dirty water splashed into his mouth, and each wave jolted his teeth together.

The punches he had taken fused with the burn on his back to make his whole body swell with pain. He tried to shuffle into a better position, but his attempts only made his head pull hopelessly against the foot that held it down. *God help me! How has this happened? Surely there's only so many things that can go wrong in a person's life! Three years a convict, shipped off to Southland, house burned down by Ijian fire, a freak storm at sea, and now this! It cannot be! What did I do to deserve it? It cannot be the end. Oh, God! They're going to kill me! Why wouldn't they? What do I need to say to save my life?*

Wesley's thoughts bounced around in his skull until their echo became white noise. Their coherent pattern devolved into pure anguish. Before long, the only thing Wesley could think about was the pain that cracked through his jaw every time the longboat slapped through another swell. It repeated itself on and on and on, beating his nerves to dust, reducing Wesley to a limp bag of bone and blood. On and on and on. Until finally the pirate lifted his boot. Solid hands wrenched him to his feet by the armpits. He was going up. He rolled his head and squinted his eyes as fuzzy vision became ever so slightly sharper. He was being lifted onto the mother ship.

Sluggishly, Wesley's racing thoughts returned, though the lingering pain in his jaw still burned even more than the burn on his back. *Is this the end?* he asked himself. *Is this what my life was leading up to? What a waste it has been!*

Once the boat was hoisted high enough, Wesley was thrown from its clutches onto the even coarser deck of the large ship. Pirates crowded around him but he dared not look up at them. Rose grunted as she was tossed to the deck by his side. Wesley felt the touch of her soft fingers. They scraped over his burn, so he violently shook them away. Rose sucked in a sharp breath, no doubt concealing yet another sob.

Wesley let his muscles to drape over the harsh wood. A sense of odd peace washed over him, inspiring him to regain his wits by letting a few throbs of pain thaw out his stiffness. That peace was cut swiftly short by unforgiving hands that forced him into a kneel. He could not help but look up then; the terrible light of the Southland sun compelled his eyes to open, to view the complete mess that he had pulled his family into.

He almost laughed; what he saw was so outlandish, so ridiculous. He was kneeling next to his wife on the deck of an oversized pirate ship, black sails billowing above his head, each flaunting the white silhouette of a giant jellyfish. All over the vessel's weathered and battle-worn surface stood glaring pirates, all clad in stinking rags, and each seeming to posses an unkempt, half-cut beard. They kept their distance from Wesley and Rose, allowing an empty circle to form around the captives. Each of their ugly faces looked into the circle with a hunger or sorts, or a wry smile that could be interpreted as any number of horrible things. Wesley urged himself not to think about what these foul creatures intended to do with him. He looked through the rigging that flew over their heads at the distant green spikes of the nearest Sentinels. His breathing was slow, but his heart was beating like a hammer in his neck.

Hold it, God! Welsey declared, silently. *I see it now! I see it! This is not how it is! You must be confused; this isn't how I end! It cannot be. It will not be! My whole life is still ahead of me. These pirates want something from me, that's all. And I will give it to them, whatever it takes!*

The circle made a small part just in front of the two Kings. A pirate squeezed through the gap, moving himself into the empty space. He looked in no particular way different from the others, aside from his beard—which was cut crudely down to little more than stubble—being almost completely white. His face was smothered in dust, his head was half balding, and the rags he wore had not been washed in years. Despite all this, he seemed to hold authority over his comrades.

He glared down at Wesley in disgust. 'You say you're not a Blackbone, huh?'

Wesley returned the stare of the white-faced pirate, but his own was weak in comparison. Pathetic, even. He held his chin up anyway, certain now that being a Blackbone carried a weight of significance with these people. *Perhaps enough to save my life*, he thought.

'Actually,' Wesley lied, 'I am a Blackbone.'

The white-faced pirate's dirty eyebrows raised in a curious smirk. 'Right then!' he said, triumphantly. 'Kill him.'

A darkly dressed pirate strode into the circle, pulled a large sword from his belt and swung it clean through Wesley's neck.

Rose screamed. The sound split the thick Southland air like thunder. She screamed a scream that yanked every last molecule of air from her lungs and throat. A hoarse, terrible and deathly scream. Then she collapsed onto the deck, just as her husband's corpse crashed beside her, spitting blood onto her gown. She gasped for air, choking on the sudden dryness of her innards. She screamed again, tears bubbling from her eyes and nose, drool slopping from her mouth. The sound this time was like a cough, the dry remnant of all her life spluttering out in fear, in horror, in pain. She knew she was dead. As dead as if it were her neck. There was no mercy here. No hope. No life. *Wes!* She could not look up, not move. Her forehead banged against the floor, her mouth open and leaking, her eyes slammed shut in denial. But she could not deny it. The world began to spin. She felt as light as an autumn leaf in the breeze, seeping into the void, losing her consciousness.

It was well after it was said that the ensuing words registered in her ears. 'Save the girl a moment longer. We'll give everyone a good go at her before we throw her overboard. No sense in wasting a good woman now!' The other pirates laughed in approval.

Sentences formed in the ever-darkening emptiness within Rose's skull, but all that spat out of her mouth was 'No! No!'

Already she was being lifted from the cold deck, her soiled gown getting ripped from her skin. 'No! No! No!' the words crumbled in her mouth, dry, lifeless, frightened.

There was no way out. She was dead, she knew. There was nothing she could put between herself and death now. All that pirates ever wanted was blood and gold. Blood and gold. She had so much of one, but none of the other.

A thought sparked in her fading psyche. As if her tongue had become fully aware of its impending doom, it allowed her to speak the one last sentence before she fainted.

'I know where Halfeye's Hoard is,' she said. 'I know where it is…'

And then came the black.

7

S he muttered a whisper-quiet curse under her breath. *What have I done?* she asked herself. *I should've listened to Wesley sooner. Traders! I'm such an idiot! It's a wonder any of them even get about in this sea. Why would anyone tread amongst so many vipers?*

She peeked around the cutter. It was a small ship's boat with a short mast that allowed it to "cut" through the waves further out to sea. Six pirates were aboard with her, all watching her movements carefully, holding themselves at a respectful distance. They tended the sail with little effort and shifted their attention occasionally to either the horizon or the distant islands that decorated it.

She had almost no idea where they were. Wesley was usually the one who knew what they were doing, or where they were going. But he was not around anymore. She was on her own.

By her reckoning it was already mid-afternoon, which meant that the sun should have been lowering itself in the region's west. By that logic, the cutter was cutting swiftly eastward, though knowing such a thing did not help her locate herself. *The Sentinels,* she thought. *That's where I am.*

Somewhere in the Sentinels, that's all that matters. In a boat with pirates. Pirates! How on Earth did I get myself here?

She let out a sigh and shuffled awkwardly on the wooden seat she was so graciously afforded at the bow of the cutter. It was the least comfortable place to sit, considering how much the front of the boat splashed up and down in the sea, but it put her as far away from the men she shared the boat with as she could get, which left her with no reason to complain.

The girl still wore the sleeping gown she had worn when her house had burned to the ground. After everything it had been through, the garment was blackened and torn so much it very barely covered her breasts. Every now and then she would notice a pirate snatching a glimpse at her half-naked torso, however to her pleasant surprise none had yet attempted a grope. In fact, none had even continued to stare once they realised they had been caught in the act. The glimpses made her uncomfortable all the same, so she turned out towards the boat's heading, despite it contorting her legs into a jarring muddle.

With the pirates wiped from her field of view, the colours of the Rainbow Sea came to life before her. The glistening water faded from deep blue to vibrant green as it neared the shores, which in turn shone white with dried coral, trimming the base of dark green mountains until they collided with bundles of twisted, brown rock formations. The vision was spectacular, though she knew it was not for these colours that the Rainbow Sea was named. In the shallower parts, nearing Southland's many beaches, the water came to life with jungles of brightly coloured plants—just below the surface—or so it was said. These underwater reefs were fabled to play home to hundreds of different aquatic species, each with their own distinct colour. Some were even rumoured to be patterned, with stripes or spots, and some others so large one could not wrap their arms around them fully and touch their fingers together on the other side. This was why the sea was so named, and she dreamed that one day she might witness such a phenomenon with her own eyes. She scarcely believed it could be so. The coral that grew on these reefs was supposed to be bursting with oranges, pinks and greens, but the stuff she saw washed up on the shore was dried, dull and white. Wesley would have professed that coral reefs were just another Southland myth, but at present she was sitting in a boat with pirates, and had seen a ghost ship the day before. She was no longer sure *what* to believe.

Eventually, the sparkling sea and the wonder of the numerous Sentinels was tainted by the appearance of a large ship. The cutter was a fair way from the thing when she saw it, but it dominated the scene with its majestic presence even so. She could not help being a little impressed, watching it draw nearer as the boat drove right toward it.

The ship was fully rigged, with its shrouds and sheets all trembling in the light wind. Its sails were almost all furled, so its body sat perfectly still in the very heart of its blue domain. In spite of their being packed away, the sails were clearly black, much like the ship from earlier in the day. *A pirate ship, for certain!* she thought. *Although this one is different. Both friendlier and… fiercer.*

Indeed, this ship was among the largest she had ever seen.

It was not so big as to rival a royal battleship back in Sirland, but it was a monster compared to the average fare down in Southland, where battleships could easily be outmanoeuvred by the smaller and the quicker. The proud vessel was fitted with a mean broadside of cannon, sporting over a dozen gunports on the one side alone, below another dozen long guns that poked over the gunwale of the ship's waist and quarterdeck. Based on the little knowledge of sailing she had retained from Wesley, she could tell that the hull was made from Sirlish White Oak, burned to a rusty grey by years of weathering. Three masts stretched up from that hull, raking the clouds with sets of yards that were each one shorter than the set beneath. Wild lines strung each mast together, creating a thick web of rope that sliced the air from the tip of the mainmast down to the sterncastle and the bowsprit.

The unexpectedly well-preserved ship was trimmed with an elegantly decorated bulwark and finished with a wooden carving of a bear's head at its bow. Curved stairs linked the vessel's upper decks flawlessly, and even the barrels aboard were neatly ordered. The beauty sat in the water like a king clothed for battle. Hard, stern and noble.

She spun towards the pirates in her cutter, despite herself. 'Is this your ship?' she asked, foolishly. One pirate spoke in reply, as proud as a mother. 'Aye. The Black Beast, 'tis called. No finer ship left afloat in Southland.'

'The Black… Beast.' She mumbled to herself. Fear struck her again. This was no trader's ship. This was no vessel to admire.

'The Blackbone family's flagship,' the pirate added. She

shut her mouth after hearing that. She turned back towards the approaching vessel, her eyes now trained on the ruthless rabble that could be seen beneath the ship's rigging.

Her apprehension made no difference, she knew. She was not likely to last more than half an hour if she tried to swim away, and the cutter was not slowing no matter what she did. Before she could even contemplate a way to escape her conundrum, the boat had been hoisted aboard the mighty Black Beast, with her sitting humbly inside it. Once it was tied into position, she was shoved onto the large ship and led promptly across its deck. The cutter's pirates escorted her up one of the curved staircases, pressed closely around her as if to protect her from the lustful inspections coming at her from every direction. She kept her head down, covered her mostly bare chest with dirty wrists, and walked forward determinedly.

When the deck fell away beneath her feet, she gave a start. She quickly realised she was being led down stairs, into the dark doorway of the sterncastle. *At least in here there should be less of them to stare at me,* she thought, hoping it was true.

Darkness blew briefly over her before the thick, damp air filled again with a light that poured in from wide windows. She peered around, irrepressibly inquisitive. The chamber she had been taken to was small by land standards, and big by sea standards. The wall on the stern side was almost entirely glass, which allowed filtered sun to splash over a large table in the room's centre. There was a long wooden bench that swept around beneath the windows, and a number of plainly dressed pirates standing by it, sober looks on their faces. A map of the Sentinels was rolled out over the table top, begging for her attention.

'Who is this?' one of the men asked, raising his eyebrows at the cutter pirates, who had lined up behind their captive, forcing her forward into the tight and muggy space. All around her the ship's oak planks creaked, and the floor swayed ever so slightly beneath her feet. She felt woozy and crowded, but she tried her best not to show it.

'We found her off the coast of Langdon Island. She's a con from Gold Harbour, stole a boat and wrecked it in a storm or something. But you have to hear what she saw, Gus! You have to!'

The man named Gus strode importantly around the table to grip her chin between his fingers. He was a stout man with a neat brown beard and dark patches around both eyes. He did not carry the stink the other pirates exuded, but his worn clothes were just as unwashed, just as faded.

He released his hand and leant back against the table, crossing scarred arms. 'Well girl,' he growled, 'tell me your name and tell me what you saw. And tell me why the bloody hell you thought stealing a boat and sailing out here was a better idea than sulking about in Gold Harbour!'

The captive swallowed, breathing slowly despite the rapid thud of her heart. *You can do this*, she told herself. *They want to know what you saw. They're not going to hurt you.* 'My name is Alice King,' she said. 'And I'm not a con anymore. I was released to help—'

'What did you *see*, girl?' Gus insisted.

Alice's words caught briefly in her throat. 'Ah, um. Another pirate ship. It was coming for our yacht, and I swam away. But

I think they got my brother, and my sister-by-law.'

'Another pirate ship, huh? That's what you saw? Anything you can tell me about it? What did it look like?'

'It had black sails... And a jellyfish painted on some of them.'

At the word "jellyfish", she knew she had struck something deep within the interrogator's core. *Please don't hurt me! I didn't mean to see it!*

Gus thrust up from his lean, urgency trickling from his head to his toes. 'Will, inform the captain. The rest of you, get out. Charlie, Roger, stay.'

Alice shifted her feet, unsure of what to do with herself.

'Girl. Sit down.' Gus drew a small wooden chair out from beneath the table. 'You need to tell us everything.'

And so she did. Whether it was due to the pirate's mean stare or simply her own nervousness, Alice's whole story was fished from her lips. She shared every detail, from her family's official pardon through to the present moment. The whole time she spoke Gus listened intently, nodding and stroking his short beard like there was no note that was not worth hearing. His dark eyes gazed aimlessly at the floor, his eyebrows scrunching up when she mentioned the ghost ship. He did not stop her though, not until she had finished explaining how the cutter had found her floundering in the water, waving for help. At that point Gus had clearly heard enough, so he cut her off as if he had no time to spare. 'You say you saw the Kraken come up the Langdon Channel then, between Langdon and Cheddar islands? Are you absolutely certain.'

Alice was far from certain. Miles from certain, if the truth were told. 'The Krak... ken?'

'Aye, the vessel you described is without doubt the Kraken, an aged Sirlish Barque commanded by Stinger Dreadwind and his brood. What's important is that you are certain you saw her in the Langdon Channel, heading north.'

'It was heading north,' Alice confirmed. 'Other than that... I... I'm not sure. I don't know the names of any islands, and I didn't know where we were. I don't know where we are *now*...'

Alice cut to silence, afraid her answer was unsatisfactory. That silence lasted too long. Gus exchanged grave looks with his two fellow pirates, turned to Alice, then shook his head, dark eyes swaying from side to side. 'I can't see how the girl could be mistaken. To me it's clear the Kraken was headed up by Langdon, with an eye out for game. But we'll have to see what Wulfric makes of it. With your pardons, Roger, Charlie, I'll go find him.'

'What of the girl?' one of the others asked. Gus was halfway out the door by the time he heard the question. He spared the moment to turn and look Alice in the eyes. 'Don't get into any trouble, girl. It's bad luck to have a woman aboard, so best you don't ruffle any feathers. Behave yourself and we'll drop you somewhere that'll have you. Roger, if you need extra hands...' he nodded his forehead at Alice. The gesture sent a shiver down the captive's spine. She certainly did not want to be used as *extra hands*, whatever that entailed.

Gus slammed the door behind him, leaving Alice alone with the strangers named Roger and Charlie. She remained seated, hoping to stay that way until she was ready to be dropped off somewhere. *How long will it be? Am I meant to sleep here tonight?*

With so many men, there's no chance in hell I'm going to shut my eyes on this ship.

She became abruptly aware of the rude stares she was receiving from the other two. 'You can't stay in here,' one of them said, as if it were obvious. Alice stumbled up from her seat almost immediately, producing only the smallest murmur of comprehension. She was afraid to leave, but even more afraid to remain stubbornly put inside a quiet box with two savage strangers spouting disapproval. Quickly shoving the chair under the table, she backed up to the room's door and zipped through to the quarterdeck before she could reconsider her actions.

The swift transition from shadow to blazing sunlight caught her off guard. After the glare in her pupils had settled down, she noticed her new company with dreadful realisation. Every one of them was looking at her. Spaced out over the long, narrow brown of the multi-level upper deck were something in the order of fifty pirates, each longing for a woman's comfort, it seemed. There were pirates in the rigging, pirates on the masts, pirates holding ropes and pirates throwing dice. Most of them, however, were sitting idly by, either upon the deck or the ship's railing, bored and dangerous.

Alice felt violated just standing there. She had nothing at her back except for the entrance to a room she was explicitly banished from, and her front was not half-shielded by the fabric of her sleeping gown. She dared not look over her shoulder, lest there were even more prying eyes atop the poop deck.

For so long now, Alice had been a convict of Southland, a

role in which she had had no control over what she were to do, or when she was to do it. Even in the women's factories, where she had been stationed for long periods, she was afforded no freedoms, given no choice. Now that she was finally liberated upon a free vessel, possesing as little instruction as an unemployed Sirlish beggar, she had become completely and utterly immobile. She had not the slightest clue of what to do or how to do it.

She noticed something ahead of her. Stamped into the main deck at the centre of the ship's waist was a pair of wide trapdoors, with stairs that led down to the lower chambers of the giant vessel. One of them had its metal grate swung open, inviting her in. *That's where I have to be,* she thought. She imagined slipping into that dark square, vanishing from view to hide between barrels in the hold. It was the escape she needed. But in order to get down there, she had to walk forward, to voluntarily bring nearer the mass of dirty criminals that lounged about beneath the furled black sails. She was wedged between desire and hesitation, completely unmoving. Filling with fear and uncertainty.

Suddenly, her bare arm was caught in the leather-gloved palm of a young man, and yanked sharply forward. It was not the jolt that bothered her; Alice was accustomed to being pushed around. But she had evaded rape through all her convicted years, mostly due to her brother's protection. The fear of its inevitable arrival now gripped her throat, threatening to jerk vomit from her wobbling stomach.

Like a rag doll being snatched away by a child, she was dragged down from the quarterdeck to the main deck, and down further through the trapdoor into wet darkness. Her legs struggled to tread along in the wake of the young man's fast-paced strides. She felt almost as if she were being held upright by his grip alone. *This is not what I wanted! Take me back up into the light!*

It was not long before Alice completely lost her bearings. She was whisked away around one corner after another, until her body was dumped eventually against the floor. Her arms flung out to break her fall, and collided harshly with the splintered base of a cabin bed. She could feel the churning of the sea through the wood, which flooded her ever the more with ill ease.

The man who had stolen her was hardly visible in the gloom of the cabin. He knelt down beside her limp body and placed a gloved hand tenderly on the spot where he had clutched tightly moments earlier. In the shadows she could only make out his face. It was soft and light, with wavy curtains of black hair at either side. He wore a stern expression, but a concerned one just the same. To Alice's surprise, he was only a little ways out of his youth, almost of an age with herself. She was not so foolish as to let it comfort her. She wriggled free of his touch, stubbornly demonstrating how unyielding she would be throughout the act that was to follow.

The man sighed. 'Sorry I was so rough with you,' he apologised. 'I needed the others to see that I was.' He shuffled away from her and let his weight fall into an unseen chair in the corner of the room. His tight clothes squeaked faintly as he moved. 'Are you alright? I didn't knock your head?'

Alice refused to answer. She tried to squeeze further into

the side of the bed.

'Don't be afraid. I'm not going to… you know. That's not why I brought you in here.'

'Then why did you?' Alice kept her tone flat and quick. As soon as she spoke, she realised how dry her mouth was. She wet her lips with her tongue.

'I saw you standing there on the quarterdeck, not moving. I thought you needed to get away from all those eyes. I can see your… your breast, you know? Well, some of it, anyway.' Alice imagined the man was smiling, even though his expression was impossible to see for the lack of light in his corner.

Could he be telling the truth? Alice wondered, turning her cheek into her exposed shoulder. *Or is he just trying to butter me up before he gets started?*

'Here, I've got some clothes for you.' The man sprang up from his seat to fossick through a heavy chest. He threw a few choice pieces out onto the floor in front of Alice. She touched them hesitantly, felt the soft, sturdy nature of the fabric. These were no rags. 'We're probably about the same size, if you ignore the shape. They should suit you right...' He paused, then turned to face the cabin's sealed door, clasping his leather-clad hands together behind his back. 'They're men's clothes, but they'll attract less attention. Are you getting them on?'

The dark was waning as Alice's eyes adjusted. She glanced up at the black waves hanging from the back of the man's head. *Maybe he is trying to help. What man would want me in more clothes, rather than less? And turn away while I was getting into them?*

She chose not to linger on the thought. She hurriedly

slipped off her sleeping gown and began dressing, starting with the underpants. The man had chosen thick breeches for her, with a belt, and a loose white shirt to fit under a tight waistcoat. There was even a pair of soft leather boots strewn out for her. She pulled them on last, happily accepting all that the stranger had gifted her.

'What's your name?' the man asked, still facing the other way.

There was a loose cord weaved through the sleeve of Alice's new shirt. She pulled it out and used it to tie her long hair back. 'Alice,' she said. 'And I'm done now.'

The man spun slowly, then returned to his seat. She could see him more clearly now. He wore almost exactly what she did, with an additional tight-breasted coat that ran down his arms to his wrists. It was an odd thing to wear in the stuffy heat of the cabin, but it did not seem to bother him.

'I'm Kit Blackbone, first mate of the Black Beast. The captain's my father. Wulfric Blackbone. But you probably know him as Captain Greyhide.'

Alice shook her head as politely as she could. 'I don't know... I haven't heard of... him.'

Kit was puzzled, but he showed no offense. 'Will told me what you're doing here, just now. And what you saw. It's very... important news. You don't need to worry, you know, you've been a good help to us. We'll drop you in Wreckrest I don't doubt, and none of the crew will hurt you before we do. They shouldn't even stare so much, not with you dressed like me!'

It was a peculiar sensation, based on little and less, but Alice felt a sudden pang of safety, even crammed as she was into a small dark cabin with a pirate. Now that Wesley, Rose and Gold Harbour were well behind her, this man Kit was her only hope. She had no choice but to trust him.

'Kit... is it?'

'Yes.'

'...What... was it that was so important about what I saw?'

'You really don't know anything about us, do you?' Kit was definitely smiling now, unable to veil his amusement. 'Do all the mainlanders know so little? Or just the convicts?'

Alice was not sure whether he had made a jest or an honest query. 'I'm not a convict anymore.'

'Oh, right, sorry.' Kit lowered his head. 'The mainlanders don't like us much, and for good reason, I guess.'

'Because you're pirates,' said Alice, without thinking. It was more of a question than an accusation, but she suspected it did not come across that way.

'I wouldn't say that to any of the crew,' Kit warned. 'That word has... connotations. My comrades are not so lawless as to be named by it. No, call them Blackbones instead; they see themselves as members of our family. My father is the head of that family, as this ship is head of the fleet. Together, our family rules the Southern Sentinels by our own law. That's what makes my father a sealord.

'Now the vessel you saw coming up the Langdon Channel, that was the flagship of the sealord James Dreadwind, the Stinger. We've long held a truce with that man. A truce that holds so long as he keeps his own family within the bounds of their own waters. If what you say is true, that he was sailing where you said you saw him, then he has been trespassing well within Blackbone territory.'

'So that's all I saw then?' asked Alice. 'The ship with the jellyfish on its sails, it was in your territory?'

'It's not as trivial as it sounds,' Kit clarified. 'For nearly half a decade Stinger has kept his family affairs north of Warhawk's Bluff. To pass it now would be no less than a deliberate breach of our agreement. It's worrying to think on why he would do that.'

'Why *would* he do that? And why did he attack our yacht?'

'You're asking more questions than I can answer. And there's no—'

'Will you go back for my brother? And Rose? Will you look for them, at least? They might have been captured by the Stinger man!'

'My father wouldn't allow it.' Kit tried on a firm expression. 'He'll soon order the crew to ready the ship for sailing. No doubt he'll want to meet with the Northern Sealord, to discuss the problem.'

Alice's stomach tightened. *Have I abandoned them? Have I left my own family in terrible danger?* 'But, can't I—'

'Listen.' Kit leaned forward, raising his breeches from the chair with a creak. As far as Alice could tell, he sympathised for her, though he did not let the feeling guide his actions. 'You'll be with us for a several days, if we're to find the Northern Sealord with his sails out. You'll want to acquaint yourself with our cook, Maurice. You'll find him in the galley at the other end of this deck… Unless you want to eat with the rest of the crew?'

Alice shook her head.

'Well then, stay out of everyone's way and you'll be fine. Can you do that?' Kit got up, placed one of his gloved hands on the door and pushed it open.

Alice was taken aback. She had only just started to settle, hidden in the depths of Kit's tiny cabin. For the shortest moment, she had thought she had found a place to finally rest, even if it were in the bowels of a pirate ship. Even if it meant she was not with her family, or on solid ground. She was clearly wrong. 'Can't I stay in here?'

Kit's eyes flashed compassion, but he sighed, 'if my father found out...' Alice could see that something bothered him. Obediently, she stood and stepped through the door frame, thinking only of what the young man wanted and not of where else in the Black Beast she might go next.

She went to thank Kit for the clothes, but he was already trudging away through the shadows, feigning disinterest. Just ahead of her, a staircase rose from the murky deck to meet with a slightly brighter one above. One of the Blackbone pirates from the room with the map was gliding down it. The man now wore a Morch naval officer's hat over his thin, hairy face. *Roger*, Alice thought he was called. *Or was it Charlie? No, Roger, I think.* Kit nodded politely at the man as he passed.

The pirate whose name was probably Roger made immediate eye contact with Alice. She subsequently felt his gaze drip down from her face to the fresh clothes hanging from her shoulders. He appeared disappointed, more than anything.

'There you are!' he declared, stepping away from the faint light. 'I was wondering where you'd scurried off to. I see you've been dressed like one of us then?' Roger gave a disapproving look at her chest. Alice was once again frozen on the spot.

'Fitting, really, as I've got a job for you that is only right for one of our own. You see, our swabbie's not so keen on doing his chores while there's a lady on board, if you get my meaning.' He gave a sly smirk. It was hard to notice at first, but under the grime on his skin this pirate was almost as young as Kit, though he carried a far more potent air of arrogance about him. 'I think the crew would be most pleased to see you pay your way by cleaning the weather deck, is what I mean. Do you think you could do that for us?'

Alice could not think of anything she would like to do less. It was plain from Roger's inflection that he was being perverted rather than friendly. *Why couldn't I stay in Kit's room?*

Alice mumbled a reply, 'ahhhh...'

'Aye, of course you can.' Roger's tone had become outright mocking. 'Here, I'll get you a mop and we can send you to work right away. You wouldn't want to refuse the boatswain now, would you?'

Roger hastily proceeded to lead Alice helplessly up to the main deck, where the scorching sun was waiting. He snatched a mouldy mop that leant by the mainmast and shoved it into her soft, unspoilt hands. A number of the Black Beast's crewmen had casually gathered around in anticipation of the spectacle. Alice wondered if they'd been waiting like that the whole time she was with Kit, mouths dripping with lust and dirt. Roger joined their ranks eagerly, nodding first at the mop, then at the near spotless deck beneath Alice's boots.

This was exactly what Kit told me not to do! Literally seconds ago! This is what he was trying to protect me from. It must be! Why couldn't I just stay in his room?!

Alice looked around fearfully. She knew mopping the deck was a bad idea, but she had no choice other than to humour Roger and his awful orders. *Unless what Kit meant was to do whatever they asked of me. If he did, then I should just do it. Do it seriously. Then they won't find as much enjoyment in it.*

Determined, Alice resolved to push on without complaint, to complete the task with her head down. She gripped the mop with two hands and scanned the wooden boards through squinting eyelashes. She had never mopped a ship before, and had no idea where to start. In Sirland, when she would wipe the floor of her family home, she would start at one side and move to the other. But she would have had a bucket of water as well. These pirates had given her nothing but a dry wad of crusty thread strung tightly to the end of a stick. Fortunately, there was a puddle of water on the deck near the starboard bulwark, so she edged over to it and starting swiping her utensil back and forth across the oak. Gradually, the mop's head filled with moisture.

Alice felt as stupid as a puppet in a fat fool's comedy show, and as helpless too. Her spectators were jeering as they watched her movements. Uneasily she continued swiping. The disguise Kit had afforded her seemed to matter little and less. Drooling stares cut slowly into her flesh like knives. *Are they so depraved that simply watching a woman sway about excites them?* she wondered. *Even the cons weren't so starved of sex.*

Alice was already questioning the truth behind Kit's assurance. Would she really remain unhurt before she was freed? It felt as though it would take a miracle of fortune to save her from the heated lusts of the Blackbone crew. The thought crippled her movements. She felt her throat turning inside her neck. There was no way out now, save to jump overboard. The idea tasted bitter, but she tossed it around her tongue anyway, giving a sidelong glance at the ship's bulwark and the expanse of water between its feet and the nearest island.

'Go on,' Roger's sickening voice taunted her. 'Put your back into it. How will the deck get cleaner if you don't bend over a little more?'

A tear pushed up behind Alice's eye. Many of the surrounding pirates were laughing greedily, though many stayed their voices, as if out of caution.

Roger petulantly urged her, 'go on!'

'What is this?!' A new voice joined the scene, dry and aghast. All other voices fell immediately silent. Only Roger could still be heard, choking on his own words.

'What game are you playing at, Roger? This is a guest, not a prisoner!'

'Ah… I… Captain, sir,' Roger said. 'I only thought she should play her part… If she's to sail with us, I mean.'

'Will cleaned the deck this morning. Now get away from me, you filth!' The newcomer cleared his throat. 'Girl!' he called out.

Alice looked up. Towering over the quarterdeck's stairs was the very image of a sealord. He was tall—nearly a foot taller than a regular man—and old enough to have been her own father. His head was wrapped in long grey hair and an illustrious beard that rivalled his great two-pointed Morch hat for chief prominence atop his figure. About his shoulders hung a dark and heavy coat with wide cuffs that were turned up. The garment was grossly out of place aboard a Southland ship, though it seemed unashamedly at home around its wearer's thick frame. Beneath it shimmered the sharpened blade of a naval skirmisher's sword, along with the same fitted leather apparel as Alice now wore, only faded from years of exposure to the salt and the sea. This was a man like those from the fairy tales Wesley had told her when she was young. Only here he was, for real, in all his authority and terror-inspiring awe, looking down at her while the breeze stirred his whiskers. 'Drop that stick,' he said, after she caught his grey eyes with her own. 'And come with me.' He turned his vicious stare toward Roger. 'Away from this undisciplined fool.'

8

'I hear you've been sleeping in the prisoner's hold,' said Salvino, as piercingly as only Salvino could. Seb gave a start, but he should not have; it was high time he became used to the Blood Hammer's quartermaster sneaking up on him while he was deep in thought. It happened especially often while he was leaning his elbows characteristically against the main deck's railing, staring off into the vacant distance. This offence offered no exception.

Seb chose not to respond. Sometimes, when Salvino made an outright statement, the man was actually posing a question, attempting to confirm whether what he suspected was fact.

'You don't deny it, then?' he chuckled, joining Seb by the railing. It was late evening, and the last light of the day was fading fast behind the Deceiver in the west. In the east, near complete blackness settled over the Snagger, another of the region's major islands. It was eastward that Seb chose to stare. Into blackness.

The night marked the first time in days the ship had been anchored. This was partly due to the atmosphere's rare tranquillity, and partly due to Salvino's efforts in insisting to the captain that the crew could not work through another full night. Ever since the hour Bart's lifeless body was dumped overboard, Captain Theodore Seablood had been utterly obsessed with hunting his so-called ghost ship, and via some misguided psychosis he had decided that the best time to find it would be when the sun was good and down. The conclusion made no sense to Seb, considering the only occasion in which any of the Blood Hammer's crew had spotted the elusive ship was in the plain light of day. Some other vessels of the Seablood fleet had sighted the thing at night, but such was not precedent enough for Ted's actions. Before now, Seb's father had taken the words of his subordinates with a grain of salt, mistrusting more often that he probably ought. It was a far better frame of mind.

Seb shuffled uncomfortably in Salvino's presence. The smug man's silence interrogated him more powerfully than any verbal assault ever could have. Seb often wondered where this strategic ability had come from. The Dorian people were known to be devious, but they weren't so untrustworthy as the Sirlish, or as stubborn as the Morch. Perhaps, Seb thought, it had something to do with the language Salvino's people had carted down from their home country of Danidor. When the quartermaster would speak in his native tongue with the other Dorian members of the Blood Hammer's crew, there was no telling what conspiracies he chewed upon. Of course, there was always a chance they were planning a mutiny, for all the rest of the crew knew! And then there were the times their brig made port at Mariscos, a whole settlement of bronze-skinned, Dorian-speaking comrades. Whenever they were there, Seb would mostly stay in his cabin.

'When we're sailing at night,' Seb finally answered, guarding his uneasiness by keeping his gaze locked on the blackness ahead. 'I like the feel of it down there. It doesn't sway as much.'

'Oh?' Salvino mocked. 'So it has nothing to do with your little woman, does it?'

Damn! Seb silently cursed. *How does he always know what's going on?*

It was true. Seb was avoiding Liz. It had not been smooth sailing since Bart's death, and Liz was not at all capable of understanding. Seb and his brother had shared a turbulent relationship, but Bart had still been his brother, regardless. Losing the arrogant fool was not something to be swept under the rug.

Liz, like Seb's father, had become obsessed, only her obsession was over Seb himself, and how he might take advantage of his new position as Ted's eldest—and only—true son. Seb was trapped. He was not so sure he wished to be the captain's golden child, now that the role was ripe for the taking. He had been envious of his brother for sure, but after seeing that carcass on the gangplank...

Seb shook the emotion from his gut and turned to his companion for a snide retort. 'You have an eye on everyone, don't you Salvino, and a hand, too?' he forced a smirk. 'But what of our captain? You're the brig's quartermaster, and you can't control the brig. Every day father searches for that bloody ghost ship, we let another handful of free traders slip through our fingers. And what of Anne? We were supposed to protect her passage, but she was torn to pieces by pirate brigands not a mile off the coast of the peninsula! It sounds a little to me like you're not doing your job.'

'Ah, but Sebastian, that is Rob's territory, you see,' Salvino quipped, thoroughly amused.

'Rob is a vassal of father, and his failure reflects on the Seablood name. That's something you both should care about.'

'You're very clever, Sebastian, but it doesn't seem to give you much authority over our captain, either. We both know I can't be to blame for his... affliction. The ghost ship has certainly whisked his fancy beyond its due end. But... it can't be denied that the presence of such a thing is... worrisome.'

'Only if it's more than a hallucination,' Seb corrected.

'Is that what you think?' Salvino pursed his lips. 'Perhaps that's what you and Liz do quarrel about.' He slid a hand over Seb's own, almost akin to how a lover might.

'It's not that,' Seb sighed. 'I'm afraid she simply doesn't—'

'Oh, save me the sob story,' said the quartermaster. 'I've arranged for Agatha to bed with her in your cabin tonight. It cost me only a few bribes. You'll find the old lady's cabin a touch more agreeable than the prisoner's hold, at least for one passing of the moon.'

Seb was speechless. He gazed at Salvino's small, narrow figure in wonder, scarcely able to conceal his relief. 'Sometimes you puzzle me, Salvino. I think you might be a good man.'

Salvino leant closer to the Blood Hammer's heir, smugly crossing his arms. 'Don't tell anyone,' he said, then slid off into the shadows.

Seb was left alone atop the brig save for the scattering of

watchmen who were still posted on duty. The soft sound of the docile water flopping about was all that penetrated the ever-darkening atmosphere. It was to be a marvelous night, with no stars, but the young man had developed a sudden urge for the promise of Agatha's lonely bed. He whirled and strode away towards her cabin in the sterncastle without giving so much as a second thought to how Salvino might have arranged the vessel's women so.

That night Seb slept deeper than he had in months. His sleep was unbroken and dreamless, just as he liked it, and it culminated with fresh rays of morning light streaming generously through Agatha's open porthole. By the time Seb had cleared the sleep from his eyes, a few drops of water could be noticed filtering through with the sun. Cheerfully, he closed the porthole, pulled his boots back over the breeches he had been wearing for weeks, and made his way immediately outside, in case Liz were to search for him.

As he expected, the black sails of the Blood Hammer were already open and bulging powerfully, pulling the vessel southward. At some point during the night, the wind had picked up. Presently, a roaring gale was dumping barrel loads of raindrops through the rigging with every gust. The erratic conditions thrust the brig from side to side as it charged over the sea, but Seb was well accustomed to keeping his feet aboard the home of his youth.

He strode along the deck, searching for his father so that he might report for duty. He found the captain fussing about at the brig's bow with his mates, the sailing master and—of course—Salvino Moreno, who was hidden in his shadow. Ted had a telescope in his hand and was leaning a little too far over the bowsprit for Seb's taste, eyeing something far off in the distance. Despite as much as a third of his crew working tirelessly to keep the vessel at its full speed, Ted had left a mate at the helm. He was not at all concerned with the goings on behind him. *God! Don't tell me he's found the ghost ship.*

Seb shuffled down the stairs to the waist and scooted over it towards his father's party as they swayed in the rain and the wind. 'What do you see?' he called out. He needed to shout, as the air was clogged with blustery roars. At first, it did not seem like anybody had heard him. Then Salvino turned to answer, noticing his captain was not like to do so. 'The Black Beast,' he said. 'It seems Greyhide has forgotten where his territory does end.'

'Or he has urgent business with us,' Seb pondered. 'You're not going to attack him, are you?'

There was a moment of silence before any responded. The moment lasted far too long, Seb decided. Far too long.

Ted eventually spoke up, neglecting to lower the telescope, or to properly acknowledge his son. 'Not unless he does first,' he grumbled irritably. 'But I ought to! What business could he have that would spur his heart to tread Seablood waters, when he could yet await my docking at Wreckrest?'

'Careful, father,' Seb warned, maintaining still the breadth of voice required to cut through the weather. He pressed up beside the others and peered through the misty air in the direction of the Blood Hammer's course. Sure enough, the beastly hull of the Blackbone flagship could be seen carving its way through the Rainbow Sea, hurtling directly at them. The

ship was unmistakeable for the giant white bear's skull painted
on its quivering black sails. The symbol mirrored the Seablood
Crown, which was itself painted on the Blood Hammer's sails
in similar fashion, distinguishing it as the fear-inducing head
of the Seablood fleet. 'The Blackbones are thick witted, but
they're as far from lawless as they come. I couldn't imagine
Greyhide leaving his den without a good reason.'

At that, Ted did lower his telescope. He turned towards his
son, shoving the sailing master aside so he could stare daggers
at the youngest present. The captain of the Blood Hammer was
even now dressed in his elaborate Sirlish finery, though the
water dripping from his wide hat had soaked almost all of it bar
the luscious wig. 'Don't tell me to be careful, boy! You'll leave
the decisions to me, you will. And I decide that the man's not
welcome here. You're not the captain yet, so don't speak like
you are.'

Salvino set aside a smile for Seb, rolling his eyes while Ted
returned to his business with the telescope. No other
crewmember had as much trouble speaking with Ted as Seb
did, but for once the captain's son let the frustration slip by
unnoticed. *Grumble all you want, father,* Seb thought. *I'm just
glad you're not still chasing after that bloody ghost ship!*

Seb shut his mouth and watched over Ted's shoulder. With
the wind streaming past in near perfect easterly flurrys, both
vessels approached one another at the same rate. When they
came close, they veered so that both were set to line up portside
to portside. Ted called out 'heave to,' and the sailors began
preparing the vessel for a sudden halt. The morning's breeze
may have been stronger than usual, but the water between the

Sentinels was never so rough as to prevent a seasoned crew from successfully executing a swift stop, even if the size of their vessels made the effort a little more taxing.

With deft hands and a dollop of shouting, the Seablood crew reorientated the foresails so that they were angled perpendicularly to those of the mainmast. While they wound up their sheets, the helmsman turned the Blood Hammer gently into the wind. Some of the sails were reduced and some of the jibs were furled too, all in quick succession. The new force generated by the turning of the foresails quickly cancelled out that of the mainsails, so in all there was no need for Seb to order the lowering of the anchor. Whilst this method of stopping risked the Blood Hammer drifting, it meant that most of the sails could remain unpacked. This, in turn, meant that the brig could take off in a hurry, if needed. Seb was certainly worried such a need might yet arise, depending on how the ensuing Blackbone meet was to pan out. He gazed carefully at the opposing ship. For the moment, the Black Beast was busy pulling the same manoeuvre, and lowering one of its ship's boats into the water.

It is to be a parley, then, Seb noted. *And we'll have the advantage on our home deck. Greyhide must be troubled out of his mind! Perhaps he too has caught the same ghostly fever that plagues father.* No matter the grounds, Seb was anxious to discover why the Black Beast had so clearly sought them out so far beyond their shared boundary. Fortunately, it seemed as though he would not have to wait long. The Blackbone ship had already dispatched its boat, which was making its way over the wobbling waves to the Blood Hammer's flank. Ted was frantically squeezing as much moisture from his prized attire as he could manage, while a handful of his crew set a rope ladder down the side of the hull for their company to climb.

Before either he or his father could find time to prepare themselves, a Blackbone had climbed the ladder and was fastening his boat to a cleat on the Blood Hammer's railing via a lengthy line. Very soon thereafter, the visiting troupe of Blackbones was scaling the ladder to alight the Seablood deck.

Ted began to arrange the important crewmen about himself. He made sure Seb was standing at his right hand, opposite Salvino. Seb also noticed that the heave to had sparked the curiosity of both Agatha and Liz, who had swiftly found their place among the welcoming party. He tried desperately not to catch his lover's eyes, a challenge made all the simpler by the sudden appearance of the Blackbone dignitaries aboard his home.

There were less than a dozen of them, in the end, that had come across from the Black Beast. First came a few familiar faces Seb had often seen in Wreckrest, followed by Gus, the Black Beast's quartermaster, then the Greyhide himself, Wulfric Blackbone. From the moment the sealord stomped his great big leather boots onto the Blood Hammer's deck, there could be no denying his authoritative and frightful presence. Despite his age, Wulfric seemed capable of snapping any other man in two, and was dangerous enough to try. Due to the wind, he had forgone his hat—an unusual sight for any Southland sailor—and its absence allowed the man's grey mane to fly around his gruff face like cold fire. It was for this monstrous fur that the captain was afforded his pet name, regardless of the colour in his bones.

The slanted rain stirred Wulfric's dark coat, partly concealing the young apprentice he had brought with him. Seb was fully aware of whom this man was. Kit Blackbone, they named him, the heir to the Blackbone fleet. He was likely to become Seb's nemesis in the times when they would both succeed their fathers.

The most curious visitor, however, was the one hiding behind Wulfic's other elbow. A girl, plain notwithstanding her hardy crewman's outfit. She was of an age no older than that of Liz, but innocent, and too scrawny for Seb's tastes. She looked as frightened as a kicked dog, though she stood straight, and did not turn her face from the assembled collection of Seablood's finest.

'Wulfric Blackbone!' Ted called through the energetic wind, before some of the visitors had yet found their feet. The Seablood captain laced his booming voice with a welcoming chortle, whilst simultaneously demonstrating his inhospitable intent by neglecting to escort his guests into the sterncastle.

'Teddy Seablood,' Wulfric replied, with equal verve.

Ted snorted. 'I'm afraid you've drifted into my territory, Greyhide! What has brought you so?'

'Ominous tidings. Ones that must be discussed, for the good of us both. May we speak in private, captain?'

Ted raised his decorated arms. 'The rain wetting your fur, is it?'

'Set your hostility aside, Seablood,' demanded Wulfric. 'I'm not the one dressed like a fool at a fool's court. It's the ears that trouble me. Must our parley be heard by everyone?'

Ted grunted. He was not happy about it, but there was no denying a decent audience without some firm basis on which to support the alternative. 'Fine. We'll meet in my cabin. Come. But have your escort wait here. I shouldn't want to risk this becoming too long winded. Diego, you have the helm.'

Reluctantly, Ted waved his entourage aside and gestured for Wulfric to go ahead of him, aft to the sterncastle. Sebastian noted with intrigue that the captain of the Black Beast brought the girl with him, as well as his son. At this, the younger Seablood stepped in beside his father, joining Salvino as the group filed in to Ted's cabin.

Having visited the Black Beast's chart room himself, Seb was embarrassed for the Blood Hammer. Though the former indoor space boasted a comparable size, it was made complete with a large table, numerous chairs and plenty of standing room. On the contrary, the cabin they now entered was no less than the sailing master's work area, the fleet's counsel chamber and the captain's own sleeping quarters, all in one. Even Salvino spent the better portion of his precious time decorating its floorboards, in spite of the small partition he was allotted elsewhere in the brig. A preposterously lavish four-poster bed was pressed up against the stern-facing windows, greeting them all. A desk sat beside the entrance and dressers lined the walls behind it. A couple of stools stood guard either side of a black rug, finishing off the musty cavern in their stumpy, pestilent way.

Uncomfortably, the six conveners pressed into the room and each found a place to stand. Seb was quick to rest his backside on the edge of the bed, while Kit dragged over a stool for the girl, who rejected his offer in the most polite manner imaginable.

'Alright, Greyhide, you've got me where you want me. Now what business do you have trampling up my way? And what business do you have escorting 'round such a young lady as this one? Don't tell me you're trying to fish out a grandson already!' Ted's face scrunched into a triumphant gloat behind a veil of wet blobs that continued to drip from the edges of his hat. Already, a pool of water was forming around his polished shoes, soaking into the dry wood beneath them.

Wulfric's features remained expressionless, though his offense was plain. 'I'm not so vulgar as you, Teddy, as you'll do good to remember. The *girl* is the reason I'm here. For weeks I've had my vassals bring me ill reports, but this woman represents the first eyewitness account.'

Ted stroked his beardless chin. 'Ill reports of what manner?'

'The Dreadwinds have been operating outside their territory,' Wulfric explained.

Ted paused, then proceeded to pace back and forth over the rug in the room's centre, so much as he was able to considering the cabin's restricted floor space. Black tufts of wool thirstily drank the droplets that fell from his soaked livery. 'Oh yes,' he said. 'That would be a grim circumstance, indeed. Bad news, it would be, bad, bad news, I fear. But how do you know it to be true? You're to trust the account of a skinny little girl? Tell me, what did she see that has you so convinced?'

'The Kraken,' Wulfric explained, not without peering sideways at the girl as if to confirm that he told it true. 'Stinger Dreadwind's barque. She saw it sailing northward through the

Langdon Channel, south of Warhawk's Bluff. There's no chance it was any other vessel, as she recalls without question the stingers upon its black sails.'

Ted stroked his chin again. 'Wulfric, my friend. On any other day, I would believe you. I would. But it so happens your girl may have been mistaken.'

Wulfric was taken aback. 'How so?'

'I know of another vessel sailing the Sentinels, sharing a similar description. I've seen it myself, trespassing upon my own sea. A ship of Sirlish oak, three masts, and black sails adorned with the sign of the Warhawk. An eagle is not a stinger, I know, but from a distance... Couldn't the two be confused?'

Seb huffed, angrily. *Not this again!*

'You speak of the Frontiere,' Wulfric confirmed. 'But you and I both were there the day Halfeye's ship sunk to the sea floor. You have your logic backwards, it seems. If you thought you saw Halfeye's ship, then perhaps it is *you* who are mistaken. Could you have spied the Kraken? It would fit well with my reports, and give us the justification we need to take action against the Dreadwinds.'

'I know the bloody difference between the Kraken and the Frontiere, Greyhide!' Ted hissed, his skin fading in hue through pink to red. His arms became animated as he spoke. 'Even at a distance! And I know it better than some pretty little girl of yours. I saw the Frontiere with my own eyes, in the daring light of day! It has returned, my friend. Returned to our plane, to our earth. A *ghost ship*.'

The Blackbone girl straightened suddenly at the thought.

Seb wondered what went through her head, but could not so much as guess where to start. Wulfric turned to face her, accusingly. 'What rubbish!' he spat. 'Tell me, Alice, could you have seen Warhawks on your attacker's sails, instead of stingers? Eagles, they are, with their wings spread out to each side?'

The girl named Alice almost completely swallowed the same words she tried to squeeze out, though with a keen ear they were able to be faintly perceived. 'Ummm... They... looked like jellyfish to me. At least I thought they did. I could have been wrong.'

'Don't be modest, Alice.' Wulfric grumbled. 'You saw what you saw, and stingers it was!' He whirled back at Ted. 'Listen here, Teddy. We have proof that Stinger has been playing outside his playground. His lot in our treaty is at the chopping block! Your own delusions are none of my business. The Frontiere is sunk and the Kraken is at large. I call on you to join me in either confronting our old brother, or punishing him.'

Ted chuckled forcedly as he gathered his thoughts. It took quite a time, but when he began to speak again, it was with conviction. 'When you see something with your own eyes, Greyhide, you know it to be true. I saw the Frontiere, resurrected before me, and you have not seen Stinger's Kraken but through the wild gossip of a... peasant girl. That's how it sounds to me. Truly, if you attack Stinger behind such petty evidence, it is *you* that has broken our treaty. And since you have so brazenly sailed into my waters on *this* day, it also seems to me that you hold little respect for our arrangement. The one we've held for so long! The last time I saw Stinger Dreadwind was at Wreckrest, where he ought be. The last time I saw you is now, right here at the heart of the Seablood fief! Now listen and hear: if you come flopping back this way once more with as much hot air up your arse, I'll take leave to deliver my own punishment, upon you. And when it comes to be, don't tell me I didn't warn you.'

Wulfric grew taller with frustration, though he restrained himself from a physical outbreak. 'I've come to you for help, captain, and you give me a lecture! Nobody keeps the treaty more than I. You criticize my morals, yet you lustily stow women aboard your brig!'

'I am not ashamed of Agatha, if that's what you mean. She suits me well, and brings no bad luck upon us. You, on the other hand, appear to have lost the very morals you hide behind, Greyhide. You have a woman with you right now! Isn't that against your precious code?'

'She's not—'

'That's enough, Blackbone! Unless you have further business, please leave us. The next time you wish to converse, we'll meet at Wreckrest, as we always have.'

Wulfric pursed his lips, suffocating his own protests. With clenched fists he stormed out of the cabin into the rain and wind without. Kit followed soon after, guiding Alice before him with leather-bound hands.

And so the parley was over.

When the Blackbone company had moved safely out of earshot, the remaining three paused for consideration. Salvino emerged softly from Ted's shadow to speak first. 'Maybe next time, captain, you could practice… a little more…'

'Patience?' Ted interrupted, gruffly. 'I hardly think he deserves it!'

Seb shifted on the bed. He felt more at ease with the captain of the Black Beast no longer present. 'But father, what if he told it true? What if Stinger Dreadwind *has* been sailing the Kraken south of Warhawk's Bluff?'

Ted scoffed. 'Nonsense! What sense would he have in doing that? The Dreadwinds get all the traffic they need from Gold Harbour. More than they need, I say! Nay, I'm not going to risk my neck up against Stinger because some girl has mistaken the Frontiere for the Kraken.'

'How many times must I say it, father. The Frontiere, the ghost ship, it cannot be!'

'Get out of here, boy. Your repetition is getting under my skin. Leave me with Salvino. At least he doesn't deny what is plain.'

Not to your face, Seb wanted to say, making his way to the cabin door. He held his tongue for Salvino's sake, considering what the quartermaster had done for him night before.

With a purposely loud slam of the door, Seb left his father alone with the shady Dorian man, and appeared once more amongst the stormy commotion outside. Sailcloth cracked above his head, fervently protesting the brig's halted stance. Elsewhere on the deck, Seablood sailors repositioned themselves following the swift departure of their visitors. The smell of hot, wet wood swirled up around them, a consequence of the persistent argument between the sun and the clouds about how wet the world should be.

Seb gazed up at the wriggling black sails. He traced the white crown painted on their surface with his pupils. *Why did he choose a crown?* he wondered. *Does he truly believe he is king over the Sentinels? What, then, would that make me? Sebastian Seablood, the Pirate Prince?*

When he looked back down he found himself face-to-face with Liz. Despite her Dorian descent, the woman's skin was so pale she was difficult to distinguish from the dull mist that engulfed them both. Only her black hair stood out, dangling in all its soggy glory over her unbearably tight corset. She wore an expression of pure scorn.

Seb flinched.

'You know I had a lovely night with Agatha, I really did.' Sarcasm dripped from Liz's pouting lips to mingle harshly with the slops of rain that spat onto her tight face.

'Please, Liz,' Seb began.

'Am I too old for you?! Is that it? Are you done with me?! Is that why you've been sleeping in the prisoner's hold? Is it?!'

'Liz, listen.'

'I don't want to listen, Seb. Not to your excuses!' She pushed on his chest, forcing him into the sterncastle's wall. Seb became rapidly aware of the onlookers. He straightened himself, stood his ground against Liz's feeble nudges.

Liz eased back, but she failed to cease her cries. 'Tell me the truth Seb! For once! Whatever it is! Do you think you're done with me?! If you do, just say it! And dump me in Wreckrest with all the other whores! Just say it! Be a man, Seb! Be a man and say it! You're better than this! You are! Don't be a fool! A fool like your brother was!'

Suddenly, impulse took him. Seb shoved Liz, sending her toppling over to slap against the deck. He rushed off, forehead converting raindrops to steam as it plowed through them. Behind, Liz's tune lingered still, transforming from aggression to apology. Seb blocked it out. *He's not a fool, he's dead! Dead dead dead dead dead dead dead! And now it's just me. Why don't you get it, Liz? It's just me! Bloody Sebastian Seablood, Pirate Prince.*

9

Rose was no more than a hollow shell. A dry, dry sponge. A sponge that had once been soaked in love and hope and life, but was now empty, cold. Even as a convict she had retained these things, so much as she was afforded. Now, she had been wrung dry. Wrung until the very last hint of moisture seeped from her bones to join the growing puddle of filth on the floor beneath her withered legs and brittle skin. Even the puddle despised her sorry carcass, soaking slowly as it was into the hull of the dark coffin in which she had wept all that a woman could weep.

She was empty. The vision of her husband's head falling from his shoulders had been all that she could see since it happened. The chilling warmth of his blood had been all that she could feel. But now she was empty. Now, all she could see was black. All she could feel was black. All that she could taste, was black.

Where at first the iron bindings that locked her wrists to the hold's wall had been cold and hard, they were now soft as jeweled bracelets. Soft and wet. She had vomited several times, some of them as the memory of her husband's murder appeared before her, and others when the rocking and sloshing of the dense ocean enveloping her prison coaxed it up from her stomach. The vile liquid had coated the remains of her sleeping gown, which had degraded to no more than a ripped, soiled scrap. The frightened girl had used her feet to pry its fragments from her bruised skin, vomit slapping over her splinters. To keep her body from utter nakedness, she managed to empty a crusted bag of potatoes, which she used to cover her legs and breasts. But now, being empty, she cared no longer whether she was naked or whether she was cloaked in the finest of silks.

And so there she was. Empty. Naked. Finished. Her hands were chained and her eyes were parched, and she draped ever so carelessly against the angled wall of the wooden vessel that had become her final destination. Though pirates frequented her dark hold, none dared touch her, nor even look at her, lest the desire to touch did overwhelm them. For from the moment she had declared knowledge of Halfeye's Hoard, she had become a treasure herself, a treasure not to be spoilt or broken. The white-faced pirate had been very clear in explaining to his comrades that Rose was not to be hurt, not until the Hoard was found. But regardless of his protection, Rose had not been fed or attended to in the slightest. Even more surprising was that nobody even sought to question her about the treasure's actual location. Instead, the girl was thrown into the vessel's hold like a piece of inanimate cargo, to be ignored thereafter.

The whole experience might have had the scent of a time when she had been a criminal, being carted off to savage Southland in a convict freighter. Then, too, she had been treated as cargo, and had been subject to mountains of vomit in sickening darkness for weeks belowdecks. Though throughout those countless days, her stomach had been filled with dried meat and sauerkraut, and either her sister or husband had warmed her side, whatever the dark hour. Now both were gone.

The memory, briefly held in her consciousness, should have sent her into a whirling vortex of tears, but she managed it now without so much as twitching. Even for the emotional wreck she had become, there was only so much she could cry, only so much one could care, before complete emptiness was all that remained. And so it was. Rose's husband was dead. Rose's sister was gone. Rose's house was burned down. Rose's home was half a world away. Rose's body was slumped in the hold of some pirate ship, somewhere deep in the Sentinels of Southland. Emptiness. Emptiness. Emptiness. Rose was empty.

Amongst the emptiness, Rose's sense of smell was the first thing to soak back in. There was no knowing how many days it had taken—not hidden away from the sun like she was—though it did eventually return. A waft of soft rot tickled her nostrils. She recognised the sensation. *Mould,* she thought. It should not have surprised her. After all, there were barrels upon barrels of food in the hold, and rags and bags and crates and cages, all dripping with moisture, some of it salty, some of it fresh. Even as close as she could touch, heavy barrels crowded the floor.

For the first time, she realised how hidden she truly was. Her narrow end of the long compartment was like a room all to itself, protected from the light, and from the goings on of the crew.

A sharp shuffle penetrated the silence. Then a scrape. The movement stirred up the stagnant air, sending additional billows of mouldy essence into Rose's face. *Somebody's down here*, she decided. They were being oddly quiet.

Out of the near pitch-black, a face appeared, hovering over one of the barrels within Rose's limited field of view. It boasted a dark beard—she could tell—and a blunt nose. She thought it looked like the man that had beheaded her Wesley, but she certainly could not be too sure.

'We could slit her throat,' a voice whispered. It was not the voice of the dark-haired man, but the voice of another. He was somewhere behind the barrels.

'Too loud!' snapped the dark-haired face, with the supple bite of a spider. His features lingered momentarily before vanishing into shadow. 'By the time she'll get the chance to say anything, it'll be too late. And if she were found dead before then… none of it may work.'

Rose swallowed. She no longer wished to live, but the talk of slitting her throat made her uneasy all the same. She stilled her disquiet by rightly convincing herself she was helpless; her hands were chained to the wall above her head, and her body was starved of all energy. There would be nothing she could do to stop it.

'None of what may work?' responded the first voice, even fainter than before. 'I've never known you to spare a life, Dagger. Not for anything. What is this about?'

'It's about sparing lives, in a way.'

'Have you gone soft, Dagger?'

'Nay, I've not gone soft. Tell me, would you really kill the girl?' The tone of the dark-bearded man was tight, direct, sharp. A dagger.

'I wouldn't.' The other man was cautious, wary, but curious. 'Not after she professed to knowing where Halfeye's Hoard is hid.'

'So you agree with Stinger's command, then?'

'Not that, neither. I would let the men have her, I would. Each and every one. So long as she can talk, the rest'a her's not worth sparing. The cap'n's duty is to his crew first, not to his captives.'

'Aye, the old Stinger's lost his edge. He's the one's gone soft.'

'I'll see that. It's not just the girl, neither. We've been tak'n our piddly share an' lettin' freighters go through to the Wimswind, when we could be kill'n their crews and tak'n the whole damn lot. That's what we used to do. Aye, you already knows this, Dagger.'

'Stinger's a good man, but perhaps a more ruthless leader would bring us more gold.'

'A new cap'n. What're you mak'n, Dagger? Be frank, you've already got me down here!'

'If it came to it, would you stand by the Stinger? That's what I've brought you here for. Where you stand, Bill, that's what I need to know.'

Silence followed. The more distant voice chewed on its thoughts before answering carefully and quietly. 'If mutiny's what you're meaning Dagger, and it sounds to me as it is, I stand for the Kraken. Not for it's cap'n.'

Rose became suddenly aware of her breathing. What she

could overhear was certainly not something she was supposed
to. She clamped her lips together and suppressed her lungs. *If
they can't trust me, they'll kill me.* She tightened her muscles.
Though she still cared not for living, an unexpected quiver said
she did not want to die, either. Not here. Not now. There was
no time to think on it; she had to keep listening.

'But the Kraken needs a cap'n. If not Stinger, then who?'

The dark-bearded man cleared his throat. 'Old Stinger's lost
his edge, but this Dagger's sharp as ever. And made of steel.'

'I could see that. That I could, that I could. Truth be told, I
was hop'n for't. Tell me, Dagger, how's it to happen?'

'We're coming on the ghost ship tomorrow, likely late in the
day if Stinger's predictions can be trusted. We'll arrange all
those whose loyalty remains to row over with him. Once they're
all on the skiff, we'll shoot them down from the main deck.
We've got the guns for it, and we'll have them all loaded before.'

'Ah, I can see that! Aye, a sight it'll make. And in front of
the ghost ship! But I must ask, Dagger, how are we to get
Stinger's cronies all in the one skiff?'

'First we've got to sniff them out. And for that we've got less
time than we can afford. A day is all. Come, Bill. We must
begin.'

The voices trailed away, fading until they blended with the
dim murmur of distant crewmen, which in turn twisted with
the creak of the hull to form a white noise Rose had been
previously deaf to. But now her ears were wide open. Her heart
was beating again, faster than it ought. *A mutiny!* she thought,
dazzled. The very idea of such a conspiracy was absurd, yet
there it was, right under her nose. It was exciting in a way, and

deathly frightening in another.

For the first time since Wesley's execution, Rose found herself thinking about something other than her late husband. As soon as she realized it, however, her mind meandered inevitably back. *Wes!* she called out silently. *Oh, Wes!* A longing for her lover returned, but no longer did it compel her to weep. There were no more tears to spare.

The white-faced man! Is he this Stinger *they were talking about? Maybe he'll get the death he deserves for ordering your murder! But it wasn't him that killed you, was it, Wes? It was the man with the dark beard, the one who was in here just now! It must be him! He's the one who needs to die! Dagger, I think. I wonder if that's his real name? Oh Wes, I will kill him for you! I will kill him! Even if I die while doing it!*

Rose's teeth clenched. Her wrists pulled at their chains, causing raw skin to rub against frosty metal, sending strikes of pain down her arms. *I will kill him! I will kill them all! Every pirate on this ship! Just give me the knife and I'll do it! I swear I will!*

Rose's back arched. Her feeble, naked body stretched away from the wooden slats at her shoulders, but the pain in her wrists exploded, and the chains would not cease their grip. She flopped back, her rage dissipating. The sack she had laid on her torso slipped from her thinning frame to the deck below. She was truly trapped. A widowed prisoner, all alone in the belly of a pirate ship, unable to move. She looked around anxiously, desperate to escape. All she could see were barrels and bags, each one shrouded in darkness. She stuck her feet out at some of the barrels to knock them over, but her legs had even less strength than she thought.

Clumsily, she retracted her feet. She recalled then Wesley's lessons on the anatomy of a ship, and decided that she could not possibly be held in the lowest compartment. The bilges would still be below her, the empty space between the hold and the base of the hull. Consequently, she started to rip at the floor with her toenails. After only a few scrapes, fierce bites stung her toes and throbbed through bulging veins into her leg. She swore aloud before running her fingers over the source of the pain. The splinters she found wedged under her nails were big enough to pinch, and were wet with blood. Carefully, she removed the chunks of wood, one at a time, still plotting how she might free herself, a process that continued until her drifting consciousness lulled her into a sort of sleep.

But if sleep ever came, it came only briefly, for the next hour was full of visitors. One by one, the dark-bearded man—who could only be identified as Dagger—brought the crew down to the hold, questioning them about their allegiance to the ship's captain, Stinger. Each meeting was essentially the same as the last. After a time, Rose thought she might have even been able to perform the routine herself. Dagger did not seem to care that she was eavesdropping from her puddle of dried vomit and blood. In fact, with every new conspirator he drew nearer and nearer to her, as if her hearing would suck the very sound from the air, preventing those from whom the meeting was kept secret from hearing anything at all.

From one pirate to the next, Dagger's conniving tongue spun word after word, each one a ripe fruit, selected delicately and delivered softly in the darkness. To begin, the mutineer would cautiously determine whether his co-conspirator was for or against their captain. Depending on the outcome, he would either inform them of his traitorous plan or convince them of their need to accompany Stinger when the man was to parley with another vessel, a vessel that was repeatedly referred to as the ghost ship.

After her terrifying experience aboard Second Chance, Rose was certainly inclined to believe such a thing could be real, but the way the pirates spoke of it simply did not add up. With every second one of them throwing the term about like seeds in spring, it was hard to believe that the ghost ship in question was anything like the one she and Wesley had witnessed. Regardless, the idea captured her imagination and she began pondering why—and how—the crew of the Kraken supposed they were to convene with such a thing. The intriguing subject was paid no heed by Dagger and his companions. It was clear from their fussing that the prime topic at hand was whether to mutiny, or whether not to, and that the dark-bearded man was at the helm of the matter, with his dark-haired hands plastered to the wheel.

Rose soon came to admire him for his clever scheming and sharp wit, though the hate for his crime against her husband never lost its bitter sting. The more Dagger proved his worth to the crew, the more she wanted to kill him, and the sweeter his blood became to her mind's tongue. But deep in all the darkness of the Kraken's bowels, Rose became only truly familiar with his voice. The image she had conjured of his face warped wildly with every imagining, and what remained bore only a dark beard, speckled with drops of Wesley's crimson blood. The voice, though, was thick with flavour. It wove through the crew, sewing its seeds of violence with chunky tones and sizzling clarity. It left few unaffected, and even fewer untroubled.

In the end there were only a handful of pirates who wished for Stinger to remain as captain of the Kraken. There were at least twenty who felt otherwise, possibly even more; Rose had not thought to count. Once the visits had ceased, the prisoner could only reason that Dagger had found his majority, and was to follow through with the mutiny come the specified moment, a time that drew nearer with every second.

A frustratingly suspenseful interlude followed, of which Rose could find no way of measuring, other than by counting each of several thousand mouldy breaths. Then a loud crack sounded above her cell. Immediately, she wondered whether the deed had been done. *Could it have been that quick? Could it have been that easy?*

The next few noises to interrupt the perpetual grind of the hull and sea aroused a similar response, though never properly revealing the outcome Rose anticipated with ever-increasing anxiety.

Another crack. This time it was closer, possibly fashioned by the sloppy boot of another visitor stomping down the nearby ladder into the hold. *Surely not another*, Rose thought.

The sound grew crisper, swelling in volume until a large man appeared in the dark and dusty air before Rose's chained, naked body. She tried to flinch, but the muscles in charge of her gut were off duty.

The visitor sniffed so loudly any sailor could have heard it from the main deck. 'It stinks down here worse than shit! And what'd you do with your clothes, woman?'

Rose arched her neck to scowl at her addresser. His face was bristling with white stubble that looked to glow as the moon did at night. *Stinger?* Rose swallowed. *Are you the captain? You're still alive?* Questions stampeded through her head, too fast to make sense of. *Should I tell him about Dagger? Does he already know? Or will that just get me killed? But I want to die! That's what I want! It is!*

Stinger's shaded pupils trailed over Rose's dried vomit to the limp pile of rags that had once been her sleeping gown. 'Ah, I see. You've been rotting in your own filth! For God's sake, wrap her in something, or she'll be worn dead by the time we board.'

A weasel of a pirate popped out from the black shadows and shoved a key into the chains at Rose's wrists. Her hands flopped to the floor as soon as they were released, throbbing with pain. The freedom felt so good Rose barely noticed the weasel's fingers grope her brazenly, even as they shrouded her skin with a coarse rag.

'Stinger?' Rose asked, but the words failed before they even left her lips. She cleared her throat to try again.

The white-faced man huffed. 'Today's your lucky day, woman! We'll prove the merit of your words, we will!'

'Stinger?' The word came out this time, bubbling and broken.

'Aye you know me, you sickly Blackbone! Stinger Dreadwind of the Western Sentinels, soon to be sealord of all the— Look at me when I speak!'

Rose's chin had drooped. She lifted it up so that Stinger's

white beard was all she could see. She made her decision. *You're going to die! I could save you... but I won't!*

'I hope you haven't forgotten, you little whore.'

Tears were creeping from Rose's eyes, though she scarcely knew why. 'Wh... What?'

Stinger's white cheeks contorted into a dry grin. 'We're anchored by the ship of an old friend,' he said. 'I'm headed over there now, and I'm taking you with me. You'll tell him the location of Halfeye's Hoard or I'll kill you on the spot, you hear?' He laughed the sadistic laugh of a madman. 'And don't you think about lying, now. This friend of mine... he'll know if you're making it up! Aye, and you'll be dead.'

Rose tried to produce another word, but her throat had given up. *He's taking me on the skiff! Oh Wes, I'm going to die! I'm going to be shot by Dagger and the rest of the crew!*

An idea struck her. Suddenly, the energy required to open her mouth surged through her blood, as a pair of pirates lifted her from her dark wallow by the armpits. 'Stinger!' she exclaimed. 'They're going to kill us!'

Stinger's white eyebrows dropped over white eyes. He slapped Rose across the face and spat onto the rag she was wrapped in. Pain tightened through her jaw as it was thrust aside. 'Don't think I care for you, woman. Not one bit.' His voice was low, threatening. 'No excuse will save you now.' He whirled and stomped hurriedly back up the ladder. The pirates holding Rose followed quickly after, dragging their prisoner so that her feet rattled over each stair. *Nothing can save me*, Rose agreed as they ascended to the decks above. *But nothing can save you, either! Today, we'll die together!*

Light ripped into her eyes, slamming her eyelids shut over them. She had been hauled from the belly of the Kraken to its main deck, where the harsh Southland sun cut through spiky clouds to jab ruthlessly at her tender skin. She attempted to shield her face from the brightness, but her stiff escort would not allow it.

A light breeze swept over them all. Where once the fresh air would have calmed her, now it made her sick. She felt vomit pester at the back of her throat. Her legs flopped helplessly over the rotting deck as the sails above smacked to and fro. Abruptly, their shadow swept over her. She felt her eyelids loosen, the bite of the sun fading. Ever so slowly, she squeezed vision out of tingling pupils, bringing the tense scene into view.

Dirt-ridden pirates were sprawled over the Kraken's main deck, soaking in the near-amber glow of late afternoon. They watched the procession with careful nonchalance. As Rose was thrust past them, she noticed a number of long-barrelled firearms strapped to belts, hidden beneath coats. *The guns that will kill us!* Ahead of her, Stinger was reversing down the side of the vessel via a flimsy rope ladder, with a number of others hot on his heels. If she had not known what was about to happen, she might have sniffed it out anyway, given the pure tangibility of the foreboding in the air. She knew it would not be long before the mutiny was accomplished now, and Rose was as dead as the Kraken's old captain. The certainty of it grew and grew.

She was shoved up to the port bulwark, where water reached out before her. The vessel had been anchored in a sheltered bay, with mountainous islands of green extending upwards in almost all directions. The Kraken was alone except for just one companion, another ship anchored within shooting range. When Rose saw it, what breath she held was briskly taken away. *The ghost ship!*

It was not the largest vessel Rose had ever seen, but it may well have been the most striking. The ship sat proud of the water like Sirlish royalty, tall and polished to a faultless lustre. To Rose's partially trained eye, the beauty looked to be nearly two hundred feet long, and was fully rigged over three huge masts with furled sails that were blacker than even the Kraken's. A full broadside of heavy long guns poked aggressively from the ship's elaborately decorated flank and over the edge of its weather decks, which themselves sat high atop dignified superstructures. What was most astonishing to Rose though, was the magnificent pair of wooden wings that fanned their oak feathers into the wind at either side of the sterncastle. They were mammoth in size, but tender in design, and flavoured the vessel with a magical presence. At the bow, just below the elongated bowsprit, flew a matching eagle, carved with equally intricate detail. Its eyes were alive and keen.

A ship from a fairy tale! Rose mused. *But not particularly ghostly. Not in this light.* A dull shock punched through her spine as a pirate elbowed her forward. 'Get down the ladder! Into the skiff!'

Rose gaped down. Below her, six pirates were shuffling about in a small rowboat, preparing to traverse the gap between vessels. Stinger was among them, impatience plain in his stance.

Hesitantly, Rose stepped free of her captor's supportive grip and lowered shaking feet onto the ladder's first rung. It twitched at her contact, wobbling more than even her muscles did. She froze, afraid. Above her, the crew of the Kraken was closing in, pressing up against the railing, loosing the straps that held their guns in place. *If I go slow, will they shoot Stinger before I get down there?* A pirate eagerly kicked her hand, and Rose almost fell from the ladder. That was answer enough. *Today I will die. What is it like, Wes? Is it really so bad? I will be with you, won't I? In only a few minutes I'll be with you. And so will the man who commanded your death!*

Rose let her foot fall to the next rung, its rope sagging under her weight. Her wrists were impossibly weak, but they held her in place. The gnarled planks of the hull gradually ascended past her, separating her from the mutineers above.

She twisted to peek over her shoulder. The pirates in the skiff were gazing up through the open rag she wore, loosing a disgusting laughter. Rose shuddered, slamming her legs against the hull, bending her knees to block the perverts' view. A lump bulged in her throat, and tears streamed from her sleepy eyes. *I cannot cry! I cannot let them see me cry!* She hung helplessly from the ladder, aware that everyone was watching her, waiting. But she could not move.

Wind brushed over her sweat. Stinger started shouting for her to hurry up. *I'm going to die,* she told herself. *I'm going to die and there's nothing I can do to stop it. So just climb down. Just move your feet. For Wes. You can do it. I can do it.*

She took another step. Then another. Soon she had half-flopped, half-dribbled her way down to the small boat, where she rolled onto a rigid seat, wordless, scraping tears and phlegm from her mouth.

Stinger glared at her with pitiless eyes, then nodded at his entourage. They each took up oars and commenced rowing. The ladder slipped from Rose's thigh to drape in the water, disconnecting them from the Kraken once and for all. Instantly, she felt the shrapnel from the rifles bite through her flesh and bone. Every inch of her body flared up in agony. But there was no sound. Startled, she opened her eyes and arched her back. She had only imagined it. The other pirates eyed her cautiously as she continued to wince and flinch. She knew that any second the guns would fire in truth, and the seven of the skiff's occupants would be immediately dead.

Ahead, the ghost ship loitered, oblivious. It did not appear to get any closer; time had slowed almost to a complete stop. Rose whirled on her seat as it rocked in the waves. The skiff was mere feet from the hull of the Kraken, the chill of the latter's shadow still falling over them. The sun sank behind it, throwing rays past the ears of the pirate crew. Rose picked out Dagger, standing egotistically over the rope ladder while his henchmen hoisted it up. His face wore an evil grin, a victorious grin, framed distinctively by his dark beard. In that moment Rose was sure, beyond all doubt. Gazing up at his face once more, even from a distance, she knew it was him. He was the one that killed Wesley.

Rage engulfed her, overcame her fear and weakness. *He deserves to die! Not me!*

'Draw!' Dagger shouted, his voice unmistakeable. It gushed from the Kraken's deck and rippled over the salty sea. *I will not let him kill me! Somebody else can, but not him. Oh Wes, save me!* The other pirates in the skiff stirred, bewildered.

Wesley's voice cracked into Rose's consciousness, as harsh as a whip. *No Rose, we have to swim!*

There was no time for second-guessing. There would be no second chance this time, as there never had been before.

Rose slipped from the skiff to the clattering of drawing guns. Warm water thundered over her body, tearing the rag from her skin. Her eyes filled with salt, blasting pain through her skull. She flailed her feeble arms through billows of rumbling bubbles, the pressure mounting in her ears and she pushed down, down, down.

A raucous clanking exploded through the deep moan of the ocean. The water filled with a fine white mist and with shooting shards of iron flecks.

Rose could not tell if she had been hit. Her body was aflame with hurt regardless.

Her lungs filled with fire. She flailed harder. Pushing, pushing, until the fire spread to her fingertips. Dark shapes swirled around her. *Stinger? No, fish!* Some of them pricked her legs as she kicked violently through the rock-hard sea. *Sharks!* she thought.

Jolting, she thrust forwards, not sure if she were even moving at all. Desperate for air, she grabbed at the thickening water above her with bloody fingers. A plume of air burst from her mouth. She swallowed hard, pressed her lips together, and squirmed in the direction she thought was up.

Her hands found the surface first, plunging from the solid sea into the chaotic air. Splashing about, she brought her mouth to the surface next and inhaled both air and water alike.

She swirled her feet around to keep balance and spluttered

through her hands. *Am I alive? Why is it so dark?* She noticed a wall beside her. Her heart went cold. Tingles leapt from her toes to the top of her scalp. She had surfaced right next to the Kraken.

She glanced up. No pirates could see her.

She glanced across. There she saw the slumping remains of the skiff. No pirate could be seen there either.

Beyond the boat, the ghost ship towered high, motionless despite the chopping waves. A single ladder hung from its side, expectant.

That's where I need to get, Rose knew. The land was too far, and the skiff appeared to be sinking.

Oh, Wes! Help me get there! And please, don't let it be a real ghost ship!

10

The first blast was the loudest. It thundered along the starboard side of the ship, pummeling through every inch of air held belowdecks. The ship shuddered as it rolled over churning waves. The smell of roasted gunpowder billowed through the filtered light of the Black Beast's gun deck. Shouts came next, as gun captains guided their respective gun crews through the process of readying the next shot.

Alice clutched the nearest cannon for stability. It seemed a just little odd to her that she could have such a weapon all to herself. Along the far edge of the long and sweaty compartment, almost half the Blackbone crew were rummaging about in extreme urgency, while on her side—the port side—a braced row of heavy long guns sat undisturbed, unloaded and otherwise entirely wasted. Here Alice crouched, spectating in terror and excitement as the gunmen executed the delicate act for which they had trained so tirelessly.

'Find a place where you can watch,' Captain Blackbone had told her. 'But stay out of our way.' She smiled to herself. The place she had found was no less than perfect. 'Today, you'll witness what happens to those who betray their own kind.'

Indeed, any vessel on the other side of that thunderous broadside volley was certain to feel the gravity of treachery. Alice wished only that she could observe the victim brigantine's reaction. From her hideaway between two of the Black Beast's unused cannons, she could barely see through the starboard gunports for the men standing in her way.

The gun deck was as full as she had ever seen it throughout her eventful week aboard the Black Beast. Where she waited, the sun's piercing light mingled with the darkness of the lower decks, streaming down as it was through open trapdoors. Rain was also pouring in where the ladder came down from the main deck, along with the reverberant howling of Wulfric Blackbone's commands. But it was not by any means a miserable day. Oft times in Southland the rain would dump over the earth and sea in thick flourishes while the sun neglected to turn its face away, or give up its warmth. Today was such a day.

As a convict, Alice had hated working in the rain, and had hated it even more when she was forced into womanly duties following its arrival. But aboard the Black Beast, the water stung her skin less and less each day. It did not matter what task Wulfric or even Roger had her complete, she managed to get sweaty completing it. After a few days, a little moisture from above came to feel more liberating than constricting. Especially after hours of hot labour on the main deck. The only reason she had chosen to monitor this day's activities from the shelter of the lower level was simply for fear of slipping on the slickened surface amongst all the commotion.

Alice peered along the floor. It seemed her reasoning had

been for naught, as the skittering feet of the powder boys had brought just about the whole of the Rainbow Sea down with them, smearing the typically dry and dusty surface with puddles of murky slop.

The powder boys themselves interested Alice greatly. Apart from weathering a few of the crueler duties not even the ship's swabbie could bear to shoulder, the powder boys were welcomed into the Blackbone crew for merely the one purpose: to keep the gunpowder from the danger of the gun deck and the main deck—where the rest of the cannons were arranged. It was stored astern in the hold, the lowest layer of the vessel. From there, the boys would carry it up to the cannons, where it could be loaded, ready for detonation.

Alice lifted her gaze as one ran past. The boys were as young as half her age, but they took to their role with the stern expression of an adult and the vigour of dedicated hounds.

'Aye!' one of Wulfric's mates bellowed.

'Fire!' came the sealord's response, from above.

In quick succession, each of the gun captains yanked their respective cords, and the full broadside of cannons both on Alice's deck and the one overhead sounded their meaty blasts, thrusting their iron frames backward, coughing smoke everywhere. The guns jerked to a halt before they could roll amidships, constrained by the chain braces that leashed them to the wall.

The explosion was probably as loud as the first, but Alice was prepared for it this time. Instead of cowering at the noise, she fixed her eyes tightly to the drills of the gunmen. Almost immediately after firing, each crew snapped into formation, preparing their long guns for another round of shots. The procedure involved an awful lot of ramming sticks down the muzzle of the weapons, for what purpose Alice was mostly unaware. After a substantial bout of fussing, the crew would finally shove bags of gunpowder down also, followed by huge metal balls. The balls were made with twenty-four pounds of solid iron, and could put holes in the hulls of most other vessels so long as they found their home at the right angle. At least Kit had told her as much. As she watched the balls disappear into the mouths of those long-snouted monsters, she could imagine it was true.

Finally, the crews would shove some rags down the muzzle before all lining up by their cannon's side to heave it through its gunport, ramming the weapon's frame against the walls of the swaying room. If nothing else, Alice was most surprised by how long it took. There were at least three hard and hurried minutes between shots, and even the quickest crews were destined to wait upon Wulfric's order before they pulled the cord and released that instant puff of smoke.

Heat blossomed through Alice's heels, begging her to slip up the ladder to the main deck so she might see clearly the effect the first two rounds had had on the other vessel. The Gallantry, it was called. Kit had told her the name when he had briefed her on the attack. Apparently, the brigantine had repeatedly forgotten to pay its fair share of loot to the Blackbone lead ship, the Black Beast. This was deemed a direct betrayal of the support Wulfric had gifted them as a representative of the Blackbone name. 'A shame, too,' Wulfric had commented, overhearing the conversation. 'That brigantine was the best vessel we had in our service, not to mention the biggest!' When Alice had suggested they save the ship and banish its insubordinate crew, the captain had only laughed. 'That's not how it works,' he had said. 'Out here in the Sentinels, if you dare tread behind a sealord's back, you'll be made an example of. The Gallantry will be sunk before the day is out. That I promise you.'

Alice stretched upward, checking for clear passage to the main deck, careful not to disturb the powder boys' rhythm. She spun left and right, saw that nobody was in the way. Then the return fire began.

The crack of a dozen cannons shook through the gun deck unhindered. The crash of half a dozen shots colliding with the Black Beast's hard flank came next. Some thumped against the solid oak bulwark, bouncing away to splash into the water below. Others made dints in the wall, colliding with a spine-tingling crunch that knocked Alice onto her backside in astonishment. Screams erupted from above, and the jangle of flintlock rifle fire filled the chasm between cannon blasts.

Alice started to fret. *Could the Gallantry sink us? Just how big is this brigantine?*

The gun crews were ready for another round. 'Fire!' Wulfric's voice ripped through the crew, inspiring the long guns to shoot once more. Alice was on her feet again, head waving about in smoke as the ship rolled heavily from side to side. Where at first she had been intrigued, now she was scared. She had not imagined return fire when she pictured the attack.

The men were back to work again, stuffing sticks and shots into their cannons. The powder boys darted still from ladder to ladder, bags of grey dust spilling from their packed arms. Two of them collided at the entrance to the hold. Another enemy round sounded. This time two shots made it into the Black Beast's guts. One smashed through oak to clang deafeningly from a portside cannon, sending flecks of sharp wood spinning through the smoke. The other hurtled straight through an open gunport and slashed past the two powder boys, collecting their legs and sending them toppling down into the hold. After a moment of silent reorientation, their chilling screeches emerged.

Alice winced. The shot had most likely shattered the boys' legs from the shins down, and the fall could not have made it better. Without thinking, she sprang from her hideaway towards the hold's ladder. The gun deck's mate strode after her.

Scrambling down into the shadowed storage room, Alice located the two boys. One was sniffling in a pile of broken barrels, the other shrieking with his hands around his legs as black blood oozed out. Alice's stomach turned when she surveyed the second boy's contorted shin. Between the knee and the ankle, a whole new joint had formed, bending the lower part of the child's leg perpendicularly to his thigh.

Alice yelped. Her hands stuttered, though she tried to make use of them.

'Leave the boys!' the mate ordered, pounding after them.

'They need help!' Alice cried.

'*We* need help! You need to carry the powder!'

'You can't leave them here, like this!'

The mate growled. 'You need to deliver the powder or we'll all die! Is that what you want?! I'll send for Maurice. You get the bags!'

'But—' Sweat frothed from Alice's forehead. The boy screamed louder, and louder.

'No buts! Get those bags! Deliver the powder! Quickly!'

Alice clenched her teeth, wiped the sweat from her hair, and snatched a few gunpowder sacks from the pile of debris at the base of the ladder. As quickly as she could, she bounced up to the gun deck.

The bags were surprisingly heavy, as if the powder within was packed to the density of stone. The adrenaline that gushed through her wrists made light work of them nevertheless. Having watched the powder boys at their duties, Alice was confident she knew how to carry them out. Skipping from one gun crew to the next, she flopped a bag into the expectant hands of the loader standing aft of each cannon. The gun deck was slick with fresh moisture beneath her boots as she darted from stern to bow, making sure every cannon was ready for the next broadside fire. She noticed that some loaders had more than one bag at their sides, and their hands could not take another. They would not place them on the wet floor either, lest the powder become soggy. She whirled after offloading her last sack. The only remaining powder boy with legs was servicing the lower deck too.

Before she could react, the mate strode urgently towards her. He had to shout to lift his voice over the clamour of gun loading and the drone of the rain without. 'To the upper deck,' he bellowed, ' to the upper deck!'

A cold chill washed over her. *To the upper deck?! Of course!* 'Yessir… Aye!' she stammered, already sprinting towards the hold to collect another armful of dust.

'Fire!' Another battery of pops rapped through the Black Beast's bones.

She had to leap right over the screaming boy to fetch more bags. His cries fuelled her rush.

The spine crunching boom of another enemy round shook the hull.

She bolted up the ladder once more. This time she scooted straight across the gun deck to the upper stairs, where she jumped quickly up into the heavy rain.

The bright scene and hammering noise struck her immediately. She almost dropped the bags in amazement. All around her the air was alive with sparkling precipitation, a shattered blue and white canvas cut with the hissing black sails of the Black Beast, the larger of which flaunted the rippling white skull of the Blackbones. The distinctive emblem appeared from below both scorching and deathly.

Soaring into the sky on either side of the ship were the jagged green walls of Langdon and Steepcliff Island, locking them in a one-way chasm course deep through the heart of Blackbone territory. Beneath their misty heights, shouts, gunfire and cannon smoke swirled together with the pounding rain to form a horrid cacophony. Alongside it all, the enemy brigantine sailed at full speed, defiant and dying, churning up the glimmering sea behind it. It was certainly smaller than the Black Beast, but was larger than Alice expected. Its two masts held smudged beige sails over a bustling crew, who slipped about amongst their broken rigging, firing their rifles as soon as they were loaded. Through the vigourous downpour the vessel remained perfectly clear, no more than a ship's width from its attacker. The smoke from its cannons was near enough to smell.

What breeze remained between the two islands held both vessels in a delicate starboard tilt, meaning the Gallantry leant askew to expose more of its hull to the Black Beast's long guns, while the latter's lean dipped its offensive flank into the water, lining up its cannons more effectively. Alice needed not to be told this was a tactical arrangement on Wulfric's part; Wesley had taught her enough to know it. The captain who had ordered the manoeuvre stood commandingly by the helm, a heavy hand on the ship's wheel as he roared instructions at his soaked army through his soaked beard.

The entire vista was so surreal—yet so real. Alice could hardly believe she was present at all. Though warm droplets pressed swiftly into her linen shirt and trickled over the skin beneath her waistcoat, and though the tilted deck rumbled unsteadily beneath her tired soles, a sense of distant numbness overtook her.

She shook herself. She had already hesitated too long. Flicking strands of floppy hair from her eyes, Alice sprang back into action. She tried to ignore the enemy cannons as she hastily delivered her powder to sopping gunmen. As soon as the loaders snatched them from her hands, the bags almost instantly disappeared down the cannon noses, to keep them dry.

'Fire!' The ship trembled. Not all of the guns ignited this time. Alice had no chance to decipher whether it was her own fault. She bounded up to the quarterdeck where she passed away her last few bags to the two gun crews there.

'Al!' Wulfric thundered from behind her. She spun to meet his dark glare, which impaled her with its tenacity.

'The boys got hit,' she barked.

Wulfric's gaze held her in paralysis for a second. Only a second. Then he looked over at the Gallantry. 'Faster,' he said.

Alice darted away. The captain's command raced in her blood. Before she could blink, she was hopping over the screaming boy again to fill her arms with powder bags. It was as if the command itself allowed her to move with greater speed.

As agile as a fish in water, Alice zipped back to the main deck, colliding with a smack against the wall of rain there. She almost knocked Roger the boatswain from his arrogant patrol as she swept over the ship. It made her smile.

After dumping the bags, she revisited the hold to reload. The newly appointed powder girl was determined to supply the full upper deck with their goods before Wulfric could order the next broadside strike. Her feet moved deftly over the ship's surface as she ran. She just about found herself enjoying the experience, when she came finally up to the quarterdeck with her last few bags. The Gallantry caught her eye. It was sitting much lower in the water than it ought, and its tilt was exaggerated. The thing was sinking. But not only that, it was no longer parallel with the Black Beast.

'It's turning!' Wulfric announced. 'Heave to! And hold your fire 'til it's all the way 'round! We'll rake this bloody traitor!'

Alice could not help but stop and stare. The Black Beast appeared to circle the stern of the Gallantry, as the smaller vessel slumped into the white surface of the Rainbow Sea. The brigantine was striving to turn away, but had lost its traction.

Its rigging whipped wildly as the sails curved far from the wind. All along its sinking surface, pirates were loosing rowboats and packing into them, abandoning their vessel as swiftly as possible. Only a few stouthearted mates stood their ground, trying hopelessly to resurrect their momentum.

Soon enough, the Gallantry was at right angles with the Black Beast, so that the greater's slender cannons leered right down the length of their prey. From there, Alice could see through the decorated windows of the Gallantry's sterncastle to its dim, empty interior.

Wulfric slapped a titanic hand onto Alice's shoulder. The shock of it made her jump. She went to move, but his grip restrained her.

'This, Al King, is why you should never turn your back to your foe.'

Alice crooked nervously, only to find Wulfric's heavy beard mere inches from her nose. 'Why?'

'Rake 'em!' Wulfric shouted, his voice carving out holes in the rain. 'Fire!'

Then the cannons let loose, and Alice saw the devastating impact right away. Several Blackbone shots smashed into the fragile rear of the Gallantry's sterncastle, their lingering crunch echoing about the wide gorge as they punched through the entire brigantine from back to front. Glass shattered and splinters burst into the air. One shot flew high and ripped a hole in the enemy's lower mainsail. Alice could hear the vessel moan as it endured its deciding blow.

'Drop the boats!' commanded Wulfric.

Lines were released instantly, and all of the Black Beast's

rowboats dropped from the ship's gunwale to the water below, colliding with a reverberant smack.

Kit materialised by Alice's side, his black hair long and straight under the weight of the heavy weather. 'Father?' he questioned.

'We can't let them get away, can we?' Wulfric was chortling, now. He discharged Alice from his huge palm. 'You were quick, Al. I need quick. Get in the boat. And you, Kit. Gus, Will, Ed, Jack.'

And with that, Captain Wulfric Blackbone shed his giant coat, stomped over to the quarterdeck's railing, and jumped off.

'Shit!' The Black Beast's quartermaster threw his own coat to the deck and climbed over the ship's side. Kit's gloved hand found Alice's. It was cold. He looked at her sympathetically. 'Are you ready?' he asked.

Alice frowned. 'No?'

Kit's fingers tightened. 'Come on!' He led her to the ship's edge, helped her place a heel on the railing, then flung the both of them overboard.

For a moment they fell at a speed with the raindrops, fetching brief respite from their constant wet battering. Then together they smashed into the salty ocean.

Alice was by no means ready for it. The frothing water shot up her nose and pounded in her ears as it rushed over her. She floundered for the surface, her clothes dragging through the flowing channel as she swept her arms forward and back. She popped out amongst the chop erupting with coughs and splutters. The calamity of sound scraping the waterlogged valley returned suddenly. She could barely suck her breath back for the immensity of the rain around her.

Kit's hand pierced her attention once more. It jabbed down from above with its partner to wrap around her armpits. Firmly in the young man's embrace, Alice fumbled her way from the water to the steeply rocking boat, unable to see through the prickling flood in her eyes.

Before she could orientate herself, a solid shaft was pushed crudely into her palms. 'Row,' Kit's voice advised. She latched on tight and began to work the oar blindly, until the fresh drizzle had swept the salt away. Head spinning, she realigned herself with the terrain. The Black Beast loomed over her, but it was fading away into the rainy mist. She was near the stern of the rowboat, sitting beside the captain's elite, rowing for her life while the small hull filled with rain. In order to see where they were going, she had to crank her head around toward the boat's heading. Wulfric was standing right on the nose, swinging an oar around like a windmill.

They passed the sinking Gallantry in no time at all, and the Blackbone ship grew rapidly smaller. Kit was bailing out the water with a wooden bucket after only a handful of strokes, leaving merely six rowers with all the work. Even still, their boat carved ahead of the other Blackbones, fervently spearheading the final assault.

Almost a dozen rowboats swept frantically along the steep gorge in a desperate chase, leaving the larger beasts in their wake. The current multiplied each rower's efforts, sending the pack hurtling through rain towards the open passage ahead of them. The sun streamed down on their advances, crowding the atmosphere with the colours of its name.

The air was impossibly humid, the sea rough but flat beneath them. Alice's back screamed murder at her, but she pulled through, forcing the boat to slip over the surface toward the enemy.

Her boat was the first to squeeze into the mob of Gallantry deserters. The fearful men pulled guns from their boats and released their fire. Kit pushed Alice to the floor, shouting 'Duck!'

Smoke mingled with the rain once more.

'Keep rowing!' Wulfric shouted. He had dropped his oar now and was brandishing his curved sword. 'Faster!' He yanked a pistol from his belt and fired it at the nearest boat. One of the Gallantry's men fell into the waves.

'Move it!' Gus growled, urging the rest of them forward. Alice was not sure she could pull any harder. Kit thumped into the seat behind her and shoved his oar into the sea.

Their boat veered towards another on their starboard side. All around them, the Black Beast's boats were catching their prey. Screams bubbled up amidst gunshots.

Alice trembled as she rowed. The boat they neared was packed to overflowing with sword-wielding Gallantry pirates. Still she rowed, faster and faster.

Before the boats collided, Wulfric leapt from his perch, his heavy shirt flying out behind him like a cape. He crashed into the dazzled targets, sword spinning, scattering them like gulls. Alice's boat rocked violently. Will sprang up too, as did Ed. The two of them bowled onto their enemies. The boats clapped into each other. Gus latched them together. Alice's head sunk deeper into her shoulders. Blood spat on her face.

Some of the Gallantry men jumped into the sea, others fell. Wulfric knocked one down with his elbow. The victim's back smacked into the small boat's half-flooded floor. He was the only traitor left aboard. Wulfric dropped his knees into the man's thighs and pointed his sword at the man's neck. 'Why did you betray me?!' he shouted.

The Gallantry sailor was crying for mercy, rain gurgling from his gaping, bloody mouth. Wulfric slapped his cheek with the back of his hand. 'Just tell me, you bloody traitor! Why did the Gallantry decide not to pay its share, huh? Did you think you could plunder the Sentinels without us?!'

Alice leant forward, curious. Other than the lingering hiss of rain on water, the scene had almost calmed right down. There were no more shouts, and the splashes of the fleeing traitors gradually trailed away. Only a couple of Black Beast crewmen were still intercepting their game, but those brawls were distant enough to pose no threat.

Gus was still holding the two boats together, and the others were pressing in around the prone sailor. Alice felt compelled to join them, though she held herself back.

'We— We didn't want to do it,' the Gallantry man answered. 'Not most of us, anyway.' He coughed up red water. 'It was just— The Kraken! It tracked us down— And Stinger Dreadwind offered us... a bigger share than you did. And he promised to protect us too.'

Wulfric grunted, clearly perturbed. He lowered his sword and stood up, the boat beneath him wobbling. The captive shuffled awkwardly. 'Don't kill me, cap'n!'

'If Stinger struck a deal with you, why didn't you go off and prance about in Dreadwind territory?' Wulfric spoke quickly, impatient to salvage the information he needed.

'We didn't want to, cap'n. Most of us didn't want to desert—'

'I don't bloody well care what most of you wanted! Why did the Gallantry rob traffic in Blackbone waters, if you were paying tribute to the Kraken?!'

'That was part of the deal, cap'n!' the captive squealed. 'We were's to work for him, but in your territory. He said he'd protect us if you found out! But he lied, cap'n! See?! We shouldn't have done it! Don't kill me!'

Wulfric erupted in a roar of unbridled rage. 'Goddamn Stinger bloody Dreadwind! I knew he was shitting all over our treaty, and now I have the proof! Proof that Teddy can't bloody well ignore! Gus, get us back to the Beast! Now!'

11

If it had sucked every last drop of life from her naked body to make the swim, it had sucked every last drop of her soul to climb the rope ladder. But whether or not the Rose that reached the top had any spirit dwelling still within that dripping, slop of a corpse, at least she had reached the top.

She flopped over the decorated railing to dribble onto the deck of the ghost ship. Her head nearly split open on the Sirlish oak planks. By now the delicate chime of night had almost overwhelmed the bay, and the moon's absence was already obvious. What were drowned mountains before were but rising black teeth now, baring their jagged edges against the fading sky. The creak of the ghost ship's wood was all that penetrated the stillness, save for the erratic puffs of breath that leaked from her lungs.

But there was another sound, trickling across the water, some distance away. Rose turned her head to peer through the regal stumps that trimmed the ship's gunwale. There she saw another vessel, sitting rudely on the sea. The Kraken, she knew. In the weak light, it was almost impossible to tell whether its black sails were flying or furled, but the thing was moving.

Further and further away it was moving, the voices of its crew dimming with the sunset. If it were coming towards her, she should have been able to see the giant jellyfish shining starkly on the face of its lower sails. Instead she spied only a dark silhouette.

She thought little of it. After all, it had been Stinger Dreadwind—the Kraken's *old* captain—who had wanted to parley with the ghost ship. Not Dagger the mutineer. Poor Stinger was now floating with the fishes somewhere between Rose's body and the shrinking hull on the horizon, with shrapnel and water to fill his lungs. Rose could hardly believe she envied him.

A soft, chilling breeze drew over the back of her thighs, coercing goose bumps from her skin.

I'm naked! she realised. *And on the deck of a ghost ship!* She emerged from her pile at once, lurching into an upright sit with her back against the ocean. She was being watched. She slapped a hand over her dripping breasts and crossed her legs. *This is truly the end of me,* she thought. *How I've come even this far, I'll never know. But now I am ruined. A naked girl on a ghost ship!*

Her eyes sifted nervously through the darkness upon the steady deck. There were men aboard, that was clear, but they made not a sound. They stood unmoving in the shadows, their pale faces reflecting the enduring purple light of the dying day. And they watched her. They did not ogle, or stare, only watched.

A shiver ran through Rose's skin. The men frightened her. In a way, she would have preferred they came lustfully onto her like a normal crew of outlawed vermin. At least that way she would have understood what was going on.

Eventually, one of the men meandered forward. He had a moustache but no beard, a waistcoat but no shirt. He appeared as though he had once been jolly, before his eyes had been closed to all that was good in the world. He shuffled his moustache, voiceless, peering down at the retreating heap of flesh that hulked before his tightly strapped boots.

The inevitable question welled up inside Rose's gut like wildfire. *Are you a ghost?* Unfortunately, the same silence that afflicted the crew seemed to grip her by the throat.

She pressed her arm deeper into her chest and brushed the other behind her back, searching for something to hold on to. Perhaps there was nothing there at all. If this were really a ghost ship, perhaps none of it was even real. Perhaps none of it could be touched, or spoken to. Perhaps she would fall through the deck at any second, to drown in the middle of a foreign bay, with nobody to know how—or where—her worthless life was snuffed out.

The ghostly figure flicked his head and raised a finger. Rose peered along his bare shoulder to the finger's tip and beyond. He was pointing at the ghost ship's sterncastle. Even under the still shade of night, the structure remained oddly discernible, like a distant tower on the horizon. It did not at all resemble the boxy sterncastle that adorned the Kraken's rear end; this was a castle in its own right, a palace wedged between the great wooden wings fanning the curious vessel's tail. Two curved staircases twisted their way to the poop deck on its roof, circling an ornately crafted doorway that was sunk deeply into the palace façade amid the dim orange glow of two lightly pulsing lanterns. Rose had to crane her neck to see the most of it over the ship's quarterdeck, which itself was both majestic and tall.

She groaned. From where she slouched, the door felt a mile away. Her legs shook at the prospect of bearing her weight. She had given everything to pull herself aboard the ship, leaving naught to spare. Even if her muscles would allow it, she did not wish to stand, for the peril of exposing more skin to the rest of the ghostly crew that surrounded her. She gawked at the prickly moustache in pleading speechlessness, unsure what to say or how to say it. *What do you want me to do in there? I don't really want to disappear into the mouth of a ghost ship, don't you know? Can't I just sit here? Can't I just sit here and wait for... and wait for...*

But the man continued to point, his finger failing to waver in the slightest. Rose's discomfort grew, despite the high dose she already suffered.

The light of evening was vanishing fast now. Soon all that would fill the night would be those lanterns, and the stars.

Another man hovered forward. This one had a bag in his hands. Or was it a rag? When he laid it on her, she pinched it between her fingers. It was a piece of sailcloth. The thing was wet, and it smelt like salt and old fish. But so did she. She pulled it onto her body enthusiastically. The moustache man scowled at the rag man, though he protested not.

The gesture sprinkled Rose with a sense of warmth, however slight. Enough to get her on her feet, at least. Moustache man firmly held his stance, pushing her to heed his command. She nodded indistinctly, swirling the sailcloth over her shoulders and squeezing its corners around her neck before rising on shaky ankles. Moustache man was jabbing his finger back and forth at the sterncastle. Rose finally turned towards it. The lanterns there were now the brightest thing on the whole ship.

She dragged a foot along the deck, letting her weight squash over it. One step. She yanked forward her other, aching pain spiralling up her calf, a tense throb grinding along the surface of her buttocks. Another. Then she was walking.

The night was not cold enough to make her shiver, though she shivered anyway, clutching the cloth tightly over her shoulders. It trailed along the wooden planks behind her as she flopped towards the quarterdeck stairs.

She tried to avoid eye contact with the various crewmen that watched her make her way towards the lanterns on the sterncastle's face, but it was impossible not to notice them. They remained completely still, never breaking their decided silence, or offering any reaction at all. Their presence invoked a deep distress within her heart. A ghostly, haunting chill.

What can they do to you? Rose asked herself. *What are you afraid of? If they kill you, what is the harm? Isn't that what you wanted?* She tightened the cloth and drove past them, wordless. Soon enough they were all behind her, and the glowing sterncastle door greeted her warmly.

A flash of hesitation gripped her as her legs threatened to give way beneath her hips. She turned from the door nervously to view a swarm of pale, frozen men soaking in the night atop the freakishly tranquil deck. She shuddered, spun back around, and fumbled her way through the archway, swinging the heavy door closed behind her.

Rose immediately pictured skeletons. Rotting flesh, piles of dust and broken furniture. Her head filled to brimming with the horrors she knew were to come bleeding from the woodwork of the ghost ship's haunted interior. She drew a deep breath to keep herself from vomiting.

But the scene before her was far from derelict. In fact, the immaculate room was dressed like a king's. Where Rose had expected spider webs, she saw only silk, quivering gently in the light of a single lantern that was placed atop a brass stand on a thickly oiled table. Its reflection caught in the far windows, its glow stretching out into the black air beyond.

Frightfully, Rose searched back and forth, making out all the furnishings one by one amongst the dim, warm atmosphere. There was a bed with four posts, a chest with gold bracings, a barrel full of fruit, an armchair with red upholstery.

Shit! Rose jumped halfway to the ceiling in shock. She almost dropped her cloth, gagging. Indeed, amid the fresh, sweet scenery there was one corpse. It reclined horribly in the room's corner, flickering in and out of the lamplight on the velvet chair there. She stumbled backward until she collided with the wall behind her. Her elbow knocked a dresser and a teacup fell from its saucer to shatter on the ground, snapping the eerie silence into dozens of pieces.

'Was it my face?' a deadly voice sounded, mean and dry. A tingle quivered through Rose's aching limbs. The corpse made a rustling sound as it moved. *It's moving! It's... Speaking to me!*

It chuckled lightly. 'Come. Closer to the light. You're a girl.

I see.'

Rose could not move.

'I said come.' The voice oozed with venom and charm alike. Rose's muscles cramped, though she eventually managed to stagger forward, too afraid to disobey the dead man's carcass. She tucked the cloth up to her chin, fingernails driving its texture into the palms of her hands.

Wes! Help me! A dead man is speaking!

'That's better,' said the dead man. As she moved nearer, she could see him clearer. The thing was old and leathery, with a rotting beard and a faded patch covering one eye. The other eye was worse yet; it peered out from a mangled scar, flaunting no colour or depth. His smile had less teeth than it should have, and the fingers that rested upon the arms of his chair were but tendrils of shrivelled skin and bone. Oddly, the animated corpse was dressed in the hardy garb of a seasoned sailor, finished with a heavy belt, short coat and tall boots, all devoid of grime or stink.

'You're not who I expected.'

Rose proceeded carefully. She did not want to tell the corpse what had happened. *But since he's dead, maybe he already knows.*

'I... I was... I was on the Kraken. The other ship. But I was... thrown overboard, and I swam here.'

The corpse revealed no emotion. 'So you are a Dreadwind. Where then, is James?'

'I don't—'

'The captain. Stinger, he's called now, aye.'

'Ahh...' Rose stepped back again, flinching. *What are you, dead man? What do you want me to say? Stinger is dead! What will you do if I tell you? Will you kill me?*

'Is he coming? Speak up.'

Rose swallowed. 'The… he… won't be coming.'

'Why?' A vicious rasp flavoured the dead man's tone.

'The crew. They… killed him.' Rose clenched her teeth in fearful anticipation of her company's reaction. 'But it wasn't me,' she quickly added. 'It was a mutiny, led by a man called… Dagger…'

The dead man chewed on the thought. 'Jack Dagger,' he mumbled under his breath. 'I know him. Sly, that one. Violent.'

Rose pressed against the dresser. The creature in front her was no less than the embodiment of a nightmare. She wanted to escape, to get back out to the ghost ship's crew.

Suddenly, the dead man sprang to his feet. A disgusting grin was plastered over his rotting face. 'The first falls,' he whispered. He sized up Rose leisurely, paralysing her attempts to nudge towards the door. His gaze cut through her soul. Approval flashed briefly over his features. 'Have a seat.' He waved his arm at the wooden chairs pushed neatly under the dark table. 'This news deserves a drink, at the least.'

'I don't th—'

'Have a seat! You can't stand there all night.' A pair of mugs materialized in the dead man's hands. He thrust them onto the table before striding to a dark cabinet beside the bed where he located a large, creamy-surfaced bottle of rum. Rose eased into one of the chairs, barely letting her weight leave the balls of her rigid feet. The other began to pour generously into both mugs. After he had emptied the bottle, he pulled out a chair for himself and reclined into it merely inches from Rose's shuddering body. The bumps on his leathery skin became painfully perceptible as he settled beside the lantern.

'Drink!' he laughed, then turned his mug upside-down over his mangled beard. Rose reached a hand out from her cloth to touch her own beverage. She dragged it across the table. She could feel the weight of the liquid slopping about.

The corpse erupted into a fit of coughs, spitting rum through the air. Cold droplets spattered onto Rose's face. She tried not to breath them in. 'You... *wanted* Stinger to die?' she asked. Even as as the words dripped from her lips, she could not believe she had uttered them. *What's wrong with you, Rose?! Just shut your mouth and try to get out of here alive!*

The corpse sucked in its coughs. 'And you didn't?' His dead, milky eye narrowed in suspicion between the bubbling scars on his brow and cheek. 'Who are you, anyway, that you would come to me with this news?' He spat phlegm onto the table and cleared his throat.

Panic flushed over Rose's damp skin. If she answered this wrong, death was sure to find her soon after. *But if he wanted Stinger dead... Wes help me! I have to tell the truth.*

'My name is Rose King,' Rose began, avoiding eye contact with that terrible white slit as much as she could. Then slowly, she told the corpse the truth. From the Ijian fire to the Kraken's mutiny she told it, careful not to include any details that might suggest her allegiance to any party other than herself. At first she stuttered, occasionally glancing at the listener's face to check if she was taking too long, but by the end her words flowed forth in a stream of emotion. The release seemed to raise her core temperature, and she ceased to shake.

The corpse drank up the story like he had the rum. When Rose finished, his mangled face winced in disappointment. He took a swig from his mug and slammed it back against the table. 'Rose King!' he exclaimed, musing.

'And who are you?' Rose blurted. Again, she castigated herself for speaking before thinking. *You don't question a corpse! You... just don't!*

Those corrupted eyebrows curved in intrigue. 'You really don't know who I am?'

'No... I told you. I'm not a pirate.'

'Neither am I,' rebutted the corpse. 'I'm a king! Don't you recognise my ship, at least?'

Rose hesitated, careful. '...No.'

'The Frontiere. Surely you know the name. And I am its master, Captain Halfeye Warhawk.'

Rose was certainly in no mood for jokes, so she chose not to reward the claim with anything more than a cursory snigger. *It's impossible. Surely he knows that. Halfeye drowned four years ago.* But the more she thought about it, the more her disbelief softened. She was aboard a ghost ship after all, and was speaking with a corpse! Rose's stare snapped onto the dead man's face. One of his eyes was hidden behind a patch, the other was half ruined. *Half an eye, that's all he's got! Oh Wes! Where in hell have I gotten myself?*

'So...' Rose asked. 'You *are* a ghost, then? You're *dead!*'

As if perfectly on cue, Halfeye let loose another explosion of coughs. Its deep rumble sounded more like a choking dog than a man with a cold.

When he straightened again, he pointed his half-eye at

Rose. 'Not yet, Rose King. But soon. It seems I'm at odds with our God; I don't think he likes me.'

'But—'

'A ghost ship? Aye, that's what I have the Dreadwinds believe. Please tell me you're smarter than they are.'

'But the crew?'

'Good Sirlish slaves from Brindia.'

'But—'

'Is it my face? Hauled from the sea floor, I know what it looks like. But I tell you, my blood's as hot as yours. I've had a hard life, and a hard life gives a man scars. None of which are skin deep, I'll say!'

Rose could not believe it. Halfeye Warhawk was dead, a Southland legend of whom the cons fabled late at night. There was no way she was truly stuck with him in the sterncastle of the Frontiere. The existence of a ghost ship was more likely.

'It doesn't make sense. How are you not dead?'

Halfeye threw another dash of rum down his haggard throat. Orange light sparkled in his beard where drops of his drink remained. 'You want to know how, Rose King? Then allow me to enlighten you. You know of the manner in which the Frontiere was sunk, aye?'

Rose's eyes widened, her face fading to white.

'Nay, you don't! By Wimsworth, you are an innocent one. I'll have to start from the beginning, if it suits you.'

Rose was still contemplating the odds of her predicament. She noticed her mug once again, the rum inside as still as glass and as black as death. *Oh Wes! I know you don't like me drinking.* She snatched the mug and stole a swig. There was no flavour, only burning. The sensation pulsed through her throat, then came spiralling up into her nose. Tears squeezed from her eyes. She slapped the mug back to the table, meeting Halfeye's half-eye squint with her own.

'That's the spirit!' the old pirate snorted. He bent over the table, almost far enough to singe his beard on the lantern. 'We were political prisoners from Sirland, each,' he whispered. 'And so were allowed to bunk with our families during transportation, a privilege not granted any regular convict.' Halfeye raised his eyebrow, assuming. Rose did not react. Instead, she raised the mug once more and filled her mouth with that warm flurry of fire.

Halfeye grinned before resuming, flaunting a crooked row of buttery teeth. 'But when we made port in Southland, we were treated just like all the other scum. Our wives and daughters were taken from us to join the women's camps, and we were left on this here Wimswind Island to turn the soil and prop up the officers' filthy houses. You see, back then the port of Wreckrest was bigger than even Gold Harbour. The bloody fools hadn't yet discovered that the gold flowed thicker on the mainland than it ever did on the islands. But fools or no, they treated us like slaves. And we were as pathetic as they told us we were. That was until April the next year, when—'

'You stole the Frontiere,' Rose interrupted.

Halfeye leant back. 'Aye, I knew you'd heard the story! It's a legend, true.'

'I've heard that part,' said Rose. 'But it doesn't explain…'

'Of course,' Halfeye went on. 'Let me go on and I'll get to it. We escaped, aye, and became lords once more. Lords of

Southland, lords of the sea. For half a decade I ruled these islands—along with my crew—striking fear into all that saw our black sails upon the horizon. While the settlers grew rich digging gold from the soil, we grew rich plucking it from the channels. We guarded those who paid us, robbed those who didn't, and sunk any bastard who questioned our authority. The Frontiere was feared by all Southlander vessels from Morchport all the way to the tip of the Barricade Reef. Or at least by those that didn't wish to share a fate with the hulks on the sea floor!

'After we claimed Wreckrest as our own, I was named the Warhawk. For the wings on my ship, I suppose. My mates took fresh names as well. Theodore Seablood, my first, Wulfric Blackbone the Beast, and James Dreadwind, the Stinger. Over time they acquired their own vessels, each as formidable as the other. That, Rose King, is where it went sour.'

Halfeye grumbled to himself and emptied the dregs from his mug.

'They grew fatigued of our arrangement. Each sealords in their own right, my companions no longer wished to pay me their share of loot, especially knowing I was stashing it some place they would never find. In the end they supposed they could rule the Sentinels without me. Without their king.

'And so, three years on from our grand escape, the three men caught me north of the Snagger. They surrounded the Frontiere. They took me on, all against one. It was more than my ship could take.' Halfeye sighed. 'Indeed, they sunk me that day. My ship, my crew, my command. All for greed. All for treachery!'

Halfeye's corpse of a body slumped in its chair. The darkness pressed in on the lantern, which seemed to lose some of its life.

Rose was upright, mouth open. *Halfeye Warhawk! How can it be?!* She filled her mouth with rum. The burn was already easier to endure, and the liquid was permeating her skin, flooding her with a warmth she had not expected to find in the depths of a ghost ship. 'So you did die! Drown, I mean.' *I knew it!*

Halfeye jolted abruptly, as if suddenly remembering where he was. 'Nay!' he exclaimed, coughing the word out. 'Nay, let me finish!' Even in the shadows of the night, Rose thought she saw Halfeye's jagged face contort in despair to hatred. 'They expected me to go down with my crew, that was their mistake. It's not a good captain who abandons his ship, even as it sinks. But I tell you, it's not a good captain who opens fire on his friend, either. Aye, the very second I knew they had me beat, I fled into the sea, before even the first cannon was fired. I left it all behind, my ship, my sails, my crew. And I floated off to the Snagger, unseen and unbroken.

'You must understand. In that moment, I could not let them win. I could not slump aboard my throne as it succumbed to its undue fate. I cast honour aside. I shed glory, love and duty, all for the burden of vengeance. Now it is all that pumps through my flesh, binding me to the realm of the living.

'That determination—along with a slice of my secret hoard—ferried me over many months to distant Brindia. There I built my revenge with cedars and Sirlish Oak. One plank at a time I had it done, until the Frontiere was created anew, a perfect replica of its predecessor. On that very ship have I now returned, undefeated, unsunk. Aye, the revived Frontiere, risen from the sea floor to exact justice! To impose the true penalty of betrayal! At least that's what it looks like. The original beauty still sleeps with the fishes, somewhere out there, it does.'

Rose shifted her bare feet on the boards below them. The floor felt harder than it had before. *A replica Frontiere? So this is not the same ship!* She looked around, marvelling at the detail in every nook. *What sort of madness is this?* She thought then of Wesley, and what she imagined she might do to Dagger if she ever found the opportunity.

'If revenge is all you care about,' she asked, 'why haven't you killed them all yet? These… traitors, I mean.'

Halfeye snorted. 'If only vengeance could be sated so simply. The sealords have since grown to a strength beyond what ever I tasted, in allies, numbers and training. On the contrary, I have but slaves to drive my sails. Open combat is not an option, as I would certainly lose. Better to make them turn on each other, aye, as they turned on me.

'It was easy enough convincing Dreadwind I was risen from the dead, and even easier convincing the fool to break his precious treaty! And all for what, a sniff of my gold?! Four years a-searching, and they still haven't found it! Ha! But his death, aye, it did not happen the way I had planned. Not if what you tell me is indeed as true as you say. But it will have to suffice. That it will. At the least, his final actions have set in motion the seed of mistrust that will topple a traitorous dynasty!'

Rose peered at Halfeye's wild stare with uneasy empathy. The decrepit captain may not have been deceased, but he was quite possibly insane. Insane with a lust for revenge.

'My reign lives on, Rose King', Halfeye hissed. 'But these bones have only the strength for one more victory.' The mad corpse coughed a blob of slimy blood onto the flickering light. 'Three sealord traitors sailing my seas. The first has fallen. Two yet will fall.'

12

'**G**oddam bloody Seablood traitor!' howled Wulfric Blackbone, the Sealord of the Southern Sentinels. He had been saying it all morning. Shouting it, really. Ever since the news came to him from the crew aboard Kit's sloop, the captain had been quivering with wrath. Under the circumstances, Alice thought the reaction was rather tempered, though despite his solid composure and unmoving expression, rage clearly boiled beneath the surface, and the curses flowed freely from his lips.

He was angry because after a long day at sea, the sloop had come back without Kit on it. Wulfric summarized the issue succinctly between tightly clenched teeth: 'I send my son to tell him of Stinger's crimes, and he bloody well kidnaps the boy! As if it were I that was breaking our treaty!'

After clawing out condemning evidence from the Gallantry's fleeing crew, Wulfric had been sure that sending Kit with as much news would spur Captain Seablood into an immediate attack on the Dreadwinds. It seemed, however, that Captain Seablood was not particularly pleased to see a Blackbone brave his territory again. And now Kit was the

Northern Sealord's prisoner. *At least Seablood didn't kill him,* Alice thought. *The man did tell Wulfric not to come back. He said to meet in Wreckrest instead!* Alice chose not to share this memory with the Blackbone captain, especially not while the Black Beast was anchored behind them in the heart of Hullbreaker Bay, and the town of Wreckrest loomed brightly over the rowboat that was ferrying her to shore.

Alice had only just begun to feel comfortable aboard the pirate ship. Since her efforts in the sinking of the Gallantry, the Black Beast's crew had treated her with an honest respect. In her mind, she had done little more than throw a few bundles of gunpowder around the swirling chaos, but the endeavour seemed to indicate something deeper to the Blackbones. Even Roger, the ship's boatswain, ceased to burden her with his petty chores and snide taunts. After only a handful of Southland sunsets, the skinny bully had pinned his filth-ridden tongue tightly behind his teeth. Wulfric was probably just as much to blame; the captain had been protecting her from the most brazen of his crew since she first came aboard. She slept in his royal cabin, and ate her food across the table from his illustrious beard. On the whole, she was treated far better than she had ever been as a convict.

Despite the greater crew's acceptance, it was in Maurice that Alice found the most comfort. The jovial giant was the ship's cook and doctor both; Lord of the Galley, in his own words. Alice first discovered him and his sanctuary while she was wandering aimlessly about the lower decks, trying to avoid Roger. He introduced himself via a casual salute with a rusty spatula poking from his bulky fist, and allowed her to watch him prepare the evening's soup. He was a passionate man who loved his work, and rarely abandoned his pots in the galley save for dinnertime.

Maurice's company served as the perfect hideaway when Blackbone life was too confronting, and Alice's presence did not seem to bother him. He listened to her stories and told some of his own. When there was no more to say he would sing, filling his cramped galley with songs of sailing and cooking, and cooking while sailing.

Sometimes, when she was neither hiding nor working, Alice would sneak up to the Black Beast's bow and climb along the bowsprit until her boots dangled over the ocean. There she would breathe in the warm, salty air, letting her long hair fly free in the breeze for as long as she could get away with. The islands of the Rainbow Sea would surround her, a stunning vista to behold at the worst of times. A sunken mountain range, Kit had called them. Whenever she was alone out on that bowsprit, the captain's son would inevitably join her. She could never tell whether he was trying to protect her or whether he simply liked the view as much as she did. Regardless, his company was not unwelcome, and he was a perfect gentleman about his intrusion.

Unfortunately, Kit was now a prisoner aboard Captain Seablood's brig, and her time with the Blackbones was all but over.

Wulfric laid a powerful yet aged hand on her shoulder, leaning into the centre of the rowboat. His huge hat swept between her eyes and the morning sun, offering a welcome respite from the already sizzling day. 'You understand why I have to leave you here, Al?' His warm tone buzzed softly in stark contrast to the curses he had been spouting all morning.

'Yes, I think,' Alice replied. *I understand why you think you have to leave me here, but that doesn't mean I agree!*

'I know you'd rather stay, but Kit... Al, you must understand. I should have taken you to land sooner. It's bad luck to have a woman aboard, and that luck has caught up with me. I can't take any more chances, not when my son is in danger. He is all I have left of my family, my blood, my own. If Seablood so much as *touches* him...' Wulfric lowered his eyes, swallowing his deepest emotions like a good captain should.

Alice pittied him. The sealord loved his son with a mighty fervour, but was too afraid to show it. *But that doesn't mean you should punish me! I haven't been bad luck. I've been a help. Haven't I? I don't want to be abandoned in Wreckrest!*

She knew that vocalising her thoughts was more trouble than it was worth. Wulfric seemed to read them in her expression, anyway. 'Al,' he said. 'You've done good. But it's not the Blackbone way to have women sail with us. It never has been.' He leant back and crossed his arms, allowing the gruff face of a lord to overcome his façade once more.

Alice looked helplessly up at Wreckrest. The town's docks were crawling closer, host to a dozen workers whose faces were only just near enough to interpret. Alice wondered whether she would find Wesley and Rose beyond them. *At least that would be better*, she thought. *Wreckrest is a convict-free settlement. We could set up a home here, and forget all about stealing that yacht.*

Heavy fingers lightly tapped Alice's sleeve. She twisted to see Wulfric nodding his forehead towards the side of the boat.

'You said you wanted to see why it was called the Rainbow Sea,' he said.

Excited, Alice spun around between the muscular shoulders of the rowing Blackbone crewmen and thrust her gaze into the calm water that slopped gently against the boat's hull. She jumped in astonishment. Moments before, the water had been a deep, dark green; now it was of a colour with pure glass, and shallow enough to see through to the sand below. But there was little sand to be seen. Beneath the rippling surface, a jungle of twirling, bulging plant life sprawled out over sunken rocks. The bizarre foliage was unlike anything she had seen before in her life. There were bright blobs of writhing tendrils, strung together like a mop, and there were heaving balls of twisted worms, squeezing up between branches made from fleshy sponge. It was all decorated in perplexing hues, in pinks, golds, deep blues and soft greens, finished brilliantly with bright purples and spots of red. Amongst the tangle of otherworldly growth, a thousand fish darted back and forth. The fish were even more vibrant, shimmering through the water like sparkling diamonds. They casually flaunted their stripes, their spots and their brightly patterned beaks. The water had come to life with colour, a true rainbow right beneath the surface, close enough to touch.

Breathless, Alice reached out a finger. It trickled through the warm water, scooting past the scattering sealife, churning up the clear surface with bubbles. A shadow nearly three feet long tumbled out from under the boat and wriggled away just as suddenly as it had appeared. Shocked, Alice snapped her hand back, turning to Wulfric in disbelief.

'It looks pretty,' the captain warned, 'but it's what wrecked Wimsworth. In this very harbour, too. The reefs are a treacherous hazard for any vessel, hiding their fangs just out of view. You best know what you're doing before you brave the Rainbow Sea.' He allowed half a smile, then stood up on heavy boots. 'Here we are. Come, Al.'

The boat had reached the docks, and a couple of sweaty workers were fixing it in place. Alice followed Wulfric's lead and climbed up behind him onto the wooden pier above. Its wooden planks felt oddly rigid under her feet, too harsh and too unmoving.

All along the wooden walkway's edge, small boats sloshed over the miniature waves, and more still sat docked beside several adjacent platforms. Most of the larger vessels were anchored in the bay with the Black Beast. It made sense, considering what Alice now knew lay just beneath the water's surface nearer the shore.

'Al,' grunted Wulfric, shaking Alice from her inquisitive trance. He whirled on the pier, his heavy coat lifting briefly around his knees, then strode off towards the town. A couple of the boat's rowers joined his side, dwarfed almost comically by the great Morch hat upon Wulfric's bear-like mane. Alice knew neither of their names. Gus had been left to manage the ship while they were gone, and with him were Roger, Charlie and Will, the other Blackbones with which she had become familiar. She recalled their faces sadly as she skipped after her escort, falling into step with the captain's bulky shadow.

Ahead, the town of Wreckrest got bigger. Before Alice had even stepped from the docks, it was clear to her that this was no simple fishing village. At either end of the isolated settlement, two peaks craned into the blue and white sky, forcing the houses on the town's flanks to rise up with them and peer down over the cramped basin of wooden buildings that formed Wreckrest's heart. Because the town was open to the sea on both its east and west fronts, it would have never fallen into either mountain's shadows, which may have been the reason for its dry, baked appearance.

Despite its surprising breadth, the town was still smaller than Gold Harbour. Much smaller. Even though the structures were bundled tightly together, and were nearly all two stories high, the small plot of Wimswind Island on which the town was built was only large enough to host a quarter the population of the mainland's grand Sirlish settlement. There weren't even any farms to keep its humble population fed. Not that could be seen.

They don't need farms, Alice reminded herself. *This is a pirate town now. They steal whatever they need. Or have it delivered, maybe.*

Heedlessly, Wulfric barrelled into the glut of buildings with Alice tailing closely behind. As he stomped his lordly boots along the dusty road, a torrent of ragged residents pushed aside to let them pass. More yet popped out from their windows and doors to see who it was that had arrived. Alice noted a similar respectfully wary look upon each citizen's face as she walked by them. She contrasted it with Wulfric's unconcerned stride. *He's royalty here,* she realised. *Or something of the like. God, they're dodging us like we're dangerous. Like* he *is dangerous.* She glanced admiringly at the long white hair hanging over Wulfric's back.

As they neared the town's centre, the smell of fresh rainforest settled upon them and the ocean breeze faded to naught, leaving only the sticky heat of the morning to moisten the inside of Alice's leather waistcoat. Above the bustling tumult of villagers, merchants and laughing drunkards, the sweet song of a thousand birds cut through from the nearby trees. It soothed Alice's nerves. *Yes, perhaps I could live here. It seems nice enough.* She started to scour through the faces on the roadside, searching for any trace of her brother or sister-in-law. *Please be here, Wesley. Please!* She felt strangely certain this was the place she would find him.

Wulfric slowed so that Alice could catch up. 'It's no Sirlish city,' he said, 'but it suits our needs.' He held out his hand casually in front of his waist and spun briskly without breaking stride. 'Wreckrest. Perfectly placed at the border of Teddy Seablood's territory and my own. Stinger Dreadwind has a port here too, on the west side of the island. But you shouldn't go visiting it.'

'How come?' Alice questioned.

'It's a little way out of town, and the Dreadwinds are… less predicatable than the rest of us.'

Alice swallowed uncomfortably. 'So, some of the people here, they're Dreadwinds too?'

'Not unless a Dreadwind vessel has docked.' Wulfric's gaze did not budge as he spoke, neither did his pace slow. Alice had to almost jog to keep up with him. 'Wreckrest is mutual territory. The people that live here belong to no one. Not Southland, not Sirland, not even Teddy. It's our safe haven. You'll be alright here.'

With that, Wulfric veered towards a large, boxy building. There was a pitched roof atop its second level, and a wide verandah across its front, sprinkled generously with empty tables and chairs. A lone man stood at the building's double doors, arms crossed. Wulfric approached the man, his coat flowing powerfully in the wake of his huge strides. Alice stepped up onto the verandah, not realising the other Blackbones had held back.

'Captain Blackbone!' the man greeted, embracing Wulfric with one arm, then remaining so close that he had to crank his neck back just to see Wulfric's face.

'Tom,' Wulfric grumbled, returning the warm spirit with half-hearted effort. 'Is Mag in? I've got somebody for her.'

Tom stepped away from Wulfric's giant chest to squint sideways at Alice. 'Aye, she's in. Busy with those Dreadwind deserters. I don't think she's had her eyes shut for more than five minutes this last week.'

Wulfric's mouth tightened, his brow dropped. 'Dreadwind deserters?'

'Those that don't like— Or hadn't you heard?'

'Sounds like I haven't. What is it?'

'Stinger,' Tom said, carefully. 'There was a mutiny. He's dead.'

'Oh.' Wulfric froze in sudden confusion and shock. He lifted a chunky hand to his forehead and closed his eyes. 'Shit!' he finally barked, teeth baring. 'Godammnit!' The captain's arms began to shiver. Alice stumbled backward, frightened. 'You bloody well better not be pulling my tail, Tom! This is no small thing!'

'Sorry to say I'm not, Captain. 'Twas led by Jack Dagger. You know the man, don't you? He's styling himself Dagger Dreadwind now. Some of the Dreadwind fleet aren't too happy about it, either. Hence the deserters.'

'Bloody Dagger! When did this happen?!'

'A few days ago,' said Tom.

Wulfric twisted his fingers together uncontrollably. 'This doesn't make any sense,' he snarled. 'Let me talk to these deserters. I need to find out what's going on.' He made a move for the doors but Tom blocked his passage, much to the larger's frustration.

'Move aside, Tom. If Stinger's really dead—'

'There's somebody else in there,' Tom added swiftly. Only now did the colour drain from the smaller man's face. Whoever was inside, this Tom did not want to be the one to tell Wulfric about it.

'Who?' Wulfric snapped.

Tom was palpably nervous. His jaw was trembling. 'P... Paddy Coupe, captain. He stopped in not ten minutes ago.'

Fury burst audibly from Wulfric's lungs, which were evidently no longer capable of containing the emotions within them. The captain threw Tom aside and crashed through the double doors, spilling light and heat into the darkness beyond. The Blackbone escorts leapt instantly into action, pulling their swords from their belts and chasing after their leader. Alice slipped inside to avoid them, darting quickly into an inconspicuous corner, behind a bench. She found herself then in what appeared to be a large and rustic common room of sorts. There were mismatched tables and chairs strewn all over the floor, and a bar by the far wall. It somewhat reminded Alice of a stable.

She poked her eyes over the furniture just in time to see Wulfric's stone fist curl through a stout man's balding head. The establishment's patron's burst from their seats, not to mitigate the violence so much as to avoid it.

The balding man went flying from his stool and fumbled into the people behind it. Those men quickly retreated, leaving the first to slump over an empty table. 'Wait,' he yelped. 'Wait!'

Wulfric kicked a stool and came down on the pleading mess, fists drawing back. In the shadows of the dim space, the captain became a hulking beast, baring his claws, growling that deep, monstrous growl. He threw another fist into the smaller man's face. This time a patch of dark red appeared on the victim's whimpering mouth.

'Captain, wait!' The words bubbled through blood.

'I've no patience for swindlers, Paddy!'

The balding man—obviously Paddy Coupe—tried to squirm free, but Wulfric gripped his hairless forehead with iron fingers and slammed the back of it into the table. Paddy's arms flailed, his skull held perfectly still against the wood, paralysed under the weight of Wulfric's arm. Spilt liquor puddled around them.

'Captain,' Paddy managed, 't— tell me what I did.'

'You think I don't see everything you do? I have eyes in the very water!'

'What... Whatever it is. I... I can explain.' Paddy's squeaking voice was so pathetic, even Alice despised it.

Wulfric leaned over Paddy's heaving chest, speaking so low

Alice had to strain to hear him. 'Tony O'Hara came to me, you fool.'

The whites in Paddy's eyes expanded. 'O– O– O'Hara?'

'Did you think he wouldn't?'

Paddy fell silent. His protests failed for naught but soft whimpers.

'*O'Hara* trades rum in Morchport, and *only O'Hara* trades rum in Morchport. That's our deal. But what about your deal, Coupe? I let you through my waters, and you spit in them!'

'I… I have rum, too. Good rum, from Brindia. Ch… Cheap. O'Hara's got none o' that… Captain… where else am I to sell it?'

'I don't bloody well care,' Wulfric snapped. 'You can empty your dirty pockets at Gold Harbour.'

'But… Captain…' Paddy's cries were little more than wet jelly beneath Wulfric's unmoving palm. 'Val would never—'

Wulfric released his hand and punched Paddy again with the other. The force was so great the balding merchant bounced off the table into the surrounding furniture. Chairs screeched across the floorboards.

'If I ever see your ship in Blackbone waters again… I'll crush it.' Wulfric kicked a table at his prey. Paddy shot to his feet, shaking and smeared with blood. He stole one last look at Wulfric's glowing beast eyes, then scampered out of the room without a sound.

Wulfric straightened, meditatively. He stood brooding for a moment, then lifted a stool slowly before throwing it ferociously into the floor. The succinct *crack* made Alice flinch. She sunk below the bench to hide.

After a minute or two of relative silence had washed through the air, she decided it was safe to emerge. When she did, she was surprised to find the room more or less empty. She had not noticed the patrons leave, though supposed they had done so throughout the commotion of Wulfric's confrontation.

There remained only a handful of drinkers. Wulfric was perched on a stool by the bar at the adjacent wall, while the other two Blackbones sat at a circular table, raising mugs to their lips. A well-nourished Dorian woman stood opposite the captain, her elbows planted firmly on the benchtop, a rag slung casually over her shoulder. She was talking to the grey-bearded behemoth. Consoling him, it seemed.

Unsure of what to do next, Alice found herself a seat by an empty table. She sat in it awkwardly. The table was sticky and rough, as was the seat, though the air was thin and cool compared to the usual Southland slosh.

Her joints relaxed, so much as was possible in such a strange place. The chair felt especially solid against her back, stable and trustworthy, however uncomfortable. It reminded her of the ecstasy she had felt when she stepped into Gold Harbour for the first time. She had been a convict, for sure, but the return to land was so impossibly welcome she had felt like crying tears of joy, of brutal contentment. Little did she know of the pain that was to come.

When Wulfric noticed her, he got up and marched over, beckoning for the other Blackbones to follow. His demeanour had retreated to its usual dormant state, though Alice detected a sprinkle of regret dusting his eyebrows.

The towering man cleared his throat before speaking. 'This

is where I leave you. Mag'll look after you.' He made eye contact with the woman behind the bar. She smiled at Alice, though it did little to comfort her.

'What will you do now?' Alice asked. She felt strangely sad for the pirate captain. *He did treat me well. He's a good man, I think. A criminal, but a good man. A man who loves his ship. And loves his son.*

Wulfric Blackbone squinted through the gloom that lurked under his hat, stone faced. 'I must see about this Dreadwind business. And work out what the hell I'm going to do about Teddy.'

He raised a log of an arm to rest a branch of a hand on Alice's little head. 'Al,' he said, somewhat fondly. He held his palm in place for no more than a moment, then sucked it away, spun on his heels and stomped towards the doors.

Alice squirmed in her seat. 'I hope you get Kit back soon,' she called after him.

Wulfric froze on the spot. Just for a second he froze, not turning, not speaking. Then he resumed his exit, vanishing into the blinding light without.

Alice took a deep breath. She looked around, disoriented. The establishment was as plain a tavern as any, a picture of the hurriedly built architecture that infected the entire Golden Coast of Southland. In Gold Harbour there was merely the one well-appointed inn, two if you counted the Salt House by the sea. Alice had frequented neither, in truth. The convicts were more like to enjoy themselves in the same sort of barrel she currently occupied, and even then Alice would not join them. *Most of them were men*, she reflected, *and Wesley would have never let us…*

'Lady,' hollered the woman from behind the bar. She flicked up her chin, summoning her newest guest.

Alice did not want to move. She had moved too much recently, when all she needed was to stay in one place, even if it were on a seat as uncomfortable as the one on which she stubbornly remained. *I'd rather be back on the Black Beast*, she thought, immediately brushing the idea from her head, embarrassed she had even dreamed it up.

'Come on, I won't bite!'

Sighing, Alice gave in. She scraped her chair across the wooden floor, stood up, and weaved her way to one of the bar's uneven stools. The woman was even fatter up close, and her curly black hair framed her bronze nose and dark eyes rather comically. She spoke with a Dorian accent, but her Sirlish was quick and confident. 'You need a drink, I say. Good ol' Greyhide prob'ly kept you dry as a dead roo.'

Why does everybody call him Greyhide? Is it just the colour of his hair? Or something else? Alice thought not to ask. 'No, thank you,' she said instead. 'I don't really like it.'

The woman chuckled. 'I won't make you pay for it, if that's what you're scared of. Not me. If Greyhide tells me to look after someone, that's just what I do. Be not a soul in Wreckrest would cross that man. So what can I get ya'?'

'No really, it's ok. I don't want anything.'

'Hm?' The woman raised a single eyebrow, an amused smile widening across her rounded chin. She leant over the bar, dropping her heavy breasts between dirty elbows. 'Suit yourself, I s'pose. What's your name, lady?'

Alice considered her answer before responding. 'Al,' she said. It was the name the Blackbones had given her. It felt right to use it.

'Well I'm Maggie,' said Maggie. 'This is my place. I've got a room upstairs you can sleep in s'long as you do some of the work around the place. Ain't get no bed for free here, even with friends like yours.'

'Thank you,' said Alice, meekly.

Maggie grinned, curious. 'You've never been to Wreckrest before, have you?'

'No.'

'Well you're in no better hands, then. I'll sort you out. Ain't no one comin' and goin' 'round here without me knowin' about it. Stick with me and you'll be fine, that you will.'

Wesley and Rose sprang swiftly back into Alice's consciousness. 'You know about everyone in Wreckrest?'

'I do.'

'Even visitors, or… new people?'

'Those especially.'

'How about a man my age, or a little older? He's thin like me. His name's Wesley. He should be with his wife, too. She's beautiful, with straight, golden hair… And they're both Sirlish.'

Maggie's lips pursed as she accessed her mind's inner vault. 'Hmmm. Can't say anybody like that's been making a fuss. There's a fair few pretty ladies 'round though. Not many with golden hair.' Maggie's dark pupils combed over Alice's sea-worn face. 'You're a bit pretty too. Most the girls we've got in Wreckrest are Morch or Dorian. You could make some gold of your own, you know? The Seabloods pay the best, when they're in.'

Alice felt her throat turn inside her neck. *You better not mean what I think you do.* 'It's fine, I was just wondering.'

Wesley and Rose reached out their limbs to fill her worrying thoughts, as if yawning after a long slumber. *If they're not here, then where are they?*

Maggie could see plainly the disquiet that plagued her guest. 'Listen Al,' she said, slapping two hands over Alice's. 'You'll be all right. I'll look after you. You don't need those others, you don't. Stay here a few days and you'll be as home as a pig in mud.'

Alice spied a dash of mud on Maggie's forehead and concealed a giggle. *This place sure is mud. But I don't know if I can be the pig.*

13

Sebastian Seablood was at the helm. His tired hands opened and closed over the wheel's handles. The Blood Hammer was flying today. North by northeast it headed, zipping by the steep half of the Snagger where not nearly as many reefs threatened to trap trespassers. With no alternate duty drawn up for the day, the Seablood brig was out solitarily for espionage. On this side of the Snagger, the outermost of the major Sentinels, the Blood Hammer could scout any vessel coming down from Southland's northern settlements, or from Brindia. Those that planned to sail through the Wimswind channel were Seablood carrion for sure, but here the brig could see those that dared take a longer route, to perhaps Gold Harbour or Morchport. The vantage gave the Blood Hammer a perfect opportunity to intercept any undefended cargo before it stumbled right up to Wulfric Blackbone's toes.

Regrettably, the protection of the Sentinels did not extend so far out into the Rainbow Sea. The surrounding waves were giants, their rolling shoulders shoving the Blood Hammer from side to side. A saner man would have taken their force head-on, but Seb was not in the mood for slow gybes; the brig was running, and running fast, carving clean through dark, green ocean.

It was a sunny day, as were many off the coast of Southland, but the breeze kept the sting at bay, so that even the crewmen who were not on duty found themselves atop the main deck, laughing whenever the brig rolled especially far to one side. Among them, suspended delicately in the quivering ratlines, was Seb's lover. Her bare legs twisted through the shrouds, plainly visible beneath the loose dress she wore—which was hiked up by the rigging that supported her.

I know what you're doing. Seb declined to surrender, but he could not take his eyes off those legs. *You're not going to win me so easily. If you would just—*

A heavy wave disrupted his train of thought, shaking the Blood Hammer to the trumpeting of amused snorts.

Liz's casual posture showed no concern.

'Having fun, boy?'

Seb turned sharply to find Captain Theodore Seablood's stupidly wide hat atop a stupidly over-complicated cladding of Sirlish robes, as per usual. 'Father. I only meant to give us more speed.'

'For what reason?'

'No reason, father.'

Ted's wrinkled cheeks screwed up as he observed his crew. Most of them were sprawled evenly over the main deck below the helm. The atmosphere on the brig was lively and warm.

'They're having a good time of it, I see,' said Ted. 'Albeit a dangerous one.'

'If you think it's too much, father…'

'I think I should take the helm for a while. That's what I think.'

'Yes, father.' Seb swung aside, waiting for Ted to grip the wheel before he loosed his own hold. Almost as soon as he transferred conrol, the brig heaved through another immense swell. The crew cheered, and a thin smile touched Ted's lips while he tried to keep his feet.

'Go on then, boy,' he huffed, 'you've had your go.' He shoed Seb aside with a heavily jeweled hand, almost falling over as he did so. Seb sighed and stepped away from the wheel. He adjusted his hat, swept his coat from his knees, and descended the stairs to the main deck.

Other than those standing idly near the belaying pins, the Seablood crew could not have looked more relaxed. The warm air soaked eagerly into their dirt-smothered skin while the rush of the sea echoed through their sores. The open sails held their curved shape stubbornly, noiselessly brandishing the Seablood crown with the wind perfectly behind them.

Seb could not share their bliss. His eyes strayed to Liz's thighs. The others knew better than to stare; she was Seb's woman, after all. But today they could not help stealing a glimpse.

Seb considered going to her. He knew she was thinking of him, though she feigned ignorance. Grumbling, he instead spun on the spot. As he did, none other than Agatha appeared on the deck before him.

The captain's woman was smaller than even the captain, and older too. Beside Seb's trunk she was barely more conspicuous than a dirty child. The brown dress she wore made up her full outfit, and her powerful scowl seemed to shrivel in the sun, even with the shade of the Blood Hammer's black sails flapping over it. Such a face was not oft spied outside the sterncastle. Today, it seemed, was to be one of those less oft spied days.

'You should go to her,' Agatha said, her cackling voice hissing through the dust in her mouth.

Seb pretended not to know what she was talking about. 'Liz, you mean?'

Agatha grimaced. 'She's worried about you, do you know? I am too.'

'Well you're not my mother. You don't need to worry.' Seb tried to squeeze past the old lady, but she sidled into his waist, blocking his movements with her tiny frame. She had a strange way of controlling him, Agatha did, almost as if she were *actually* his mother.

'Yes,' she scolded, 'and how many times must you remind me? I don't know why it bothers you, really. The only blood you now share on this ship pumps through that self-righteous bull's testicle up there.' She nodded at Ted, who was holding the wheel forcefully between chubby fingers. Salvino was behind, blending with the main mast. How he had gotten there unnoticed was beyond Seb. The Dorian man promptly caught his eye. Seb looked away.

Agatha cleared her mouth with a horrible, gagging rasp. 'You ought to lie with her, Seb. You never know when she'll dry up. It could happen any moment, just like that!' She clicked her rusty fingers. 'Besides, it'll get your head straight again. You've been pondering on this... *trouble* of yours for too long now. I'm telling you, it does a man no good to keep worrying so.'

'Agatha, it's not—'

'Oh, shut it, Seb. You don't want to end up like your pathetic excuse for a father, do you? Always whinging about this and that? You're better than him and you know it. The crew knows it too. And you're better than Bart was. Don't tell me I'm wrong.' Her nose twitched. 'Go and see your woman. For God's sake, do it before every Seablood aboard looks up her dress!'

'Is that vulture out of her aviary again?' Ted shouted down from the wheel. 'Send her back inside, boy, if she's causing you bother.'

Seb glanced apologetically into the lady's pale eyes, which were angled steeply at his lofty head. 'No need,' he called back, without turning. He pushed past Agatha, ignoring her continued efforts to halt him. Hurriedly, he strode down the ladder to belowdecks, the sun flickering out from view behind him.

Everyone's on her side! Seb cursed as he trudged lower and lower, into the prisoner's hold. *What if I don't want her? What if I can't help not wanting her? I just want Bart! Why can't Bart be captain, and me his mate? He'd make the descisions and I'd do the killing!*

Seb fingered the hilt of his cutlass. He pulled it free and swung it through the musty air as he descended. Once he reached the hold, he started pacing back and forth, slicing the dormant stink into a hundred pieces while the floor swayed and the walls creaked. The rumble of the Rainbow Sea shuddered through thick oak in every direction, though it could not be seen. Deep in the Blood Hammer's hold, there was less light than there would be in the belly of a whale. Even during midday's stark onslaught, the hold was a cavern of damp shadows, where the stale air relentlessly shuddered, overwhelmed as it was by the deep churning of the sea. The chamber was especially unpleasant whilst the brig was in flight, with the bilges rattling underfoot. But such was the very reason Sebastian sought the location, more and more and more.

Soon his arm lost its energy, and his furious pacing continued up and down the hold's length with his sword at his hip. Thoughts swirled around in his head, darting away from his every snatch like a school of fish. The hull groaned, mimicking the pained tension that wracked the pirate prince's dizzy skull.

He paused at the stern end, near a neatly piled stack of barrels, grappling one's edge as the hull rolled vigorously, shaking his balance.

That's not like me, Seb thought. *I never lose my feet!*

A tight scrape pierced the dull drone of the hold. A pasty face peered up at him, its dark eyes no more than black splotches.

Seb jumped, startled. *Who the shit else is down here?!* He thrust his cutlass out in front of his chest, the sharpened tip collecting a sparkle from the filtered glow that dribbled in from the hold's entrance. *This is my place. I deserve that much, at least!*

He eased forward, toward the intruder. The sword caught in midair, clinking against metal. *Shit!* Seb cursed as he realised. He was standing before the prison cells. The gloomy compartments were reminisient of dog kennels, built crudely but sturdily into the bones of the brig's bowel. They were the defining feature that distinguished this hold from the main one. Seb could not help but feel as if he should have known better.

We had to go and get ourselves a hostage, didn't we?! Now where the bloody hell am I going to hide? Where the bloody hell am I going to sleep?!

Seb retracted the cutlass, fitting it sheepishly back into his belt. He had made a fool of himself in front of Captain Blackbone's very own son.

This was my sanctuary! Seb thought. *My oasis!* He grimaced at the prisoner, whose pale face was divided by the grey lines of the cell's iron bars. The prisoner glared back, tenaciously piercing him with those black blotches.

Seb straightened, raising his head and decorating it with a dry smirk. 'Having fun, I assume?' he sniggered, then whirled and strode away toward the ladder.

As his muffled footsteps drew nearer the feeble light, the prisoner called after him. 'What will you do with me?' His voice was hoarse, and carried with it a weight of honour that only a Blackbone could conjure.

Seb slowed. He did not want to answer, less acknowledge the prisoner any longer than he already had, but a Seablood was scooting across the mess deck overhead, and Seb shied into the hold's darkness. He angled his shoulders towards the cell and answered with a tone as cocky as he could spit. 'Whatever we want.'

Seb returned to the ladder, stepping up with heavy feet.

'Sebastian Seablood,' the prisoner's voice followed him. 'Am I right?'

At that, Seb sprang again into the hold, stormed hurriedly over the moist floor, and pulled his blade free to poke it through the iron cage. 'I'll kill you right now,' Seb warned, his teeth grinding together with annoyance. 'Is that what you desire?!'

'I am right then,' the prisoner clarified.

Seb growled. 'You know my name. What of it? I know yours. Kit. Greyhide's pup. But knowing names doesn't matter down here. Not when you're on the wrong side of this.' He tapped an iron bar with the blunt edge of his weapon.

Kit huffed, his pale face motionless but for the slow rocking of the hull. It floated eerily above naught but a shade in his dark cell. 'You don't need to worry, Seablood. Go and drink with your women and forget I'm even down here. I won't tell.'

'Tell what?' Seb could scarecely veil his anxiety, though he tried.

'That you sneak down here for sword practice.'

'I need no practice,' Seb scoffed. He tucked his cutlass into his belt again, as if to make a statement. 'I could best you and all of your Blackbone litter with a hand tied to my back.'

'Open the door, then. Prove it.' Kit was not joking.

'Is this why you came paddling into Seablood territory? To make jests from a cage?'

'I came because my father told me to, not because I wanted it. I knew what it meant.'

Seb's throat contracted, snagging his words. He pressed his lips together and stepped back from the cell. His eyes were now adjusting to the dark, so he could at last see Kit in his entirety, however faintly. The young man was slouched against the cell's rear wall, dressed in well-fitted black cladding from his neck to the tips of his fingers. His dark hair flowed by his ears in jarring contrast with the white of his face. On the whole, he seemed more Morch than he ought, given his Sirland-born father, though he bore the fierce aura of a true Blackbone.

Seb swallowed. 'You knew you'd end up here?' He was more impressed than pitiful, and more curious than either. 'Yet... Here you are.'

Kit's expression, however increasingly opaque, refused to change. 'My father's ideas do not always match my own. But a good sailor obeys them, no matter.'

Seb leant against one of the barrels, careful not to stare in Kit's direction. He crossed his arms and sighed. 'Then we share a fate, it would seem.' *Who would have thought?*

The sounds of the sea swept over them, drowning their exchange. For a time, they sat together in bottomless reflection, two heirs of the Rainbow Sea squashed into a little box with nothing to say. The bars between them grew darker as the faint light from above soaked into the hull. Over the roaring thunder of the water that pressed in on every side, not even the hoots of the crew could be heard; they might as well have been completely alone.

Seb preferred it when *alone* meant only his self and no other, but he was beginning to wonder whether this Blackbone's company was as blood curdling as he had first imagined. *Hell, he didn't even know Bart. Not that I know of, anyway. And he definitely doesn't know Liz. He probably doesn't know father. Not really. And he doesn't know Agatha, or Salvino, or Bill. He doesn't know the Snagger like I do, or how to trap foes in the Teeth. He doesn't know the settlements along the Del Continente Peninsula, and probably doesn't even know how to speak Dorian.*

'Your father,' Kit interjected, eventually. 'Captain Seablood. He's asked you to do something. Kill me, was it?'

Seb smirked. 'If only.' He wiggled against his barrel until his lean was as comfortable as it was ever going to get. 'Killing is what I do best. Killing without getting killed myself. That's the secret. You're only as good as what you can get away with unharmed.' Seb paused to touch his cutlass. 'This sword has been the end for dozens of good men. Too many to count. And it has saved my life as many times. My life. My crew's. And my brother's.'

'Is that what you tell yourself at night?' Kit mocked. 'To justify the comfort of your bed?'

'I don't sleep!' Seb snapped. 'It keeps me up.' His eyes lost their focus, and his fingers loosened unconsciously from his sword's hilt. He felt his mind sink into the abyss, spiralling into that black pit of souls, where there was no forgiveness, no compassion. 'I think about them. All of them. All the time. All those people, all those men. Merely a passing thorn in my side. Yet to them, I was the ultimate villain. The end of their story. Those final seconds…'

Kit went silent.

Seb shook himself. 'Nay, my father doesn't want me to kill for him. He wants me to be captain.'

'An honour,' conceded the prisoner.

'It's only a bloody honour if you want it.'

'You don't want it?'

'Do *you?*' Seb swiveled toward the dark shape behind the

iron bars. Kit's eyes were wide, sucking in all the light of the hold. Seb frowned, realising suddenly the gravity of what he had said. *Maybe I should kill you,* he thought, *so you can't speak a word of this to anyone! Shit, but what would father do then?*

Kit's voice came back at him, harsh and stubborn. 'If you think you can lure me to speak against my own, Seablood, you're mistaken. I will never turn on my father, or on his ways. You best leave me be. If you aren't going to kill me—'

'Demands from a prisoner?!' Seb forced a laugh. 'I'll do what I like. It's my vessel here, Blackbone. I'll stay if I want to.'

Kit grumbled. 'I'd rather be alone.'

'As would I,' admitted the other. 'But it seems even I am a prisoner. Locked on this brig with more than a hundred inmates. At least here, you are free of your fool father.'

'Wulfric Blackbone is no fool. You'd be a fool to think it. Take your disrespect elsewhere and leave me be.'

'You still defend him, even when you have no need.' Seb was talking to himself more than to his addressee.

'What do you want from me, Seablood?' Kit had become visibly disturbed, the soft sound of his agitated movement grating with the hold's deep hum.

Seb pondered the query before answering. 'Nothing,' he eventually spat. 'Shut your mouth,' he later added, then stood up and left the hold.

The remainder of the day blew past like a hot westerly wind, enduring in its gusts enough of Ted Seablood to send any man insane. The afternoon brought not a single vessel into view, either. Not even one of their own could be spotted scouring the crisp horizon.

When the brig finally veered off between Compass Rock and the distant yet fearsome Rainbow Dagger—two rugged stone formations near the Snagger's northern coast—Ted at last relieved himself of the helm's responsibility, posting Seb at the wheel once more. The younger Seablood had to then beat the brig to windward as the subsequent change of heading sent them almost right into the same breeze that bore them through the morning. The process was rather painful for the Blood Hammer, requiring an excessive number of tacks and turns to keep the vessel on target without ever facing it directly into the wind. Each tack begged the attention of most men on duty, and called for a hefty dollop of management from the helmsman. Such was most likely the reason Ted was not particularly interested in overseeing the task.

By the time the sun had set in a fiery cabaret of pinks and purples, the Blood Hammer had circled the full northern quarter of the Snagger, and was anchored in Blackfish Bay, a coral-riddled inlet that provided excellent protection from the ocean's forces. It was to be a still night, and one of the first where Ted forgot to mention the ghost ship.

It was also going to be a loud one. The crew had been drinking for the most part of the sun's presence, and there was no indication that the moon's was going to be treated any differently. Seb was in no mood to join them, but neither was he inclined to crawl into bed with Liz. Instead, he loitered about the quarterdeck for a good couple of hours, hoping Salvino would appear as he had a few nights ago, to offer him someone else's bed. As he waited, most of the crew could be heard rolling dice and spilling rum all over the mess deck below.

The happy noise echoed through the inlet, and sent a shiver through Seb's skin. Even in the warm clutches of the Snagger's embrace, the man felt the prickle of cold stir his hair.

When it became evident the quartermaster was not going to turn up, Seb resolved to waste not the rare stillness, and snuck down to the prisoner's hold. That dark place may have still been occupied, but it was preferable to the confrontation he would have to suffer were he to retire in his own cabin.

Cautiously, Seb slipped over the hold's ladder into thick shadows. The cavern was even darker than it had been during the day, and was no longer swamped by the rumble of the ocean. The perfect place for peace and solitude.

Pressing his feet softly against wooden planks with every step, Seb was careful not to alert Kit of his return. He had come to sleep, not to converse, and was certainly not disposed to share any more of his troubles with the vessel's lowly hostage.

He felt his way forward with hands outstretched. They slid along the hull's port wall until they collided with a pile of empty sacks, squashed up between a series of heavy barrels. It was the bed he had adopted as his own. The nest was hardly a suitable resting place for a pirate prince, but its solid, cold rigidity delivered Seb the tiniest semblence of cosiness.

Silently, he stretched out over the rough sackcloth, praying he had been stealthy enough to avoid tickling the prisoner's attention. Night finally settled on his tired muscles, the peace of it blocking out the muffled frivolity still buzzing through the brig's Sirlish oak frame. He shut his eyes. The hold's distinctive damp scent wafted over him.

'Sebastian?' whispered Kit.

Seb's forhead tightened. *Damnit!*

'I know you're there, Seablood. It's halfway through the night. What are you doing?'

Seb was tired of hiding it. He faced the black shadows of the prison cells and kept his voice low. 'I'm sleeping down here. The reason why is none of your bloody concern!'

Kit went quiet. *Good!* Seb closed his eyes once more. *Shut up and go to sleep, you Blackbone fool.*

But after a few seconds, Kit spoke again. 'You were right,' he said. 'I don't want to be captain either.'

14

'**M**ore rum!' commanded Captain Halfeye Warhawk from across the table. The ghostly crew cheered as Halfeye's first mate emptied a bottle into his master's mug. The decrepit old man swung the drink above his gaping mouth and let the clear liquid cascade over it. As he attempted to swallow, his whole body jerked, and all that had made it into his narrow throat came shooting out again with a rattling cough. Rum, phlegm and blood alike spat over the table and over the food layered on top of it.

Rose recoiled, disgusted, wiping the spray from her cheeks. She had taken her seat opposite the legendary pirate captain, meaning she was in prime position to collect his periodic fits of explosive body gunk. Halfeye had already grown fond of her and hence had reserved the spot. She may have been an outsider, but she was the only human aboard with whom the corpse of a man could suitably vent his spleen.

Though the crew was technically Sirlish—or looked the part, at the least—none of them spoke it as well as they should. The truth was that they were all Brindians. Slaves, no less. Halfeye had purchased them from the Brindian docklands where he had rebuilt the Frontiere. He had apparently been extraordinarily particular about the subjects he enlisted, since slaves were almost never of Sirlish descent. The slavery trade had vanished from the Western Nations over a century ago, so distant countries such as Brindia had to pluck most of their goods from their own population. As a result, slaves usually wore the dark-brown complexion that most Brindians were like to share. Others were dredged from elsewhere in the world, where the native peoples were darker still. No doubt the govenor of Gold Harbour had considered taking some of Southland's native inhabitants as slaves, though the Ijians would most likely prove too wild for his pompous purposes. Besides, the man already had access to a plethora of convicts who could give him whatever he needed.

Halfeye's crew laughed even harder as their captain wiped away the mucus to take another swig. They certainly did not act like slaves, Rose noted. Or ghosts. Halfeye had explained this by spouting that the Frontiere's crew were not hired to be either; they were hired to be sailors. The rabble had only initially appeared spectral to Rose's eyes simply because Halfeye had instructed them to stay silent in the presence of strangers, lest their accent reveal their true identity. Now that they were comfortable around her, they had become as boisterous as a pack of cons.

The table at which they sat was more a pile than anything else. A few spare planks of oak were heaved atop crates to form a long surface on which mounds of food were strewn. The food consisted mostly of raw fruit and vegetables, though there were three giant pots of pork stew that poked out from the indiscriminate mess like towering, iron centrepieces.

The table itself stretched from fore to aft of the Frontiere's waist, hosting near thirty feasters whilst the crisp night sky hovered overhead. The crowd was small, even accounting for those who slept and those who were posted on watch. Usually, a similar-sized ship would host a much larger number, though Rose supposed the ship on which she had been transported to Southland probably did not offer a completely fair comparison. On that journey, she had barely been afforded enough room to stretch her legs.

Suspiciously, she checked her bowl for stray flecks of Halfeye's phlegm, then pressed its dry edge to her lips and drew up a mouthful. The warm, salty flavour flowed through her, and a juicy chunk of meat slipped between her teeth. She replaced the bowl and finished her mouthful with a drop of rum. She was getting used to the drink's fierce bite, and liked the calming rush she felt after drinking it.

This is luxury, she decided, surprising herself. Aboard a strange and dangerous pirate ship, the widow was more comfortable and free than she had ever been since her innocent backside was shoved unduly into Sirland's overflowing penal mess.

Wesley popped back into her head. Every time she felt the remotest sense of peace, Wesley's ghost appeared before her and that peace turned to anger, her course realigning with revenge. The sensation of her husband's hot blood spitting onto her skin flooded her. She glanced up at Halfeye, his face half stuffed with a carrot. 'You don't get to eat like this on no ship out yonder!' he said. 'You'd be sucking down salted beef

strips day after day. Nay, such is the joy of plundering the
Sentinels. You're never too far from port!'

Rose sighed. *Perhaps he's the only one who understands what
it's like to have everything you've ever loved taken from you.* She
felt empathy for Halfeye, and pity.

'Ho!' A sailor shouted behind her. A barrel of mirth
followed, and a faint thud. Rose spun on her crate of a seat, the
rum in her belly making everything a little blurry. A handful of
crewmen were standing in a tight-knit bundle, slapping
eachother on the back. One of them pulled a worn dagger from
his waistcoat and threw it swiftly across the deck. The weapon's
hilt clapped into the quarterdeck's stumpy wall, and fell to the
ground rather disappointingly.

The crew laughed again. Smiling, Rose noticed the
pumpkin that had been propped against the wall atop a pillar
of narrow boxes. Its yellow skin glowed in the lamplight, a
perfect target.

When Halfeye saw what they were doing, he shot up from
his seat and wobbled over to them. 'You scumbags don't know
half o' how's done! I'll show you, aye! I'll show you how's done!'

He crashed into the group as they handed him a fresh
dagger. Halfeye took it graciously and attempted to straighten
his sickly body.

Rose could not help but applaud along with the others. She
could barely focus her eyes for the rum, but she was, at least,
still in possession of the two of them. She cleared her throat
unintentionally. 'You've only got one eye!' she heckled. At that,
the crew guffawed as hard as ever.

Halfeye glared at her crossly, his one mangled pupil barely

able to find her amongst the night's shifting shadows. 'I don't need two eyes, Miss Rose!' he declared. 'You just watch!' He faced the pumpkin and threw the dagger. It zipped through the air with astonishing speed and lodged itself point-first into the quarterdeck, even further from the pumpkin than the previous thrower had managed. The captain cursed unintelligibly.

One of the crewmen darted forward to fetch the blades, while another turned to Rose. 'You have go!' he said. 'Show us how lady throw!' A Brindian accent cut through his words, though they were sober enough to be understood. Rose shied away nevertheless.

'Aye, Rose!' Halfeye exclaimed. 'Get up here an' give it a throw. See how funny it is then, ha!'

Rose groaned, but stood. Evidently, she did not need much convincing. She stumbled over to the others, accepting the rounded pommel of a battered dagger in her right palm. A sailor jabbed his finger at the pumpkin, over twelve feet away. 'Go on,' he said, 'hit it!'

Rose wound her hand over one shoulder, sparing a second to visualize Dagger's face on the pumpkin's blotchy surface before throwing. The dark eyes of her husband's murderer leered back at her. She loosed the blade. Before she could see where it had gone, a short thump bounced back at her, the sound of the blade's tip puncturing vegetable flesh. She strained her eyes to make out the target. She had hit Dagger right in the nose.

'Good shot!' commended a bewildered crewman, springing aft to pull the weapon from the impaled vegetable. Another crewman thrust towards Rose, extending a pale hand as he did so. 'Oh, I like girl with good aim!' But before he could finish his vulgar gesture, Rose caught him by the wrist and slapped her hand into his chest. The man flew over backwards and crashed into the deck. The crew surrounding her jolted in surprise. Even Rose could not believe what she had just done. She stared at the pervert on the floor, unable to interpret his features. There was no laughter this time, only confusion.

After the fallen crewman had scampered to his feet, Halfeye stepped in to break the stunned silence. 'She's stronger than she looks, aye!' he announced. 'Don't nobody mess with Rose King! That's what I say!' He pretended to straighten his coat, but his hands merely flapped about in their lacy sleeves, straightening nothing. 'Now whose throw is next?'

Joyous bustling promptly returned to the crowd, while Rose slunk to her seat. She let another slurp of rum trickle over her tongue. Her head was spinning. The feeling was odd, though even more odd was how comfortable she felt within it. The food, the table, the two rows of deadly criminals within spitting distance of her soft skin. She was comfortable with it all. Wesley's death had emptied her, but she was being filled again. Filled with rum.

The feaster beside her flopped a broth-soaked slice of bread into his mouth and leant in her direction. It was the man with the moustache, the first of the Frontiere's crew she had met. 'Where you learn how to do that?' he asked, rather gently for a world-weary slave.

Rose held her gaze on the mug before her, barely hearing the question. 'What?'

'The push! You make that man fall. Where you learn it?'

A pause indicated Rose was either unsure of the answer, or too drunk to utter it. The hiatus teemed with the raucous chatter of happy pirates all around. The supple atmosphere was cool, dark and still, allowing the voices, the bumps and the ever-present shush of the sea to permeate through it in a delicate swirl of unexpected nothingness.

Rose shook her head to focus. 'Nowhere,' she eventually answered.

'So how you do it?' The moustache man was more interested than Rose could be bothered caring for. She elected not to answer, choosing rather to pour herself more rum, all the while envisioning Dagger's face on that pumpkin, with her own dagger stuck right through it. *I'll kill him,* she told herself. *The first chance I get!* She pulled her mug to her lips and drank once more.

Rose was sick the next morning. She refrained from dropping her stomach's contents all over the cabin floor, but she felt like she ought to. Her skull seemed to shrink around her brain, and an unquenchable nausea stretched from her bladder to the roof of her mouth. The illness kept her inside for hours after she had woken, even as the ship soothed into the day's course.

Well after midday, Halfeye sent for her, and the wreck of a woman pulled herself up to the captain's chamber, where the corpse of a man was reclining by his small table with a bottle of rum. It was the image Rose had come to expect.

Daylight had a strong effect on the room, transforming it into a very different place compared to what it had been during Rose's first visit. Generous windows allowed the royal palace to come alive with sparkling clarity, highlighting the silk curtains on the four-poster bed and the crimson rug beneath a crowded bundle of powerful furniture.

Instead of launching into his usual, bland delineation, Halfeye revealed that he had something else drawn up on the agenda for the day. After a brief bout of meaningless prattle— and more than one lengthy coughing session—he assigned her a task, one which was to be carried out on the largest of the Sentinels, Wimswind Island. Located on this island was the region's only settlement not connected to the Southland mainland. This particular settlement was founded when explorer Captain Winston Wimsworth temporarily wrecked his ship on the coral reefs of Hullbreaker Bay. Since then, the town—aptly named as Wreckrest—had become the centre of trade for vessels under the sealords' control. Halfeye took the time to carefully clarify these details before getting around to his actual intentions.

'There's a tavern in the middle of the town,' explained the legendary captain. 'It's said that if a rumour finds footing there, it'll spread from Morchport to Mariscos in a matter o' hours.'

Rose soaked up the instructions as Halfeye spurted them out. Humouring his flowery twists and turns, she deduced that the assignment was, in fact, quite a simple one. She was to plant the seed of a lie into the guts of the pirate haven and get out as quickly as possible. All to loose havoc on the town.

She asked all the questions she needed to ask, keen to succeed in her first role as a Warhawk, though she refrained from voicing the one that plagued her the most: would Dagger be there? In a way she hoped he would not be, as it would only serve to interrupt this opportunity to prove her worth. In another way, it was all she wanted.

'This is an important piece in my plan, Miss Rose,' warned Halfeye. 'I'd do it myself, you know, but I'd be recognised for who I am the moment I step into Wreckrest. God only knows what would happen then, and I intend to let Him keep it a secret.' He wiped a drop of blood onto his sleeve after the bead had dripped into the hair at the corner of his mouth. 'Can I trust you? That's what I mean. Will you do't and do't right?'

'I will,' Rose responded.

'Good!' exclaimed the captain. 'Aye, when it's done we'll be one step closer. Before you know it, I tell you, we'll have a Seablood *and* a Blackbone head mounted on these here walls!'

In truth, victory was not to be so hasty. As the Frontiere could not anchor in Hullbreaker Bay for the danger of being needlessly recognised, Rose had to ride in one of the ship's cutters from a nearby inlet for almost three hours simply to arrive within the jaws of Wreckrest's harbour, let alone approach the town. The little boat possessed only a small sail— and only five of Halfeye's men to weigh it down—so the journey was not only slow, but unstable.

It was nearing dusk when they finally began to pass through the huddle of anchored vessels that surrounded the quaint town. Many eyes distrustfully followed her as Rose's band crept past their floating fortresses, inspiring her muscles to nervously flicker. It would have been worse were the Kraken present, though it was nowhere to be seen, an observation that considerably calmed her anxiety. Instead, the bay was crowded with smaller sloops and schooners, mostly pressed close to land where the waters of the Rainbow Sea remained helpfully deep. The patch immediately surrounding the town's docks, however, was as barren as the open ocean. *Reefs*, Rose knew. While most of the channels between the Sentinels were as bottomless as the islands were tall, some places were made dangerously shallow by jagged coral shelves. This was apparently one of those places. A feeling of loneliness overtook her as the boat edged tentatively towards the clearing. *Oh Wes*, she longed. Ahead, Wreckrest beckoned from its seat in the saddle of the island's huge, mountainous peaks.

Pffff! A sudden snort sounded beside the cutter. Rose spun toward the sound, releasing a shriek when she spotted the dark eye of a sea monster breaking the still surface on which they sailed. It lingered in the sun's fading rays for a few seconds before vanishing into the ripples. Her heart thumped in her chest and her hands flung out beside her to grasp whatever they could find.

Halfeye's men laughed. 'A… turtle!' one of them managed between snorts. 'Be quiet, you see more.'

With that, the men muffled their voices and joined Rose in surveying the shifting blue. Sure enough, another sniff sounded, and a tiny head popped out of the water, more distant this time. Rose pointed it out when she found it and the others smiled at her. Their teeth said more than their fragile Sirlish ever could have.

The turtle soon dipped under the water and was gone. For just a flash, Rose forgot herself, completely lost in the magic of the moment. Then they were at the docks, and the sail was pulled down. Neither her mind nor her body could escape her cruel fate for longer than a minute.

And so it was that Rose arrived at Wreckrest, stepping over the docks into the town's thoroughfare between a pair of Warhawk pirate slaves. If an onlooker were to spy her, they would surely have mistaken her for one of them. Below the chin, she was clad in the uniform of Southland's free men, sporting hardy boots and a weathered but expensive waistcoat. She had unbuttoned the top portion of her shirt to ease the thick heat, fearing not that it betray her gender since her hair had already done so, flowing brazenly over her ears. It was most likely those golden wisps that truly set her apart from her companions, eventually attracting more attention than Halfeye had suggested she attract. For in the town of Wreckrest there were indeed onlookers, and many at that.

Though the sun had fallen asleep behind looming trees, the street was alive with activity. Atop the rotting wood of veranda after veranda, suspicious men and women were standing idly, guzzling liquor or advertising their nightly services. Windows were afire with bright light, and a constant trickle of foot traffic buzzed from one end to the other.

Rose paced into the creature, marvelling. It had been years since she had seen a place with such energy. It reminded her of Sirland, and walking along the main street by their old home, Wesley's arm firmy intertwined with her own. Gold Harbour had exactly none of the charm afforded this cheap settlement. Where the former was littered with sullen cons, Wreckrest was packed tightly with cheers and freedom.

How can a town on an island have so many people? Rose decidedly ceased the thought. She knew the answer. In her own way, she was now a part of the answer. But only if she completed her mission. Sternly, she squashed her wonder and picked up her pace. Her fingers clenched around themselves, pretending to grip her husband's.

As the Warhawk trio pressed deeper into the wooden metropolis, Rose lost count of how many people ogled at her peculiar arrival. She began to fret over her decision to wear her hair out. *I should have worn a hat*, she thought. But then she saw it. To her right, not twenty yards ahead, the patrons of a thriving tavern spilt out onto the street, soaking the air with their boisterous chants. Where the tavern kissed the path, a circular opening formed between the cramped buildings, punctured in the middle by a single stone monument. *This is the one.*

Rose whirled toward her tail. 'You two stay back,' she commanded. 'I need to do this alone.'

The slaves nodded in comprehension and retreated into the shadows. Rose swallowed hard, then swiveled back toward the tavern. *Oh Wes, don't let this be harder than it needs to be.*

As quickly as she could, she stomped up to the busy establishment and wove her way through its crowd until she was pushing open the double doors. The interior was even busier.

She now became excruciatingly aware of her hair. There was not a single golden head in sight, though the faint lamplight made it somewhat difficult to tell for sure. Rather, the room appeared to be packed with men of Morch or Dorian blood. The ones that noticed her arrival sized her up greedily. She met their stares straight on with a sneer as cold as she could muster.

The look compelled most of them to avert their eyes, but it did nothing to prevent a wayward hand from clutching her rear.

Rose spun to face her groper, fingertips ready to grapple. In that instant, she remembered what she had done to the man on the Frontiere. She smothered her fury before it followed through, reminding herself that this was no time for a fight. *Or an imasculation.*

The guilty Morchman was leaning against the wall by the entrance, thick arms now folded and a saucy smirk on his pasty face. He lifted an eyebrow at Rose's raised hands, which might have been ready to throw him to the floor had the man not been of such mammoth size.

'Oh, you didn't like it?' the man mocked. He had to shout through his Morch accent to be heard over the clamour, but his haughty composure remained intact. He flicked his chin up. 'How much gold would I have to spill before you did?'

Offended, Rose edged nearer the heavy stranger and held her ground there despite the current flowing through the tavern's doorway. 'I'm married,' she growled.

'Then why're you here, girly?'

Rose concealed her wrath. *It's not what I'm here for.* She replaced her frown with a smirk, poised to play her role. 'Can't I have a drink?'

The man was impressed by this. 'Aye, you can. If you can pay for't. But how you goin' a pay for't if you're married an' do no workin'?'

'I can pay,' Rose replied.

'A pretty girly that can pay! Why haven't I seen you before?'

'It's my first time here.'

'Aye, your first time. A new girl in Wreckrest! Come, let's get a drink then. You can pay for us both.'

Rose was not about to argue. If the offer meant getting the job done sooner, she had to accept. She followed sheepishly in the huge man's wake as he carved a path through the solid, sweaty bustle.

He slammed his palm against the tavern's bar, almost violently, and a plump Dorian woman pounced over to attend them. Her searching eyes radiated a sort of friendly, mothering character. It was welcome respite from the burly villainousness of the tavern's many patrons. *This is where I must do it*, Rose told herself. *The barmaid!*

'Who's this you've got, Vic? You can't find no Sirlish beauty like that in Morchport!'

'She's not mine, Mag. Found her just here. She's pay'n for our drinks, she says.'

Rose shuffled uneasily as the woman inspected her over the bench. 'Another new girl, huh? I got somebody here was looking for one like you.'

'Nobody here would know me,' Rose stated, definitively. *And nobody will remember!* She quickly realised she had no reason to get so defensive, as the serving woman was already distracted pouring some sort of vile liquid into a pair of mugs. She slapped them onto the bar. The Morchman hooted and snatched one before the foam had settled. Rose left hers alone.

'What brings you to Wreckrest, then? Escaped Gold Harbour on a Dreadwind sloop, did ya? I'll bet you're well worn-in if that's the case, knowing what they're like.' The woman gave Rose a shrewd smile, one that magnificently combined sympathy with empathy. But the woman was wrong. None of the Kraken's Dreadwinds had *worn her in*, and she had escaped Gold Harbour with her husband, not pirates. But there was no sense in sharing the truth. Now was the time for lies.

'Not quite,' Rose corrected. 'I escaped Gold Harbour on a merchant ship, but it was caught by pirates. Seabloods, they called themselves. And they left me here once they'd… you know…'

The woman chuckled. 'Seabloods'll do that. Better off with them than Dreadwinds, though.' She took one last look at Rose's mug. 'Drink up,' she urged, then turned away to serve some other impatient customer.

Rose panicked. She could not lose the barmaid's attention, not before she had finished. 'We were headed south!' she blurted, shouting to be absolutely sure she was heard over the noise. 'Via Morchport.'

The barmaid's head snapped around, that warm expression replaced by a stern grimace. The Morchman beside her dropped his mug. Even the man on her opposite side whirled abruptly, his toothless Dorian face filled with horror and hate.

The plump woman slid back to Rose, pushing her big breasts firmly against the bench so she could keep her voice low. A sweat broke out on Rose's forehead. She was being watched.

'Shush!' the woman begged. 'Do you realise what you've just said?'

Rose was fully aware of what she had said. 'No. I only said we were headed south. Via Morchport.'

'Then you were taken by Blackbones, girly!' interrupted the Morchman, white spots appearing on his monstrous hand as he gripped the handle of his mug with immeasurable force. 'Aye, it must've been!'

Rose could barely veil her nerves now, but it was far too late to back out. 'They said they were Seabloods. Teddy Seablood... was their leader. I've never heard of Blackbones before.'

The men around her drew sharp breaths, their muscles contracting so tightly that she could feel their rigidity tickle her shoulders. The barmaid grasped Rose's quivering hands and leant in further. 'I'm warning you, girl,' she whispered. 'Look around, can't you see? This place is packed to the rafters with men either sworn to Blackbone or Seablood, and you're suggesting one has betrayed the other... Seabloods would never plunder south of Gold Harbour. That's Blackbone territory. It just wouldn't happen. End of story. The bloodshed you'd cause... Just keep your mouth shut!'

Rose plucked the gold from her pocket and dropped it onto the bench in payment for her drinks. It was a chunk the size of her finger, with more than enough weight to pay for the whole crowd. The mangled thing had been hacked from a golden brick with her captain's axe, but shimmered gorgeously in the lamplight nonetheless. *I hope you're happy, Halfeye!* She closed her eyes and drew a shaky breath. 'It was a schooner, I think, and they had a black flag. With a white crown on it.'

'She's a bloody liar!' the Dorian man howled. The words landed on deaf ears. The Morchman's mouth was already foaming with rage.

Before anything else could happen, Rose was whisked away into the kitchen behind the bar. The plump woman kicked open the back door as she slipped the chunk of gold into her apron's pouch. A swift shove in the back saw Rose stumble out into the warm night air of a narrow Wreckrest alleyway. Her boots splashed through a black puddle.

'If you value your life, girl,' the woman said, 'run! Get out of Wreckrest as quickly as you can.'

Rose did not need to be told twice. The seed had been sown.

It was time to flee.

15

A shrill cry scratched through the dull buzz emanating from the town's centre. A shiver teased Alice's skin. *Just another fight*, she thought. She had been a resident of Wreckrest for less time than she spent aboard Second Chance, but already she had learnt enough to not be frazzled by yet another routine drunken brawl.

Maggie had explained it to her in the simplest way. In Wreckrest—she had said—the three pirate clans came together in peace, but the tension between them was ever strung so tightly that a foul whisper here, or a misplaced elbow there, could spark an instant punch-up.

The plump woman had been more than accommodating to her young guest. She wasn't kidding when she told Wulfric Blackbone she would look after Alice, that much was certain. The bed Alice was given was cosier than any she had previously alighted upon, and the hot meal she had eaten for breakfast was unspeakably heart warming. More importantly still, Maggie had stifled Alice's fears concerning the sea-girt town's rough residents, casually passing off each worry with a cursory flick of her heavily jewelled wrist. 'Ain't nobody hurt you here,' she had said. 'Those mainlanders would call us outlaws, and aye, I s'pose we are, but we're s'far from the West and all its laws that it don't matter! Truth is, we're free people, and free people don't hurt ya 'less ya try tak'n away their freedom.' Alice smiled at the memory.

She may well have been finally counted among the free, but Alice still had to work. The heavy sack slung around her neck was testament to it. The lumpy bag tapped pesteringly at her gut as she walked. *Carrots*, she knew.

After spending the greater part of the afternoon washing dishes, she had eventually been sent to collect vegetables from a woman named Rita. The woman had been growing a number of crops in a large garden near the edge of town, where the slopes of Wimswind Peak set their toes.

Alice had little trouble finding the place, but had a lot of trouble trying to leave. Firstly, there was the matter of the payment. Alice had been sent with two bottles of rum to trade for the bag of carrots, and Rita had been expecting three. Then, by the time Alice had convinced the other there were no more bottles to give, the mildly crazy gardener had launched into a vicious rant about the island's Ijian population. Apparently, the very carrots Alice sought to purchase had caught their attention weeks prior. The vegetables' orange colour and sweet flavour had been no less than irresistible to the simple forest dwellers— so the story went—and had inspired several night-borne burglaries.

'I'll be damned if I grow another batch o' those terrors!' Rita had screeched. 'From now on, I'll be growing only cabbages. See how they like that! You best tell Maggie she won't be making her carrot soup no more. Not unless she gets out here and helps my husband build a thief-proof fence!'

The cloudy sky had been swept away by darkness when Alice eventually left, sack of carrots in hand. It was not for soup that she had collected it; Maggie planned on boiling the roots to serve alongside some pork she had smuggled from Gold Harbour. The juicy prospect of the approaching feast dripped onto Alice's tongue, tempting her senses with salty warmth. The thought alone made the sack lighter, and the mounting sound of the tavern's thriving commotion only meant the meal was nearer.

The silhouette of a woman in a puffy petticoat skipped around the corner ahead of Alice. It strode up the alleyway with curious urgency, gliding quickly between the wooden structures that towered over them both. When the woman noticed Alice, she halted cautiously, allowing the soft light that radiated from the town centre to settle on her well-dressed shoulders. Despite her expensive outfit, the woman was most likely a prostitute, though the working women of Wreckrest were not bound to the lower class like they were in Sirland, so it was difficult to be sure. Alice—on the other hand—was yet dressed in the sailor's garb Kit Blackbone had gifted her, and would have made a much stranger sight.

'Don't go that way,' the woman warned, partially breathless. 'There's trouble at Maggie's tavern.'

A worried tingle zipped along the surface of Alice's arms. She recalled Maggie's reassurances to sooth herself. 'That's where I was going,' she said. She lifted the carrots from her torso, as if to offer an excuse for her wandering the streets so late.

The prostitute was in a hurry to move along, but something held her back. She gave Alice a sideways look, noting the waistcoat and the breeches. 'You're the girl, aren't you?' There was an indecipherable bite in those words.

'What girl?'

'The girl from the tavern.'

'Yes. I mean... I came from there.'

The woman's eyes widened, soaking up the alleyway's light. 'You! Do you know what you've done?!'

Alice hesitated, shaking. *No! I don't know what I've done!* 'What do you mean? What happened? I haven't been there for hours...'

The stranger's scowl lessened, though only mildly. 'Oh, you're not the girl then. You can't be. Although...'

'What girl?'

'A new girl, dressed like you.' The prostitute was still in a flustered hurry. 'She came into the tavern saying that the Seabloods have been fishing in Blackbone waters.' She shivered.

Alice did not really understand what that meant, but she knew it was bad. She had seen enough to be assured of it, especially having recently witnessed a particularly bitter parley between the two families. *After all that mess with Kit!* 'It wasn't me,' she defended.

'Good,' snapped the other. 'But keep clear, anyway. It got dirty. Quickly. More than usual.' She shot Alice a final, suspicious glare, then floated off into the dense maze of wood and brick beyond the alley.

Alice was inclined to believe the prostitute; a woman like

that would have no cause to deceive her. But despite the judgement, she could not turn back. There was not a soul in Wreckrest she could fully trust—besides perhaps Maggie— and she dared not linger in the dark streets for longer than she needed to.

Oh well, Alice submitted, stepping back into motion. *Danger or no, Maggie said she'd look after me. That's more than I can say for anyone else. I'll be safer with her than I was on the Black Beast, I'm sure!*

She rounded the last corner, curving into the comparably open expanse of the town centre. Its battered gravel was locked in perpetual dusk by the numerous lanterns dotted around it. Under this light, every detail of the gory scene was distinguishable. Alice froze on the spot. Her lungs collapsed in her chest, smothering a horrified gasp. She would have dropped the sack if it had not been tied to her neck.

What she saw could barely be fathomed. In all her years as a convict, she had never seen more than one dead body at a time, and yet here there were nearly ten! A few were strewn over pools of glistening black, sleeping involuntarily against the dust in the shadow of Maggie's front porch. Another was draped over the statue in the middle of the clearing. Another still appeared to yet be moving, though not for long.

Alice's bulging eyes swept from the corpses to the crowd. Every sort of man was there, most fleeing in tight clumps. Shouts bounced from each corner of the road, and sweaty heat crawled over to her nostrils on the soft breeze, igniting within her nose the stink of an old butcher's shop.

Swords twinkled as they swung about through the angry

throng; the fighting had stopped, but the threatening had not. Wherever there were blades, there were men guarding them, urging their comrades to stay their hands. 'This is bloody Wreckrest!' one shouted. 'They're traitors!' called another.

While the violence had seemingly concluded, the lingering combatants were clearly too riled up to be interfered with. The brawl had been far more devastating than Alice was prepared for, and there was yet enough rage in the atmosphere to suffocate a girl like her. She therefore decided that moving any closer was not a good idea. *I don't want to go anywhere near those dead bodies!*

She whirled to run off. As she spun, someone noticed her.

'Hey!' the man called. Though her instincts scolded her for it, her reflexes interrupted her feet. She flicked her head back to glimpse the man, dark hair whipping around her face. He was halfway across the clearing, but his features sliced through the night to form a visible frown. A pack of Dorian men were stacked behind him, their bronze skin heaving under the warm glow of the lamps. *Seabloods*, Alice assumed, though she intended not to stay long enough to find out if she was right.

Before she had time to flee, the man raised his pointer until it was aimed right at Alice's nose. 'It's her,' he snapped. 'The lying bitch!' Then in perfect unison, the batch of Seablood thugs ripped swords from their belts.

One single, impossibly furious heartbeat pounded through every inch of Alice's body, flooding her senses with cold fire.

Then she was gone.

She sprinted with all her might in the opposite direction, too hurried to drop the sack of carrots. She sprang into the nearest alleyway. Her hip cracked against a wooden wall as she skidded around the corner. Shouting blasted through the dark crevice. A beastly, savage roar.

Stumbling, she launched off the wall. Her feet slapped over the gravel as she rushed around another corner. There was no time to think. No time to fear. Only time to run.

They want to kill me! They're going to kill me!

Footsteps rumbled behind her, the sound of death fast approaching. Alice leapt over a toppled barrel and lost her balance. The trip sent her crashing into a stack of crates. Her fingers pressed deep into rough edges and brought the stack down into the alley behind her. Splinters raked through her palms. She cursed and leapt off again. The stench of her pursuers exploded into the alley, bouldering through the crates. Alice let loose a shriek as she sensed their advance, and stifled its echo with urgent panting. Another corner. Her legs coursed with energy. Another corner. She could see almost nothing. She held a hand out in front of the sack to stop herself from running face-first into anything. She could do nothing to stop her shins from collecting smaller obstacles as she went; there was no time for pain. Another corner.

She burst into a wider street. Diving for the other side, Alice could nearly feel the breath of the murderous gang at her heels, ripping through the warm air that gushed around her speeding limbs. They spilt into the street, their grunts fading only to be replaced by the deep trampling of their boots. *They're not giving up!*

The fugitive zipped into another alley on the street's opposite bank, her feet swiping past each other so fast she could hardly believe she stayed upright.

She slid around a bend, scraping her waistcoast on a verandah railing as she went. Her knees felt numb. They would not be able to keep up the pace for long, and the Seabloods seemed to be gaining on her. She pushed forward regardless, desperate to shove as much distance between her neck and the pirates as possible. She knew it was hopeless. The town was not big enough to sustain a long chase. Not if she kept on in the same direction.

With no time to reconsider, Alice sprang aside at the next junction, bursting down an alleyway that led back towards the town centre.

Then *thuck!* She had launched onto the wide street and bounced into a cluster of heavy-gutted thugs. Rock hard fingers grappled her shoulders and threw her into the air. All sense of direction vanished, and her flesh was battered from every side. *I'm dead! I'm dead! I'm dead!* A dusty wall cracked against her skull.

'Get off me, scum!' The voice was thick with sleazy accent. The others scoffed at her rudely. *Morchmen!* Alice forced open a bleeding eyelid. *Not dead!*

She was strewn over the dusty ground as the dead bodies had been, though she was less than half as lifeless. Above her, the mob of Seabloods leaked onto the street, its path colliding with the Morchmen. More shouting thundered. Its vicious threat lifted her to her feet, and she was running again. Away from the town's heart now. The Seabloods would be on her trail again soon enough. She knew that much. So she heaved forward, disappearing into the forest of houses.

Her pace slowed as the urgent clatter of her pursuers subsided. Blood dripped down her side and sweat sparkled on her forehead.

She decelerated into a stumble-jog. The buildings were growing further apart, and though her eyelids were clogged with dirt and grime, she could see clearer for the footing the moonlight found between roofs. The structures she trod by were reminiscent of shacks, built with haste and scant resources. Between their precarious roots, the island's trees found their own, blurring the boundary between civilisation and nature. She was close to the edge of town on the south side, supposing her bearings had not completely abandoned her. Already, the deathly roars of Wreckrest had been culled to a dull murmur.

She halted, leaning over her knees to let her breath cascade from her lungs in awful lurches. The pain in her ribs and hands was finally safe to surface. It wriggled in her skin, biting and scratching, soaking up any sense of relief she might have hoped for.

She rubbed her eyes with splintered fingers, freeing her vision. Once she could make out her surroundings, she began searching for places to hide. There were no lights this far from the main stretch, so every crevice was acceptable, however Alice was careful not to squeeze into any place that might noisily alert a local resident to her presence.

In the end, she bundled her burning body behind a stack of firewood that was packed tightly beneath a poorly built shelter of crumbling half logs. There she remained, perfectly silent, while a dormant hour crept by. Midway through, she allowed herself to start picking at her splinters. The activity was short lived—given her hiding place was blacker than the blood outside Maggie's tavern. Hence, she soon returned to silent waiting, weathering the throbs of pain as they kept her awake.

This isn't fair, she told herself, over and over again. *Can't I explain to them that it wasn't me?* She knew the answer was an unyielding no, but she did not cease to question it. *I didn't say anything about the Seabloods! Not that I can remember, anyway. But maybe I did. Maybe I said something without realising, and now innocent people are dead! Because of me!*

Alice's musings did not resolve pleasantly. All she had wanted was to sit down in front of Maggie's hot pork and stuff her mouth with it. That juicy dream had since been replaced by the memory of slaughter in the town centre, and the stink of it. She felt as though she ought to be lying on the ground with those dead men. She felt it was now her inevitable fate. It seemed that she was alone in a town full of people who would kill her, and that when the sun came up, the swords would come out, points first. *How did it change so quickly?* she wondered, glumly. *Everything has gone from good to bad, bad to worse. Maybe Wulfric will come back and save me, and everything will be alright!*

Wulfric's image drew a salty tear from her dry eyes. She knew he was not coming back. He was off saving his son. Nobody would protect her now.

But what about Wesley? She scrapped the idea almost as soon as she had come up with it. There was no hope left. *That's the smart answer,* she thought.

Approaching footsteps sent her heart into her throat. She shrivelled into a tight knot and held her breath. Amongst the night's quiet, it was impossible to tell how distant the legs were; their plodding rang crisp through the darkness. The voices chimed even louder.

'We've gotta get back t'the sloop,' one mumbled.

'You think I'm a bloody fool?!' retorted another. 'O' course we gotta get t'it. By Wimsworth! You wanna go back that way, do ya? Huh? Get gutted by those Blackbones an' everyone else?'

'Shit Ped, we're going the bloody wrong direction!' Both men were attempting—poorly—to mute their speech. To a certain degree, their breathy whispers only served to carry their voices further.

'Didn't you see what they did to Don? You want to try your luck, huh? Godammit, the whole bloody town's gone mad. Killin' on the streets o' Wreckrest! Is that what it's come to?'

'Seablood shoulda never tak'n that Blackbone boy pris'ner. That's what's it! He done it to us 'imself.'

'Don't say shit like that! It was Dagger Dreadwind started it, killin' the Stinger an' all.'

'Pah, what's that gotta do with't?'

The voices grew so loud they rattled Alice's bones. She thought it impossible that they would fail to see her. Lifting her eyes over the pile of wood, she searched. Her vision adjusted to the night's colour, revealing not two, but three wandering silhouettes, each gliding along the crooked earth towards her rapidly weakening cover.

Heartbeats pulsed so ferociously through her skin she could hear the thumps. *I should've gotten further away!* she rebuked herself. *I should've fled the town while I had the chance!* She dared not imagine what the men would do when they stumbled into her. If the scene in the town centre were any indication, she was in trouble. She had to escape.

Scrambling for ideas, she rustled her hands through the soil beneath her. The first thing that dropped into her panicking head was hardly a calculated plan. Her fingers found a rock, then it all happened before she could hold herself back.

The rock flew through the air. A sharp *whoosh* sped away to strike a leafy branch somewhere in the distance. The crash ripped the silent night in two.

'What was that?!' a Seablood gasped with perfect comedic timing. Alice wasted not a second of it. She shot out from her shelter and bolted toward the trees, generating more noise than the rock possibly could have. Boiling adrenaline whisked her up the rising slope that blended with the town's border until all semblance of Wreckrest had left her behind. It was not until she waded knee deep in the shrubs of the island's mountainous rainforest that she realised nobody was chasing her.

Her heart still pounded in her chest, though the atmosphere had morphed into something new, something altogether different. The air had thickened—as impossible as it seemed—and the fleeting moonlight had been snatched away by greedy treetops.

Alice whirled nervously, convinced the Seabloods would not simply allow her to run off. She shut her dusty eyes and let her ears do the probing. Where she sought the rustles and murmurs of would-be killers, she heard only the light hiss of snoring leaves, speckled with the soft chirps of Southland birds.

Birds, Alice marvelled. *It's the middle of the night!* Their songs made her suspicious. She weighed them in her mind, wondering whether her trackers might be using the sounds as secret communication, or whether she was merely alone in a dark and uninhabited wood. Both options frightened her.

She opened her eyes. It made little difference to what she could see. The ground was so squashed under plant and shade that not even the stars could monitor the terrain. *How did I get here without tripping?*

Tightening prickly lips, Alice resolved to keep moving. She waved her arms out before her as she strode through the foliage, climbing higher up the slope. Tickling spines slid through her sticky sweat and caught in her hair. She became grateful for the carrot sack, which acted as a shield for her torso, deflecting the many branches that attempted to hinder her progress.

At first, Alice's boots sunk into soft debris with each step. As she pressed on, the debris gave way to packed soil and grimy stone. Soon enough, she was heaving her body over mossy boulders while the bubbling of a stream drew closer.

The calm noise stirred the dark, and a sense of misguided peace settled on her fumbling frame. She could even— almost—see where she was going again. The grey of wet rocks caught the timid light from high above, glistening beautifully. Over there, the stream emerged, over there, a tree trunk, over there, a sharpened stick.

Her boot lost its hold and slipped from a rock's surface to jam into dried leaves between the rock and its neighbour. Despite the fall, she managed to keep upright, however clumsily. When her vision refocused, the sharpened stick was still there.

Alice went cold. She was stunned, frozen as ice. In that

moment, time stood still, gracing her with a generous handful of precious breaths before her death. But her faculties sluggishly came back to her as she realized the stick was not moving. The stream bubbled on but the stick was not moving. Not yet.

She traced the length of the spear back to its shadowy bearer. Wrapped in the forest's hazy veil, the man's midnight skin was perfectly camouflaged.

Alice shuddered, stumbled backwards. There was nowhere to go. Through the darkness she could see more faces. Dark faces, with darker shadows over their eyes. They wore next to no clothes and bore nothing but spears, each raised, ready to strike. These were no Seabloods. Nor were they trees.

Ijians!

Tears rolled down her cheeks. She knew now she was doomed. There was not a word she could throw at them, not when they did not speak her language. She had not a single thing to wedge between herself and those spear points. *Except…*

Alice pulled the carrot sack gently over her head, and cast it onto the rocks beside the nearest Ijian. The Ijian looked at it apprehensively, never lowering his weapon. He used his toes to fiddle with the sack, until even Alice could see the orange flesh of the prize within.

The Ijian's gaze returned to Alice's rigid figure.

He lowered his spear.

16

'This one's fresh from Danidor,' he said as he passed it through the iron bars. Pale hands clutched the bottle thankfully and brought it to pale lips.

'It's good,' came the reply.

'Is it?' asked the first. 'I've never been able to tell the difference. It gets you drunk, that's the main thing. That's all I've ever cared about.'

'Getting drunk's all you've ever cared about?'

Both chuckled. Their spirit filled the hold with warmth, and fed life to the lamp that illuminated its contents. Though there was iron between them, the men leant against the lining of the Blood Hammer's hull as if friends, and threw back their rum with the world.

They never faced each other. They instead sat adjacent, one on a crate and one on a bench, staring at the opposite wall. Seb could see a clump of barrels there, with a bucket on top and a mop beside it. One of the barrels' iron rings was broken, and could not quite wrap the whole way around the container's hips. He thought he could have painted the clump from memory. He had certainly looked at it enough. There was no doubt Kit could paint it, from his altered perspective, of course; Kit's painting would have been sliced several times by unmoving black lines.

Seb's smile faded. He sucked another mouthful from his own bottle and answered thoughtfully. 'I wish.'

Kit grunted in partial agreement. The sounds of night flowed over the ensuing silence, smothering their worries. Planks creaked, the sea whispered, and the thick hull rocked the crew to sleep atop its anchored bed in Dain Bay, a wide bite on the south face of the Deceiver. The smell of fermentation was heavy in the brig's hold, and the day's heat had been trapped within, soaking that smell in a bath of moist warmth.

A few sailors were still awake, throwing dice on the mess deck overhead. Their chants had subsided in respect for those with early morning duties that needed to rest. It was probably past midnight, though Seb truly had no way of knowing.

Kit shuffled on his bench and stuck his bottle under it. He pushed his hair back and crossed his arms, leather-gloved hands vanishing into elbows. 'Have you ever thought about running away?' he asked.

'Deserting?' Seb scoffed.

'You could call it that,' Kit pondered, going quiet once more. He knew the question had been answered.

'My blood's as salty as my father's. I belong on this brig.'

'Who told you to say that? Your father?'

'It's what he said to Bart.'

Kit exhaled sympathetically, reacquainting himself with the bottle. In the dim light, the glass sparkled with a soft, emerald magic. 'I hear Gold Harbour is the land of new beginnings.

And there's enough work in Mariscos for all of Danidor. I've often wondered… but of course I would never. I could never… Not leave my father, my family.'

'Not Morchport?' Seb asked.

Kit snorted. 'Even in my dreams I couldn't flee there. The Black Beast docks there too often, and the crew spends too much time in its streets.'

'You dock at Morchport?' Seb was astonished. 'If the Blood Hammer came anywhere *near* Mariscos, we'd be sunk before we could go about.'

'The Blackbones have a good relationship with the Morchmen,' said Kit. 'They don't see us as criminals so much as businessmen. They respect us. Aye, if I could live there, I suppose I would. I'd build a house on the outskirts, and work a farm. Have children too. I'd be well rid of the water, and more than happy to never see Wreckrest again. God knows I've enough gold for it!'

Seb shook his head, though the motion probably went unnoticed. 'I could never leave the sea,' he admitted. 'Sailing is my life, and my love. If I were ever to escape father, I would sail across the ocean, discovering new lands and visiting old ones. Not twist around in the Sentinels forever as I'm so doomed to do. I've ridden the Blood Hammer for half my life, and I've never ventured beyond the Barricade Reef!' He flung his head back to let more of the smooth rum run over his tongue. 'It's a curse.'

Kit smiled. A warm smile. 'You're not stuck behind these bars, as I am. You can flee if you wish. Go, leave this all behind and have your adventure.'

Seb sniggered, mocking. 'And if our places were switched? Would you do it?' The question needed no answer. 'I cannot leave my father alone. If only Bart were still alive, the fool!'

They laughed then. An uncomfortable laugh, but a laugh nonetheless. It crumbled into stillness in seconds, replaced by the restrained murmurs that pulsed down from the deck above.

A cold wind seemed to weave through the hold. It clawed at Seb's soul, casting ice over what joy he thought he knew. Cold reality, it was.

Kit sensed it too. He turned on his bench to face the Seablood, his cheeks illuminated beyond their prison bars. 'You're a good man,' he told Seb. 'I wouldn't have thought it, but you are.'

Seb's throat twisted in his neck, but he showed it not.

'Tell me something honest,' the Blackbone continued. 'What is to be done with me? Am I to be killed?'

Seb sat up straight, matching the other's stare. 'Not without me knowing about it,' he said. 'And for the company you've given me, you shouldn't be paid so poorly. You're our hostage, aye, but that's where it ends. You will not be killed, that's a promise. I won't let it happen.'

'A dangerous promise,' Kit remarked.

A smirk crept onto Seb's expression. 'Just watch me keep it.'

A shadow blew then into the hold, quiet and unremarkable. A shadow in the shape of a simple Dorian man in a simple, dark coat.

'Sebastian,' Salvino said. 'Your father beckons.'

'What is it now?' Seb asked, pained.

'Word from Wreckrest. Bad news, I'm afraid.'

Seb grumbled. Standing, he brushed his shirt and adjusted his shoulders. Before leaving he sent Kit a silent nod. The prisoner returned the gesture kindly, and watched helplessly as Seb followed the brig's quartermaster up the ladder, out of the hold.

'How did I know I'd find you down there?' Salvino whispered as they sidestepped their way through the gamblers at their dice. Most of them scurried away at the approach of the brig's royalty, though a couple were far too engrossed in their game to even notice the intruders slip past them.

'It's where I sleep,' stated Seb, bluntly.

'Of course. You wouldn't go down there to share supper with the Blackbone kid, I'm sure.'

Seb's temperature rose, but he continued alongside his shady companion as if it hardly troubled him. 'You know why I go down there, Salvino. Not for the Blackbone. For the silence. I thought you understood.'

'Oh please, Sebastian!' Salvino hissed. 'The whole crew knows you and the boy have become chums. You've been down there half the day of late. Tell me, what is it you talk about that's so juicy?'

'He's no *boy*,' Seb retorted. 'He's a man my age, and heir to the Black Beast. I give him the respect he deserves.'

Salvino smirked, as smug as a child who had discovered his mother's secret candy. He gently repressed a jest, though one tickled his lips.

'And it's not the whole crew,' continued the taller of the two. 'My father knows nothing, as usual.' He glared at the other.

'Worry not, Sebastian,' assured Salvino. 'I won't tell Ted of your treasons. Not today.'

They climbed the final ladder onto the brig's main deck. The heads of those on duty turned their way, otherwise they were alone beneath the silver-soaked masts. To the north, the Deceiver's sharp summits cut the sky. To the South, the distant Wimswind Island was not more than a faded smudge between a swirling, black sky and a humming, glassy sea. A smaller vessel was anchored nearby, swaying ever so slightly in the light breeze.

Salvino's bronze features blended seamlessly with the hues of the night, and his coat became invisible, as if it were not there at all.

'Who are you tonight?' Seb asked, quizzically. 'My friend… or my father's?'

'Neither,' the invisible man was quick to answer. 'As always. I'm friends with the Blood Hammer. And the Seablood crown borne by her sails.'

'My crown,' Seb grimaced.

'Is it now?' Salvino raised an eyebrow.

'It's mine as much as his. I've my father's same blood.'

'Do you now?' An impossibly suspicious smile contorted Salvino's thin lips.

'What does that mean?'

'Here we are,' Salvino declared with satisfied amusement. Indeed, they had reached the Blood Hammer's sterncastle. Salvino descended into the cramped doorway and held the door ajar for the pirate prince.

Captain Theodore Seablood was bunched up inside, cowering behind his desk with a flustered, red face. His ridiculous wig looked lonely without its usual wide-brimmed counterpart to keep it company, and even odder yet hanging over the shoulders of the captain's sleeping gown.

A Dorian sailor stood close by. Seb knew not his name, but recognised his self-important posture. The sailor nodded politely at the newcomers. Seb neglected to return acknowledgement. Behind, Salvino closed the cabin's door and vanished into the flickering corner.

The room was still dressed as much like a king's as any palace in Sirland, which was disasterously inappropriate considering its size and function. The illustrious four-poster bed relinquished barely enough space to house the rest of the captain's oversized furtniture. The result was an inhospitable clutter, made only the worse by the tug of war between the shadows and the lamplight.

Amongst the mess, it was impossible to engage in conversation from any reasonable distance, so Seb paced onto the plush rug right beneath Ted's desk and met his captain's watery gaze from awkwardly near. 'What news from Wreckrest, father?'

'What took you so long, boy?' Ted snapped, tapping the desk impatiently. 'I send Salvino for you, and you go off drinking first?'

'I came straight here.'

'Did you? I don't believe it.'

Seb sighed. 'What is it? Why am I here?'

'Cleto sailed right up from Wreckrest.'

'I got here as quickly as I could,' the sailor added. Ted grunted rudely at the interruption, never shifting his precious attention from Seb.

'There's been trouble. Big trouble,' said the captain.

I can see that, Seb thought, unsure whether to bother fretting. Trouble in Wreckrest never boded well for business, and a Seablood sloop sailing all the way from Hullbreaker Bay to the Blood Hammer in the middle of the night meant the trouble was no lemon tart.

'A Blackbone felon has been blabbering about Seablood vessels crossing into their territory.'

Seb felt the fuzzy prick of relief. 'Is that all? A week hardly goes by without—'

'You'd think so!' Ted cut in, adjusting his wig with needless force. 'Apparently it's stirred up quite a tustle. Seems there's a bit of tension about.'

'Well, we do have Wulfric's son belowdecks.'

'Aye, we do,' Ted agreed. 'I've half a mind to take his head so we can show them this is no game.'

Seb flinched. Merely minutes earlier he had promised to keep Kit alive. 'What?' he exclaimed, as warily as he could. 'Kill Kit Blackbone? Over a brawl?' He could feel Salvino's perceptive grin jeer at him, even if he could not see it.

'Not just a brawl,' complained the captain. 'Several Seabloods dead. And all the rest fled from Wreckrest.'

'Several dead?!' Seb remarked in disbelief. 'In *Wreckrest?*'

'Aye, over a bloody rumour!'

Seb glanced now at the sailor, who was still standing by Ted's desk like an upright dignitary from the West. The man nodded in agreement. 'How are we supposed to keep up our work,' he questioned, 'if we can't dock at Wreckrest?'

'Well… was it true?' Seb asked. 'Perhaps we deserve it.'

'We don't bloody well deserve it!' Ted shouted. The steam rising from his ears was almost tangible. 'And I'll be damned if some pathetic lie like that were ever to be true! Nay, never! We must set it straight, boy. No Seablood should be afraid of resting his arse in the capital!'

Seb huffed and brought a pained hand to his forehead. 'Let me guess. That's where I come in?'

Ted slapped a fist twice against the desk he so inflexibly slumped at. 'Right you are, boy. If we allow this to drag on, we'll look no more than squealing piglets in Greyhide's eyes. The Blood Hammer can sail again at break of day, though Salvino implores we act sooner. Cleto's sloop is ready to move now. It can be docked at Wreckrest before dawn.'

Seb finally located Salvino's face, so cleverly veiled in the crevice between the captain's dresser and the starboard curtains. The former threw an accusing glare, but the other shrugged it off. A cheeky grin was all the quartermaster would allow.

What game are you playing? Seb silently interrogated. *Are you jealous that I've found a friend aboard the Blood Hammer, other than yourself? How childish.*

Salvino maintained a fixed expression.

Seb spun back at his father. 'You truly wish for me to ride this sloop to Wreckrest… tonight?'

'We'll arrive at midday,' Ted grumbled. 'Surely you can last a few hours, wrenched from your whore's breasts!'

Seb gritted his teeth. *Oh father, how little you know me!* 'Of course, father. Though what would you have me do when I get there? Why should my word hold more sway than any other

Seablood's? Or do you mean for me to throw some sort of Ijian peace party?'

'Are you trying to be funny or have you gone insane? I hope it's the latter, because you've failed at the first. Use your head, boy. Figure it out!' Ted stood up so abruptly his chair fell backward onto the floor. Cleto recoiled. 'If I knew I'd need feed you your brains as well as your slop, I would never have suffered years of your incessant crying! You were a whiny child, and you've grown into a whiny man.'

'I have not,' Seb barked. 'Fine. I will do it. Cleto, come. Get me out of here.'

The Seablood sailor bounced into action, leaping ahead of Seb as he barged out of the captain's cabin. Salvino slunk after them.

Hurriedly, Cleto collected his rowing party from beneath the brig's starlit surface and directed Seb towards the port flank, below which the sloop's skiff was tied. It sloshed about in the water, knocking softly against the Blood Hammer's giant belly.

Seb waited for the others to climb down the rope ladder first. He strode over to Salvino, who was perched in the shadows, camouflaged beside the mainmast. 'Did you come out to see me off?'

'Watch yourself, Sebastian,' said the quartermaster, ignoring the question. 'Ted may not appreciate it, but you are the heir to his fleet. If anything were to happen to you…'

'Moments ago, you would have had me believe he was not my father at all,' Seb sneered. 'So which is it?'

Salvino's dark eyes narrowed. 'Stay safe.'

Seb nodded. 'I don't want anything happening to Kit

Blackbone while I'm gone. No matter how red hot my father glows.'

At Seb's solemnity, Salvino chuckled. 'It'll only be one sunrise. I'm sure we can last that long without an eruption!'

Seb grumbled, then stepped towards the ladder where Cleto was beckoning. He wondered whether he should say a farewell to Kit before he so suddenly departed. The thought caught him by surprise; never before had he considered something so impractical. *Perhaps he is the first friend I've ever had.*

Salvino peered vigilantly through the mild breeze as the Blood Hammer's heir slipped from view. His hand was inside his coat, tickling the hilt of his concealed dagger. The other hand stroked the mast.

Once the commotion sank away, Salvino dipped down the nearby steps to belowdecks, unseen. Avoiding eyes was what Salvino was best at, especially at night. Even if he were to be spotted, a man so oft suspicious was never really suspected of being where he should not. Despite this, he could not evade worry. His gaze darted from side to side as he navigated his way through the dark layers of the Seablood brig.

Soon, he arrived. He was almost entirely confident he had not been noticed, which was not perfect but had to be enough. With a light touch, he laid his fingers on the handle and urged the door forward. His boots tapped ever so peacefully against the mangled rug beneath them, ferrying his body into the tight cabin.

Harsh snores echoed off the enclosing walls. A lump heaved up and down slowly beneath a thin blanket. A bead of sweat carved down Salvino's forehead, threatening to blur his acute vision.

The door edged closed, and the warm room drained of all light. The smell was toxic. Salvino ceased his breath. Were the cabin's owner a wet hound, the air might have been fresher. All the same, the quartermaster pressed on.

His hand hovered over the sleeping woman. Stray hairs scraped his palm as it neared her face. The other drew the dagger.

He felt warm, moist breaths pump through his fingers. Sad, helpless breaths.

With one swift motion, Salvino's hand pressed hard against the woman's mouth. The other pressed the dagger's point in quickly.

Salvino shut his eyes.

When he was done, he blew silently out of the cabin, trickled swiftly through the mess deck and swept down darkly into the prisoner's hold.

Kit Blackbone was still awake, as expected. He was mulling over his pointless thoughts, bathed in the lingering radiance of a single lamp.

'Seb?' Kit asked, breaking free from his contemplation. Salvino emerged, looking upon the prisoner with sorrow and amusement both.

'Seb has left the Blood Hammer,' Salvino curtly announced.

Kit's apprehension was suddenly palpable. 'Where has he gone?'

'You two have become friends, haven't you?'

'What of it?' The prisoner shied away from the cell's bars.

'Don't fret, Blackbone,' sung the Dorian man. 'I can be your friend too. In fact, I've brought you a present.'

The hold filled with quiet, hushing to hear the tinkle of keys sprout from Salvino's coat. The quartermaster threw the entire ring through the prison bars. The keys bounced unceremoniously off Kit's shin and plopped against the ground. The prisoner peered at them with distrust.

'Congratulations,' Salvino said. 'You're free.'

Then he left, dabbing at the blood on his sleeve with his handkerchief.

17

The deep green horizon stretched out beyond his sight into the twisted white of the morning. From that white flowed the soft scent of salty sea, washing over his face, clearing his lungs.

Hullbreaker Bay was littered with vessels. Sloops, mostly. Their masts pointed up from their narrow bodies, touching the swirling chaos of clouds that rummaged through the endless blue far beyond. With sails furled and anchors set, there remained only small flags atop each spire to revel in the day's generous breeze. Out from Wreckrest's eastern docks where he waited, only two types of flags flew. The crown and the skull, the respective emblems of Seablood and Blackbone. At this hour, there were only two crowns to be seen. One floated above Cleto's sloop—the vessel that had borne him—and the other was painted on the Blood Hammer's fore course sail. The brig was by far the largest in the bay, and the only one to flaunt its sails. *Father wishes to leave as quickly as possible,* Seb deduced. *He probably doesn't trust I've done my job.*

Warm gusts rippled through Seb's shirt, sucking the sweat from his skin. Despite its brutality, the wind calmed him. It was Seb's true love, the wind. It had never left his side. Unlike Ted. And Liz. And Bart.

He raised his arms, allowing the air to claw at his elbows. He cared not how he looked. Nobody would dare question Sebastian Seablood lest they soon taste the sharp edge of his hungry cutlass. Perhaps it was for this fear that Seb had survived the night. Perhaps it was simply for his name. Either way, it did not matter. Wreckrest hunkered behind him now, yawning as it woke from unrestful slumber.

Beside him was Cleto's skiff. It rocked about beneath six Seablood thugs as they argued over whether it was safe to wander back into town for one last drink. A couple of them were assured that returning to their sloop was a better idea, but were tempted nevertheless. Seb tried to ignore their squabbling; soon enough the Blood Hammer's boat would reach the pier, and Seb would be ferried back to his home aboard the giant brig for whom those petty pirates served.

That very boat was almost upon him. The familiar shape of its minature hull sliced through the sparkling water, transporting a number of well-known faces over the coral shelf. At its stern was the bronze, inscrutable façade of Salvino Moreno. Upon noticing the man, Seb knew something was amiss. Salvino rarely left the Blood Hammer.

The quartermaster's approach started Seb's heart racing. He lowered his arms and felt the sun's sting burn through his breeches. He put on promptly the smug visage of self-assuredness that he knew so well, and nodded politely to his crewmen as they bumped into the pier. What made Seb's heart truly lurch was how quickly Salvino leapt from the boat, landing his black boots on the pier with cat-like swiftness.

Seb was too impatient to remain silent. 'Are you lost?' he joked, masking his eager curiosity. 'I don't think I've ever seen you this far from the brig.'

Salvino's eyes laughed, but he replied with a tone thick in solemnity. 'Walk with me.' He placed a hand on Seb's arm and lightly turned him around. The two strolled cautiously along the pier toward the town, leaving the others to tie up the boat. As soon as they had escaped earshot of their comrades, Seb pressed his teeth together and glared accusingly at the seemingly detached Dorian. 'Tell me. What is it?'

The quartermaster would have typically inserted a dry and wit-soaked gag. This time he cut straight to business. 'Sebastian,' he said, 'how is Wreckrest? Did you clean up the mess?'

Is that really what's on your mind? Something has happened! Tell me what it is! 'As well as I could have,' Seb replied. 'Tempers had eased by the time I arrived, so the Blackbones who weren't asleep were sober enough to hear what I had to say, at the least. No Blackbone lackey would ever hurt me, besides. Not unless they were ordered to by Greyhide himself.'

'That's why you were sent,' agreed Salvino.

'That I know,' said Seb, 'though I cannot tell whether the bitterness will start up again once my presence has vanished. I'm telling you, Salvino, the Blackbones are none too happy about Kit's capture. And rightly so.'

They reached the end of the pier and veered off towards the mix of dried coral and dust that formed a sloping beach between the water and the outer footholds of Wreckrest. Their boots crunched over uneven lumps as they traced the shore southward.

'It wasn't meant to make them happy,' Salvino said.

'Of course it wasn't. But don't you think it would all but solve this trouble if we were to release him? We've gained nothing by taking him prisoner.'

Salvino ceased his slow pacing and looked deep into Seb's eyes, his own twinkling with mystery. They were now alone, although still visible to those at the docks. At their toes, the incessant lapping of the bay's little waves cloaked their voices. Behind, green talons stretched out from the island's mangled canopy, swaying side-to-side in perpetual disquiet.

'Unfortunately,' answered Salvino, 'we cannot do that.'

'We can,' Seb snapped. 'And we should. We will, in fact.'

Salvino raised his eyebrows and lowered his nose, never breaking eye contact with the other. 'Kit is no longer with us.'

'What do you mean?'

'He is dead.'

'You *killed* him?'

'I didn't... The captain did.'

Seb whirled, slamming his jaw tightly shut. He could feel his fingernails carve into his palms, and his heart push into his throat. He swallowed several times to keep it down. Its pulses squirted tears onto his cheeks, which were speedily whisked away by hot gusts.

Out on the rippling water, the flags taunted him; Blackbone skulls glaring in his direction. Among them, the Blood Hammer sat pompously high, its great black sails writhing. Beyond it all, the Rainbow Sea washed into that blurry horizon, where the clouds were not so sharp.

'I told you…' Seb mumbled through locked teeth. '…Not to let anything happen.'

Fingers came to rest on Seb's burning shoulder. He shrugged them off. 'Why?!' he demanded.

'The boy escaped,' Salvino explained. 'He was found sneaking up to the main deck. And… Agatha. She was… We found her dead.'

'Agatha too!' *Shit!* 'I don't believe it!' Seb was beyond furious. 'It's not bloody true!' *Why would Kit kill Agatha? There is no way. No way!* 'Why didn't you wait 'till I was back? I told you not to let anything happen! I *told* you!' Seb clenched his anger within twitching flesh. His joints strained against the pressure.

'Ted's fury was untamable, I'm afraid.'

'Untamable! Shit!' Seb lashed out. He swung his cutlass from his belt and threw it with all his might into the dried coral. When he realised he had probably ruined its edge, he kicked the beach. Pieces of white-grey sprayed into the waves. 'Shit! Shit! Shit! It was one bloody night! One bloody night! I *told* you! Why couldn't you hold him off 'till morning?!'

'Sebastian,' Salvino interjected, his tone cool, his position on the beach unmoving. 'The crew suspects you.'

'Me?!' Seb exclaimed. 'I was here all night! In bloody Wreckrest!'

'Not that you killed Agatha. Nay. That you let Kit free.'

'Why would I—'

'Everyone knows, Sebastian. That you two had become… friendly.'

Sebastian went still. He had forgotten himself. He squashed

his emotion into its rightful corner and glared back at the quartermaster. *Are you accusing me, Salvino?* The Dorian man was too smug to be thinking anything so treacherous. 'What about my father?'

'All he knows is that his woman is dead.'

'His woman? He despised her!'

'Nevertheless,' Salvino sighed.

A gust blew Seb's hair into his sweating face, forcing him to turn away. All he could hear now was the deep urgency of his own breath. He closed his eyes and let his shoulders drop. Gradually, he managed to slow his lungs. This was no time for hot-headedness, he knew; such brash attitudes were the realm of his abominable father. *How has this happened?* he wondered. *Why would Kit do such a thing? He can't have. He's been framed by one of the crew! But Agatha? Dead! Is it even true? What do I do if it is? What would Bart have done?* His forehead crumpled. *He'd probably have killed Kit days ago.*

'Sebastian?' Salvino calmly enquired after allowing a few moments of windy quiet. 'If you would, I have gathered a considerable portion of our crew to my side, over the past few weeks. They would do anything I request, I daresay. Even a mutiny, if that's what it came to. Some are equally as unhappy with our captain's recent... madness.'

Seb spat, ignoring the comment. 'Last night you made me question my lineage. Well now I need to know. Is Ted really my father?'

Salvino seemed to anticipate the question. 'Don't be foolish,' he said. 'Ted stole you from your mother, aye, but he was certain you were his. Just like with Bart.' He raised an eyebrow.

'Is that what you wanted to hear? I'm afraid I can't be more definite than that.'

'I can,' Seb growled. 'He's not my father. Not anymore. Not if what you say is true. I'm sick of it all. I'm sick of him.' He waved a loose hand at the distant brig and its floppy, white crown. 'Go back. I'm not coming with you.'

'Sebastian—'

'I won't be swayed. I'm done with the Blood Hammer. I'm done with the whole business. I cannot drift on this black tide a day more.'

Salvino nodded in respect, at last misplacing his cheeky grin. 'Well, you can't stay here. Once the Blackbones find out—'

Seb scanned the bay. There was only one other means by which to flee the island safely. 'I'll board with Cleto,' he said, then spun on the spot and marched toward the docks. Salvino sprang after him, gliding in Seb's shadow until they both had returned to the end of the pier where their boats were tied.

No further words were exchanged between the two. Salvino bequeathed Seb a thin smile and nothing else, watching warily as the pirate prince stepped into Cleto's skiff and commanded its inhabitants to ferry him back to their sloop. Sebastian regarded the quartermaster not at all, choosing rather to be carried away in silent anguish, glistening eyes held forward.

And so it is that I will never become Captain Seablood, mused Captain Seablood's heir. *Farewell, father. Farewell, Bart.*

Cleto's sloop was anchored as close to Hullbreaker Bay's reef as was safe. It was a well-built vessel, for sure. It was small, sporting only a single mast and a shallow draft that allowed it to sneak through some of the Sentinels' more hazardous passages. The thing's bowsprit was almost as long as its hull, allowing for a monstrous headsail that won the vessel its unrivalled speed, however difficult to manage.

Sloops like Cleto's were the vessel most favoured by each of the three sealords' various subordinates. Between the Pinnacle and the Rainbow Dagger, they could be spotted zipping from Sentinel to Sentinel, harassing any stranger that strayed off course. Unlike their bulkier masters, sloops backed away from complicated trade deals and intimidation rackets, choosing instead to feed off the region's smaller game, catching their prey by surprise to claim their loot. In that sense, a sloop's crew were true pirates, though they were never left alone to pursue their craft in peace. After years of weaving, the Rainbow Sea had become a political tangle, forcing many pirates to attack each other, or act as errand boys for their respective sealord. An errand boy is exactly what Cleto had become.

Despite himself, Seb smirked as his boat neared the sloop. The name painted on the vessel's flank could not have been less original, or more conceited. *Cleto*, it was named.

The skiff shuddered as it rammed into the awful lettering. Exerting his authority, Seb stood before the crew had even grappled the skiff's lines, and was the first to climb aboard Cleto herself. Some twenty Dorian pirates called the vessel their own, although most of them were presently belowdecks, recouping the sleep they had lost the night before. Fortunately, Cleto the man was not among them. He was balanced self-importantly by the helm, and had already given the order to hoist the anchor. It did not take him long to notice Seb's return.

He muttered something indecipherable in his native

language. While Seb was versed in Dorian as well as any, he could not quite catch the remark. 'Surprised to see me?' he forced a grin and inhaled his ruminating mind deeply into his chest.

'Aye, surprised. What brings you back, sir?' The words were civil, but the expression on Cleto's dark features betrayed irritation.

Seb paced along the deck's edge toward's the sloop's captain. 'I've need of a fast vessel. One that can outrun the Blood Hammer.'

'Begging your pardon,' Cleto retorted, as politely as possible for the pirate he was. 'But we've business to attend to. I'm sure the Blood Hammer can get you any place you need, in almost as much time.'

'What business do you mean?' Seb interrogated. 'Seablood business, or your own?'

'We're Seabloods too, sir. We may not share the blood, but we share the name. What I'm sayin's, all our business be Seablood business.'

'Then you'll follow my orders?'

'I follow the orders of your father, sir.'

'And I speak for him at this time,' Seb stated. 'I've need to head south out of Hullbreaker Bay. Away from the Blood Hammer, beyond the Sentinels.'

'Sir! That be Blackbone territory, and the wind will be against us. It's too dangerous!'

Seb cleared his throat, his fingers searching for the hilt of his cutlass. When they could not find it, confidence slipped off his skin. The bare patch it exposed was hastily smeared over with anger. 'Do you mean to question me at every turn,' he shouted, 'or will you obey your master?!'

The sudden change in Seb's temperament saw Cleto flinch. His crew froze, expectant of either retaliation or concession—both worryingly unsafe. Their leader's face screwed up as he wrestled internally with the outcome of both options. In the end, he elected the more tactful of the two. 'Hoist the mailsail!' he called. A pair of eager sailors snatched the halyard, and the sail clattered up into the wind.

Cleto challenged Seb with a greasy nod. The latter returned the gesture stone faced, then spun to watch the undersized crew lift the sloop into motion. It began to sway the moment the skiff's hull was drawn from the water. Within minutes, the agile vessel was soaring past the bay's anchored tenants with a healthy portside lean.

Seb refused to look at the Blood Hammer as he overtook it. To distract himself, he focussed his vision on the spiky shadows of Wreckrest, so small between the two peaks of Wimswind Island. As the town shrunk, he could not help but wonder if he would ever see it again. He certainly hoped not to.

Cleto tapped Seb's shoulder. 'Sir, we'll need to tack soon if we're to head south down Wimswind passage. Are you sure you need do this?'

Seb turned, a fire in his eyes. He slurped up a lungful of fresh wind before speaking. 'There is no choice to be unsure about,' he said. 'I want this island out of sight before nightfall.'

Cleto moaned, resigned. 'Very well, sir.' He faced the sea and grumbled to himself. 'The Blackbones will be unpleased, to say the least. You better know what you're doing, sir.'

Of course I don't! Seb wrapped his hand around the belt where his cutlass had been, wishing he had not disposed of it. *I don't have a bloody clue. Just get me away.*

And away they sailed.

Over the next few hours, Seb took it upon himself to compose the plan Cleto rightly expected him to already possess. There were settlements south of Morchport, he knew. If Cleto were able to get through Blackbone's waters trouble free, there would undoubtedly be scope for a new life down there. The only problem with such an idea was that such remote townships would offer nearly nothing for Seb to busy himself with. Tendering trade between local ports would undoubtedly twist him back into the pirate web he was now so close to escaping, and the sloop was not by any stretch of the imagination built to survive long voyages to Brindia or beyond.

A sudden lurch sent him stumbling into the shrouds. He clutched the lines with deft hands and swung himself into a slouch, with his feet hanging over the edge of the sloop's gunwale. Embarassed, Seb peeked over his shoulder. None of the crew gave any indication they had noticed his stumble, though he was sure they had. Growing up on a heavy brig like the Blood Hammer had fostered a less-sensitive breed of sea legs in the pirate prince, a condition only apparent aboard such a light interceptor.

Seb shuffled uncomfortably but indifferently in his new seat. The sudden drop had left a dull sting in his backside, but he refused to show it. *Soon, I'll have escaped it all*, he reminded himself. *Then I'll have no need to be so self-aware. Never again will I need to live up to the cursed name of my fool father.*

A pang of sadness popped against his chest, the gravity of his decision soaking in. He contemplated his father's face. *Will I never see it again? I didn't even give him a chance to defend himself!* He clenched his fists and shook his salt-ridden hair. *No! I mustn't think on it. The Seablood life… I want it no longer! Kit was right.* A tear squeezed free of his squinting eyes. *Kit! A soul as lost as my own, yet so sure of itself. I shouldn't have left you, brother. I promised that you wouldn't be killed, but my words were naught but wind without a sail. No! They were more than that; I am not my father! I will make it up to you, Blackbone. That I will! One day, when my father is dead, I will. My promises are not broke so easily.*

Another tear. He wiped it away in anger. Kit was dead, as dead as his brother, and there was nothing he could do to change that. Nothing to do but flee.

Seb's stare fell to the water. It churned peacefully against the sloop's port flank, bubbling up in soft flakes of white beneath his dangling boots. At present the vessel was sliding along a southward tack. The southeasterly trade wind was forcing Seb's seat to rise high above the rough green fields around him. The fugitive kept his head down, musing over the wake. *Blackbone water*, he knew, reflecting with an ever-deepening gloom. He had rarely traversed such territory. It filled him with a feeling of melancholic adventure.

Hours passed, creeping by in an orderly fashion, each to the tune of the sea splashing against hard oak. Seb did not leave his seat, even as the sky sank hesitantly behind him. His woes began to leak quietly from his heart, dripping ever so leisurely onto his breeches. *Could it be this easy? This easy to run away?*

And could it really be so simple, whipping through Blackbone territory unnoticed?

'Ship ahead!'

Of course not.

Seb's head flicked up. It was almost sundown, but the nearing lump of a round-topped island was crisp against the comparatively faded shape of the Sentinel behind it. Unless Seb's sense of distance had evaded him completely, the mass was indeed Cecil Island, a sloping chunk of earth plopped in the mouth of Dusty's Beach, itself a pale stroke of dried coral that wrapped the west coast of the Watcher. Just south of the island, slithering into view, the faint silhouette of a ship floated unashamedly on the glowing waves.

'Captain, shall we change course?'

'That's for our master to decide,' Cleto called back, his voice layered with contempt. 'Sebastian, sir, what do you say?'

Seb got up, pulling himself erect with the stays. He squinted at the distant ship. It was a ways away, but noticeably sizeable. 'The only ship that big in these parts is the Black Beast,' he stated. 'It's too slow to catch us, so long as we hold our course.' He waved a hand forward, eyeing the crew. 'Go on.'

He turned back to watch the ship. The diminutive shape scraped the dull horizon, its dangerous presence thick in the air, even at such a distance. It appeared to be anchored, though there was no telling for sure until Cleto's vessel drew nearer. Regardless, the ship was clearly in no position to launch into motion; its sails were furled and its bow was angled directly at the beach.

'Are you sure it's the Black Beast, sir?' Cleto questioned,

swinging from the helm to Seb's side. His condescending tone had given way to curious observation. 'It's big, for sure. But it looks different to me… Brighter, maybe. Not so bulky.'

Seb stroked his face. He was unsure. The figure was not particularly reminiscent of the Black Beast, though it radiated a perculiar sense of familiarity. It grew more distinct with every second. 'Have you got a scope?' he asked.

'Aye we did, sir, but no longer. We'd have replaced it too, but our usual business doesn't so much need it.'

Seb grumbled, straining his eyes.

'Sir, are we holding course?'

'Yes,' Seb blurted, though he was not really listening. His mind was transfixed on the oncoming vessel. Something about it… was…

Seb made out the subject's rear. A giant wooden wing seemed to sweep out from the hull and fold up by the sterncastle. *By Bloody Wimsworth, it's the ghost ship! The bloody ghost ship at Dusty's Beach! Father would—*

'Wait… I've changed my mind!' Seb stammered, cold adreneline rushing through his muscles. 'Change course!'

'Aye aye,' Cleto replied with enthusiasm, the relief plain. 'Starboard!' he shouted at the mate who was manning the wheel.

'No, not starboard!' barked Seb. 'Go about. Portside.'

'But that'll take us…'

'…Directly towards it.'

'But— But—' The crew's muffled complaints echoed their captain's.

'Can't you see? It's the Frontiere! Halfeye Warhawk's ship.

The one we sunk four years ago!'

Cleto fell silent, realisation washing over him. The crew may not have recognised it, but Cleto was aboard the Blood Hammer the day Seablood, Blackbone and Dreadwind conspired to take down the legendary tyrant. He would never forget the vessel's wings, or what they looked like when they sunk, broken, into the ravenous waves of the Rainbow Sea.

'Today we will catch the ghost ship,' Seb murmured, then laughed. The laugh was mad and greedy, and so fearsome the crew ceased their questioning to scurry about the sloop's lines, preparing it for an eastward veer.

Wonder sparkling in his eyes, Cleto slid wordlessly up to the helm and took the wheel for himself. He thrust its handles to his left, shouting 'Go about!'

The lines keeping the foresails taught were left to drop, and the sloop's hands hauled them quickly back on the port side of the mast. Sails snapped as the bowsprit sliced directly through the wind's flow, forcing the boom to sweep over the deck. Sailcloth billowed out as the vessel settled into its new heading.

The manouver was slick, and little speed was lost. Cleto grinned at its success and straightened the wheel, seaspray now sprinkling his opposite cheek. 'I'll say it again, Sebastian, sir!' the sloop's captain bellowed while his sailors tied down the lines. 'You better know what you're doing!'

'It's a bloody ghost ship,' Seb responded, pushing his way to the bow. 'I haven't got the slightest idea!' His boots came to the foot of the staysail. Before him, the ever-expanding image of the Frontiere beckoned, laughing as he was.

There had been no time for second-guessing. As soon as

Seb had seen those wings, he knew he must chance it. All his dreams of a new life drifted away to the south, and brave stupidity found root. *Father thought it a ghost ship. He was mad with lust for it, the fool! Wouldn't he froth if he knew I would find it first, and see for real what it truly is?* He marvelled at how quickly his course had shifted, how quickly the Frontiere had sucked him in. *It cannot be!* Halfeye Warhawk danced on the edge of memory, his eye patch dark beneath his long, curled locks. His was a face Seb had meant to forget. Instead, he was rapidly forgetting Kit's, and Bart's, and all the others. *I must know what trick this is! I must know!*

The sloop beat through the waves, the late light catching each disturbed droplet before it fell back to its family. The Frontiere grew clearer and clearer, and bigger and bigger. Seb could not tear his eyes from it. *There's no way! It cannot be!*

The ship was firmly anchored between Dusty's beach and Cecil Island. Its crew were worrying about atop its decks, undoubtedly concerned for the oncoming vessel. *They don't look like ghosts to me*, Seb smirked.

'Sir!' Cleto's hurried voice bounced along the sloop's length. 'What action shall we take?'

Seb retreated from his outpost, stomping amidships toward the helm. 'Ready the skiff. I want to board the ship before it can get its sails down.'

'What of the cannons, sir?'

'Cannons?' Seb whirled. Indeed, the Frontiere was readying its artiliary. Gunports were opening and men were lifting carronades over the starboard bulwark. 'They won't be ready in time.' He hesitated. 'But forget the skiff. Head around and approach from behind. Get as close as you can. I will board this ship, at any cost!'

'They'll kill us!' Cleto resisted. 'They're probably... immortal, or—'

'They're not ghosts!' Seb roared. *They can't be!* He stopped beside the wheel. The sound of panicked shouting reached into to his ears. There was no turning back. He gripped his chin, breath heavy. 'They won't attack one man,' he stated. 'I'll go alone. Get me a grapple. And reef the sails. There's no sense in hitting them too hard.'

Cleto gasped, a cocktail of excitement and fear coursing through him and his men. It was all insane. 'What do you mean to do, sir?'

'I don't know,' Seb chuckled. He stabbed a crazed scowl at one of Cleto's mates. 'Get me a grapple!' he repeated.

Cleto swallowed. 'You better know what—'

'Stop saying that!' Seb shouted, his world spinning. *Is this even real?*

The Frontiere's masts rose now above the sloop. Cleto's crew dashed over the deck, pulling down half of each sail to slow it. As carefully as he could, given their enduring speed, Cleto guided his vessel up beside the ship, and began to pass it.

The Frontiere's broadside soared over the sloop's flank, a wall of oak and iron. Seb at last found himself face-to-face with the elusive ghost. *Got you!*

Cleto's mate materialized with the grapple and rope. Seb seized them hungrily. The sloop was hurtling past the larger vessel with unforgiving pace, allowing only a few seconds for Seb to make the jump. Cleto was calling after him, though the pirate prince could no longer hear the words. All he knew was the Frontiere's railing, high above. A pack of blunderbusses peeked over it, paired with the terrified faces of would-be spirits. Seb was mindful to avoid them when he thrust the grapple's hook into the air.

All sounds ceased as the hook zipped through salt and wind. Seb's heart stopped. Time stopped. All senses vanished. The sloop's deck faded. The sky blackened. The warm sting of the evening air was gone. Even the gushing friction of the rope as it rushed through Seb's loose palm had all but disappeared.

Then the hook caught, squarely around the ghost ship's railing. Seb tugged it to make sure it held. It did. *Not a bloody ghost ship at all!* The world jolted as it started up again, in all its noisy chaos.

Seb leapt from the Sloop's deck, feet flailing through the spray at the end of the grapple's rope. His fingers worked themselves deeper into course strands, bracing as he smashed against the Fontiere's hull. Beneath, the sloop was already gliding away.

He twisted his body, lifting his feet to the oak, hauling himself higher. The guns did not fire, he noticed. Whether it was due to the angle or general confusion, he could not be sure. Thankful nevertheless, he walked up the wall, his practiced elbows yanking his weight up and up the rope.

It was only a matter of seconds before Seb was clambering over the ship's gunwale to alight briskly on the main deck. A sense of accomplishment flushed over his features. He had boarded many a ship by grapple, but never from such a small vessel.

His elation sank when he became aware of his surroundings. Brushing away his hair, he whirled cautiously. He was circled by gruff sailors, each with either a blade or blunderbuss pointed at his chest. They carried a fresh eagerness on their expressions, tinged with a drop of trepidation. They awaited the intruder's next move with teeth clenched.

After a pause, Seb's tension eased. His decision to board alone was already validated. If there had been even one intruder more, the seemingly volatile crew may not have been so restrained.

He cleared his throat, testing not the depth of his host's patience. 'I am Sebastian Seablood, son of Theodore Seablood, captain of the Seablood Fleet and Sealord of the Northern Sentinels. I come to parley with your master.' *Whomever that might be.*

Some of the Frontiere's crew dropped their weapons, though not enough. A strange look of recognition overwhelmed the assembly. It was a look of expectant lustfulness, a look that troubled Seb even more than the swords. He opened his mouth, but could think of nothing more to say.

Consequently, those gathered stood still, as if caught in stalemate. The creaking of the dormant ship floated into the darkening sky, where the breeze fluttered around the ship's tall and magnificent masts. The only sound that stood abreast of the calm was the muffled cry of Cleto's sloop, which was scrambling around somewhere below, trying not to run aground on Dusty's Beach.

Seb drew a deep breath, filling his lungs with wet air. He centered himself, his hand reaching instinctively for the hilt of his cutlass. He forced it away before he even remembered it was not there at all. *What am I meant to do now? Are we going to stand here all night?*

He went to repeat his title and intention, when one of the silent crew finally moved. Without a word, the sailor pushed into his companions, opening a passage through their ranks. He pointed a pale finger uncertainly at the giant sterncastle. When the others realised what their comrade was doing, they folded back, weapons still held firmly in their hands.

Seb had no idea what to think. *I'm on the bloody Frontiere! That sterncastle should be on the bottom of the ocean. This cannot be!*

He stepped forward. Before he could stop himself, he was pacing with fierce determination up the quarterdeck's stairs toward the ornately decorated entrance of the ship's chunky tower. *I will solve this mystery. I will.* Throwing caution to the wind, he swung open the door and charged inside. A fistful of ghostly sailors poured in behind him, pressing their blades right up to his back.

Within, no lamps had been lit, yet the fading light that hummed through the windows illuminated enough for Seb to perceive the important details. It was the captain's chamber—no doubt—which was lavishly decorated and immaculately maintained. Oddly, there were only two occupants, besides those who had entered with him. A striking woman was nestled by the open curtains of a four-poster bed, though she could not hold Seb's attention for long. Not beside the man in the bed.

Even in the evening obscurity, the man's features drew Seb

in, a maelstrom pulling at his memories. The man was no more than a rotting corpse, but his wiry beard was unforgettable, and over one eye he wore a patch. The other eye was only really half an eye, mangled as it was. It peered through terrible pain at its newest visitor.

Halfeye Warhawk! Seb could not believe it. *It can't be. It can't be! He is dead!* His jaw dropped, and the floodgates of reminiscence burst open. He could remember standing in the same very room, with all the particulars—the ones he could see—completely unchanged. The only difference was that the old man was even older, dangling over the very edge of life.

'Halfeye.' Seb's voice was no more than a breath. He stumbled forward to reveal his own façade. The woman refused to move, so Seb knelt beside her. He felt as though he might faint at the slightest provocation. Halfeye's half-eye widened in recognition, but he did not speak. Perhaps he could not speak, Seb realised.

'If you're really Halfeye,' said Seb, 'you'll remember me. Sebastian Seablood.'

Halfeye's crusty head rolled toward him, and a crusty voice dripped out of it, crackling like the last embers of a fire well finished. 'I remember you. Sebby. You're... Teddy...'

Abruptly, it hit him. Ted had betrayed this man. Taken everything from him. Killed him! Seb jolted back, realising who he was in the eye of the old face before him. He scrambled to explain himself. To explain away the most horrible of mutinies. 'I've left my father,' he said, as if it would help. 'I've left him, the Blood Hammer, I've left it all. I want no more of it. We should never have sunk your ship.'

Seb had never felt remorse at what the three sealords had done to Halfeye. In truth, he had never encountered a need to think about it before this exact moment. What was done was done. But presently, he coud not help feeling sorry for the dying captain. He could not help but feel like the man's fate was Seb's own doing. Emotion choked him, and wonder blinded his two eyes. He struggled to convince himself it was not real. Or that it was.

The old man smiled through his mossy beard. 'You were always a good boy,' he said, as breathless as his visitor. His eye rolled up and down. 'But see. Ted never sank my ship. Here it is. See? See?'

Seb could barely accept what he was hearing, what he was seeing. *But it has to be real! It has to be!* He nodded. 'Yes. I see.'

Halfeye coughed a weak and deathly cough. 'I thought God had turned his... back on me.' His voice shook with both sadness and joy. 'Soon, I will meet him face to face. Sooner than I had hoped.'

Seb leant forward, head spinning as fast as it could spin.

'I was going to die, Sebby... with nobody to take my place... nobody to finish my work. All I needed was an heir. A son. And now...' He coughed. 'Thank you, God.'

18

A bed of sticks, a leg bristling with thorns, and now the old man was dead. At least they were not blaming it on her, she was relieved to discover. It was just as likely they would suppose the man's death was brought about through some magical curse she had carried with her. It would have been fair, she reflected. So many an Ijian death had been caused by sickness brought south by the people of the West.

The lady with the big cheeks gave her a polite nudge. Remembering herself, Alice picked up the pace. Her boots—tough as they were—had a hard time competing with the other women. Where her heels sought solid footing, the Ijians' dark-skinned toes merely kissed the ground, as if hovering through the brush. Still, she was compelled to maintain her position in the line. It wormed its way swiftly downward. Determined, she forced herself on, her breath heavy and her skin dripping with sweat.

Some of the women behind her giggled, making hushed comments in their positively impenetrable language. Alice deduced by their tone that they were weaving jests about her uncoordination, or something of the sort. *One of your elders has just died!* Alice thought. *Shouldn't you be crying, or sad, at least?* She shook her head. *Don't question it. Just go along with it. They might yet let you go free. That is, if they don't burn you as a living sacrifice.* She shook her head again. So far, the Ijians had not alluded in the slightest to any intention of harming her.

The big-cheeked woman nudged her again, this time with a little more force.

'I'm trying, I'm trying!' Alice complained, letting her feet fall with even more weight into the tangled foliage beneath them. She proceeded to trudge down the slope as fast as she could, following the head of the line. When a safe gap had emerged between her back and the lady behind it, she spared a moment to peek up from the rough path. The evening light was fading to naught over the distant smudge of the mainland, where a curtain of orange and purple hung low in the sky, filtering through the spindly branches overhead. Just down from where she stood, she could see the same light tickling the water, forming a thousand shards of colour that flicked in and out of existence. Between the water and the trees, a great fire curled upwards, spitting its sparks into the surreal vista. *Fire*, she thought, and shivered. Heat came gushing through her skin as she mentally relived her family's narrow escape from their burning house in Gold Harbour. It had been Ijian fire that led her to this place, only to be confronted with it once more.

The footsteps of the big-cheeked woman approached, so Alice sped off down the path again. *Ijians chased us from the mainland,* she mused. *Who would have thought they were on the islands too?!*

A light crunch sounded as her boot sank into dried coral. She had made it to the beach. What sadness Alice had expected from the Ijians following the death of one of their eldest seemed finally to smack her in the nose. The women's light-hearted chuckles floated away on the soft breeze, which coated the coarse beach in a deep reverence, a solemn silence. All that sounded now was the persistent rippling of the waves and the focussed labour of the men who tended the crackling fire.

A sandy hand clasped Alice's wrist and dragged her into position. Like most of the others, she soon found herself part of a large semi-circle that embraced a few important men and women who remained in the middle by the fire. Their arms and chests were decorated with thick white stripes and circles. Already, Alice could sense something magical. She surrendered herself unconsciously to the spectacle, absorbing every curious detail as the warmth of the flames caressed her tired flesh.

The beach was decorated like nothing she had ever experienced. Wooden poles and leaf-shaped boards sprouted from the pale coral all around, which itself was soaked in the ashes of a thousand fires. A dozen canoes fashioned of bark sheets snuggled up near the trees, where beautiful oars formed a fence of sorts, protecting the exposed coast from the leaves. Closer to the fire, the men had jammed spears into the ground so that their points pricked the purple clouds. The spears formed a ring around the inner circle, keeping Alice and the other women at bay. Within the ring, the dead body lay atop a nest of sticks and leaves, as naked as the rest of the tribe, glistening with an odd moisture.

The outer Ijians sat, cross legged. Big Cheeks made sure to guide Alice in mimicking. The coral felt sharp even through her breeches. She imagined how uncomfortable it must have been for the bare backsides of those around her. They did not appear to notice, however; they rocked about as if sitting on cushions.

Once everyone had settled into their rightful positions, the ceremony began without delay. At first there was humming. It swelled from the participants' throats in smooth pulses of sound. Then the voices' pitch slowly rose, forming a deep and harmonious buzz that vibrated in Alice's bones. One by one mouths opened, and hums became chants. The usual noises of the beach fell away, as if the water itself wished to listen to the tantalising charm that wound through the music. While the voices were afflicted with a nasal harshness, they came together to create something powerful, raw and wonderous. Alice could not help holding her breath.

Bursting next into the mix was the sound of sticks, clapping against each other in loose rhythm. Several Ijians in the outer circle held the stumpy instruments in tight fists, their dark arms shimmering in firelight as they struck them together. Gradually, the chants changed, feeling for the rhythm of the sticks until all sound and sight—even the waving sails of fire—pulsed together.

Alice's sense of misplacement evaporated. She was alone with the music, the night, the great fire's heat. The painted ones had started to dance. Their movements were harsh, fierce and repetitive, like the music. But beautiful. Their patterned flesh wobbled and their limbs jolted. They each rotated around the dead man, their faces averted.

Alice's heart pumped rhythmically in her chest. While the scene was layered with magnificence, there was anxiety too. The peaceful chiming seemed to get faster and more urgent. Before Alice could pinpoint what was happening, she was watching the dancers jump about in extreme arcs, poking their legs in the air and jabbing their noses forward and backward. Fear joined the other emotions. Alice was suddenly uncomfortable. She realised again who she was. A white ghost among dark strangers, trespassing on a ritual of obvious significance. She wanted to hide her face or run away, but she could not tear her eyes from the eccentric dancing.

The men began to stomp the coral. A pair of them crouched by the dead body, collected it under their forearms and hurled it into the fire. A cloud of sparks flowed from the flames, swaying into the blackening sky. Alice swallowed nervously, eyes now pinned to the staunch corpse of the old man, cushioned as it was by soft tongues of orange and red. *Ijian fire*, she thought angrily, whilst simultaneously knowing there was something quite spiritual about it, something that was not worth her anger. Hesitantly, she allowed her body to relax again, submitting to the layers of peace she unquestionably sensed.

The ceremony's energy eventually lulled, though it did not cease for the better part of an hour. By its end, Alice's legs were numb, and the comforting warmth of the fire had become sticky and awkward.

A couple of days earlier, Alice would have told any who asked that the Ijians were no more than a race of barbarous animals, envious of the Westerners and their advanced technologies, though of these opinions she was no longer sure. There was something in the dancing and the way the wild people traversed the slopes of Wimswind Island that made her wonder whether she had got it all the wrong way around. *But why would they burn down our house?* she reminded herself. *These Ijians may be friendly, but the ones near Gold Harbour…*

Big Cheeks helped her up as the gathering dispersed. While some men remained to watch the fire, most were combing into the island's forest, each maintaining purpoted silence as they left. Alice and the women with her soon joined them, and climbed up the island's side at a much slower pace than they had employed on the way down.

Alice became completely sightless under the clouded night sky, though she could tell when she reached the cave. The rustling of the island's canopy dimmed as the rock that jutted over the tribe's sleeping pit came nearer. A distinct and cool stillness wrapped her clothes. Tittering at the pale girl's disorientation, Big Cheeks set her down on her bed of crunchy foliage and disappeared into the shadows. With her head— now nestled against a pillow of twigs—both full of questions and as empty as ever it had been, Alice slipped into another uncomfortable night of dreamless sleep.

She awoke with the same incredulity she had experienced the morning before. *An Ijian camp! I can't believe it!* The fresh forest scent itched her nostrils. Already she could feel the strain in her neck, caused undoubtedly by the rigidity of her sleeping position. She tried stretching her muscles to alleviate some of the ache that wiggled into the back of her skull, though the sounds made it hard to focus on the task. She had overslept, she knew, despite her bed of sticks. The Ijians were already up and about, bothering around the cave with rustles and broken chatter. She wished she could have understood exactly what they were saying. She hardly needed terrible smarts to know they often discussed their guest, and probably what fate they might cook up for her. She opened her eyes to check on them. Almost immediately, the morning sun forced them closed again, filling her eyelids with dusty brightness. The cave was completely open on one edge, aside from the infrequent barriers that leant up against its rocky roof, so the morning glow was rudely allowed to cut through and harass those within. Even in the shade, atop the radiant chill of rocky soil, Southland's warmth reached out to her too, especially wet and dense this morning.

Alice rolled over, forcing back her eyelids. Twigs pricked at her waist and caught in her hair. Carefully, she picked them out and viciously rubbed her eyes. The fabric hanging from her shoulders felt heavy with sweat. She had discarded Kit's waistcoat, though her bulky breeches still smothered her—and she was certainly not ready to dispose of those, even if most of the Ijians managed without.

She wrung her fists over her eyes once more, blinking away the sandy sensation there. When she finally felt as though they might stay open on their own, she spun around to peer through the cave. *An Ijian camp! How have I ended up here?!* Her mind ambled back to where she had come from. *We were convicts… in Gold Harbour. That was only days ago… or was it weeks? God, and in that time… A ghost ship, a pirate ship, an outlaw's tavern, and now... this!* That last word stayed with her. Of all the places she could have thought to land, an Ijian camp on Wimswind Island was amongst the last.

When the hunters had found her two nights prior, she had thought her adventure had finally reached its end. The native people of Southland were infamous for their irritable nature and aggressive behaviour towards the pale peoples of the Western Nations. As a convict, she had often spied their dark-skinned figures prancing about the sparse edges of her coastal settlement, and had thought little of them. The officers kept them away, and made sure to keep the convicts from befriending them, in turn. Nevertheless, their violence became inescapably apparent when they burned down her family's new house. Alice had therefore expected a similarly violent reception when she barrelled into the Ijian hunting party after fleeing Wreckrest earlier that night, though her expectations had been bewilderingly far from fair.

After the hunters seemingly accepted her sack of carrots as a peace offereing, they had given her a long sideways look, and had tried to ask her questions in that sharp language of theirs. Eventually, they escorted her to their camp with crude but gentle guidance. She was then presented to the old men, who sat weakly beside a dying fire amongst an army of mostly naked tribespeople. She would never forget the smiles they gave her. Even by the wavering glow of hot coals, she could see their white teeth clearly. She had wondered at the time whether those smiles were more welcoming or menacing, but it had since become difficult to imagine them as ill-intentioned in the slightest, or to imagine herself a prisoner, for that matter.

Especially after some of the fiercer Ijians made every effort to construct her a comfortable bed, and left her alone to sleep with the women.

The next day bore events even more shocking. Despite her status as an intruder, the Ijian women had treated her like a daughter, sticking to her side and directing her when she was confused. They were kind natured and were always smiling. Whilst their mannerisms were harsh and their instructions strict, they would often touch her tenderly to check that she was unafraid.

They led Alice to a nearby stream, where she filled her stomach to overflowing with juicy water. Afterwards, the women took her on a foraging expedition along the contours of the island, each equipped with a light basket woven from fibrous roots. They trekked a lengthy distance through valleys bristling with thorny shrubs and sharp-pointed bushes before they found any fruit worth picking, but when they did there seemed to be something to pick from just about every tree. Alice had never before seen most of the fruits and seeds the women sought. Some were like small berries, and others were large and woody. One woman took a special interest in demonstrating how to locate the best brown seedpods from within the branches of a particularly gangling tree. Like all the Ijian women, it was hard to distinguish her from any other, except for her unusually bulbous cheeks. Big Cheeks thereafter became Alice's primary guardian, although many of the other women also took notable interest in her. There was the one with the flat nose, the one with the grey hair, and even one whose bare breasts hung almost six inches lower than anybody else's.

It was well into the hottest part of the day when they arrived back at the cave. Shortly after, Alice was left to her own devices while the women reclined lazily against green boulders. Instead of escaping, Alice could not help but linger, partially afraid the remarkably peaceful tribe might turn were she to try something unsavoury. She even joined them in a midday nap.

Food was prepared by late afternoon, once the men had returned from their own morning activities. The Ijians neglected to include Alice in this process, though she did not hold it against them. From all appearences, the strange seed grinding rituals performed with rocks and sticks by an open fireplace were too complicated for an outsider. Once it was over, Grey Hair shared some of her vegetables with Alice— including one of her own glistening carrots—and Big Cheeks brought her a handful of oysters with a lump of browned paste on a stick. Alice slurped down the oysters greedily, unsurprised by their lusciously fresh flavour, but nibbled slowly at the stick goop between chunks of carrot. The brown subtance was plain to taste and abnormally dense. She suspected it contained more than a few traces of dirt.

She managed to ingest a good half of her lunch before retiring her stick by the oyster shells. She peeked up to check that she had not offended anyone. As expected, a few pairs of near-black eyes quickly met her own, but instead of disgust, they were drowned in curiosity, and perhaps wariness. She noted interestingly that what she saw then was not a pack of beasts gnawing at their spoils, but a gathering of free people, sharing a civilised meal. The men and women—most of whom were still completely unclothed—sat intertwined in a casual ring around the cave, chatting to each other as they passed food from hand to hand.

Alice had thought the Ijian people were savages. *But they aren't*, she thought for the first time, eyeing the neat bundle of spears left just outside the camp. *They're just...* Something about the spears pierced her attention. Where there ought to have been a whittled point, something grey caught the filtered sunlight. Alice crumpled her cheeks and focussed her pupils on the spearheads. They were not stone, either. The bright detail was more reminiscent of something much less expected. *Nails!* she realised. The more she stared, the more she was certain; the spears had metal nails fixed to their ends. *How did they get those?* Her gaze then carved around the campsite, noticing things she had not thought to look for. There were bricks trimming the fireplace, lengths of string in the dust, and the barriers that leant against the cave's open edge were covered in cloth and tied down with rope. *Did they steal these things? Or did they...* An old, distraught woman hobbled out from behind the barrier Alice had been surveying. The outsider swiftly dumped her train of thought to watch what happened next with only the smallest portion of understanding.

It was a good hour after that before she finally realised one of the old men had died. She neither knew how nor whom it was, but after much commotion a pair of men filed out of the cave with the old soul's corpse slung between them, confirming her conclusion. They disappeared into the trees quickly enough, though the subtle unrest among the tribe lasted until dark. Then came the funeral ceremony.

Alice's skin tingled at the memory. Of all the strange things that had happened to her, the previous night's escapade on the beach was the most perculiar. She shivered, bringing herself back to the present.

Big Cheeks was standing outside the cave, examining baskets with Flat Nose. Alice gathered herself and got up, ducking so as not to hit her head on the cave's ceiling. She again considered removing her breeches—or even her shirt—as the day's muddy air was already becoming stifling. She lowered thumbs into the laces beneath her sweating stomach, hesitated, retracted. *I'm not an Ijian,* she told herself. *I just can't do it.*

She strode out from the cave hastily lest Big Cheeks leave her behind. She stretched again in the open air, the knots in her shoulders creaking as she pulled at them.

Big Cheeks' big cheeks bunched up above the corners of her glowing white teeth. She thrust one of her baskets into Alice's chest. And so the day began as it had the day before. Skipping breakfast, the women visited the stream for a drink then set off right away for the morning's foraging effort. This time they did not travel so far, a change for which Alice's legs were duly thankful. They wound down to the beach, following a half-beaten trail that looked to be shaped by nature rather than humans, and halted in a thick patch of foliage so near the water Alice could see rippling waves through the branches.

Unlike her first expedition, Alice was now awarded the freedom to forage alone. Big Cheeks and Flat Nose kept an eye on her at first, but later became wholly absorbed in their own delicate work, letting their apprentice fly unbound. Noticing this, Alice wandered gradually further away, acting as if she knew what she was doing, or where she was going. In truth, she did not recognise a single species of tree. She wormed through the tangled forest hoping to find one she was sure Big Cheeks had shown her the day before, but stumbled upon no such luck. Most of what she saw was gnarled trunks wrapped in crusty bark and scratchy bushes with thin leaves. After a time, she discovered an unfamiliar shrub with tiny berries in it, all arranged together in clusters. Embarassed that her basket was yet empty, she started breaking off some of its minature red and green branches.

Once her basket had accumulated some weight, Alice abandoned the shrub to dawdle toward the beach, driven more by fancy than duty. Crisp, white coral shone through the leaves as she neared, and the soft churning of the Rainbow Sea trickled ever clearer into her ears. A man's voice weaved through the sea's song. Alice jumped at the sound, unsure if she was intruding on something she should not. Curious nevertheless, she crept closer still to the beach, pressing into the green of a low-drooping tree branch to conceal her approach. When she was near enough, she could see partially along the bay's coast through the leafy shelter of her hiding spot. She gasped when she realised what was there, quickly throwing a hand over her lips to muffle the leak.

Where the fire had been the night before, fresh ashes were now splayed, dry and motionless, shielded from the southeasterly wind by the island's peak. The decorations were still there, poking out from the bleached coral like they themelves were sentinels, hired to guard the row of precious canoes adorning the edge of the jungle. One of those canoes, however, was out of place. It was half buried in the lapping waves that stroked the shore. Beside it lingered three Ijian men, their lean and dark bodies naked but for a few furry arm bands. There was no hope of recognising their faces, especially so far away, but Alice decided they could not have possibly been from any tribe other than her own.

At their feet was a turtle. Big and brown, finished with beige. It slumped atop the coral, dead. Alice paid it little attention. It was not the turtle that grappled her curiosity so. It was the pirates.

She knew they were pirates for their hardy clothes, their sickly posture, and for the white jellyfish painted on the bow of their tiny rowboat, which was hauled over the coral halfway between her hideout and the naked men.

Three Ijians against four pirates! Alice bit her lip. *Surely the pirates have the advantage.* But there was no violence to be seen. Where she expected blood, there were only voices. Muffled voices, too distant to decipher. Each one talking over another. At first, she thought the two parties did not understand each other, but their body language soon said different. From where Alice spied, it almost seemed as though they were haggling.

Suddenly, one of the pirates cried out and raised a sword. Surprisingly, the Ijians flinched not at all. That was when Alice noticed the curved blades on the ground. They were aligned as if they had been affectionately placed there, just outside the decorated stretch of beach.

Alice's forehead wrinkled. Her gaze returned to the leaf-shaped boards that circled the ashes. *It's sacred land,* she thought. *And the pirates know it. They must.* The Ijians' spears were visible too, thrust into the dirt by the canoes. She looked back at the pirate who had shouted. It was not a sword in his hand. *A chain,* she saw. *They're trading!* The concept was so unexpected she heard herself gasp. *I didn't think that… I didn't know… I never would have thought…* It was less so the pirates' civilised demeanour that shocked her—she had witnessed such aboard the Black Beast—but rather the immovable amity of the Ijians. Here stood a handful of those wild tribesmen, making peace with pirates in the heart of their sacred temple. At every turn, the savages had proven just how little they were like savages at all. The officers from Gold Harbour had painted a very different picture. Her fingers curled unintentionally into a fist as her eyes were drawn into the marvel of the extraordinary exchange.

The turtle's shell shrugged as an Ijian shoved it through the coral with his foot. *How did they get that? They must be mighty fisherman if they were to catch one of those in one of… those.* The bark-built canoe bobbed up and down in the waves, giggling.

Two pirates lifted the turtle between them, its paddles hanging limp over their shoulders. The four then parted from the naked men and shifted their feet over the beach respectfully as they retrieved their swords. Prize in arm, they subsequently made their way back towards their boat. Towards Alice.

Oh! Oh no! Alice snatched her basket and pounced into the bushes. Coral cracked beneath her quick steps. She did not have time to check if the pirates had heard her. She sprinted through the trees, sticks whipping her breeches, tearing new holes in her shirt. Sweat coated her immediately, collecting dust as she bounced up the steepening slope. *Not again*, she thought, the sores from her last chase spinning to the forefront of her consciousness.

A shadowy figure swooped in before her. Alice shrieked and tried to dodge, but solid hands caught her, forced her to stop.

Alice waved her head. 'No no no!' she cried.

Big Cheeks shook her. 'Aaah!' she growled. She kept shaking until Alice ceased her struggles. When the outsider realised who it was, her heartbeat slowed, though the sweat went nowhere. 'You,' she sighed, tears in her nose. 'It's just you!'

Big Cheeks loosed her grip, frowning at Alice's basket. Sheepishly, Alice lifted it to her chest with arms sore from Big Cheeks' tight embrace. The basket was empty.

Instincively, Alice spun to see if her berries had dropped nearby. They were nowhere to be seen.

She turned back to Big Cheeks. 'Sorry,' she said.

The woman laughed, touching Alice on the forehead to wipe away some of the sweat.

Alice resisted awkwardly. 'Aren't you angry?!' she snapped.

Big Cheeks stared at her with those deep, black eyes. Unreadable, unemotional.

'I don't get it!' Alice cast aside the basket to sign with her hands, supposing it would bolster her communication. 'Why are you so nice?! Why are you treating me like one of your own?! Like nothing is out of place? Well, I'm not! I'm not an Ijian. I'm Sirlish! I'm from another world! I don't know how to pick your... nuts... from your trees, or sing your... songs. We should be enemies! So what are you doing with me? Tell me, please. What do you want from me? Please, just let me know.'

Those black eyes did not flinch, did not waver. They held their ground, as did Big Cheeks' lanky limbs, still and soundless. It was impossible to tell whether the woman was attempting to interpret the younger's insane babbling, or whether she was simply waiting for it to finish. Only the birds replied, chirping their answer over and over again in perfect rhythm: 'Huh? Huh? Huh? Huh? Huh? Huh? Huh?'

Alice let her breath ease from her lungs. She dropped her head. 'I just don't understand what is happening.' She swallowed. 'You're meant to be dangerous. But you're friendly. But then... our house, it was burned down by Ijian fire. Why would you do that?'

'Fire?' Big Cheeks responded, handling her speech like hot coals.

Alice squinted, surprised. 'Fire? You understand that word?' She made flames with her fingers.

'Fire,' said Big Cheeks. It might as well have been a *yes*.

Memories of searing heat tore through Alice's skull. She recalled the panic, her brother's shouts, and the burn she wore on her arm. 'Oh,' she said, flipping her left wrist to show Big Cheeks. Where the flames had licked her, the skin was smooth and spotted, but not as red as it had been. The meagre smudge was not nearly as serious as the injury Wesley had suffered.

'Ijian fire,' Alice explained, pointing to the burn with her right hand.

Big Cheeks drew a sharp breath, moaned. She held Alice's arm softly as those black eyes filled with moisture. To Alice's complete amazement, she saw that the Ijian was crying.

'Fire,' she sobbed.

19

The Frontiere was headed west through the Blackbone Passage. Langdon Island towered to the south, and the mammoth mass of Wimswind Peak bulged into the swirling sky in the north, sliced into a hundred pieces by the ship's rigging. Clouds had amassed directly above, allowing not a streak of blue between them. *As if they know! Even the sea... it's restless... mourning.*

It would rain soon. That much was certain. And when it rained in Southland, it never simply rained. The heavens would open, and an ocean from above would crash down onto the ocean below, perhaps for an hour, perhaps for a week. But rain was certain.

The shrouds are shaking, the hatches are shut. And me! I feel so...

Wind swept hair drenched in muggy moisture over his face. It was a wind that ought carry him past Warhawk's Bluff before nightfall. But the sails were packed away, and the ship was slowing. This was no time to hurry. Even so deep within the heart of Wulfric Blackbone's feeding ground, respect had to be paid.

The King of the Rainbow Sea was dead.

And this time, it was no mutiny. Nor murder. No swords, no guns, no waves. God himself had called Halfeye Warhawk beyond life, to the lands outside knowledge and time. In his wake braced Sebastian Seablood, boots planted before the helm of the deceased's legendary ship, sleeves rippling about sturdy forearms. His grim expression waited patiently as the unruly crew huddled together in the vessel's waist.

They shifted nervously. Under the circumstances, they knew not what to do. None of them were true Southlanders, nor pirates at all. Those who could bear weapons with even the slightest competence were assembled closely by the pirate prince's rear, their blades drawn beside loaded pistols. Even of those, few were fluent in Sirlish.

A rabble! Seb cursed. He could scarecely accept the great Halfeye Warhawk would hire such an unqualified pack of commoners to tame the most revered vessel south of Brindia, though his propensity for disbelief had all but melted of late. After all, here he stood aboard the very ship he had watched sink four years prior. He did not know how it was possible— not yet—but there was positively no denying the truth in it. The planks were solid beneath his soles, and the sailors peered up at him with the lost eyes of the living rather than the cold gawk of the dead.

I never saw him die, Seb reminded himself, as he had been forced to do countless times over the course of the night. *Not back then. I watched the ship sink, but I never saw Halfeye's body. Nobody did.* He swallowed. *But now I have. I saw it this time. I felt it.* The leathery touch of Halfeye's lifeless flesh still lingered on his fingertips. *No! This is no time for emotions! I must be strong.*

I must show them that I am strong. Or else…

Halfeye's woman was beside him, her expression as rigid as his own. Her face was as perfectly shaped as the Frontiere itself. Her golden hair fluttered softly in the breeze, and her sailor's outfit failed to hide the enthralling curves of her flawlessly figured trunk. *She is hiding it too,* he realised. *The pain. She's better at it than I am. Maybe it's her. Maybe she should be—* He scrapped the thought, returned to the eager mass beneath him.

'Your captain, Halfeye Warhawk, is dead,' he confirmed, with a loud voice devoid of sentiment. 'His illness took him where we cannot follow, just this night gone.'

The crew rustled, a whisper humming through their ranks. The news was not wholly unexpected, so many attentions remained unbroken.

'Your captain…' he drew an extended breath. *Just… Ahh! What else can you do now? Perhaps— No! No! It's too late!* '…He named me his heir. To captain the Frontiere. And the Warhawk legacy.'

His mouth shut, formed a straight line. He tensed, his body motionless, prepared for anything that might be hurled at his unfamiliar face.

Whispers now hissed amidst the crowd, louder than before. But that was all. The clouds continued their silent gathering, and the ship settled into its position in the channel, exhibiting no eagerness to press on. Worried faces glared at him. Faces that would neither object nor trust. Faces lost.

'My name is Sebastian—' he cut himself off. His credentials would be of no use, he decided. He felt for his cutlass. It was not there. His heart leapt into his throat.

'It's true,' the woman shouted, smashing the tension. Rose, she had called herself. Her beautiful eyes sparkled with suspended tears. 'Anyone there when Halfeye died will say so,' she said, gesturing at those behind her. 'This is what he wanted.' She shot a piercing scowl at Seb, who caught it with brow lowered. He barely noticed the sting in her pupils, marvelling instead at the striking way her voice combined harsh authority with sweet femininity. *No!* he hounded himself. *This is not the time to be thinking about... her... Halfeye Warhawk has died! He was alive again, and now he is dead again! Just like that!*

Rose spun ferociously and forced her way through the line of armed sailors to vanish behind the sterncastle's royal door. She might as well have wailed, for all the stomping she made.

Seb wanted to follow her, to ask how she felt, but he knew it was a bad idea. Not only were nearly fifty men watching his every movement, he was entirely positive she did not want to be followed.

He regarded the crowd, all squashed together on the near motionless deck. Opening his mouth, his tried to discharge his first order. But no words came. *What am I bloody well meant to do now?* He took half a step away from the helm, all too aware the crew was waiting on his next move.

The temptation to drive the Frontiere further south whisked through his consciousness, an opportunity so juicy he almost reached for it right away. *I wanted to escape, but here I am. Captain of the Frontiere. Bloody captain of the ghost ship!* His thoughts lifted from his skull and drifted through the heavy air, to imagine the Sentinels from high above as a navigator would view them on a chart. He saw Cleto's sloop, safely back in Seablood waters, on its way to notify Ted of his son's ghostly fate. He saw Kit's waterlogged corpse, cushioned by coral as it wasted away beneath the sea where it was dumped. He saw Salvino skulking in his father's shadow, smiling his toothless smile. He wanted nothing to do with it.

His imagination veered southward, where the chart's lines were blurred and unknown. *This is truly where I wish to go! It's where I was headed and where I must head. I'll take the Frontiere with me. As soon as I can, I'll do it!* His thoughts finally floated down, resting now on the image of Halfeye's cold, lifeless body. It was yet tucked into the sheets of the sterncastle's illustrious bed. *But first… The captain must be laid to rest. The way he ought. Not where he was betrayed, nay. North of there, with Bart. So the ocean can drag him far away.* Seb nodded to himself. *But we can't double-back, in case we've caught the attention of a Blackbone scout. So…*

Seb leaned forward, craning. All eyes that had wandered returned now to the new captain.

'Loose the sails. All hands on duty, back to your stations. We'll stay on course. If the weather's kind, we'll yet make it to Stinger's Bay before we set anchor for the night.'

A tentative 'aye aye' trickled from the Frontiere's waist. It was more than enough enthusiasm for Seb, who felt not to hold even the slightest authority over the men below him.

Somewhat satisfied, the captain whirled to face the Sirlishmen at his back. He eyed them warily, asking with his stare whether what he had commanded was indeed acceptable. He assessed their cutlasses, and the fingers held firmly against pistol triggers. 'Put those away,' he said, 'and get some rest.' Most of them had been up all night, witnessing Halfeye draw his final breaths, yet they appeared not in the slightest way eager to retire. Instead, the weary soldiers held their ground, frozen in either defiance or confused uncertainty. Seb narrowed his gaze, challenging them, then turned away. *If they want to stab me in the back, let them do it now.* But no such thing occurred. To Seb's partial relief.

A heavy flapping poured forth as the great square sails dropped from their spars and heaved in the foreboding wind. As their black surfaces straightened, so did the white emblem painted upon them: a ferocious eagle with wings spread wide. *Halfeye's Warhawk...* Seb frowned. *Or is it mine now?*

He tilted his head and let the thick afternoon air flood tired lungs. Then, allowing no time to reconsider, he scrubbed his hands on his breeches and placed them on the ship's wheel.

The rain came soon after. It soaked Seb's shirt before he had a chance to take it off, and filled his boots so they were twice as heavy. Fortunately, the wind remained agreeable, meaning the Frontiere was free to run through the storm unhindered and unseen. Like the ghost it was, the ship slipped secretly past Warhawk's Bluff to sneak into Sting Bay before the grey light faded to black. The journey was dangerous, curving as it did through tight channels while visibility was all but nonexistent, but the crew proved surprisingly adept. They observed Seb's orders with meticulous obedience.

When finally the anchor dropped, not even the moon could be spied upon the water. No lamps were lit abovedeck, not even for the few sailors that remained to pursue their pointless watch.

Even the ruckus from the mess deck where the crew was undoubtedly drowning in rum was swallowed by the tremendous hiss of rain.

On and on that rain went, rolling over the ocean, darting through the darkness and frothing up the Frontiere's surface. Seb lingered by the helm, even as his clothes tried to pull him belowdecks with their water-soaked weight. Hair was stuck to the side of his face, and droplets hammered at his shoulders.

His mind was empty. At last, the absurdity of his circumstance had grown so massive he had nothing left to ruminate over. To think on it was to risk going insane. He was tired, spent, and amidst his wilful flight he had suddenly become the captain of Halfeye Warhawk's kingly ship—a ship that ought not exist at all—for reasons he was want to understand. If long-dead Winston Wimsworth were subsequently to sidle up beside his muscular shoulder, he would not have blinked at all.

A lone figure snagged his attention. It looked nothing like the famed Sirlish explorer, but rather more soft. It was perched on the main deck just below, leaning over the ship's delicate railing to stare off into the blackness beyond. The figure was scarcely more than a smudge to Seb's eyes, yet the hue of its golden hair shone just brightly enough to cut through the mist, betraying its identity. Most intruigingly, she was leaning in the same spot Seb used to frequent of a night on the Blood Hammer.

The woman had forgone her coat, and the rain stretched her loose shirt tightly over her skin. She seemed not to notice it. Neither did she react to Seb's approach, which was plainly heralded by the slop of his waterlogged footsteps.

Her unmoving stance prompted Seb to hesitate. He halted outside her view while the rain pounded everything, shutting the two of them off from the world. He had not thought about what he would say, or that perhaps he should not say anything at all. In the end, he simply stood there, waiting.

When she obstinately sustained her silence, Seb knew she was angry with him. 'I didn't want this,' he said, raising his voice to combat the rain's incessant noise. 'I didn't want to be named captain. When I said yes to Halfeye, I—'

'You think *I* wanted it?' Rose snapped. Her jaw barely budged when she spoke.

Seb choked on the rain, briefly.

'You're the only one here who knows how to run a ship like this,' the girl added. 'And you came to us right at the last minute… And if you hadn't…' She paused. 'Maybe it was… meant to be…' Her forehead lowered, the rain draping golden strands over her nose.

Slowly, Seb stepped up to the railing and leant his elbows against it. *I don't know what she wants. But I didn't ask, either way.* He abruptly realised that the two, in fact, had not really spoken at all.

Rose finally turned, to glare through the rain and shadow at her captain. Seb evaded her eyes. He knew that looking upon them was to gaze into one of the most beautiful faces he had yet discovered, and he dared not be distracted by it. Her features were soft, her skin smooth, and her mouth came together at each end in sweet little points that held between them lips neither too full nor too thin. And those eyes. They were so pure, yet behind them lurked something dark and mysterious that begged to be studied. He had noticed it the first time he had seen her. That her breasts matched perfectly with her hips, her luscious curves only lightly hidden behind the raiment of a deck-bound sailor. That her dead-straight hair hung over one cheek, dangling just shy of her rounded shoulders. To Seb, she was breathtaking. But she had been so cold to him, so indifferent.

'There's just one thing…' she said, her voice hard. 'You're going to continue his… work… aren't you? That's what he wanted.'

Seb huffed, still staring into the wet, wet black.

'Aren't you?' Concern flavoured the contempt in Rose's tone.

'How can I say? I don't know what the man was up to. I suppose you do.'

'I do. We have to finish what he started, we have to—'

'Don't… stress about it. I'll gather the mates in the morning. We'll discuss plans then.'

'But it—'

'Give me this one night. Rose. Please. It's been an impossible day. Bloody Halfeye Warhawk died, if I'm not completely mistaken. Doesn't that… I mean… My brother died. Not long ago, he died. He was killed, actually. And we dropped his mangled body into the ocean. I watched it disappear right below me. The man who had always been there. My whole life. Always there… After that I… I didn't want to do… anything! Not for…'

This time it was Rose's turn to choke on the rain. She shut her mouth and blinked out to sea. Seb stopped, unable to continue.

And so, the two strangers slumped, voiceless, while the rain tore through the rigging to cascade over their stunned bodies. Beneath its drone, the Frontiere's deck was solid and slick. There was no breeze in the bay to make them cold, and nothing dry that could get any more drenched. Seb wondered if they could lean there all night.

'I didn't know him for long,' Rose stated eventually, snapping the roar of silence in two.

Seb's eyes came open when he heard her voice. He had not realised they were closed. 'Who, Halfeye?'

She nodded, and drew a breath full of rain and wet air. 'But I had a husband.'

Seb finally faced the girl. Everything drooped from her body like seaweed, especially her sloppy hair. It was impossible to tell whether there were tears amongst the buckets of water running down her neck. He imagined there might have been.

'And, now Halfeye...' She loosed a few sobs, but was astonishingly quick to suck them up into a stone-hard expression. 'Nobody cares,' she growled, replacing sadness with frustration. 'Even when you were named captain. Nobody cared. They just accepted it! They didn't yell, or fight, or... anything! And now they're all asleep. Probably. He was their *captain!* Their whole *purpose!*'

Now that he was looking at them, Seb could not pry his eyes from Rose's. They were so full of passion, of hurt. They overflowed with black water, like they were full to the brim with the stuff. He felt so sorry for her, so empty.

When Rose's steam had subdued, he saw it fit to speak again, though he did so carefully. 'Nobody cared about Bart, either,' he said, his words bubbling through the black water on his own face. 'Not even my father. Not enough, at least.'

Rose's stare pierced Seb's own, burning with a hot flame as unquenchable as the anger that fuelled it.

'Everyone turned to me,' said Seb. 'As if I would take his place. I was better than him. Better at sailing. Better at commanding. Better at boarding. Better at fighting. Better at surviving. But I would never take his place. Never. He was the fleet's future. He was the only one. The only one my father cared about. But then… when he died… it was like his name vanished. Gone. To be replaced by my own. And they all thought I'd be happy about it. Happy about my brother's death.' His fists tightened. 'It came so easily to them. Forgetting. They were sad, I'm sure… but then they saw this ship floating on the horizon, and it all just… blew away.'

Seb could tell his prattling only served to feed Rose's already palpable anger, but he could not seal the leak now. He tried to stop, but the pressure quickly grew, backing up until the blabber came flowing once again. 'I talk to him sometimes,' he blurted. 'In my head I talk to him. I talk to him because… it seems like he's the only one who knows. The only one who cares. The only one who understands what it's like for me. But he doesn't understand. He's dead.' He hesitated. 'No one understands.'

Rose's eyes were locked with Seb's. Even through the black they sparkled, burning hotter and hotter. She pressed closer to him, the flames engulfing them. Then her chin came up, and she kissed him.

Cold, wet lips clutched at his, and her cheek dabbed softly against his nose. Water coursed over them. He turned his chest towards her, making no effort to pull back. His hands fell into her waist, and pressed on the saturated shirt that stuck to her sides. He pulled her closer, free of any resistence.

Lips working, she traced fingers up his arms, wrapped them around his neck. The curves of her hips began to move, writhing slowly against his hardening lump.

Seb's mind was no longer empty, but filled with the sweet taste of Rose's mouth. Unconciously, he let his hands scrape down and slide back up underneath her shirt. Though drenched and layered with tense goosebumps, her skin was impossibly smooth. Its chilled surface cushioned his palms as they edged around to the small of her back.

Suddenly, after the shortest time in the world, Rose pulled away. Seb leant with her, unable to give her up. She continued to retract until Seb's face came apart from her lips. Her eyes opened—still flaunting those intense flames—and looked at Seb with a sort of ferocious challenge. She was not pulling away, Seb realised. She was pulling *him*.

Her hair draped over her features in thin, dark spikes, shooting beams of water from their tips to her heaving chest and shoulders. Between those spikes, her expression was firm, cold, beautiful. Seb could not resist her invitation. He surrendered himself to the moment, and followed her into the sterncastle.

After their departure, only the heavy gush of black water remained, thundering in thick sheets against the shimmering deck of the Frontiere.

20

It was still raining when Rose's boots clapped against the longboat's hull. The feel of crusty bark crunching under the weight of her axe had not yet ceased vibrating through her elbows. It filled her with warmth, with satisfaction.

She dropped the weighty tool into the boat, its head splashing in the rapidly widening pool of water there. 'Off!' she commanded, striding swiftly to the bow. The men jerked into motion, heaving the boat, knee-deep in Sting Bay's spiky chop. When they had built up enough momentum, they hauled themselves aboard and each collected an oar from their respective flanks.

The other longboat was ahead of them, already gliding through the mist towards the ship's glorious silhouette. Eight paddles stirred the water beneath it. Soon, her own eight joined them.

The hammering noise of rain over water swallowed the boat. Rose spun to survey the shore they had left in their wake, but the weather already obscured it. Only the island's peak dared peep through the grey curtains of falling sky, illuminated from behind by the dull glow of morning's first light. Rose huffed crossly. She wished only to gaze upon her handiwork once more. *It is done,* she reminded herself. *The final pieces have been set.* A smile crept into her cheeks. Just as it knicked the edges of her lips, it fell again from her face. Her hand dropped to the place where her thighs met. She could still feel something there. So foreign. So uncomfortable. *Oh Wes,* she thought, but quickly stopped thinking it. More than a dozen pirates rowed at her command, pirates with swords and axes and strong arms. She straightened, shuffled her slippery shoulders. Weak emotions were no longer welcome.

Shouts sounded from the nearing ship's upper decks. The rain-smothered outlines of its busy sailors shimmered into view. Eveything was a shade of grey now. Not just the sky, but the ship, the horizon and the sea itself. Towards that dreary vision the longboat progressed, charging along grey waves until grey spars pricked out over Rose's head. Her boat curved around to huddle beside the Frontiere's daunting port wall. A rope ladder dribbled down to greet her, drenched and heavy. She swung onto it as soon as it licked the water, taking leave of the eight men that had rowed her from the shore. She had no knowledge of operating the davits—or in any part of hoisting the longboat back aboard the ship—and she had no interest in learning.

Despite feeling as if she were dragging her body through a waterfall, Rose managed to pull herself over the bulwark, where she had to squeeze through a clot of the Frontiere's iritating sailors before she could properly exhale. The men went about their fussing behind her, calling out to the passangers of the boats below, casting them ropes.

Out of the wet greyness that plagued the deck, a tall and

rugged pirate strode forth to meet her. His drenched hair was tucked behind his ears, and a great coat hung from his handsome shoulders, flapping wetly below him in big swells. This was a different man from the one she had previously met, though the grave glower pasted to his features hinted he still possessed the same underpinning soul.

'Where have you been?' he questioned before taking a breath. 'Where are the other boats?' He was trying to be angry. In fact, he was definitely angry, Rose resolved. But he interrogated her with a sort of rushed gentleness. It was pitiful.

The captain drew up within arm's length. He eyed Rose suspiciously and lowered his voice, somewhat emabrassed. 'You... You left. While I slept... I would have sent men searching... but all the boats are gone!' His lips shifted in puzzlement. 'What did you do?'

'I took them,' stated Rose, as firmly and as proudly as she could. She locked eyes with the captain, challenging him to dicipline her. She knew he would not.

The captain took the bait only half-heartedly, speaking with just a little more volume. 'I'm now the master of this ship, aren't I?' His neck twitched, allowing him to count how many onlookers were listening through the grey rain. The curious ears clearly troubled him. 'Maybe I'm mistaken, but shouldn't you have—perhaps—consulted me before pinching all our boats?' His tone was so thick with sarcasm it made the air sticky.

Rose groaned. She could see the master's forehead crumple; he was terribly uncomfortable, yet he refused to properly demonstrate his anger.

'Come with me,' he commanded. He swivelled on the heels

of his boots and stormed off toward Halfeye's cabin. His great big coat bounced around his ankles.

Rose followed with her head held high. Rain splashed up her legs and streamed down her sides as she squelched along the Frontiere's grey planks. Leaving the crew outside, she trailed the captain into his chamber, swinging its delicate door wide as she went through it. The buzz of the storm racked the atmosphere within, though it was dry, and not so grey. Aside from the chill of beads still dripping from the tips of her hair, it was also warm.

The sheets of the four-poster bed were a mess, Rose noticed. *That bed,* she thought. Merely one day prior, it had played host to the dead carcass of the legendary Halfeye Warhawk. Even more recently, she had lain upon it with the Frontiere's newest captain, giving to that man what she had only ever given to her husband. At the time, she had felt no shame in defiling the old fool's resting place. Now, she looked at it with an agitated sense of regret. She wished Halfeye's body had not been moved, and that she had weathered the preceding night in solitude. *Oh Halfeye, what did I do?*

Captain Sebastian Seablood swooped past her and slammed the door shut, his hair dripping just as much as hers did. 'Rose, what have you done to me?' He circled her and plopped his backside onto the edge of the dishevelled bed, not before throwing his coat aggressively at the rug in the centre of the room. 'If you were using me, just say it!'

Rose did not say it. She tightened her lips and peered out the window at the greyness there.

'Rose... I woke up, and you were gone. Gone from my bed.

Gone with all the ship's boats. Every one! I was… worried…'
Seb paused in thought, then looked up at Rose. 'I'm giving you
a chance to explain yourself. One chance. Where are my boats?'

Rose met Seb's stare, then shied away in disgust. Who she
was disgusted at, she could not detect. She longed to erase what
had happened the night before. In that moment, she had felt
as if someone finally understood her pain. She had brushed the
edge of empathy, tasted the first drop of compassion to come
near her tongue since Wes left the living to their own devices.
And she lusted for it. Hungered for its flavour so fiercely she
had pounced on it. She had taken that comfort by the lips,
surrendering herself to passion and desire and the animal
within her. What followed was naught but empty sex. With a
hollow mind she had lain beneath Sebastian's panting body,
focussed only on the sweet pulse of his manhood within her,
and the fleeting ecstasy with which it came. But here was the
captain, sitting under her nostrils, restraining his wrath like he
owed her something. Like what they did was more than a blind
thrill.

But it meant nothing, Rose told herself. *It meant nothing. It
meant nothing! Nothing at all! You're not my lover, Sebastian, and
you never will be! Wes was my lover. And he was taken from me!*
The feeling between her legs still sizzled.

'Well?!' Seb was getting visibly mad. Finally.

'I took the longboats to shore,' Rose coldly explained.
'That's where I've been.'

'Aye, you took the longboats to shore,' Seb nodded, almost
contemptuously. 'And why, exactly?'

Rose straightened, as if she could will herself taller. Her fists tapped rigidly against her hips. 'We landed at the home of the island's Ijian tribe. We demolished their sacred beach, and broke all of their boats.'

'You...' Seb stood slowly, involuntarily. 'You... But... *Why?*' His eyes pleaded with her, begging for any excuse to keep his fury furled. Rose held that very excuse in her palm, though whether Seb would accept it was yet to be determined. 'It's part of Halfeye's plan,' she said.

'Halfeye's plan?' Seb paced over the cabin's luscious rug. 'I told you we'd discuss that in the morning!'

'Well, we had to do it while we were still in Sting Bay,' Rose rebutted. 'I tried to tell you—'

'And why in God's name would Halfeye want to... do... *that?*'

'To anger them,' Rose answered. 'So they would fight back and attack the town.'

'Halfeye wanted the Ijians to attack Wreckrest?! They'll bloody burn it to the ground!'

'Not if there's pirates there to stop them.'

'Pirates?! What pirates? Wreckrest is full of women, children, and grandfathers who've forgotten their own name!' Seb froze. His muscles rippled with tension and his teeth peeked out from behind stretched lips. He turned measuredly toward Rose's braced façade, his face still dripping with rain. 'Rose... What did he do to you? What are you doing for this dead man? You have to tell me. Tell me everything. Right now. I am your captain.'

Rose hesitated not. 'He wants justice,' she snarled.

'He's dead, Rose. Whatever he wanted... He doesn't want

it anymore.'

'So we should just forget about him?!' Rose's own fury began to surface. The stain of Wesley's blood burned hot on her skin.

Seb went to argue, but his mouth shut before the words spilled out.

'The three sealords ruined him,' Rose said. 'They left him for dead.' Warm droplets formed in her eyelids, mingling with the cold ones already there. 'And now he's actually dead. But his work isn't finished. The sealords must die! It was Halfeye's final wish!'

'Halfeye?' Seb spat. 'The revered legend of the Sentinels wanted Ijians to do his dirty work for him? Is that it? Really?'

Rose felt her insides rumble. 'The Ijians won't kill them. The sealords will kill each other. That's what they deserve!' She spoke with unhindered certainty. 'Both the Seablood and Blackbone traitors are angry enough now, and Stinger Dreadwind is already dead. All they need is to be brought together.'

'Bu—'

'That's where the other boats are. The cutters. They've gone to warn them. Dreadwind, Seablood and Blackbone. To warn them that Wreckrest is under attack.'

'By Ijians?!' Seb exclaimed. 'If you think they'll be lured like that… They just won't!'

'They'll go! They'll all go! And they'll all die!'

Seb gaped. 'Rose…' He was still, stunned and dumb. Rose could hardly believe she had let the man inside her. He was being so pathetic, so weak. For all his captainly accessories, he could not comprehend the harsh necessity of justice.

His brother was killed! How can he not understand?

'Rose…' Seb said again. He had become so calm, so mellow. Rose could not understand how it was possible. 'Can't you see?' he continued. 'It's madness. If this was truly all that stirred Halfeye's dying heart, then he was nothing but a madman. Not someone to feel pity for. Don't fall for it, Rose. Please. Don't get trapped in a madman's folly.'

He's trying to comfort me, Rose realised. *He is weak!*

'He was not mad!' she barked. 'He wanted revenge. It's only fair! He built this ship for it! He hired this crew for it!'

'He built thi—'

'Yes, he built it! An exact copy of the one they sank! And now you're its captain! If you don't want it, why are you even here? For his treasure?!' She was shouting now, her hoarse words scraping at her tender throat.

Seb gasped. 'Halfeye's Hoard?!'

'That's all you want, isn't it?! He told you where it is, and now it's all you care about!'

'He didn't tell me. Did he tell you?'

'You want to tear it out of me?! Do you?! Go ahead! I've got nothing else left! Nothing!'

Seb's composure burst. 'I don't bloody well want his treasure!' he exploded. He swiped at the mugs on the cabin's table. They clattered against the delicate cabinetry. Despite desiring such passion, Rose could not help but flinch at its sudden eruption.

The captain spun fiercely, waving his arms and gripping the air with dangerous, shaking fingers. 'I don't bloody want any of it! I was leaving! Running away! I didn't want this ship and I didn't want you! I didn't want any of this shit!' He kicked the wall so hard Rose thought his boot might have gone right through it. Its thump echoed about the Sirlish Oak alongside the roar of the torrential weather without. The noise swelled in a brutal crescendo, perfectly mirroring Captain Sebastian Seablood's fury.

Tentatively, Rose weighed back in, her temper steady. 'Then leave,' she said. 'Take the ship and sail away. The sealords will kill each other no matter what you do, and Wreckrest will be destroyed. It is done. There's nothing holding you here anymore.'

Seb stomped up to her, grim. His lordly presence towered high, his stormy hair dangling over her quivering forehead. 'One of those sealords was my father. Theodore Seablood. Nay! Bloody damn fool, he still is my father! And I will not leave him to die. Not by the hands of some dead man and his servant girl!'

Rose coughed, incredulous. *I am not a dead man's servant!*

'Get out,' Seb demanded. 'Get out! Get out!' He barreled past Rose's elbow to snatch at the door before shoving her through it.

'Bu—'

'Is this what your dead husband wants?' Seb scoffed. 'More death?'

Rose seized up.

'I didn't think so,' hissed the man, and he slammed the door in her face.

Rose almost fell over, the water on the grey deck slick beneath her soles. *Wes?! Wes?! Is he right, Wes?* She tried to recall her husband's face, yet all she could envision about was Seb's own, sneering back at her. Seb's face groaning over her naked trunk. *How dare you?* she thought. *You're weak! Halfeye's work must be finished! I shouldn't have let you become captain!*

Rage boiled within her chest. She reached a hand for the door, but stopped herself. She screamed in frustration, then pounced away from the richly decorated structure.

Across the deck she scrambled, indignantly scooting past the ship's prying sailors. *It's too late, Halfeye! He can't stop it now. They'll die. They'll all die!* She thrust heaving arms through the ratlines that ascended into the rain above the Frontiere's starboard extremity and yanked her way up. *Get me away! Just get me away!*

Her fingers burned as they clambered for grip, and her mouth filled with the tainted water that splashed in spears from the mast. Grey sheets of mist thickened under her sloshing boots as she climbed high into the ship's rigging. Twenty feet up, the sway was already sickening. She ceased her scurries to hang limp in the ropes. The bulk of the legendary ship slept heavily below her, shifting awkwardly from side to side. Rose dropped her face towards it and roared.

She had climbed the ratlines to escape the dry minds of the captain and his crew, yet even through the sharp fog she could still see them buzzing about. They cast her glances from here, from there. They continued until Seb came hurdling into the scene.

The freshly crowned captain plopped callously from the entrance to his distinguished cabin and zipped straight across to the forecastle, where he disappeared just as fast. Rose's acrobatics were quickly forgotten. The mindless rabble of sailors below was stirring in its captain's wake, distressed. *Half of them followed me like that, just a few days ago. But he's the captain. Of course they'd forget me to follow him. They'll forget Halfeye soon too, and everything he dreamed of! Even the gold he promised for their stupid pockets! Idiots! At least I had them wreck that Ijian beach before Sebastian could tell them otherwise.*

She ground her teeth to stop them from chattering. The breeze in the rigging was chilling her to the core, blowing as it was on her saturated shirt. The tenacious warmth of the heavy air was all that stopped her from retreating belowdecks. That terrible Southland humidity that banished the truest cold. Not like the bitter frost of Sirland in a lifetime long passed.

But I, Rose reminded herself, *will never forget. I'll kill them all for you Wes, and for Halfeye too.* She conjured Wesley's face in her mind's eye, but again failed to picture it with the clarity she desired. She could not remember how he looked when he laughed, or how he reacted when she cried, or what it felt like to have his arms cradle her neck while she drifted into dreamless sleep. The thought troubled her. It triggered Seb's words to resound in her head. *Is this what your dead husband wants?* She fought back tears. *Is this what you want, Wes? Or am I being stupid? I'm doing it for you. Really, I am... But is it really what you want? Halfeye was not my husband. You were! I'm not doing it for him, Wes, I'm doing it for you. I'm getting revenge. Isn't that what you want?*

Rose curled up, tangled in the ship's shrouds. She was alone and wet. Grey air twirled around her, and strangers scuttled below, guns and swords peeking out from under the lining of their waistcoats. In every other direction, the grey, chopping waters of the Rainbow Sea extended outward until their edges blended completely with the encroaching sky. *Oh Wes! What do you want?! What am I meant to do?!* In spite of her best efforts, she started to cry. Her sobs were noticed by some of the crew, though she could hardly summon the energy to care.

Is this what your dead husband wants? The words played over and over, bouncing around in her hollow skull like a rattle. *Wes! I wasn't doing it for Halfeye. He was the only one who… And his… But I don't care about him! Only you!*

Is this what your dead husband wants?

Oh Wes! They don't have to die! What have I done? Halfeye's enemies are not our own! Only… Dagger's face appeared to her, and the rattling ceased. She had witnessed that wicked face only a few times, but she could remember its every detail. The face of Wesley King's killer. *Dagger,* she cursed. *He is the only one that counts. If I can kill him, it will be enough.*

The commotion on the deck broke Rose's concentration. With the black sails tightly furled, her elevated vantage point gave her scope to view the entire ship from bow to stern. All over it, she watched the crew tense in concern.

Seb had returned. He marched now before four of the men that had accompanied her to the Ijian beach. Between them was suspended Halfeye's corpse, wrapped in dreary grey cloth. Hastily, Seb moved amidships to the gap in the bulwark meant for the gangplank. He tossed aside the wooden barrier latched there like it was no more than a scrap of paper. He nodded. When the crewmen hesitated, their captain drew a sword from his belt. The blade had been hidden by Seb's coat, now shining through the grey like lightning. It was Halfeye's sword, longer and less curved than a regular one.

'It's not as practical,' Halfeye had told her, during one of their numbered nights spent warm in his cabin. 'But if your crew thinks you can use it, then it's fearsome, and you may well never have to. That's one of my little secrets!' The memory of his laugh made her smile—just a little—and the taste of rum emerged in the back of her throat. *He was a good man.*

The crewmen threw his body overboard. And so Halfeye Warhawk was again cast into the ocean, vanishing beneath the waves to a symphony of raindrops. But he was not gone for long. After a few seconds, the legendary pirate's corpse bobbed up again to float rudely on the water's surface, flopping about in the storm.

Rose gasped. *Halfeye!* The vision of his stiffly wrapped carcass was repulsive, yet she dared not look away. Regardless of any irreverence the ship's new captain so suffered, Halfeye had deserved a proper funeral. That much was plain. He was a great man, a king among criminals. But now he wobbled in the sea like a rotted log, like broken debris that ought be cleared away. Looking at that *thing*, Rose at last wondered if he had ever truly been as magnificent as the stories supposed he was, or if he really was just another chunk of misplaced flesh. She searched for pity, but only disgust found her. Only hate.

'All hands on first duty,' called Seb. 'Ready the sails! We make south, back through the Blackbone Channel!' He turned his back on the place where Halfeye was dumped, and barrelled through the storm towards the helm, where he claimed his solitary post behind the ship's wheel.

The Blackbone Channel! Even Rose knew that was not the fastest way to Wreckrest. The main port may have pricked the far side of the island, but there was another on the west coast. Another that the Kraken used. *It's not right! What is he doing?*

Springing to action, she yanked her legs from the ratlines and slid down soggy shrouds to the railing. She dismounted swiftly into the tumult. Her heels splashed along the deck and stairs as she raced to Captain Sebastian Seablood's side.

'You cannot stop me,' he hissed as she neared. 'And don't even think about—'

'The Blackbone Channel? You're taking us to... the... away!'

'Away from what? My father will undoubtedly be chasing me. Especially if he knows which ship I've found. It would be quicker to double back if we're to keep him from Wreckrest.'

'But... Won't he head straight there?! If it's under attack?!'

Seb grimaced. His face was lathered with water and impatience both, his features stone cold. 'This ship'll be faster than the Blood Hammer in running winds. We'll catch him no matter which way he sails. Now back off.'

'What if he didn't chase you?' Rose questioned, resisting his dismissal. 'The Kraken! Doesn't it have a port on this side of the island? Wouldn't that be quicker?'

'Whatever you think you can do to stop me, it won't work!'

'I'm not trying to stop you. It would be quicker! Wouldn't it?'

'The Dreadwind port in Box Harbour?!' Seb was practically shouting at her, consumed with distaste for the girl. 'Why do you want us there, Rose? Why?!'

That's where I'll find him! Dagger! 'I changed my mind!' Rose exclaimed.

'You changed your mind? I don't believe you.'

'It's like you said! It's not what my husband would have wanted! All this death!' *The only death I need is Dagger's. That's all I need. Just give me this one thing!* 'We need to get there quickly! To stop the Ijians!'

At Rose's insistence, Seb released his hands from the ship's wheel and paced briskly back and forth in the space before her. His boots kicked heavy spray into her breeches, making them heavier and colder than they already were. 'You're right,' he said. 'We need to be quick. But I need to reach my father even quicker! The Ijians can wait.'

'No!' Rose pleaded. 'We have to get to Wreckrest!' *Bring me to Dagger! It's all I want! Just bring me to Dagger!* 'I sent messengers! He'll have a head start!'

'It's decided.' Seb cleared his throat. 'Faster!' he bellowed ferociously at his crew. 'We must intercept the Blood Hammer wherever we find it!' He glanced at Rose's tormented expression, his face hard, drained of all tolerance and gentleness.

He lowered his voice to wallow in the dark tones of his grey mood, paralysing Rose with a piercing glare that sliced through the rain like a sword. 'You'll get away from me,' he said. 'But first...' He hesistated, curled his fingers into a fist before his squinting eyes. 'Just tell me.'

Rose stuttered.

'Go on. Tell me where Halfeye hid his bloody gold.'

21

Outrage vibrated through their dark skin, coursed freely through their Ijian blood. Alice did not blame them. She, too, felt its heat spread to her fingers and toes, despite the torrential rain that beat at them. *Why would anyone do this?* she pondered, heatedly. *Pirates! But not Wulfric... He would never do such a thing. And Kit wouldn't stand for it if he did! No, it has to be one of the other two. Seablood or Dreadwind. But Seablood... Isn't their territory in the north?*

Howls poured from Ijian mouths. Men scurried about the beach like ants, inexorably spurring themselves into deeper, wetter fury. They circled the course earth, examining every wound. Alice traced their well-worn feet from amongst a bundle of squabbling women, watching in horror as, one by one, they knelt beside the defiled fireplace and wailed.

Neither was it just the fire, whose dusty coals were strewn carelessly all over the dried coral; the strange decorations that had made the quaint plot so sacred had been snapped in half, each cast down with a greater sense of disregard than the last. Worst of all were the canoes. Those carefully crafted boats of bark and natural twine had been smashed to naught but shards, and were smothered in the tribe's revered ashes. The work was not that of a lone madman. The canoes had been ripped apart by perhaps a whole gang of pirates, wielding axes, clubs and hatred.

No, it couldn't have been the Black Beast. There's no way! Why would they do this? Why would anybody do this? These Ijians... They're gentle, and... Alice's thoughts revisited the recent transaction she had witnessed between a clump of Ijians and pirates. By all accounts, the two parties had been amicable. They were civil, at least. The vandalism that had taken place before her, however, was an act of pure malice.

If she had not been present for the old man's funeral, she perhaps would not have thought much of the outlandish site. It was primitive, dirty, and seemingly unorganised. But she knew now that the ground here was alive with spirit and memory, in a manner she supposed she would never understand. Whoever had defaced it had obviously known of its significance, whilst simultaneously bearing so heartless a soul as to not be bothered by the fact.

The women could no longer contain their hysterical bickering within their ranks. They pushed out to mingle with the men, crying, shouting and muttering in their harsh, foreign tongue. There was no order to their grieving, no sense, but their grief was plain, fierce. They stomped about in an absolute frenzy, shaking their wrists in the air, even while their mouths erupted in sorrow.

Alice wanted to join them as a demonstration of solidarity, to show she was as disgusted as they were. *But...* The tips of her fingers filled with freezing needles. *What if they think I did it? Or what if they blame me anyway? I came from Wreckrest, didn't I? And my skin…* She edged backward. *I should run. Before they kill me!*

She twisted her neck, surveyed the escape routes that trailed off into the island's dense foliage. The slope was thick with sticks and shrubs, all soaked from top to bottom in Southland's sticky rain. Only the path to the cave betrayed even the slightest hint of a solid footing. *I would never get away,* she realised, returning her gaze to the cacophony on the beach. Her sweaty, tingling hands gripped one another. *They would catch me before I'd made it ten steps!*

Grey Hair produced an enormous noise that rose above the mess. Gradually, the racket faded, and the Ijians spiralled towards each other. Their arms waved uncontrollably and their voices sparred like battling warhawks, but it was evident they had commenced a coherent discussion.

Alice peered over their heads at the pale morning sky beyond the bubbling waves. The impenetrable weather had turned the horizon a dull grey, and any detail more than a hundred feet away was hazy and indistinct. The sun should have been high enough to illuminate the mainland across the narrow patch of sea ahead, yet no evidence of any such land could even be imagined. *You're out there somewhere,* Alice thought, grimacing. *How could you do this?!*

The perplexing din was blending now with a more rhymical chanting. A surge of fear swept over Alice. She gripped the nearest tree. Its soggy bark stung her shaking fingertips.

The Ijians were marching towards her. Amongst them she noticed one of the taller men throw a curved sword into the ground, point first. The gesture appeared to mean something. *A pirate sword! Maybe it was left behind! Maybe the Ijians know it wasn't me!*

The troop approached, their anger sizzling under heavy raindrops, woven tactlessly into their vicious chanting. Alice wanted to run. Her hands clutched the bark even tighter, squeezing all the blood in them back to her heart. *It's stupid,* she knew. *I could never outrun them!*

Then, suddenly, as if she were not even there, the Ijians strode right past her. They stormed up the path to the cave, and their chants flowed up the hill with them. Their passage sounded like thunder amid the rain and the sloshing treetops.

Alice was paralysed beside the column, too afraid she would be noticed if she were to move. Not even the rain made her shiver now. Its water felt almost warm on her pale, frozen skin. And the leather rags that had once been Kit's only hugged her tighter the wetter they got.

Big Cheeks hovered near the back of the group, lagging behind with some of the other women Alice recognised. When they eventually shifted past her, Alice sprang from her immobility to grip the large Ijian's arm.

'Where are they going?' asked the younger. She knew full well Big Cheeks could not understand her, but the words sprayed out nevertheless, all full of rain and saliva.

Big Cheeks ceased her chanting to scrutinse the pale girl. She held a thumb and forefinger to Alice's temple and squeezed lightly, a blank look in her impossibly dark eyes. Already, the majority of the Ijian clan had moved on, crawling up the hill like one giant, clacking insect. Only Flat Nose remained, sticking to Big Cheeks' side like a sister of sorts. Perhaps they were sisters in truth, or perhaps Ijians did not recognize family the way Western people did. Alice was unsure.

'What should I do?' she asked, her query equally as useless as the one before.

A scowl formed on Big Cheeks' big features. The woman's face was seldom affected. Even her hair refused droop in the rain the way it should have. But the scowl was unmistakeable. It was frightening.

'Fire,' she said.

'Fire?' Alice asked.

'Fire,' grumbled Big Cheeks.

Understanding hit Alice right in the teeth. 'Fire! No! You can't!' She jerked her chest closer to that of Big Cheeks. 'You can't burn Wreckrest! They didn't do it! There's innocent people there!'

Alice shoved her finger urgently at the beach, where grey mist shuddered over the water. 'They're out *there*! The people that did this! They're on the ocean! You can't just—' Alice cut herself off. Big Cheeks was not listening. She had already turned her back, and was hastily waddling up the path behind Flat Nose.

Faces flashed past Alice's inner eye. Faces she had seen in Wreckrest. Peaceful faces, belonging to people who worked gardens, cooked dinners, and to those that sold themselves in the alleys beside the main street. She remembered the violence too; so many dead men sleeping in complete motionlessness, their barren cheeks squashed against the dusty surface of the town centre. That image she had tried to push from her consciousness, yet there it was, pushing back. She pondered briefly whether they all, in fact, deserved to die.

But Maggie... The tavern owner's face appeared last, overwhelming the violence. Her boisterous black hair stretched to the edges of Alice's imagination. *She is good,* she told herself. *Good, she is good!* She thought again about the prostitutes, and her heart filled with pity. 'No!' she shouted. 'You can't burn it! You can't!'

Heat surged through Alice's veins, spurring her into action. Her squelching feet carried her uncontrollably up the hill toward the Ijian column. Sticks ripped through her breeches and bushes grabbed at her shoulders. Raindrops seemed to puncture her skin as she slapped into them, running with all her might for the cave.

She felt as though she was gliding through the forest with the dexterity of an animal, necessity guiding her movements rather than careful consideration. But the Ijians got no closer. Not until she had ascended to the cave itself did she catch the swarm. There, they swirled about collecting wooden tools with dreadful purpose. Their chanting had concluded, so only the persistent noise of endless rain billowed into the air around their dark figures.

Alice froze at the edge of the clearing, across from the slanting rock formation that completed the Ijian home. She had chased them to put a stop to their rampage, but she quickly realised she knew nothing of how to do so. Helplessness besieged her. Her body ached more than it had as a convict. All over her skin, cuts stung, and beneath, bones ached. The girl had suffered so very many a trial throughout the past week.

Now she was no more than a worn sack of flesh, hot, small, and so remarkably… wet.

'Wet!' she impulsively exclaimed, bounding forwards into the clearing's guts. 'It's too wet! You can't burn the town while it's raining!'

The Ijians ignored her ramblings. They brushed by in an almighty hurry, leaving her to spin on the spot.

A band of eager men was gathering itself at the northern end of the cave, where a wide sheet of rock formed a stage of sorts. It reached horizontally out from the soaking soil, glistening. The Ijians not among this tight pack were instead handing it sticks, spears and a couple of baskets full of something Alice could not make out.

She sliced through the crowd toward the stage, a headache swelling within her skull. 'No fire,' she demanded, directly at the tuft of warriors. The simple phrase snatched the attention of some among them. Those that looked at her brandished a frown so terrible she felt as though every hair upon her body sucked back into her core.

What am I doing?! With a frightened tone, she forced herself to reiterate the command. 'No fire,' she said, then pointed to the sky from whence came the steady flow of water. 'Rain,' she explained. 'No fire. Rain. No fire.'

One of the Ijians bared his teeth, forcing dark cheeks to rise into his dark eyes. 'Fire!' he agreed. He regarded his fellow Ijians. 'Fire!' he cried, raising his spear. Then the chanting started again. The gathered band flexed their bulging arms with war-like enthusiasm, and turned from the cave before hopping off their platform to stomp away into the trees. And just like that, the men were gone.

Alice made to follow them, but a forceful hand shot past her neck and clenched her chest. 'Aaaah!' Big Cheeks warned, her voice ruffling the back of Alice's thorn-ridden hair.

Frantically, Alice squirmed in the woman's embrace, arguing with the only word she knew Big Cheeks would understand. 'Fire,' she proposed. 'Fire. Fire.' She drew her ripped sleeve back from her arm to expose the burn she had received from the Ijians on the mainland.

Big Cheeks' grip loosened enough for Alice to slip out of it. The woman scoured her with a characteristic blank stare, a near complete tribe of furious Ijians heaving in the background. Even some of the children were present, gripped by curiosity if not by comprehension.

'Thank you,' Alice muttered, then nodded. 'Fire.'

With that, she sprang off into the bushes after the departed band. *I have to go with them,* she knew. Even if she had not yet thought of what she meant to do to stop the fire, she knew she must go. *I can't let them burn down Wreckrest. The people there don't deserve it!*

Sticks ripped through her breeches once more, and the bushes grabbed at her shoulders, but this time she overtook her target with ease. Not only was she surprised the Ijians at the cave had not pursued her, she was surprised at how calmly the outbound band strolled through the rain. To confuse her further, the men barely blinked at her arrival, instead allowing her to join their ranks as if their excursion were for nothing more than lazy foraging. They managed to acknowledge her with a solemn 'fire', and a foreign hand signal that was welcoming enough to satisfy any stranger's misgivings.

After that, the whole affair slowed drastically. Urgency melted away to drip from Alice's elbows in heavy streams as she strode evenly beside the group of Ijians through dense, deep green. The band's unexpected composure astounded her so much as to shock her into silent compliance at first. Soon after, she reasoned herself into it, deciding that a protest was unlikely to halt her companions. She settled instead for the hope that she could find something to dissuade them once they drew nearer to the pirate town.

And so Alice found herself marching alongside an army of Ijians through the jungle of Wimswind Island, bound for Wreckrest with tools of war. The path they picked was winding, and stuck mostly to the high ground where the slopes were more forgiving and the earth was not so smothered in scratchy undergrowth. The rain kept her gaze low for the first part of the journey—not only so she could keep the water from her eyes, but so she could carefully place each footstep to avoid slipping on one of the slick boulders that littered the path. Then, some time after what was probably midday, the rain stopped. In an instant it stopped.

Alice failed to notice it at first. Sweat and rainwater were so thickly mashed into her clothes that the battering from above was no longer worth consideration. It was only when the sun peered out from the curling Southland clouds that she paid first attention. Fresh light beamed on her back, leeching the chill from her bones as soon as it made contact. The sensation was so welcome it further postponed her realising what had happened. *Fire!* she then thought. The rainy weather would have certainly put a stopper in the little Ijian campaign even if she were unable to, though the instability of the region's climate had once more acted to spite humanity, as always it seemed to.

But it's still wet, Alice assessed, clinging to hope. Indeed, the ground was so soaked with moisture any large fire would have been either sluggish or downright impossible to light. Such became less so as the day wore on. The sun glowed hotter and hotter, and the sky parted to let it through. By mid-afternoon, the outer layer of Alice's outfit was completely dry. Her knees ached also, and her stomach was pulling at her insides like a petulant child, for despite their leisurely pace, the Ijians had not stopped for lunch—or for any other breed of snack. Only briefly did the column deviate, when the band rested by a stream for the briefest moment before pressing on anew.

Alice managed not to realise the journey from Wreckrest to the Ijian camp had been so lengthy when first she made it. On such occasion, she had run part of the way and been deathly frightened for the remainder, ferried through the night by a lightweight hunting troop. This time, the same distance took her the greater part of the day to cover. After spanning through grey rain into blue skies, it stretched finally into the magenta of early sunset, where every muscle within Alice's limp body was poised to collapse. After that, her only respite came when the band would file over a treeless peak. There, she could pause and gaze out upon astonishing vistas of distant islands, all snuggled up in perpetual slumber atop the shimmering orange waters that overpowered the horizon. She had never known the Sentinels to look so beautiful as they did from so high atop

Wimswind Island. Their magic embraced her spirit, even as her ankles crunched downward in heavy treads.

Suddenly, the band stopped. Alice collided with an Ijian's rear, and focus came rushing up to slap her. She jumped away, apologising profusely in her futile language. The man was unbothered, choosing rather to join the others in a sort of busy scrambling. Near-naked, muscular bodies began to shuffle, kneel and even vanish completely, their dark skin blending with the ever-darkening atmosphere.

What's happening? Alice panicked. Then she saw the angular roofs, the solid walls of wide planks, the fences made with stakes. *Wreckrest!* The edge of the town had, indeed, become passably visible through the tangled shadows of the forest. It peeked at Alice humbly from further down the steep hill.

Fear flared up, washing through her. Her ears tingled. *We're here! I... I have to stop it!* She whirled to face the busy army of Ijian warriors. She could tell now that they were preparing for attack. She knew not exactly how they intended to conjure their Ijian fire, but she knew it was soon to arrive. Wet as the island remained, the morning's rain showed no signs of returning, and the air was as dry as it ever got.

Some Ijians were presently lowering their baskets while their comrades hurriedly fished through the things within.

Alice went to move, but unsurprisingly found herself paralysed, completely unable to think a way forward. *They're men! Strong men! Ijian men! All of them! What am I going to do? How can I stop them now?! They barely even realise that I'm here! I might as well be invisible!* Then an idea struck her. At last, she knew what she had to do.

She leapt suddenly through the shrubs and flew through the trees, spending every drop of effort she could muster. *Let me get away,* she prayed, *let me get away!* Sticks ripped through her breeches, bushes grabbed at her shoulders, tears burst from her eyes. She paid no mind to stealth, to subtlety, only to speed. She swerved by trunk after trunk, bounding down the uneven slope. Away from the Ijians. Shadows whisked past her furious face. Shadows of trees, shadows of shelters, shadows of pitched roofs. She was in the town now, going deeper. A barrow handle clipped her toe, she fell to her knees, her breeches slid four feet through mud before she came to a halt. Her legs burned even as the cold softness of the grime cradled them.

Then it was still, quiet. She flicked her hair from her face and anxiously checked behind her. The Ijians were nowhere to be seen, their rustling masked by the faint chirp of evening birds. *I got away! I got away! I've escaped!* A vision of fire spoilt her delight. She was surrounded by small buildings. Storage sheds, mostly. All made of wood. *I have to warn the town! Before it burns! If I can't stop the Ijians, I at least have—*

'Where did you come from?'

It was a tall man, heavyset behind a wiry beard that was crudely cut to within an inch of his dirt-smothered chin. He wore a crusty waistcoat, bulky boots and a monstrous belt. In the belt was stuffed a sword, just as his hands were so stuffed with a half-drunk liquor bottle and a loaded blunderbuss. The waning pink light left one half of his figure in shadow. He was not one of Wulfric's pirates, but a pirate all the same.

Alice shook, stuttered.

'Why were you runnin'? Go on, tell me.' He tossed his chin

up.

Alice's mind raced. 'I need to get to Maggie's tavern,' she blurted. *I need to tell him about the Ijians!* 'I was… I need to see her.' *He's too dangerous. He'll kill me!* 'I… She wanted me back before dark.' *He'll blame it on me if I tell him. He's a pirate!* 'Please… I work for her.'

The pirate raised a mangled eyebrow. 'Not a good day t' be runnin' 'bout out this way.' Something made him pause. 'No time f'it,' he grumbled, as if to himself instead of to Alice.

As confidently as she could, Alice stood. She tried not to show that her knees burned with grazes. Neither did she try to wipe the mud from her breeches. 'Please. I need to go.' She attempted weakly to push past the man.

'Not s'fast, girly,' said the pirate. He threw the bottle against a pile of stones, shattering the glass. Alice flinched as his meaty fingers latched onto her wrist. 'Maybe I needs to take ye t' ol' Mag's m'self. Jus' t' check tha' ye really… one o' hers…' A savage smile crept into his beard, a smile that frightened Alice more than any Ijian ever had. Or any fellow convict.

Alice struggled, attempted to wrench herself free.

'Don't be scared, girly,' the pirate soothed. 'If ye one o' Mag's. Shouldn't be any prob'em. Ye get ye gold too, uh? Come on.'

The man kicked into motion, dragging Alice behind him. *You should tell him. Tell him about the Ijians! But he's bringing me to Maggie… I'll tell her. Yes. And she'll protect me. She promised Wulfric she would. And she can warn everyone else. Not me.*

The man's strides were as large as any giant's; Alice had to scuttle in his wake to keep her legs from dangling against the dirty road. As they weaved through the tightly crammed town, the ground flattened under Alice's boots, and she began to recognise alleyways. The last time she had seen those narrow passages, she had been running from pirates. She remembered it all too vividly. And now she had been caught by one, though it was most likely for a different reason. The pirate in question certainly did not appear to belong to the faction that had pursued her. He possessed no clear Dorian or Morch traits, but rather flaunted a rough, generic look akin to that heralded by simple traders back in Sirland. There were others like him as well, stomping out from behind dark corners, lining the streets and wriggling their fingers around rusty firearms. They nodded enviously at Alice's captor as he trudged past them.

A curious face caught the captive's attention, even as it rushed by. *I've seen that man before*, she realised.

Her soles stumbled into the town centre, where she made a special effort to keep her eyes down. The worn road was soft with moisture from the rain, and emanated a sickly warmth that smelt of vomit, or rot, or something else like it. Days prior, blood and death had stained the very walls that surrounded her. She chose not to look at them, or even at Maggie's tavern, the only place in the pirate haven she knew would be safe.

Abruptly, she recalled from where she knew that face. *He was there! On our yacht! With Wesley! And Rose! These pirates, they're from that ship! They're...* Her toes clapped against wooden stairs, and she fell. Her limp arm caught in the unrelenting fist of her captor.

She cried out, hastily levering her body to its feet with her free hand. They were at the door to Maggie's rugged establishment. The pirate burst inside without hesitation. The doors nearly snapped closed before Alice could slip through them.

Wesley! Rose! Are you here? Are you safe? You have to be here! You have to be! These are Dreadwind pirates! She cranked her head from side to side, the movements shooting pains into her skull. Her family was not there. And neither was Maggie.

A few rough characters were scattered amongst the tables, each more vile looking than the last. One had a black waistcoat with a white jellyfish painted on its back. While he was hardly the most derelict of the bunch, his face drooped heaviest with evil as it turned to glimpse the newcomers. He eyed Alice's frame as a dog would a scrap of fleshy bone. 'Who's this?' he asked.

'She says she's one 'o Mag's,' Alice's captor told him.

'She's not,' confirmed the jellyfish man. 'I've never seen her. Mag's not here to claim her own, anyway.'

Alice's blood filled with ice.

22

Out of the raw violet in the east, under the belly of swirling clouds and over water shattered by the warm light of the dying sun, a skull appeared, as clear as day, floating menacingly through the heavy air in royal splendour, grinning as much as it glowered. The Blackbone skull, the skull of the Black Beast. At night, the ship's black sails would have made it nearly invisible—a trait once treasured by such outlaws—though the white emblem now fixed upon them glared openly through the dim atmosphere, a luminous warning for any that dare fall into the ship's path. Like the stinger of the Kraken or the crown of the Blood Hammer, it was not an image any sailor wanted to see barrelling at them. Not even if they stood below the latter.

Sunset tickled the oncoming vessel's bowsprit as it glided into imperfect focus. Its body steadily followed. Lanterns aboard its deck echoed the orange notes of the western sky, divulging its details. So proud, so powerful. It was the most beautiful ship to have ever sailed the Rainbow Sea, save for the Frontiere. Beautiful, and strong.

Captain Theodore Seablood grumbled as he watched it. He adjusted the illustrious wig he had chosen for the occasion so that it sat more comfortably below his magnificent hat. His polished shoes twinkled in the glow of both the sunset and the lanterns upon his own vessel, and tapped the brig's Sirlish Oak deck as he swivelled toward the quartermaster, who was—as ever—waiting patiently behind him.

'Damn this bloody farce! We should not be here.'

Salvino smirked the kind of smirk he reserved for times when frustration boiled just beneath the surface, though the captain was too irritable to notice it. He opened his mouth, 'My captain—'

'Yes, yes! I know,' groaned Ted. 'You've done nothing but nag about it since those dirty spies drifted aboard. But look!' He jabbed a chubby finger at the approaching Black Beast. 'The Greyhide has come to round up the Ijian rabble himself. We're scarcely needed, I'll say. The sooner we get back on my boy's trail, the better. Let us raise the anchor and be on our way!'

A weary sigh emanated from Salvino's slim chest. 'My captain, Sebastian has fled south. It was a fruitless venture, chasing him, and still is.'

'Aye he has run off, to board the ghost ship before his old man could! Cleto made that very clear. My son, Salvino! Aboard the ghost ship! Can you believe it?! How he tricked us all with his witty distractions and his petty whining!'

'Of course, the ghost ship. It yet plagues you, my captain. Tell me, what is more believable, that your son drinks now from the skull of a long-dead legend, or that Cleto has gone as mad as I ought think you have? Calm my nerves, my captain. Tell me you don't truly believe it.'

Ted growled. 'And what about you? You believed those *messengers*, when you should have seen them flogged for insolence! Perhaps I should have you join them belowdecks, for all your insistence we follow their course.'

Salvino sighed again. 'My captain, must I always voice reason to deaf ears? Look behind me! They were right, were they not?'

Ted huffed at the quartermaster, unhappily defeated. Indeed, the orange air above Wreckrest was obscured by charred smoke, a giant column of it that stretched from the town's southern flank to the muddled clouds looming overhead. Ijian fire. Many a time had it plagued Mariscos while the Blood Hammer sailed nearby, but never Wreckrest. *Why now?* The Ijians were fickle, Ted knew, but they were never as brutal as the mainlanders seemed to think they were. The free sailors of the Sentinels held quite the respectful working relationship with the native inhabitants of Wimswind Island. The Dreadwinds especially.

Ted looked around, returning his attention to his immediate surroundings. From where he and Salvino lingered at the Blood Hammer's bow, the whole of Hullbreaker Bay could be surveyed. The brig was anchored as close to the coral as was safe, so that the endangered town was within swimming distance. There were a number of smaller vessels just as near. Their vacated crews had already been positioned beyond the shoreline.

The Blood Hammer's boats were either in the davits being lowered into the water, or full of men ready to row for the docks. Sparkling lanterns fluttered around them, lit hastily in preparation for the unavoidable darkness between the brig and the beach. Their radiance highlighted puddles of water now spilt on the brig's deck; storm water that had collected in the boats while they had rested their hulls.

In all, over half the crew were waiting to go ashore, more than should rightly fit in four longboats. Ted wondered whether they were properly invested in smothering the fire, or whether they simply ached for a night on solid ground. Regardless, there was a queer urgency on their faces, each of which reflected splinters of the eerily coloured sky. They were quiet too. The usual chatter had been replaced by the subtle plop of the sea, and a sort of soft expectancy. It was as if they each held their breaths.

A small man approached his superiors, one of the few Sirlish sailors under Ted's employ. He had a patch of mousy hair atop his balding head that looked to have a life of its own.

'Smith,' Ted nodded, shuffling around Salvino so the Dorian's shadowy frame did not get in the way. 'Are you ready to get going? I suppose we've got to blot out that bloody Ijian fire before Greyhide does. Aye, we're too deep now to let that fool claim all the glory.'

'Aye, captain,' Smith confirmed before turning courteously and immediatly towards Salvino. 'Are you ready, sir?'

Offended, Ted straightened his back to make his distinguished stomach poke out further than his nose. 'What are you asking him for?! Of course he's ready. He's ready whenever I am!'

The quartermaster raised his eyebrows cheekily. 'Certainly, my captain. Though he doesn't mean it like that. I'm taking his boat, you see.'

Ted was astounded. 'You're going to shore?!'

'Wreckrest is in danger,' said Salvino, 'and I intend to help. Besides, you can take care of the Blood Hammer all by yourself, can't you?'

Ted grunted. He stroked his shaven face unconsciously, trying to make sense of Salvino's expression. 'Well, aren't you a bloody hero then?' he said. 'What has come over you these last few days, huh? What happened to the always-cautious Salvino I used to know? Skipping off to save Wreckrest! Pah! And before, with the Blackbone boy! I would never have killed him so fast if it hadn't been for your ceaseless pestering on the matter. You forced my hand, you worm! Since when were you so brash?'

'Not brash, my captain,' defended the quartermaster, chuckling. 'I merely offered you the choice. You know it as well as I. If Sebastian had returned, he would never have allowed you to kill the prisoner. And the boy deserved it, I should say. He murdered your lady.'

'Bloody hag,' barked Ted. He crossed his arms and wrinkled his mouth. 'Aye, he killed Agatha, the fool. The boy had to die, I know, but I dare say after this bout in Wreckrest, Greyhide will want back what was his. Where will you be then? Still in town? Poking your cock from corner to corner? It may be I should send you to tell him what we did, seeing as it was your idea. See if you think it wasn't brash then!'

Salvino smirked. 'Of course, my captain. I will do it. I will tell him.'

'Uh, Salv...' Smith cleared his throat to remind the others

of his presence.

Salvino allowed the short man to grapple his attention. 'Right you are,' he noted. 'I'm coming.' The quartermaster's eyes twinkled as he shot Ted one last sly look. 'Take care, my captain,' he said, then swept away with his hands held behind his back. His dark coat vanished into the busy rabble amidships.

Ted whirled crossly, and so forcefully his royal hat almost fell off. *Bloody hero! Who's he trying to impress? The girl?!* He remembered Liz. Since Agatha had been wrecked, he remembered Liz often, speculating on whether he could coerce her into his bed. It was obvious Seb had no further use for her.

A gust of cool wind sifted through the captain's curls. It carried with it the voices of many a Blackbone, several of which were laden with the spitting tones of a Morch accent. The Black Beast was almost upon him. Its grand sails were curved like a woman's thighs, cuddling the breeze. There was no sign the ship was slowing at all. *At this rate, Greyhide'll drive himself into the reef! Ah, I'll be glad to see it! Even if he furled his sails now, his hull is doomed for sure!* His forehead tightened. Something troubled him. *Why is he in such a hurry? Cannot he see us ahead of him? Does the fool think me ill capable of handling a few wayward Ijians?*

He whirled again to voice his thoughts. But nobody was there. *Damned Salvino! Where have you gone?!* He peered across the glowing deck, watching suspiciously as the last of the longboats was lowered into the sea. It overflowed with Seablood warriors. *Half the bloody crew! And most of the fighters! Who do they think they're up against?*

Something itched at the edge of his mind. Something

terrible. He felt unexpectedly alone. He could no longer feel Salvino's breath on the back of his neck, could no longer hear the boy's voice as it bossed around his crew, could no longer smell the rancid stink of his woman's knotted hair. The Black Beast was completely visible now, plowing through the bay at full speed.

Ted shifted his shoes impatiently, locking his eyes on the Black Beast's deck, where he knew Wulfric Blackbone would be returning the favour.

Greyhide cannot know! We've told not a soul! And those spies... His stomach turned. *They are safe. They are safe! No Blackbone yet knows their pup is dead, save for the spies. And they are safe!* Yet the Black Beast did not slow.

'Cap'n, sir,' a weedy voice addressed him.

Ted had to lift his nose to discover the face of the dirty man who had interrupted his train of thought. 'What is it?' he snapped.

'Beggin' yer pardon, cap'n, but the boats r'all off.'

'I can see that myself. I'm not blind!' Ted snorted. 'Go and have your bloody dinner and leave me be.'

The man departed as quickly as he arrived. While he scuttled away to join the other men that had been left aboard, the Black Beast's foresails finally began to ripple.

Ted realised then that the Blackbone ship had no intention of anchoring at all. It was to pull up rapidly and temporarily, never settling.

What is this game, Greyhide?

With swift and deft accuracy, the nearing ship was pulled hove to. The sails were crooked to oppose each other, forcing the great vessel to shudder in tension. It lost its momentum instantly, twisting as it concluded its rampage through the bay's protected waters. Ever so slowly, the Black Beast swung into the wind, its sails roaring. It edged right over to the Blood Hammer's side. Closer than ever a ship so large should come.

Ted could see its whole length now, and every sailor atop its weather decks. The Sirlish Oak glistened beneath the fiery sky, and its sails loomed like midnight against it. There were ship's boats already in its davits, and a couple in the water, dangling in their mother's wake like a pair of testicles. Before the Black Beast even came to a halt, its boats filled with Blackbones. With swords, pistols and frowns.

You cannot stay here, Greyhide! Not without anchoring. You're too close to the reef! Or do you plan on abandoning your men while they rescue our port? What of your honour, then? Your precious honour?

A grey mop stood out amongst the opposing crew. It shone dazzlingly below its black hat, and pointed down at thunderous feet, which were wrapped smugly in the train of a monstrous coat. Wulfric Blackbone. The Greyhide. The beast did not bother looking Ted's way. He crudely leapt from the gunwale of his ship to crash into one of its boats, even as the thing hung suspended beside the bulwark.

Ted spat. *First Salvino, now you! A good captain never leaves his ship. That's what I say! Not for Wreckrest. Not for anything!*

His heart rumbled, reminding him of his uneasiness. *They are safe! They are safe! As far as Greyhide is concerned, his boy is chomping on carrots and stew as we speak.*

Wulfric's boat slapped into the blackening water between

the two vessels, more than a dozen Blackbone thugs within it.

'Damned spies!' Ted cursed, aloud. *I'll check them myself, I will! They are safe, I know it!*

He launched into action, stomping along the deck to the main ladder. The residual crew folded away so he could charge unhindered through their ranks.

The orange sunset was replaced by the orange of flickering lamps as the captain trampled down to the lower decks where he so seldom visited. He had to wrench a lamp from its sconce before descending to the lowest level, where the darkness was locked tightly in place by the water's pressure without. Here, the commotion outside was utterly squashed by the muted groan of the bay that purred through the walls.

Lamplight flooded the prisoner's hold, illuminating the debris and setting afire the stench of dusty mould. A makeshift bed was nearby, dishevelled in the corner beside a leaning stack of crates, begging to be discovered. But Ted was there for one purpose only.

He raised the lamp to let its radiance cut through the prison bars at the hold's end. Orange stars gazed back at him through the tired eyes of eight Sirlishmen. *Eight!* He counted again. And again. And again. *Eight! Eight! Eight! Of course there are. What was I thinking?*

His lungs deflated, and the folds on his forehead eased. *They're all here. They are safe! Damn my suspicions, of course they are!*

The eight spies began to stir. They called out to Ted in wasted, raspy voices. The sound echoed dully around the tight cavern. Stick-thin arms were thrust through the prison bars, wiggling their fingers. Even if Ted were willing to listen, he would barely have understood. It seemed to him that merely half of the spies could speak Sirlish at all. The others spoke with a sort of Brindian gibberish.

Such did not fool the great Theodore Seablood. Despite their protests, Ted knew full well what these men were. They were Blackbones. When the group had arrived in their cutter to warn his crew of the impending Ijian attack, he knew right away that they were liars—at least in part—come in peace purely as an excuse to check on the health of Greyhide's son. *And how that has played out for you!* Ted sneered at the prisoners, turning his back on them. The pathetic messengers had never even attempted to offer an alternate explanation for their presence. They were stubbornly mute, speaking only when they saw a chance to coerce the captain to set sail for Wreckrest. Ted would not have heeded their warning if it were not for Salvino. Oddly though, the spies' forboding had proven accurate.

Eight. He nodded. *They are all here, safe. Sealed away with my secret. Teddy, you worry too much.*

'Cap'n! Cap'n! They're boarding! The Blackbones!'

'Boarding what? The brig?!' Ted dropped the lamp and scuttled up the ladder. *Boarding?! Surely not! There's no way!*

Screams tore down through the mess deck. Thumping, rattling, battering. *Crack!* Gunfire!

Sweat exploded from Ted's face. His hands and feet worked faster and faster, yanking his old frame up the next ladder, up to the surface.

He fumbled onto the main deck panting like a dog. The

swirling sky was full of smoke, the Blood Hammer's masts stretching high into it, up, up. Beneath them, the scant sailors were huddled along the starboard bulwark, desperately packing gunpowder into their blunderbusses, or swinging their cutlasses wildly over the edge.

It cannot be! He wouldn't dare! He wouldn't dare!

The Seablood line drew back as Blackbone heads appeared at its heels. Ted puffed out his chest, stood his ground amidships. 'Hold them back!' he demanded, frazzled. 'Cut their ladders!'

The rest of Ted's crew spewed out from belowdecks to join the effort. Some thirty men they made altogether.

'There's too many,' a voice shouted. And needless it was, for Ted could see a wave of hostile bodies crunch over the bulwark even as it was shouted. *Greyhide! Why are you doing this?! You're meant to be saving Wreckrest!*

The Seablood line broke promptly, and Blackbones leaked onto the deck, blades raised. They were flowing aboard from at least five access points all along the Blood Hammer's flank, having scaled grappling lines or scrappy ladders.

Ted's crew scattered. Their guns fired. Their teeth came out. More smoke poured into the atmosphere to squirm through the shrouds.

No! Ted stumbled backward.

An oversized Blackbone's devilish soles clapped onto the deck, its eyes devouring the fear in Ted's.

No! Ted spun, darted for his cabin. 'No yielding!' he screamed as his polished legs carried him swiftly over the shivering deck to the sterncastle's door. 'Defend the brig!

Defend the brig!' He slammed the door shut behind him. His numb fingers were shaking as he hurried to lock it. He bashed the door's bolt with a fist in frustration until the cold metal slid home. Then he bounced away from the thick wood.

It was as gloomy in his cabin as ever it had been. He ran to its far wall where he crammed his shoulder blades against the cloudy windows. It was quieter now, all but for the rattling of his trembling belt against the Blood Hammer's stern panelling.

Shit! cursed the captain. *How am I going to survive this one?*

Out in the wind, it was getting darker, both for the hour and for the growing stream of smoke that poured from the rooftops of Wreckrest. Salvino knew there was coral beneath him, but he could not see it. The water glistened like pitch, but scratched the longboat's hull like claws.

A sound could be heard behind him. Shouting. Gunfire.

'Salvino, sir!' Diego stood up amongst the rowers of a nearby longboat—so small amid the wide expanse of Hullbreaker Bay. The Dorian's bronze skin rendered him nearly imperceptible though he was merely yards away. 'Greyhide be boarding the Blood Hammer,' he finished in flawless Sirlish, a courtesy spared for the minority among the conspirators who yet spoke one language.

'Aye!' Salvino replied. *As I suspected.* 'Keep on!' he yelled back.

Oars slopped again into the sea. Salvino neither looked back nor forward. He held his gaze on the boat's wet floor as he was ferried ever closer to the burning town. He had always hated traversing the water in smaller boats. They were unstable, dirty, and completely inescapable. Though screams bounced at him from all directions, the unrest of the waves had them beat, had his muscles all tight.

'Salv!' Diego's shady tones cut through the chop once more. 'It seems me the whole damn Blackbone crew be boarding, sir! If we ain't turnin' back now... There may be no Blood Hammer left at all!'

Grumbling, Salvino finally spun. Cool ocean spray greeted his features as he did so. The four Seablood longboats were still nearer their brig than the shore, plopping slowly along the bay's surface. Across the water in the east, both Blood Hammer and Black Beast appeared to reach over Salvino's head, parked beside each other like warring brothers. Between them, he could see an army of critters speeding up the side of his beloved vessel. Indeed, there were a large number. This was no mere sortie.

His gaze centred on the black sails of the enemy ship, where the great white skull still quivered, tense. It was the only image not succumbing to the power of the encroaching gloom.

'What say you? Salv! What say you?!'

The quartermaster cleared his throat and raised his voice so the rowers in all four boats could hear. 'Aye, forget Wreckrest! We turn back! Turn back!' The brutality of his tone did not suit his usual manner, though its use was critical in this moment. Now was the time. His time. At long last. 'I have a new plan!'

Wulfric Blackbone kicked down the cabin's door. Splinters exploded from the lock as the big wooden rectangle spun halfway across the room before crashing into Ted's desk. The sound obliterated the quiet.

In the now ruined doorway, Wulfric's unmistakeable silhouette heaved. It blotted out most of the light still lingering about the air behind the man's mammoth shoulders. His majestic beard soaked up the rest of it. From beyond, the howling and thunder of battle rushed in, drowning the cramped furniture in pained screams.

Theodore Seablood stepped proudly from the stern wall. He took a deep breath, pointed his chin up, and adjusted his wig. 'Greyhide,' he said. 'How dare you board my brig?'

Wulfric stomped fearlessly into the cabin and drew his cutlass. 'You killed my son, Teddy.'

Ted choked on a gasp. Swallowed it. Wulfric's daunting figure moved closer, his enormous coat blending with the shadows. 'What?! Aye I took him prisoner, but I would never! Come, I'll take you to him. He's in the hold.'

'Shut your bloody mouth, pig!'

Ted whimpered, stumbled sideways. 'Wulfric! How dare you?! This is my brig! You're attacking me! Your men... Outside!'

'Yesterday, Teddy. One of your own servants came to me. They told me themselves.' Saliva dripped from the Blackbone's mouth.

'Told you what?!' Ted edged further aside, circling the room, circling his adversary. *A traitor! A snitch! But who? And why? Bloody arse, why?!* 'Rat! You shouldn't believe everything you hear, Greyhide! Besides, the boy killed my woman, Agatha. He murdered her in cold blood! What was I to do?! Tell me!

Bloody well tell me! What else was I to do?! What else?!' *Who did this to me?! I will kill him myself! Nobody betrays Captain Theodore Seablood and lives to tell of it! Nobody!* His dirk had fallen from the broken desk. It nudged his shoe.

'You killed my son, Teddy!' Wulfric's canine teeth emerged from the nest of grey thorns on his cheeks. 'You *killed* my *son!*'

Ted snapped to the floor, snatched the dirk in chubby fingers, and bounded from the room in one brisk motion. His hat fell from his wig as he glided into the open air.

The Blood Hammer's main deck stretched out before him, bathed in utter chaos, slashed lengthways and widthways by rope, blood and steel. Half-dead corpses decorated the planks—pleading for mercy—whilst Blackbone and Seablood alike danced over their faces, stabbing at one another. The stink of hot viscera blended with that of sweat and smoke.

We're outnumbered, Ted saw, shoving the point of his dirk towards the battle. Some of his men were retreating up the rigging, others had vanished belowdecks. The cowards among them were diving into the bay. Blackbones chased them wherever they fled. The villains swarmed over every inch of the vessel's surface, hungry for death. In the fading light they seemed to join together as a black mass, lumbering, swallowing, devouring.

A Blackbone appeared beside the captain. He swung a pistol at Ted's head. Dropping suddenly, Ted shoved his dirk into the attacker's bare ankle. A loud pop blared, followed by a loud curse. The Blackbone smacked into the sterncastle's wall, shouting.

Wulfric leapt from the cabin doorway with an almighty roar.

Ted had no time to hesitate. He bounced up and darted forward.

A pair of duelling sailors barred his path. Barely wavering, the captain poked the enemy in the back. The other jolted harshly, falling victim to Wulfric's enormous fist. His chest bowled into the main mast before flopping around it into a pack of approaching boarders.

Ted ducked beside the mast just as Wulfric's blade came after him. It chipped into the wood. Ted flinched, tried to stab at Wulfric's knees from below. Wulfric kicked the hand aside and swooped around the mast's base to get at his prey. Ted rolled to port and tore away once more, shooting this time for the poop deck stairs that led to the brig's uppermost and sternmost shelf.

A number of Seablood combatants broke from their sparring to launch at the Blackbone leader. Wulfric dismissed them with an effortless swipe of his sword. He spun through the fray and trudged alone after Ted. Fresh boarders combed into the Seabloods to keep them busy.

The sky was almost black now. No starlight made it through the surging pillar of smoke, and no moonlight flickered on the water. Ted scrambled up the stairs to the poop deck and ripped loose the lantern that hung there. He threw it wildly at Wulfric's advancing outline. The Blackbone dodged, and the lantern sped down to wallop an unsuspecting boarder in the back of the head. Ted's surroundings were consumed instantly by darkness.

Bang! The Blood Hammer shook. The world shook. Wulfric fell to his knees on the stairs.

For a moment, the battle took pause. Every eye aboard the Seablood brig tuned to the neighbouring Black Beast. Beneath that vessel's startling skulls, its body was a hulking monster. There were plenty of men atop its deck. But they were not Blackbones.

Bang! Another. The deathly crash of exploding wood ripped open the night. The brig shook again. *Bang!* This time the cannonball shot just high of the hull, smashing through the port gunwale and gliding into a pair of unfortunate heads. Bodies dropped to the deck, splinters flicked into faces.

Ted's eyes widened impossibly. *Cannons! But why would he? Most of his men are aboard this—* His heart skipped a beat. He dashed to the railing, where he glared across the narrow chasm between the Blood Hammer and the Black Beast. *Bang!* He clasped the quaking barrier to keep his balance, frantically scanning the enemy deck. *They're not Blackbones! They can't be!* Then he saw who it was. The indubitable presence. Thin, dark, smug. His plain coat glistened under the lanterns at the Black Beast's helm. A handful of Ted's best fighters were with him. *Salvino?*

Wulfric's footsteps approached. *Salvino? What are you doing over there? No! No! It cannot be! You wouldn't!*

The captain whirled. 'Greyhide! They've taken your ship! They're shooting us down with your cannons! My own bloody men! They've taken it, the shit-eating rats!' *Salvino! Not you! Salvino! My Salvino! What are you doing?!*

Bang! A deep shot, aimed low. The sound of gushing water chilled Ted's soul. 'Traitor!' he thundered, loud enough for Salvino's distant and pitiable ears to hear. 'Coward! What blood runs in your veins but poison?!' He turned to the other captain. 'You must reclaim your ship! My men have stolen it, the traitors! Stolen the Black Beast!' He spat profusely as he spoke. 'Cease this folly and salvage what is yours! Or we'll all go down together!' *Salvino! My Salvino!* 'Kill him, Greyhide! Kill him!'

Bang! Wulfric tripped as cannon fire thrust through the stern. He recovered promptly to stand tall before his opponent, his cutlass still wedged between unmoving fingers. 'You killed my son,' he growled. 'Damn the Black Beast.'

Ted gaped, incredulous. Wulfric's blade came hurtling towards him. He slid along the railing and thrust his dirk defensively in front of his quivering face. 'No!' He leapt across the deck. 'Greyhide! Your ship! Your duty! Your honour!'

'Damn it all!' roared Captain Blackbone, savagely slicing his blade through the smoke.

'You fool!' Ted scooped a line from a starboard pin and threw it at Wulfric. 'Bloody reckless dog! Where's your honour?! Where's it gone?!'

Wulfric cut the rope. Ted pounced on him, stabbing with his dirk. Wulfric responded by kicking Ted in the gut and elbowing him in the face. Ted's wig spun free and floated overboard. His exposed, knotted hair went cold.

Wulfric swung his blade again, only to have it parried by the other. 'You killed my son!'

Ted scurried away from subsequent strikes. 'I had a bloody son too, and he pissed off! See how I care!'

Bang! Wulfric fell. Ted lunged. Wulfric tumbled into his shins. Cries sounded all around. The rest of the crew had resumed their fighting. *Nobody is saving the Black Beast! Nobody!*

Bang! Crack! The Blood Hammer creaked in pain. The deck wobbled, began to lean.

The foes jumped to their feet. They scuffled, pressing backwards and forwards into each other, waving their weapons like madmen. Their feet scooted over the poop deck, alone. They parried, struck, parried, lunged. The two blades glittered as Captains Blackbone and Seablood duelled for their lives.

Bang! Ted lost his footing. He jerked away to evade Wulfric's attack, felt the railing at his back. *Bang!* A cannonball smashed through the sterncastle just beneath them. Ted's body toppled over the edge. His free hand grasped for the railing, but slipped. He dropped the dirk and fell, flailing. He managed to quickly jam his soft arm into the newly blasted hole just below, where once a window had been. A shard of smashed oak impaled his palm, catching him. His body thumped against the brig's side. 'Gaaargh!' he screamed, struggling. His shoes kicked against slick wood, nothing more than black water below them. Pain raked through his arm, shooting fire into every inch of his being. He tried to lift himself up, but the spike pushed further through his flesh. Blood streamed down onto his neck.

Above, Wulfric cut the end of a line and wrapped it around his fist. He leapt over the edge after Ted, discarding his sword as he dropped. Great big boots pounded into the broken wall as the Blackbone swung down to where Ted hung. Rope dug into his skin as it suspended his beastly weight.

The two bumped shoulders, squabbling, cursing, scratching. Against the side of the Blood Hammer they fought, whilst the brig was brought low by the Black Beast's broadside. Their feet scraped the hull, each man clawing at the other with their spare fingers.

Ted felt his grip slip. The hot wetness in his hand was burning. He flung up his other arm to pull himself through the hole, but Wulfric slapped at the first.

Ted screeched. Wulfric howled and whacked it again, somewhat dislodging Ted's tendons from their wooden hook. He stuck a hand into the jagged hole and snapped off a shard of oak, which he forced deep into the limp capain's eye. Then he swung away on his rope. Twirling back, Captain Blackbone charged, allowing his entire weight to crash into Ted's hips. With a confused gulp, Theodore Seablood came free of his hold, and fell to the black below.

Salvino smiled as he watched Ted's body plop into Hullbreaker Bay. He dusted his sleeves and strolled along the Black Beast's quarterdeck, gracefully brushing his fingers against the polished railing. He stepped tenderly over the bloody carcass of an unfortunate Blackbone who had been left to guard his ship.

Before him, the Blood Hammer was sinking, along with the remainder of the Blackbone crew. *Though I tried,* he thought sadly, *I will never have you, it turns out. My sweet brig.* His attention returned to the smooth oak beneath his palms. *But you will do well in her stead, my ship, my newest love.*

The fighting had stopped. All those aboard the Blood Hammer were either dead or fleeing on what scraps of luggage they could find. The Black Beast was drifting away from it now, though it mattered little since the cannons were no longer required. The brig would be sunk within the hour, no matter what.

'Tell them to cease fire,' Salvino commanded Diego, who stood patiently in his shadow. 'We must away. Unlash the wheel and set course for east. And keep clear of the reef; there's no sense in spoiling our prize so quickly.'

'Aye aye, cap'n,' said Diego.

And so the Black Beast sailed peacefully from Hullbreaker Bay, a trail of smoke in its wake.

23

Broken pieces of pine and oak clattered into the Frontiere's bow. The broken bones of a lifeless vessel, whose nose still gasped for air above the black skin of the restless Rainbow Sea, and whose belly now rested upon the coral shelf lining the aptly named Hullbreaker Bay.

Sebastian's knees almost gave way when he discerned whose vessel it had been. The emotional wreck threw wits to the smoky wind, losing his composure, his temper, his vigilance. It was the perfect opportunity to slip by him, to go where he had assured her she was not allowed to go. Thus, she did. The captain may have arrived too late to save his father's brig, but Rose's task remained achievable. Its fulfilment grew closer by the second.

She beamed when her petite longboat floated past the sinking shell of the Blood Hammer. Its jagged silhouette penetrated the night's bleakness, black on black. It was beautiful, perfect. Not only had Halfeye's dreams of destruction come to fruition, Rose was finally free to pursue the murderer for whom she lusted.

The ten men with her muttered nervously amongst

themselves while they heaved oars through the bay's chop. Their Brindian speech was incomprehensible to Rose's ears, but their anxiety was plain. Indeed, they were fast approaching Wreckrest, a town positively luminescent with energy, noise and fire. So much fire.

Rose gripped the hilt of her sword and pictured his face. That dark, short-cropped beard. Those feral, unflinching eyes.

The boat pulled up to the edge of the longest pier, clapping hurriedly into a number of other boats left dawdling in the same spot. Rose immediately rose to step over her escort.

'Miss,' one of the rowers raised his voice. 'The captain's orders! We come to save as many people as we can. Are you going to help?'

Clambering onto the pier before the boat was even tied down, Rose spun to scowl at the pathetic clump of weak sailors that had carried her this far, and this far only. *How quickly you've turned from Halfeye!* 'That's not what I heard,' she said.

'Aye, that's right what he said. I know it!'

Rose groaned. 'Well, he's not my captain.' She spun back— golden hair flicking her in the eyes—and took off down the pier.

Directly ahead, Wreckrest was writhing in a state of pure devastation. The southern half of the town was completely afire, radiating mountains of smoke that billowed into the crusty air and twitched in the vibrant glow of the flames below them. All along the beach, pirates were crawling out from the waves, having swum despairingly from wreck to shore. They emerged all drenched, and collapsed on the dried coral beneath the flaming ruins of their home. Between their slumping bodies and the raging fire, clumps of frightened townspeople had gathered, mostly women and children. They were wailing, screaming, and fussing about, unsure where to go or what to do.

Rose rushed past them all, racing for the centre of the fiery town. She never took her hand off the hilt of her sword, which was thrust through her belt to rest—exposed—on her breeches, in the same fashion as the other pirates.

The heat hit her like a brick wall. Her ankles seemed to crumble as it cascaded over her body, forcing her to halt before her soles had yet tread onto the main street. She held a forearm to her eyes. Even at a distance, pain trickled through her bare skin. She pulled her shirt's sleeves down to her wrists. It was not enough.

She turned back towards the beach by the docks. One of the pirates there was bobbing face-first in the shallows, his limbs motionless while his companions squirmed and coughed. Rose bounded down to him, gliding over rocks and gravel, crunching over coral. She splashed into the cold sea, liquid ice seeping soothingly into her boots as she grapped the waterlogged figure. She held her breath and slid her fingers under his sloppy armpits to shuffle his coat from his shoulders. The heavy garment objected as if it were nailed to the man's back, though some aggressive shakes eventually convinced it to come free. The man suddenly kicked his feet.

Rose screeched in shock, yanking the coat to her chin. The dead pirate began to struggle, flapping about, splattering, choking. Rose whirled, suppressing vomit, and rushed out of the water. She fed her arms into the wet coat as she again slipped past the squealing children and charged toward the town's guts. The coat was long and weighed down with barrel-loads of seawater, yet it felt like armour on her skin, shielding her from the fire's fury.

Fiercely, the dripping woman strode now into the mouth of Wreckrest's main stretch. She kept to the right, where the buildings were still somewhat moist from the morning's downpour. The flames that licked the sides of almost every building on the street's opposite bank seemed almost to puncture her pale flesh. Their deathly warmth pushed at her left cheek, soaking into her skull. Her eyes begged to be shut, but she propped them open with stern determination. As she progessed down the street, her gaze zipped back and forth. *Where are you? Show yourself! You must be here! You must!*

Deep inside the town, the excitement was even more palpable. Men darted in and out of alleyways, hurling buckets of water at fresh spears of quivering white-yellow. Others were shepherding the weaker through the streets to safety, or dragging injured friends across the dusty ground while they croaked in extreme agony. More still were brawling, for reasons Rose could only imagine. They were punching each other, or gripping each other's faces as they spun about into burning buildings. None of them were Ijians. *Cowards!* Rose thought. *Setting their Ijian fire and retreating! Weak cowards!*

Everywhere around the town's hysteric residents, roofs were collapsing into brittle black walls that sported radiant orange tips. Clouds of sparks blew into the street, where hot embers were scattered freely. The surrounding structures were built so closely together it took mere seconds for the fire to leap from one to another, save for where the town's central channel cut the clutter in half. But now, even the main street seemed to boast insufficient width.

Smoke choked the atmosphere, blocking any hope of distant vision. It quickly drowned Rose's lungs with its woody stink and its searing heat. She coughed to get it out. *Where are you?! You must be here! It's your town! You must be saving it!*

Those hopping about the street appeared to be pirates more often than townsfolk. They were heavyset, gruff, strong, Sirlish. *Dreadwinds! They're Dreadwinds!* Everything was so hot. Sweat accumulated under all of Rose's sailing gear, even as it dried out. Her coat warmed, roasting her slowly. She sensed her hair was ready to combust. It was dry and hard. But still she pressed on. Her legs were aching. Her lips were trembling with vengeance and fear alike. The roar of the flames was like a rushing wind, deafening her, complimented only by urgent shouting that came from all directions.

I'm in a burning town! Why would he be here? Why did I think he would be here?!

Her body flew involuntarily into a shaded alleyway and smacked against a wooden wall. There was no fire where she paused, and the faded light there appeared blue in contrast. Not until a couple of seconds had passed did Rose notice she was being held in place. 'Hello there, girly,' the perpetrator hissed. 'Does this lady need to be rescued, does she? I know the way to go. Aye.' The foul man grinned as he spoke.

'I'm looking for someone,' Rose stated coldly, her voice hoarse. Already, the man's dirty hand was slipping crudely past her wet neck to her chest, his yellow teeth bared and his glistening eyes wide.

'Ooh, she's dressed like a man *and* she barks like a man. But we'll see if she's really a man under all—' Rose kneed him between the legs, palmed his face, and drove him to the ground. His head thumped against the dust and blood popped out of his mouth. Rose slid her sword from her belt and held it to the man's nose, straddling his waist. His eyes were even wider now. And he was silent.

'Where is Dagger?! Tell me where he is!'

'D… D… Dagger Dreadwind? C… C… Captain Dagger?'

Rose's heart burned. Her blood chilled. 'Dagger! Yes! Where is he?!'

'I… I… I…'

Rose pushed the point into the pirate's nose. It slid onto his cheek, leaving a line of red where it went.

'Argh! Bitch!' He struggled, but Rose punched him in the stomach. His mouth gaped, his stuggles ceased.

'Where is he!?' Rose yelled.

The pirate gasped for air. 'The… Tavern… In… Town… Centre… Maggie's!'

Maggie's tavern!

Hern's soggy fingers grasped at Seb's wrist. Hastily, Seb pulled the former shipmate aboard the Frontiere's deck. Half-drowned, the Seablood did not even recognise his prince. His arms flopped about on the wooden planks like they were his lover. Seb soon ignored him to peer once more into the thrashing darkness that surrounded the sunken Blood Hammer. He searched for the woman who had once been his own.

Another figure ascended to the top of the rope ladder. *Liz?! Is that you?* Seb seized the figure's shoulders and threw it beside Hern. The ugly man groaned and rolled onto his back. Cursing, Seb returned to the ladder. 'That's all 'em,' a voice called up. Seb leant over the ship's bulwark to look down at the longboat drifting by the ladder's feet. A lone lamp was held aboard the small boat, illuminating the faces of Halfeye's men and the jagged shards of Hullbreaker Bay around them. Weariness was clear upon their expressions.

'It's not all of them!' Seb shouted. 'Half my father's crew is still out there, my father with them! Hold—' he paused. Straightening, he faced the other way. Less than a dozen Seabloods had been dragged onto the Frontiere, dripping bloodstained salt onto the ship's regal surface. *More than half!*

A sailor stepped over the sagging Seabloods towards Seb. 'Captain, sir. The anchor is set.'

'Good,' Seb replied. 'Get these men into the— Into *my* cabin. Get them whatever blankets you can find.'

'Aye aye,' the sailor diligently replied, moving to rush off.

'But get Rose out first,' Seb added.

The sailor hesitated. Were it not for the weakness of the surrounding light, panic could have been seen to swallow his Sirlish features. 'Captain. She's not in there.'

'Then where is she?'

'She got on the longboat. Headed for the town, sir.'

'Gah!' Seb shivered in anger. He spun toward Wreckrest. The fire there was so fierce now its peaks were almost twice the height of the tallest building. The water between the ship and the docks sparkled with its orange reflection. *You'll get yourself killed, Rose! What were you thinking?!* But he knew exactly what she was thinking. *Revenge!*

'Sir?' The crewman in the longboat hailed once more. 'Sir? What we to do?'

The wreck of the Blood Hammer yet reached its dark spires into the air before the furnace, sinking slowly. Where the firelight danced upon the waves around its flooding hull, barely a blemish stood to be noticed. If more of his brothers were out there, they had already drowned. Or washed ashore, at the least.

Further ahead, the bones of Wreckrest were crumbling, wasting away to the roar of Ijian fire while their old hides were whisked through the air as glowing fragments, to assemble in the sky and swirl round and round above the hellish misery that had conquered the haven where once they belonged. From this turmoil, the screams. They could not be erased by the sounds of the bay. Even the heat seemed near enough to warm Seb's cheeks. *That's where you are, father, isn't it? And Liz, and Rose as well.*

'Sir?'

Seb cleared his throat. 'Hold the ladder, I'm coming down.'

And with that, the Frontiere's captain slipped down the ropes, crashing urgently into the longboat's navel. 'Make for the docks,' he commanded. 'We've done all we can out here. We'll be more use ashore.' *I'm coming for you,* Seb grimaced. *I'm coming!*

Alice opened her eyes reluctantly. The shrieks were like nails being driven into her ear holes. She had heard such a thing in Gold Harbour many times, though it was now somehow worse. So much worse. The sheer terror in the girl's cries. It was as if she expected to have her throat slit afterward. *Perhaps*, Alice thought, *she might*.

Presently, the dark-haired man with the jellyfish emblem on his waistcoat was ripping the other girl's dress right down the back.

'Like what ya see, girly? Yer next up. Cap'n Dagger likes 'em thin.' The pirate wrapped his hands around Alice's waist and rubbed them back and forth. Alice ripped an arm free from his perverted cuddle and lashed out at his face. White scratch marks formed instantly on his lip, mere moments before he sent his fist flying into her own mouth.

She came free of her captor's embrace and thudded against the floor. The world went black, then returned all blurry, spinning in circles. Laughter mingled with the other girl's cries.

The tables drifted down. The floor came away from her head. She had been lifted back up, and was hanging limp in dirty forearms.

'Ye better not do that to Dagger!' the pirate snarled at her. 'Or he'll chop off yer hand. Don' think he won't!' He waggled his wrist in front of Alice's nose. She shook it away, barely able to perceive what had blocked her vision.

Tears peeked out from her eyes and rolled down her soon-to-be-bruised jaw. She would have sobbed, but she had neither the energy nor the incentive. All she possessed now was the certainty that she was next. That the foul man across the room would have his way with her, and that her body would be forever spoiled by a filthy Dreadwind.

She told herself she would not scream. Not like this girl did. She dared not give him the satisfaction. She would be strong, and when it was over, perhaps he would let her go. *But where would I go? Nowhere is safe. Nowhere!* Her throat tried to turn upside down in her neck. But she did not cry. She clenched her jaw, forced weight back into her toes. The grip around her loosened.

Slowly, the room came again into focus, however shrouded by nausea. It was the same tavern that had briefly made her feel so safe. Now it felt like an oven.

Heat billowed over the tables and chairs, where half a dozen crazed pirates spectated, adding their jeers to the squeals that bounced from wall to wall. Through the windows, Alice could see fire. Already it was overwhelming the other side of the town centre. If the Dreadwinds with her remained for much longer, Maggie's Tavern would be burning around them.

'We have to get out…' she tried to warn them. Her words were little more than drool.

'Oh, the girly's scared! Don't ye worry, girly. There's 'nuff time for yer turn 'fore we have t'get out. Don't ye worry.'

Alice let her eyes slam shut, and she sank into dizzying black.

Crack! The double doors whipped against the walls and a flurry of smoky air gushed in, filling Alice's nostrils with woody heat. Startled, she drove open her eyelids, even as the smoke stung her pupils. A new pirate had charged through the tavern's entrance, completely smothered with soot and mud. For a split second, Alice thought it was Rose, though she swiftly realigned with reality, so much as she was feebly able.

At the other end of the rustic room, the lead pirate named

Dagger irately dropped his half-naked victim, who scuttled to the far corner as quick as a mouse. 'Who dares?!'

'You don't remember me?'

It sounded like Rose's voice. But it also did not. It was different, in a way. Darker.

'Nay, should I?' Dagger laughed, prompting his comrades to chuckle along with him.

The intruder stepped confidently into the smoky space beside Alice. 'You don't remember my husband either, do you?'

Dagger began picking his way through the tables, and stopped when he finally recognised his foe. 'Oh, I remember, yes! You're that girl! The one who claimed to know where Halfeye's Hoard was hid. Didn't we kill you? Truly, I cannot recall. Remind me, will you kindly.'

'You killed my husband.'

Wesley?

The woman pointed her sword at Dagger's chest. Her coat was massive and daunting. Her golden hair was tangled. Her scowl was so stubborn.

'Rose!' Alice wailed, her words slurring, her mind spinning, her eyes unbelieving. 'Rose, it's—' Alice's captor slapped a hand over her mouth. She screamed into it. Bitter, dirty sweat coated her lips.

Rose chose not to notice. As did Dagger. 'Ho ho,' he snickered. 'I killed your man, did I? What of it? This Dagger's killed more men than he can count.'

'And now I'll kill you!'

A pirate snatched his blade from a nearby table and started at Rose.

'Woah! Hold on there, Bill!' Dagger fended the pirate away with a wave of his hand. 'The girl has issued me a challenge. A challenge I'd be heartless to deny. She wants to die the same way her husband did, can't you see?' The other pirates hooted, agreeing. 'The dagger, Bill. And stand back.'

'Cap'n, it's only a dagger,' the first cautioned, but tossed the weapon nevertheless. Rose's sword was indeed twice the length.

'Don't you know I'm more than that,' Dagger growled. 'Now come at me, girl, time is against us.'

'Rose! No!' Alice screeched, but her cry was caught in the thick fingers pressed against her lips. She kicked her feet, trying to release herself.

Rose lunged at Dagger, sword flailing. The pirate dodged. Rose's thrusts sent her careening into a table. Smoke swirled around it as it collapsed. Its wood hammered the floor. Rose collapsed too. The audience laughed.

Dagger brought his blade down to finish his opponent.

'Rose!' Alice felt her captor's fingers ease.

As quick as lightning, Rose rolled away from Dagger's blow, eyes narrowing, muscles tensing. She swung at his shins. He leapt into the air, landing with a crash into a stack of chairs. The encircling crowd recoiled, their laughter cut off as if Rose had cut it herself.

Dagger sprang to his feet, rubbing his eyes. Rose gave him no chance to recoup; she launched forward in a crazed gale of stabs and swipes, her eyes burning with determined insanity. 'Die!' she was shouting. Alice could barely believe it was her. *Not the Rose I know! Who is this woman?*

Dagger evaded every stroke with deft but drowsy

movements. He looked for an opening through which to force his own blade forward. He could not find one. The room held its breath. Alice ceased her struggles. More smoke poured in. Rose jabbed and jabbed. Then came the opening.

Dagger twisted his arm past one of Rose's clumsy slashes, and sent his dagger right at her breast. It slid into her shoulder instead. To Alice, it seemed like the pirate had missed. It made not a sound, and was so fast. Not until Rose shrieked in pain did she know.

Alice screamed with her. Terror consumed her thoughts, though it was something else entirely that had ignited within the other woman. Hate.

Rose's shriek transformed into an ear-piercing roar. She swooped under Dagger's ensuing thrust and jammed her sword into his dagger hand. He released his own yelp as Rose grabbed him by the neck and rode him to the floor. She wrested the dagger from his shaking fist where blood bubbled profusely, and her knees dug holes in his gut.

He shrivelled into a ball, overwhelmed by searing pain. Rose aimed the blood-soaked dagger at his neck. The room was stunned, motionless, unsure how to respond. All except for Alice. Seizing the opportunity, she kicked her heels into her captor's shins and at last squirmed free of his arms. She pounced across the room, scrambling over upturned tables towards Rose. The air stung her eyes and her skin burned as it had in Gold Harbour. But she forced her way through. She shot up to Rose's back, clutched her arm, and pulled her from the cowering jellyfish pirate. The two women flopped onto the floor. 'Rose!' Alice begged. 'Don't do it!'

A falling beam smashed one of the tavern's windows. Sparks sprayed into the murk. Orange flashes flavoured the air, finished with ever-building heat.

'Leave him,' she continued. 'Let's get out!'

Rose's ferocious resistance subsided when she noticed Alice's face. Recognising eyes squinted up from within her ash-smothered face. So familiar, yet so different. There was a hollowness to Rose's stare, an emptiness, as if life itself had been squeezed from her very being.

'Alice?' Rose was confused.

'Yes!' Alice exclaimed. 'It's me! Come on, we have to go!' She tugged at Rose's elbow.

A loud pop echoed through the tavern and more sparks exploded into it. The surrounding pirates kept their distance. Some of them scrambled eagerly for the entrance. The half-naked girl had already vanished.

'But...' Rose complained. 'He killed... He killed...' Her expression pleaded.

'No Rose! You're not a killer! Let's get out of here!' Alice yanked more fiercely at the other's drooping body. Dagger was dragging himself away from them.

'Killer? But he... He... He killed Wes!' Rose's face went from soft to hard. Her forehead crumpled. 'He has to die!'

'No!'

Rose howled, tried to get at Dagger.

Alice grabbed at her, tried to top her.

Rose's teeth came out. She swung her blade at Alice. Its tip sliced through the target's face. Hot liquid poured over Alice's chin. Rose shoved her aside, rushing after Dagger, yearning for his death.

The pirates were well on the move now. Shouting, cursing, scuttling. Most were fleeing, while a couple raced towards either Rose or Dagger. Alice could not see any of it. Blood and smoke and tears blinded her. An enormous swell of pain tore through her cheek, sizzling like fresh embers. She clambered across the floor. Footsteps ran circles around her. The doors slapped open, closed, open. Her palms slipped on red water. Her boots scraped soot. She was up, stumbling. She crashed through the doorway. Heat smacked her cheek. Fire crackled, gusted, rumbled. Everything was orange and black. She fell from the verandah. The street was hot to the touch. She leant towards it. Dust stuck to her bloody fingers. Fire was eating the air. It was eating everything. She shuddered. Let her tension go. Dropped flat on the ground. Lost her concentration. Will. Feeling.

A man lifted her from the burning dust. 'Rose?!' he asked, frantic.

She knew that voice. She had heard it before. 'Wesley?'

'Wesley? No. Seb.' He turned away. 'Get over here! This one's hurt!' He turned back. 'Was there another woman in there? Young, with light hair?'

'Rose?' asked Alice, her frail voice barely squeezing through the blood in her mouth.

'You know her?' the man questioned. 'Is she in there?!'

Alice swallowed, gritty pain trampling down her throat, her cheek throbbing unbearably. She pried open an eye, through which she could see Maggie's Tavern. It was burning now, like everything else.

'No,' she said. 'She's not.' *That is somebody else.*

24

It was a beautiful day. As perfect as Southland could offer. The ground glittered with the memory of morning showers, and the bright sky—an evenly folded broth of snowy white and crisp azure—shone happily down on midday with a gentle warmth and a sprinkling of soft breeze. Even the charred frames of the countless ruined homes radiated their own breed of quaint tranquility. It was difficult to picture how chaotic the street had been the night before.

Seb's lungs bathed in moist air as he drew each breath. The scent of leaves, earth and ash touched his nose. Birds were chirping their oblivious and blissful songs, whist the crunching of his boots sounded over the blackened street.

To his left and right, sailors and townsfolk alike rummaged through the remnants of Wreckrest, searching for items lost. Only a few buildings remained, standing alone amongst the wreckage of the night's Ijian fire. Within those buildings, a handful of kindhearted villagers tended to the burns of the less fortunate.

Seb's feet halted as he came up to Maggie's tavern. The structure was only half razed, though its roof and upper level had completely buckled. It had been a meeting place for Seablood, Blackbone and Dreadwind all, where those with a thirst came to share a drink. And so it remained, Seb was surprised to notice, for upon its broken floor a clump of survivors sat together in harmony, trying to make sense of what they ought do next, mugs in hand.

Seb eyed the Seabloods among them. Those few that had made it to shore were certainly not the most valued of the Blood Hammer's crew, though they had been quick to inform their prince of what had happened aboard the sinking brig.

Salvino, Seb was reminded, painfully. He had, of course, been informed of the quartermaster's misbehaviour. His mind twitched in anger. *I always knew you were a sly worm, but...*

'Seb,' a man called out. Seb swivelled toward the voice to see a grave-faced Rob stepping over a mound of sooty wood. The young sailor had ever been friendly with Seb before he recently became captain of a schooner under the employ of the Seablood fleet. After the fire was quenched sometime during the morning's brief rainfall, the man had been invaluable in assisting the Frontiere's scrappy crew as they salvaged what they could from the town's rubble.

'Did you find them?' Seb asked eagerly, his heart skipping a beat.

Rob sifted through the town's derelict heart to approach Seb's side. His expression was answer enough. 'Nay, Seb. Though some of your ghost ship's crew say they saw the girl Rose leaving with the last of the Dreadwinds.'

Seb's fingernails dug into his palms. He cursed. 'They'll kill her.'

'Not from what I hear,' Rob remarked. 'They could just as well have been mistaken, but your ghost men swear she was no prisoner. That she was leading them, even. To the Kraken, no doubt.'

Seb's forehead ruffled. 'That doesn't make any sense.'

'As I said, Seb. Your ghost men, they could be mistaken.'

'They're not ghost men,' Seb snapped.

'Aye. All the same, you'll want to see what they dragged up.'

Father! Liz! 'You said you hadn't found them yet.'

'Aye not those, but someone else.' Rob beckoned. 'Please. Come and see.'

Dubious, Seb fell in step with his old friend, and the two wound their way through the black town until they reached the the docks of Hullbreaker Bay. There were dozens of people gathered on the beach, and more crowding one of the piers. As Seb neared, he saw that the busy wooden platform was smothered mostly with crewmen from the Frontiere, men under his own command. A young woman stood among them, seeming out of place.

The crunch of Seb's boots was replaced by tapping as he left the shore and made his way down the pier. Rob held back, allowing space for the other to push his way through the pack. When Seb finally reached the pier's end, the girl confronted him immediately. Her face was wrapped in a wide and bloody bandage, and her untidy sailor's clothes were strangely reminiscent of a late Blackbone prisoner. She was one of the people Seb had pulled from the fire. One of the last.

'Don't kill him,' she begged. It clearly pained her to speak, though her resolve was so strong she cared not a bit. 'Please don't kill him!'

Don't kill who? Seb tenderly nudged the girl aside to gaze at the man she was supposedly protecting. Sure enough, there was a figure kneeling on the pier's wooden planks. His hands were tied, and a circle of the Frontiere's crew stood rigidly around his frame, locking him in place with sword points.

The man was tall, even kneeling he was tall. His enormous grey beard was soggy, and his lordly coat was absent, yet still he was beastly. He looked up at Seb with hard eyes. Provoking eyes.

Seb lost his breath.

'Please, captain, sir.'

Seb was speechless. He was gripped in the old man's inscrutable countenance. The latter was just as silent. There was naught to say.

'Sir, he's a good man. Please.'

Seb shook his head, forced his mouth to open. 'She says you're a good man,' he commented. 'Should I believe her, Wulfric Blackbone?'

Wulfric matched Seb's glare, his features bent in the gritty snarl of a captured bear, hungry for its inevitable death.

One of Seb's crewmen piped up. 'He says he killed your father,' he said. 'Theodore Seablood.'

Seb's heart dropped. His face dropped. His mouth gaped. His knees trembled. His toes curled. The girl went quiet.

And Wulfric held his glare. Challenging.

Seb felt his skin prickle all over. His bones rattled. 'Is this true?' he asked of the captive sealord. *Of course it's true.*

'Aye,' Wulfric replied. He cleared his throat. 'He killed my son.'

Seb could not find words.

Wulfric growled and went on. 'Wreckrest is destroyed. The Blood Hammer is sunk. The Black Beast is stolen. The sealords are no more.' He paused. 'It's over, Seablood. It's all over. Finish it and be done.'

Seb looked away. He faced the man who had informed him of Wulfric's crime, and spoke in an even tone. 'Where did you find him?'

'We pulled him from the water,' was the reply. 'Like all the others.'

Seb sighed. He shut his eyes, brooding. The air was heavy. Solid. It pressed in on him from every angle. He could feel the breath of every assembled man as they stared at him in waiting. He could hear the water lap against the pier's foundations. He could smell the sea dripping from Wulfric's beard. *Father, I'm sorry.*

'What should we do with him, captain?' the informant probed.

Seb opened his eyes. He craned over the sealord, losing himself in that wolfish glare once more. 'I have an idea.' He spun on the spot. 'Load him onto the Frontiere. Chain him down and prepare for sail. It's time to leave this place.'

With that, Seb slipped away down the pier towards the dusty heap of Wreckrest. *It's over.* Wulfric's words rung vividly in his head. *Is it really?*

'Captain Seablood,' a voice hollered.

Captain Seablood is dead, Seb thought. *You've got the wrong man.* He turned towards the voice anyway.

The girl with the bandaged face was scooting after him, her gait weary and hurt. 'You're not going to. Kill him. Are you?' She spoke softly now, carefully. She tenderly touched her cheek as her lips moved.

'Why do you care so much?'

'He was kind to me. He took me in. Protected me. I guess. It's a long story. Really, though. I've just. Had enough. Of all the killing. Of all the death. And I can't—'

'What's your name?'

The girl hesitated. Her dark hair was long and straight, and it flowed behind small, pointed ears. Seb felt as though he had seen her before. Perhaps with Wulfric. 'Al King,' she said.

Seb flicked his head back. 'Well then, Al King. I'm taking the ship south beyond the Sentinels, where there's less gold and less death. If you'll come with us, you can tell me the whole story, however long.'

Al delivered him a quizzical look.

Seb raised his eyebrows. 'I'd appreciate having someone to talk to. There's nothing left for you here, besides. Might as well—'

'I'll come,' she said. 'But only if.' She exhaled. 'You don't kill him.'

25

The Frontiere sparkled as she drifted away with her bow pointed southwest. The huge eagles painted on her black sails curved in the morning's trade winds. She sat so elegantly atop the glassy green of the Rainbow Sea, the finest ship to ever grace the Southland coast. Huge oak wings caressed her flanks, waving at him, bidding him farewell. Elsewhere upon her shining deck, Sebastian Seablood was undoubtedly looking back with the same pompous smirk on his face. Also bidding him farewell.

'You treat her right, you bloody coward.' Wulfric cursed. He still could scarcely believe what he saw. 'I've seen her sunk once before, and I don't ever want to see it again.'

The vessel was so real, so present, yet so impossible. It was the ghost of a ship long dead, no matter what unlikely story its crew spun to mask the truth, or how solid the thing had felt beneath his black bones as it conveyed him away from Wreckrest forever. *A ghost ship. A beautiful ghost ship. Captained by a spineless fool.*

Fury stirred within his fiery belly. 'Coward!' he shouted. His roar thundered over the calm water that stroked the shore's white coat. 'You're a coward!' He kicked the beach, sending pieces of dried coral flying through the breeze. Pale shards plopped into the waves, with nothing to answer but the rustle of the palms overhead. Wulfric was alone. Naught was going to change that now.

In the end, Sebastian had been too weak to kill Wulfric with his own hands. The freshly crowned captain could have run him through with the point of his cutlass, he could have dropped him into the sea, hung him from the mast, even smashed his head with an oar until it popped open on the deck. But the fool had opted for the most gutless of death sentences: to maroon his victim upon an uninhabited island, leaving him to slowly die out of sight and mind. The Seablood boy had not even granted him a pistol with which to end it early.

Such was not an honourable end for Wulfric Blackbone, Sealord of the Southern Setinels. Even if the sentence was unlikely to be paid in full, as the eastern borders of the Watcher were oft traversed by traders heading to Morchport, traders who might spy his lonesome shadow upon the island's coast. No. It was a betrayal, plain and simple. Straight up skulduggery. A fate Wulfric knew he ought not suffer. That he did not deserve. He had had no choice but to kill Teddy. It was justice. For Wulfric's own son. For Kit.

Wulfric shut his mind. He knew that if he were to think on Kit for more than a second, his life might well end before the heat or hunger had chance to take it. He huffed and whirled, casting his gaze into the island on which he had been abandoned. He remembered its name, though had cared little for it in the past. The Djun Cay, it was called, one of the many coral islands right on the border of Seablood and Blackbone territory. It was small enough to circle briskly on foot, though not so petite as to be swallowed by the high tide. In truth, it was perchance not a proper cay at all, as the island's centre seemed a solid lump of sandy rock, dressed with a handful of shrubs and palms that towered over the round beach.

It was a quaint place, a bright and handsome oasis on the outer edge of the Sentinels. As good a place as any to be marooned, in a sense. There would undoubtedly be coconuts on the palms, and maybe a puddle of fresh water somewhere beneath them.

Presently, the sun showered down on Wulfric's tired shoulders, warming his body beyond comfort. He grudgingly lifted his boots from the sandy coral and trudged over to the thicket surrounding the island's heart. There was little shade to be had, but he found a soft place to sit with his back pressed against the hardy stem of a heavy palm. There, at least, he could rest his sore muscles. They creaked with age and self-pity as they lowered his trunk to the earth.

From his new vantage point, Wulric could see far into the ocean beyond the Sentinels. Its empty expanse resonated with the hollowness of his soul. He wished for rum to wash out the grief, but found that the vista was somewhat satiating for the time being. Its shifting textures soothed him, complimented by the persistent hushing of the sea. Slowly, Wulfric's anger began to ease. The tension crawling through his skin soaked into the warm soil, even as beads of salty water still dripped from the tip of his beard. *Kit*, he thought again.

Birds called to him from somewhere behind. Their

miniature chirps were impossibly upbeat, singing to each other—it seemed—about the joys of living, and the wonderful adventures they were yet to share. Their song was alluring, and soon enough had Wulfric turning his head to glimpse at where it came from.

His old eyes could not locate the creatures, but in scanning for them he noticed a series of rock pools wedged between ragged boulders. Upon spotting the fresh water, his throat became instantly and immeasurably parched. He knew that if he were not to drink, he might not even last the day. So, with a deep sigh, he forced himself to stand once more.

Oversized boots flopped through the shrubs under tired knees and a monstrous silver mane. The sealord drew himself to the nearest pool, where he stood tightly, peering down at the harsh reflection of his battered features. The island's mangled greenery now hid his location from the world beyond, yet still he was loath to crouch, to lap water from the ground like an animal. *No. I am Wulfric Blackbone*, he told himself. *No coward boy is going to force this disgrace upon me!* Sebastian's face appeared in his mind. *Yes, you! You cannot make me do it.* The boy's expression was smug. Too smug. *I am a sealord of Southland! I would sooner die!* Sebastian's face suddenly gave way to that of his son. That black hair. Those brown eyes. *Kit!* Wulfric dropped to his knees. He bent over the pond and dug his bulky hands into its smooth surface, splashing liquid at his mouth.

The water was cool and sharp. It sprayed over his dry beard, stinging his lips. It was not enough. He dropped his whole face into the pond, sucking it up in mouthfuls. Water coursed down his throat, swirling in his stomach. He drank until his breath ran out then pulled away gasping, water bubbling out onto the rocks.

Wheezing madly, he slumped against bruised elbows. He stared blankly at the rippling pond. His whole body drooped in misery and defeat. Water dribbled down his chest while sand ground into his tattered breeches. He wondered if he should have instead let himself die. He wondered it as the water stilled, and his ragged face came back into view. He squinted at the reflection. His nose was swollen and burnt. His mouth was cracked and red. His cheeks were dirty and rough. Then he saw it. Something else in the water's reflection. Something out of place.

He sat up, curious. Beside the puddles, a natural rocky shelf reached over a cluster of shrubs to form a shelter of sorts. Beneath it was a square edge stained with old lichen.

Wulfric clambered over to it. As he closed in, he saw that the edge belonged to a wooden box, braced with iron and weathered with neglect. He brushed aside a few scratchy branches to get at it, and stumbled abruptly into a small hollow beneath the shelter. His eyes widened as he regained his balance, squatting to fit his huge frame into the tight space. Nearly a dozen chests had been stacked there, all three feet long and swallowed by shadow. They were half-buried in dirt and half-ruined by rot.

Wulfric ran a hand over their crusty surfaces. He fingered one of the rusted latches and ripped it open, swinging back the lid. Dust cascaded over the chest's cloth-wrapped contents. Eagerly, he swept the dust and cloth aside to reveal rows upon rows of tightly packed gold ingots. Their metallic lustre was dark and crisp. 'Halfeye's Hoard,' he whispered.

He thrust open another. And another. It was all the same. Rows upon rows upon rows.

'Did you know this was here?' He laughed. 'You bloody fool. You bloody goddamn lunatic!'

www.ingramcontent.com/pod-product-compliance
Lightning Source LLC
Chambersburg PA
CBHW020252120726
47904CB00001B/170